Secret Paths Editions presents

Chimera

Alan McCluskey

First published in May 2019
Secret Paths Editions, Mureta 2, CH-2072 Saint-Blaise
Copyright © Alan McCluskey
Cover illustration by Alan McCluskey

ISBN 978-2-940553-13-6

Other books by the author

Stories People Tell

Boy & Girl
In Search of Lost Girls

The Reaches - The Storyteller's Quest Book One
The Keeper's Daughter - The Storyteller's Quest Book Two
The Starless Square - The Storyteller's Quest Book Three

Coming soon
Local Voices

1.

:: tiny squiggles of silver light worm their way through the darkness and hiss nonsense - squirming messages spawned by kids dashing in senseless circles - their agitation addles my brain - I no longer know who or what or when I am - I crouch between coats in a cupboard amid the smell of Nan my teacher - her pretty perfume gets on my hands and follows me about - backwards and forwards I rock, like a boat praying for the storm to stop

"Sam?"

:: no - I won't go out - it is not safe - only confusion and tears lie out there - I stuff fingers in my ears and listen to the pulse of my heart - when I am under assault, when I find no refuge, I fear my heart will falter or flicker out - where would Sam be then? - in the unending dark I say - in bright heaven says Nan, but how does she know?

"Sam, are you coming out?"

:: I bury my head between my knees and cup my hands over my ears - if only I could think Nan away - not that I want to be rid of her - she's my favourite, after dad - but I will not go out, not for her, not for anyone - she moves away and the din diminishes

Oooouuieeeeee!

:: the scream has me lurching sideways, my heart clamouring in my chest, my breath wheezing in and out - several dark monsters pounce wrapping cottony wings around my head and set about strangling me - I lash out, arms flailing like a crazed windmill - the more I fight the more the monsters attack - I lurch forward desperate to get free - light floods over me as I hit the floor with a thud and keel forward trussed up in a knot of coats and scarves - I skitter to a halt in front of Nan - at her back, a tight group of kids stare wide-eyed - several point fingers - a number mutter rude remarks

"Oh Sam," Nan says, disengaging me from the clothes and setting me on my feet. "Whatever happened?"

:: how should I know? - a pained scream echoes in my head - inside my head - it was inside my head - my knees tremble and give way as I slither to the ground - several children giggle behind cupped hands - I stick out my tongue, but pull it back, terror gripping my guts - a form is unfurling inside me, stretching and yawning - a form that is not me - I scuttle on all fours towards the cupboard bowling over two kids - they scream - who cares? - only one scream holds my attention and it is inside my head - in the cupboard I slam the door, curl up in a ball and press my eyes with clenched fists

"Sam!" Nan calls out, a thin sliver of light penetrating the dark.

:: I cringe from her hand snaking towards me - perfumed fingers find my shoulder, brush up my neck and caresses my head - with each touch waves of horror shudder through me as if those fingers could reach inside and grab my soul

"Everything is going to be alright."

:: never - nothing is ever going to be right again - in the shadows of my head a pair of eyes flick open, large and round - I see alarm and hurt and confusion - I scream and scream and scream only to be lifted from the cupboard, Nan's arms about my waist, my arms clinging around her neck, my screams muffled as tears stream down my cheeks

"There … there."

:: Nan's perfume wraps itself around me, familiar and comforting - it flows into my nose, my mouth, my throat, my lungs - deep inside that alien presence shifts, sniffing the air, enjoying the scent and with that pleasure it grows and takes shape - I try to block my nose and wrestle free of Nan's embrace to rob it of the scent, but I cannot shut out the smell - something akin to a smile spreads through every cell of my body - I slam up defences, pull down blinds, draw across bolts in a desperate struggle to resist

"Sam, stop struggling. You'll hurt us."

:: what do I care if Nan gets hurt - of course I do, but I am being invaded - how did it get in?

Sam? a voice says softly in my mind, a girl's voice, questioning, uncertain, as if sounding out my name. *Sam.*

:: get out - get out - I kick with all my force - I hit out with clenched fists but it is beyond reach - I hear Nan cry out as she lets me fall to the floor - kids are screaming, others are crying - to hell with them - I hate them all - I thrash out - a raging battle of legs and arms and desks and books and over it all the smell blood

Stop Sam! The girl's voice says. *Please stop.*

:: leave me alone I scream - my bruised arms and the pain in my legs scream back - my movements slow, my strength fades as does the light - as obscurity claims me, I mouth one last word - never

2.

A scream shattered the silence. Jon broke into a run, the pounding of his boots echoing off the unadorned walls. At the only door not obstructed by wooden panels he halted, uncertain. The lesson was not yet over and parents were not allowed in. Sticky-taped to the door a government poster portrayed an insane hag brandishing shrivelled plants. He shook his head. The caption read: Alternative medicine is deadly! Someone had crossed out 'alternative medicine' and scrawled 'synthetic food'. Jon couldn't help glancing over his shoulder to see if anyone was watching.

Hearing a groan within, he pushed open the door. To his horror, Sam lay on the floor, his eyes rolled up in his head, his fists clenched and bloody. A short distance away sat the teacher, her back propped against the wall, her right arm cradled in her left. Her black hair, always so tidy in a knot behind her head, was loose and dishevelled. Her face was pinched in pain and her left eye swollen. She glanced up and their eyes met. In that brief moment he caught a glimpse of pain and despair and fear, but also tenderness and longing. Her expression was so intense, he had to look away.

Books were scattered across the floor and chairs upturned. Several children lay groaning as they grasped heads or legs or hands. The rest huddled in a corner, some crying softly, but most cringing wide-eyed. Jon shuddered. Each of these children would tell their parents and their parents would whisper to their neighbours and someone, somewhere would do their duty and inform

the police. The last thing he needed was trouble with the authorities.

He kneeled next to the teacher and, out of some distant
reflex, moved to place a reassuring hand on her shoulder, only to
stop short.

"What happened?" he asked pulling back.

She dragged a hand across her forehead that was creased
with worry. "Sam went wild and hit out." Her voice was raw with
emotion. It unsettled him.

Sam had his difficulties, but never had he been violent. The
authorities knew about him, of course they did, especially after
the trouble with his mother during the Disaster, but, for some
reason, they did not intervene. When word of this violence
reached them, they wouldn't hesitate. Sam would be carted off
to what people politely called a 'special school' and never seen
again.

"Give me a hand," the teacher said.

Her out-stretched hand startled him. He shied away. Like
everyone else, he avoided physical contact for fear he might catch
the Disaster. Had it not killed so many? She looked at him, her
hand quivering but her eyes challenging and, despite himself, he
grasped it, pulling her to her feet. Her fingers were moist as if
she had a fever. At the thought of the millions who had died, he
released her hand and wiped his fingers on his trousers, hoping
she wouldn't notice.

She looked around, her eyes settling on Sam. "You should
take him home. I will try to sort out this mess."

"You won't …" He couldn't finish the sentence. Of course
she would. If she didn't report this she would probably forfeit
her job. Work was not easy to come by, especially not in one of
the last private schools in town.

"I will do what I can," she said, shuffling towards one of the
children lying on the floor.

Without another word, he scooped up Sam's limp body and
headed for the door. Alone in the corridor and out of earshot,
he leant against the wall and stared at Sam. The boy's eyes were

closed, as if he were asleep. His long neck and oval face reminded Jon of his late wife, Jane. She had had the same thick-set eyebrows, the same long, dark lashes. It had been twelve years; twelve years during which he had managed to keep Sam from the predatory grasp of the authorities.

"Oh Sam. What have you done?" The boy's unmoving form offered no response. Jon pushed off the wall and headed for the exit.

Outside the air was dull and lifeless, almost grey. The wreak of chemicals invaded everything. You'd think you'd get used to it after so much time. But it was subtly changing, as if the chemists knew blood hounds were on to them and were set on throwing them off the scent.

He stepped from the porch and moved cautiously away from the school. Sam was heavy and the pavement was cracked and uneven, but at least no grass grew between the paving stones to trip him up. He could thank the Food Police and their herbicides for that.

The buildings that flanked the walkway leaned away as if afraid of him. Shutters hung from their hinges at odd angles, windows were boarded up and scraps of paper had collected around entrances and piled up in dark corners. He peered into the shadows each time he passed a narrow alley. Someone might be lurking there. Caution had got him thus far. This afternoon no monsters surged out to greet them.

His building was not so different from the others. He had bought it shortly before the Disaster when he still had money, thanks to a major concert tour. Fissures were forming in the walls and paint on the shutters and window frames was peeling, but at least it was cleaner than neighbouring buildings and no windows were boarded up. Even if he still had the means to repair it and the materials could be found, it would not do to have it stand out. Flaunting wealth, however paltry, was asking for trouble.

A shout wrenched him from his thoughts. A man in tatters burst from a nearby alley and dashed in Jon's direction. Sam stirred but did not wake. Close on the tramp's heels thundered a pair of guards, all muscles bulging, their truncheons raised, panting like dogs with their tongues hanging out. Jon struggled to reach the key in his pocket, balancing Sam on one knee. He almost dropped the boy several times but dared not put him down. With clumsy fingers he fumbled the key into the lock. The fugitive was closing fast. Finally, the door swung open and Jon hurried inside. Laying Sam on the floor, he slammed the glass door and flipped the lock once, twice. Hunched over Sam, his breath coming hard, he watched.

The man was barely feet away when he was overtaken. The guards thrust him to the ground, setting about him with truncheons, raining blows on his shoulders, his back, his head. Blood flowed thickly over his face. His eyes locked momentarily with Jon's, beseeching, then rolled up leaving only the whites in view.

The guards knew no restraint. They laboured the man like a vengeful storm. Curled up in a ball, the tramp made no move to resist. Maybe he was already dead.

Enough. Jon might have been glad to pay guards to patrol their quarter, but to see the violence close up was sickening. He turned his back, picked up Sam and headed for the stairs. Climbing the four flights, he was forced to stop several times as the boy began to slip from his aching arms.

Once inside, he lay Sam on the sofa, hurried to the window and peered out. No tramp or guards were in sight. Returning to the sofa, he sat next to his son, closed his eyes and let out a shuddery sigh.

3.

:: bumps, battles 'nd bruises - cease your bleating oversized lump - is that all you can do, moan and groan - whinger - is it not enough that my stomach growls and my ears roar and my head throbs and my lips smart and my hands sting - wise the fool that keeps his eyes closed in the dark - I sniff - the air smells of shelves upon shelves of dusty books and candles long snuffed out and the Persian rug that covers my sofa at home - how did I get here - pianissimo dad plays piano - despite muted fingers the music is sharp and cutting to my ears - unpredictable rhythms trouble me - deep inside a sigh surges, inundating me with nostalgia and delight - HER! - how could I have forgotten - she followed me home - she wheedled her way into my house - her joy at the music has me doubting - I sense centuries of misty memories spreading before me like so many winding paths coaxing me to step back in time - get out intruder - this is my body - I don't want your memories - leave me in peace - I fling myself to the floor - lashing out, my fists connect with the sofa - I cry out in pain

"Stop that Sam!" Dad orders.

:: firm hands nail my arms to the carpet - I buck up with my hips and writhe like a serpent struggling to slither free - it is not me, it is her - get her out of me - I want to scream, but only inarticulate grunts and groans issue from my mouth - when a hand covers my mouth I bite hard tasting blood - dad screams and slaps me knocking my head sideways - I cease struggling - my limbs rigid - never has he hit me - I cry - it is unjust - it is not me - it is her - please dad, take her away

"Oh Sam," Dad says and sobs.

:: my eyes fly open at the unfamiliar sound - I stare into his face only inches from mine - tears roll between the folds of his skin, disappear into his beard then fall onto my cheeks mingling with my own - his mouth opens in short gasps - terror grips me - is he going to flicker out and pass away - did I do this to him? - do not leave me dad - I love you - he leans forward, pressing his lips lightly on my forehead - my whole body heaves - she too is grieving - all of us are - and through the mists I see the lifeless bodies of children old and young carried away by an immense wave

"I'm so sorry, Sam," Dad says wiping the tears from my face. He leans back against the sofa. "I didn't mean to…" Fresh tears flow. "It's been too much." He brushes them angrily from his face. "I wish your mother were here. She was so good in a crisis."

:: mother - an unfathomable word - a dark hole in my being from which only absence makes itself felt - I peer in from time to time - the emptiness makes my head spin - I wonder what would happen if I threw myself in - other kids have mothers - people who bring them to school - people who fetch them afterwards - but who hardly ever take them in their arms

"I have never talked about her, Sam. It is not safe. What she did could get us in trouble, but I think you should know what a wonderful person she was."

:: the girl is on the move again - she has stopped crying and I sense her shifting forward, greedy for dad's words - he is not your dad - she backs away retreating into a distant corner of my mind - you cannot hide from me - I know you are there - get out and leave me alone

"You won't remember the Disaster, Sam. It was shortly after you were born. You and I were lucky, this part of town was spared the illness. There were few vigilantes bent on ridding us of the infected. Your mother wanted to tend the ill. It was her calling. She would have saved many lives had they let her. Healing was not yet illegal, but it was getting more and more dangerous to do. People were so frightened. They hunted down anyone in contact with the ill. Despite the dangers, she insisted on visiting parts of town where many were dying. She was such a lovely person. She would never have hurt anyone. All she wanted was to help the sick and for that they shot her in the back…"

:: dad breaks off and begins crying again - his tears are greeted by a thoughtful silence - the girl has ceased her round, her grief abated - I hold my breath trying to still my twitching fingers - the whole world hangs suspended, waiting to see what comes next - ring softly ring - someone is at the front door downstairs - dad looks up wide-eyed

"That can't be them," he says. "They wouldn't ring. They'd kick down the door."

:: he scrambles to his feet and, tugging at his beard, hurries to the window - hiding behind the frame, he looks out - he cmutters a word I don't understand, then rushes to the door and is swallowed by the stairwell - I crawl behind the sofa and peer out, afraid of what he will bring back - I hear him on the stairs - he's not alone - then he hurries in closely followed by Nan, her breath coming hard - she pushes the door shut, making sure it is locked

4.

Nan halted in the entrance, struggling to regain her breath. She had run from the school, leaving the moment she received the message. She'd been lucky. A minute later and she would have missed it.

"Miss Arandale?" Jon asked, a look of surprise and worry on his face. He must have been wondering what she was doing out so close to curfew.

Nan hardly knew him and had never been to his flat. She glanced around. The layout fit the plans she'd seen. The shelves of books caught her attention. A grand piano stood amongst the sparse yet tasteful furniture. But what struck her most was the tidiness. For a man raising a child alone, especially one so unpredictable, such orderliness was a miracle.

Her attention returned to him. He stared at her, his look guarded as if she were a harbinger of bad news, which she was.

"Can I sit down?" she asked, still struggling to regain her breath.

"Please do. My apologies. You startled me."

She sat on the settee while he went to fetch Sam curled up behind the sofa. "Come out, Sam. Say goodnight to your teacher." When Sam refused to budge, Jon took a step closer, but the boy scuttled away and hid under the grand piano, knocking over the piano stool as he did. "Stop that, Sam. You've already caused enough damage today."

He glanced at her and shrugged. The prospect of chasing the boy around the flat with her watching clearly embarrassed him. Sam could be difficult, she knew only too well. That was why she had brought the remedy tucked in her coat pocket.

"You wouldn't happen to have a cup or a glass stashed away, would you?" she asked.

He looked alarmed. Asking him was a risk. No sane person would be caught with such a thing. Eating anything other than the synthetic pills prescribed by the Food Ministry was punishable by death. Seeing the fear in his eyes, she explained, "I need something to put a little liquid in."

The moment she said it, she realised she'd made things worse. Only prescribed water produced by approved suppliers was allowed.

"What are you playing at?" he asked, glaring at her. "I need to get Sam to bed. I have no time for dangerous games."

Afraid he would kick her out before she had time to deliver her message, she ploughed on.

"Both your lives are in grave danger," she said, beckoning to Sam who crouched near the pedals of the piano. When Sam edged closer, Jon scowled.

"After what happened at school, you mean?"

She nodded. "The police have already questioned several parents. If you are lucky they won't come till tomorrow."

"What does that have to do with giving you a cup?"

"It's complicated. Why don't you sit down and let me explain."

He crossed his arms, as if to say he was having nothing of it. His reaction made sense. All he wanted was for her to leave. But she couldn't. He sat down across from her, keeping his arms folded over his chest.

"When the police come, they'll lock Sam up." She spoke in whispers, hoping there were no concealed microphones. "Sam is no criminal. He's ill. But they can't cure illness. They are not interested in caring for the ill. Their only response is to eradicate illness by getting rid of those who are ill."

She felt a shiver run down her spine. Not Sam. They couldn't get Sam. He was special. She was sure of it. She wished she didn't have to be so forthright, but there was no time to be diplomatic. She feared Jon might reject her explanations and call the police.

He shrugged and sank deeper in his chair. "There is very little I can do."

"Jane would never have given up so easily," she said, playing her trump card.

He sat bolt upright and spun to look at her. "What do you know about my wife?"

"I am a healer. We worked together during the Disaster."

Jon slumped back in his chair, mumbling, "Healer, teacher, who are you?" Now she was not only a nuisance, but a dangerous outlaw, a wanted criminal. Would he turn her in? Maybe not if she stressed her friendship with Jane.

"I knew Jane well. She would never have balked at finding a solution."

He nodded. "She was always attempting the impossible."

Out of the corner of her eye she spotted Sam rounding the edge of the settee.

"Come and sit next to me, Sam," she said, patting the sofa. When he crawled over, she lifted him from the ground and planted him next to her. Turning to Jon, she said, "I want your permission to give Sam medicine that will calm him. If he gets agitated we stand no chance."

He looked away, wary. She pictured the poster on the class door: Alternative medicine is deadly. He probably didn't believe the propaganda, but everyone was cautious.

"He's always been like this. How could your remedy help?" he asked.

"It will calm him. We can talk about it later. Now we need to get you both to safety."

"Safety?" he scoffed, his eyebrows raised at such a ludicrous idea. "No one is safe from the Food Police. They have spies in every shadow."

"Not everywhere. Once I have given my potion to Sam, I will take you both to a safe haven. I know nowhere is completely safe, but it will be safer than here."

Jon shook his head. "Listen. I am an ex-concert pianist, turned translator with a severely handicapped child, not an adventurer or an outlaw that can dash into hiding from the police." He paused to look at his long, slender fingers. "Jane was always much more adventurous than me, more courageous too." He sighed. "I wish I had had the strength of character to stop her going to her death in the suburbs."

A distant drone had them on their feet moving to the window. Peering round the curtains, they searched for its source.

"That's odd," he whispered. "This is always such a quiet neighbourhood. No one has vehicles. And anyway, where would they get the petrol?"

She could just make out the open area out front. All was still. Then an armoured vehicle burst from between two buildings its motor roaring, careened along the walkway heading for their building, skidded to a halt in front of the entrance and a squad of food police tumbled out.

"We're trapped," he said, his voice strangled.

"No we're not." She pulled the flask from her pocket and brandished it at him.

"Go ahead," he said, capitulating.

"Whatever happens," she said, "Sam needs to stay calm."

The boy struggled when she tried to give him the medicine. She was obliged to prise his mouth open, but at least he didn't spit it out. Scooping him up, she handed him to Jon. "Find sturdy shoes and a good coat for both of you," she ordered.

Hurrying into the hall, she went in search of the service hatch she'd seen on the plans. It hadn't been used in years. She pulled a flashlight from her pocket and drew a large knife from a sheath hidden under her coat. The hatch had been painted over many times and she had to scratch away a thick layer of paint before she could slide her knife between the frame and the hatch. Despite her efforts it wouldn't budge. Below she could hear a crash as the police forced their way into the building and boots resonated in the stairwell. To her relief, the hatch slid up revealing a shaft with rusty metal rungs on the far wall.

"Listen carefully Sam. You are going to ride on my back." Not waiting to see if he agreed, she pulled the large scarf from around her neck and said to Jon, "Hold him on my back while I wrap this round us both." The moment he was lashed to her back, she climbed into the shaft and began her descent.

"Close the hatch after you, Jon," she whispered, "and whatever you do don't make a noise."

5.

Jon felt his way from rung to rung in the dark. Unevenly spaced, the bars were rough and chafed his hands. Half way down he searched for the next step only to miss, his foot flailing in empty space. He clung to the rung, his heart hammering in his chest.

Above, the Food Police were thundering at his front door, demanding to be let in. Only seconds later, a violent crash marked the limit of their patience. Jon swore, thinking of his books, the product of years of perseverance. They had survived the Disaster when other libraries had gone up in smoke. Now they were being destroyed by brutes who couldn't even read. Above all he regretted his grand piano, probably the last one in town.

He was so intent on the noise above that his boot bounced off Nan's head. He heard her suck in air, but she made no other sound. She pulled Sam out of the way just in time as Jon descended the final rungs and joined them.

Nan switched on her torch revealing a basement, the walls of which were grey with grime and the floor flecked with mould. In one corner, a fluorescent mushroom thrived under an air vent.

Sam's arms were firmly clasped around Nan's neck and his feet had snaked around her waist. The sight disturbed Jon, who pointed at Sam and mimed carrying him. When Nan shook her head, he felt at a loss. He had been carrying Sam for years.

Going from one exit to another Nan pressed her ear against the door and listened. Selecting one, she opened it and stepped into a narrow corridor that sloped gently down. He followed.

Air vents appeared periodically in the ceiling, but they provided no light. Night must have fallen. Nan turned off the torch, no doubt worried it might attract attention. He heard the scratch of her fingers trailing along the wall finding her way by touch. One hand placed on Sam's shoulder, he walked close behind.

In the dark the only sounds were their laboured breathing and the dull sucking of their shoes in the mud under foot. That there were no signs of pursuit was worrying. The police had been in such a hurry. They'd wasted no time breaking in. Surely they wouldn't give up now.

After a good ten minutes plodding, the sound of Nan's hand scraping along the wall ceased. She switched on her torch. They were standing at the middle of a crossing of several tunnels.

"Let me take Sam," Jon whispered.

To his relief, she accepted and, untying Sam, Jon took the boy in his arms.

"Let me tie him on your back," she said, holding out the scarf.

He waved a hand in dismissal. Sam curled up in Jon's arms, his head pressed against Jon's chest and closed his eyes. Thank heavens Nan's potion worked.

Nan opted for the tunnel that continued in the same direction and they moved in single file, faster now that they had the torch to light their way. The tunnel was littered with refuse. Worst were the dead animals. They stank. The place would surely give him nightmares. Several times they stumbled on sections where the wall had caved in, but they managed to squeeze past.

Whenever they paused, Jon listened for pursuit. He heard nothing, although they were not alone. A rat scuttled in front of them. It glared, then darted away into the shadows. He spotted a snake, but it slithered off before he got a good look. He was glad it did. Pushing snakes and their slit eyes from his mind, he fixed Nan's back.

She halted at a round metallic door as large as the tunnel. In its middle a king-sized handle pointed its rusty arms up and down. Nan grabbed one end and pushed it anticlockwise, groaning with the effort, but the handle resisted. Only when he helped did it shift in jerks with painful squeaks. Once opened, he caught sight of a small hallway leading to other tunnels. They stepped through and Nan closed the door.

"We are no longer under your quarter," Nan said.

"Where are we going?"

"A way house, a temporary refuge where we can rest and get something to eat."

"And after that?"

"We head for the safest place in town."

Jon raised his eyebrows. For ten years his home had been one such place, but he doubted there were many others.

"Baxter," she said.

"Baxter!" he spluttered, taking a step back. He almost toppled under Sam's weight. Baxter with its charred ruins! Rumour had it was rife with the withering sickness that had caused the Disaster. It had long been cordoned off and abandoned.

"That's where you are taking us?" His voice rose in disbelief.

"Yes. It's the safest place in town."

"Safe!" He almost choked on the word. "How can it possibly be safe?"

"Firstly, there is none of the illness people imagine..."

She was so confident, it irritated him. "How can you be so sure?"

"Because I lived there and I know a lot of others who live there and none are ill."

He tried to take in what she said. She had lived in Baxter! She might be contaminated. Had he avoided the sickness so long only to be claimed by it now?

"Secondly," she went on, "there are no Food Police. That's why I say it is the safest place in town."

Sam shifted in Jon's arms as if he were about to wake. Jon looked down at him, surprised to be so moved by the sleeping face. The boy seemed so vulnerable. Jon couldn't take the risk of exposing him to Baxter. "I can't do it."

"Are you going to be ruled by fear based on rumour? Or are you going to trust me and accept my knowledge and experience? The choice is simple. Either it's the Food Police and their torture chambers or Baxter and a possible route to freedom and safety."

He would not have called himself narrow-minded, but even though her arguments sounded plausible, the idea of leading Sam into Baxter was beyond him. He shook his head.

"Anyway we are not there yet," Nan said. "First we have to make it to the way house."

6.

I feel it on my skin like a velvet caress that has goose flesh forming on my arms. I taste it in my mouth, both bitter and sweet; cerulean blue, deep and vibrant, reaching through my eyes to the depths inside, setting my soul yearning to break free. Every cell hums to its music. I want to jump and dance and shout. I want to cry and laugh. I don't know what I want. My body will shatter if I contemplate it much longer.

Edelweiss? No. That's white. Spring gentian. That's it. Five upturned petals, curved gracefully outwards, reaching for the sun. A single flower in an earthenware pot alone on a window sill. Never to be picked, a distant memory warns. It brings death.

Death. I shudder. Where am I? Who am I?

:: out - out - out - this is my body - my world - there is enough confusion in here without cramming your muddled emotions into my ears - foul intruder - pick your blasted flower and die somewhere else

His voice, for all its ferocity, curls around me. Rather than pushing me away, it invites closer inspection. I wet my lips in anticipation. I taste the 't' of 'out' and sense the rush of air driven by a short, sharp tightening of the muscles of his belly. The 't' hisses between the tongue and the roof of his mouth darting out like the forked tongue of a snake.

:: it is your tongue that is forked, not mine, blockhead - the sound you hear is the slamming of the door in your face - get - out - I am the master - the sole occupant here

You're wrong. I am here too.

:: not for much longer

He does control this body, so maybe he is the master, or is he? His shoulders are slumped and his arms are slender, too slender for me; a little exercise would do him good. As for his hands, the long fingers are interlaced in a tense pyramid. Bone presses against bone, squashing muscles and flesh. I feel the hurt, but he is insensitive to it. His hand? My hand. Yes. My hand. I flex the muscles, unlacing my fingers and relax, delighting in a sense of achievement.

:: hey - stop that

He wrenches back control and clenches his fists, lashing out at the gentian. *No!* I tear back control, narrowly missing the plant, hitting the wall instead. Both of us yell in pain and crumple to the floor.

Hearing the door fly open, Sam scurries away just as Jon rushes in closely followed by Nan. Seeing us clasping our hand in pain, Jon sighs. "You're hopeless, Sam. What have you done now?"

Nan steps past him and kneels beside us. "Let me look," she says, reaching out to hold our hand.

Sam, who is in control, jerks the hand out of reach, narrowly missing smashing into the wall again. I wrest control from him and let Nan examine our hand.

:: you snivelling noserag - you limp lamppost bent over double - you - you - you earwig smeared with rancid butter

He wishes he could hit out, I can feel it, but he doesn't want to hurt Nan and I am well in control. Instead, he splutters meaningless abuse with all the venom he can muster.

Nan extends our fingers then folds them again. "They are not broken. But your hand is grazed and bruised. Maybe our hosts have something for that."

She helps us to our feet and joins Jon by the door where she turns and waits for us to follow. I take a tentative step, wobbling precariously. Nan stretches out a hand to help, but I shake my head. She's used to Sam's clumsiness so my unsteadiness won't surprise her and I want to walk on my own.

:: you will fall - as apples and pears do, so will you - down down down

No I won't.

I take a second step. Sam is trying to confuse me with a muddle of nonsense, but I ignore him.

There are so many sensations in this walking: the soles of my feet on the cold floor; the pressure under my toes and on my heels constantly changing; the tensing of my leg muscles that gives birth to a gentle swaying of my hips. Oh the pleasure of it. Then there are the tiny adjustments of my shoulders and my arms shooting out for balance. I feel my lips pursed in concentration and even my eyes and ears strive to move me forward. Above all, I sense my centre of balance shifting forwards and backwards, but also sideways like a sedate but erratic pendulum.

Jon and Nan watch my hesitant progression wide-eyed. This is as new for them as it is for me. In six hesitant steps I reach Nan and lay my head against her chest.

"Well done," she says, folding her arms around my shoulders. I feel an immense longing and a host of past memories surge, blurry images of times when I was loved and held like this. I can hear Nan's heart beat. I feel her warm embrace and beyond that warmth I sense something I can't put words to. Like a soft breeze, or the shifting of coloured light bathing me in its glow.

"Being away from home seems to do you good," Nan says, running a hand through my short hair.

"Let's go," Jon says wrapping an arm around me and leading me away from Nan, much to my disappointment. He sounds upset. Did I do something wrong?

:: course you did blubber head - everything about you is wrong - you are nothing but a monumental mistake

"Indeed," Nan says, shocking me till I realise she was replying to Jon not agreeing with Sam. "Our hosts are waiting for us. They've prepared a meal."

7.

Jon and the others wove their way across the courtyard. So many neat rows of vegetables and well-tended bushes heavy with fruit. How on earth had their hosts managed to conceal such a pleasant and productive dwelling behind the facade of a ruin?

Sam had insisted on going with Nan but refused to hold her hand. The relative ease with which he walked unaided astounded Jon. Maybe Nan was right. The change had done him good. But that didn't make his violent outbreaks any less worrying. When Sam slipped and fell, Jon couldn't help wincing as the boy's knee hit a stone. Jon expected him to cry, but Sam sat where he had fallen, unperturbed.

"Getting the first seeds was the difficult task," one of their hosts, Ralph, said helping Sam to his feet. Like his wife, Gertrude, who picked a couple of tomatoes and piled them in her up-turned apron, both looked unexceptional: short, slightly stooped, greying and above all mild. Like their home, you'd never have guessed that two ferocious opponents of the Food Police resided behind such facades.

Most of the living quarters were below ground, although carefully placed windows high in the walls let in some light. The dining room was just large enough to hold five around a bare wooden table. Jon moved to sit next to Sam. He would have to help the boy eat. But Sam insisted on sitting with Nan.

Jon caught Nan's eye, raising his shoulders by way of apology. She smiled and shook her head before lacing an arm around Sam's shoulder.

"Here, Sam," she said, pulling a flask from her pocket. "Take a couple of drops."

"What is it?" Gertrude asked, leaning forward to sniff the contents. "Smells of alcohol."

"A tincture of plants designed to reduce anxiety."

"Anxiety?" Jon asked.

"The world is an anxious place for the likes of Sam."

"Surely it is not anxiety, but anger we need to deal with," Jon replied.

"My guess is that his anger is rooted in anxiety," Nan said.

"Well, whatever the explanation, your potion is having an effect," Jon said, begrudgingly. He had never seen Sam so calm for such a long period.

His son raised the flask to his lips, then leaned his back as if to down the whole bottle.

"Just a little," Nan said, putting out a hand to restrain him. "It's got to last."

Gertrude had made a cold soup with tomatoes and herbs accompanied by a salad and something that looked like a cross between a thick biscuit and a small loaf.

"We are cautious when it comes to cooking," she said, "who knows who might smell the food and search for its source."

Jon contemplated the bowl of soup in front of him, his stomach churning. He picked up the spoon, turning it over in his fingers, but didn't eat. Years of government propaganda rang in his ears: Natural food kills.

He looked at Sam across the table. The boy had none of his qualms. He was spooning soup into his mouth with remarkable facility for someone who, until yesterday, had had difficulties putting a food tablet in his mouth.

Gertrude smiled at Sam then turned to Jon. "Is this the first time you've eaten such food since the Disaster?" she asked. There was no accusation in her question, only kindness. "It won't harm you, but I wouldn't eat too much."

Jon dipped the spoon in the soup, scraped the underside on the edge of the bowl and raised a little to his mouth. It smelt rich, far too rich. He sipped a tiny drop, steeling himself to resist the urge to throw up. Instead, he was surprised by the taste which brought a raft of memories flooding back. Jane had been such a good cook.

Just as he was about to sip a second mouthful, Sam's spoon slipped from his fingers and crashed into the bowl splattering soup across the table.

"Never mind," Gertrude said as she hurried to fetch a wet cloth.

Sam had curled up into a ball and was trying to burrow into Nan's arms. "You are doing very well," she told him, stroking his hair.

"Sam has some difficulty managing walking and eating," Jon explained.

"Don't worry about the soup, Sam," Gertrude said. "There's more if you'd like."

Sam stayed with his head wrapped in his arms next to Nan.

"Let's go next door," Ralph said once the meal was over. Nan and Jon helped Gertrude clear away while Ralph took Sam next door. Jon was amazed the boy accepted to go with a complete stranger.

The room, which was no bigger than the dining room, was filled by two broad settees and an upright piano. It was odd to see such an instrument there. However had they got it in? And where did it come from? Intrigued, he opened the fallboard and was about the run his fingers over the keys when it struck him that anyone lurking outside might hear. Closing the piano he turned to Ralph and asked, "Do you ever play it?"

"Oh yes." He grinned. "We just have to take some precautions."

He closed a shutter on the small window and drew a thick curtain over it. Then he pulled an equally thick curtain over the door. "Now you can play."

Jon opened the fallboard again and played a series of arpeggios. "It is well tuned."

"I was a piano tuner before the Disaster," Ralph said.

Jon wondered if they'd ever met back then. He didn't look familiar.

"We saw you in concert," Gertrude said as she sat next to Sam and Nan.

He was surprised she recognised him. He'd aged a lot since the Disaster.

"I remember it well. You played several pieces of Bach," Gertrude said. "The Disaster has robbed us of many good things."

"My biggest regret is that all my sheet music got destroyed," Ralph said.

"How did you manage to save the piano?" Jon asked.

"Luck really. I was supposed to repair it, but I had no time. So I stored it in an outhouse not far from here. For some weird reason it escaped the fire."

"Not all the music was destroyed," Gertrude said. She hurried out into the dining room and returned carrying a tattered score. "We found this hidden inside the piano." She handed it to Jon.

It was a complicated keyboard piece, probably written by a contemporary of Bach, but he didn't recognise the composer.

"Fat lot of good that does me," Ralph said. "It is far too difficult for me to play."

Jon placed the score on the music rack and sat on the piano stool. He had been playing for a while when he felt someone standing next to him. Stopping, he saw it was Sam. The boy had never shown the slightest interest in music, much to Jon's regret. Yet there he was staring intently at the keyboard. Jon turned back to the music and continued playing. When he had finished and stood to acknowledge the muted applause, Sam was still standing next to him.

To Jon's surprise, Sam slid onto the vacated stool and held his hands suspended over the key board. He was afraid the boy would damage the keys, but instead he pressed one, middle C. No one spoke. Sam struggled to control twisted fingers and tried other keys. Jon recognised the sequence. It was one of the ancient modes that existed before pianos were invented; each mode another voice, a different emotion. Surely Sam's choice was pure coincidence.

Sam closed his eyes, his fingers gliding over the keys as he added notes around the basic mode forming a complex melody that varied each time he returned to it. Jon forced himself to close his mouth which had fallen open. Then Sam's left hand got to work accompanying the notes with a measured bass. An extraordinary counterpoint unfolded, the simplicity and the beauty of which moved Jon to tears. As the boy neared the end, he broke off, thumped the keyboard with a clenched fist and flung himself to the floor, thrashing about as he had done earlier.

8.

:: insufferable show-off

Jealous, I want to say, but I keep the thought to myself. We are stretched out on the settee our head in Nan's lap, our eyes closed. She is idly twisting her fingers through our hair. I find it comforting.

:: meddling fingers muddling my hair messing with my thoughts

Across from us, Jon, Ralph and Gertrude are squashed onto the other settee.

"That was extraordinary," Ralph says. "How long has he been playing?"

Jon sighs. "He has never played."

"Come off it."

"I assure you, he has never touched a piano, except when he bumped into it or fell over the pedals."

:: blasted noise box is always sticking out its feet to trip me up

"But that's not possible," Gertrude says.

It's amazing how people talk about you without restraint when you don't speak, as if not speaking means you are dumb.

:: what do you expect? - the dumb are dumb - they do not count

"It could well be autism," Nan says. "Some children who have great difficulties being in the world can be brilliant artists or musicians or scientists. It's as if they focus on one activity."

"But why should it surface now?" Jon asks. He sounds almost annoyed.

It would be easy to set them right, but that might not be wise. For starters, they probably wouldn't believe me and who knows how they would react if they did. Playing the piano had been silly, but I couldn't resist. The music was so enticing.

:: enticing, my foot, smart-aleck showing off

"It's not so much the piano playing that worries me as the outbursts of violence," Jon says. "Somebody is going to get hurt."

"It can't be easy to live with the frustration," Nan says.

"Frustration?" Ralph asks.

"Imagine you are a genius but can only express yourself through a piano."

"I wish I could express myself like that," Ralph says, getting to his feet and closing the piano.

"You forget that you wouldn't be able to talk and most physical activities would be nigh on impossible," Nan points out.

What a horrible thought. If I were locked in like that, I think I'd go crazy.

:: wrong again intruder - why leave such a snug fortress to risk myself in their chaos?

"Nan told me you had a brush with the Food Police," Ralph says.

"They came to fetch Sam and we had to run."

"I gather there was something before that."

There is a long pause. I sneak a look at Jon, whose brows are knit in thought. Across from him, Ralph has shifted to the edge of his seat eager to hear Jon's answer. They are so engrossed in their conversation no one bothers with us.

"The work you were supposed to do," Nan jogs his memory.

"Oh that! They wanted me to translate a scroll."

"Did you see it?" Nan asked.

"I did. It was really old. At first the ministry bloke didn't want me to touch it, but I explained I had to be sure I could do the translation."

"So what was it about?" Ralph asked.

"It told the story of an island beset by troubles that someone was going to save…"

The mention of an island sends a shiver down my spine.

:: go back to your island and drown with all the others

Come off it, Sam. You have no idea how awful that was. What good will it do you to hurt me?

:: hurting is not enough - destroying would be too good for you

I sigh mentally. I know time is on my side, but I will have to put up with his abuse till then.

"Someone?" Nan asks.

"I'm not sure of the translation. Something like lumens or luminar."

"Luminaries!" Both Nan and Ralph say in chorus. Nan ceases playing with our hair and leans forward.

"Luminaries?" Jon asks. "What's that? Some sort of light people?"

Ralph glances at Nan before replying. "A luminary is a special being who comes into the world at a time of crisis to set things right."

"A sort of saviour?" Jon asks.

I sense Nan nod in agreement.

"Why would the Food Police be interested in such a myth?"

"Because they don't want anyone to set things right," Nan replies. "It's always the same. Once a luminary emerges, those in power try to track him down and eliminate him."

"But surely such beings exist only in myths," Jon says.

Ralph glances at Nan again, an unspoken question passing between them.

"They are real enough!" Ralph says.

Jon laughs, his laughter sounding strained as he shakes his head. "How can you be so sure?"

"Because we have been waiting ages for the luminary to return," Ralph says, a wistful smile on his lips.

"We?"

"There's a group of people dedicated to helping the luminary when he or she arrives and we are part of it," Ralph tells him.

Jon looks at them incredulous. "You too?" he asks Nan.

"Me too," she replies. "How do you think I knew about this way house?"

"So you aren't a teacher?"

"Sure I am. But that is not all I am."

"Hold on a moment," Jon says. "How can you tell who this person is? What if you make a mistake?"

"No set of factors distinguishes a luminary from everyone else," Nan says. "But there is one characteristic found in all luminaries. The medical term is chimera."

"You mean they have two heads or have various animal parts?" Jon laughs.

"That is the mythological meaning," Nan explains. "But the medical term refers to people who have two distinct sets of genes."

:: so that is how you sneaked in - left over junk jerked into life by mistake

"I didn't know that was possible."

"On a much smaller scale, it is surprisingly common. Most of us have traces of genes from our family and ancestors. With the luminaries that other set of genes is complete and lies dormant for centuries."

"Two people in one to save the world," Jon says.

"Normally it is only one of the two that is a luminary."

Their words are troubling. This chimera business sounds very much like Sam and I. Not that we have anything to do with saving the world.

9.

Two beds stood in the narrow room, a small one for Sam and a slightly larger one. Nan shot a glance at Jon who looked away, blushing. What would it be like to share a bed with him? She quickly pushed the question aside. What was she thinking? What about Sam?

"That's far too small for two people," Jon mumbled, making for the door. "I'll lie down on the settee."

He halted at the sight of Sam wrestling with his jacket preparing for bed. She thought he might remain, if only to help Sam. Not that the boy needed extra help with her there.

"Keep it on, Sam," she said. "Just in case we need to leave in a hurry."

The boy immediately ceased struggling but his arms and legs began twitching. Blast. She had to be more careful. The last thing they needed was another fit of anxiety. At least her potion would help fend off the worst.

Jon moved to reassure Sam. Maybe she should have let him, but she was eager to comfort the boy and got there first, taking Sam in her arms. Jon's shoulders slumped. "I'll let you handle this," he said, turning to go. "See you tomorrow."

If she were to get Sam to safety, she couldn't afford to have Jon sulking, or worse, turn against her. She unclasped Sam's hands from around her neck and left him on the bed.

"Jon," she said, laying a hand on Jon's shoulder. "Why don't you stay a while?"

He made to shrug off her hand, but she held it there, saying, "Please."

Reluctantly, he took his place on the larger bed, perching on its very edge. She joined him, sitting a few feet away.

"This is not easy, is it?" she said.

He nodded, staring at the floor for a long moment. She waited.

"Only a couple of days ago life was predictable," he said. "Despite the difficulties, I knew what to do. Now nothing makes sense. I can no longer trust myself to make the right decision." He rubbed his eyes.

She shifted to his side and put an arm round his shoulders. He held himself stiff as if that could ward off the emotions. Tears formed in his eyes.

"It's all very well giving Sam this potion, but what happens when it runs out? Will he lash out and hurt someone?" he asked, his voice breaking as he wiped the back of his hand across his face. "He gets completely out of control." He pulled a handkerchief from his pocket and blew his nose. "Maybe it would be better if we let the authorities look after him."

She gasped, pulling away. "Never!"

Jon continued talking, ignoring her reaction. "I've managed to care for him for twelve years, ever since Jane died. I think I've done a good job." He got to his feet and began to pace. "But this violence is too much."

"You can't hand Sam to the Food Police."

He glanced at Sam who had begun rocking backwards and forwards on his bed. "I can't handle it any more," Jon said, lowering his voice. "I'm not made for this."

"Then I will look after him," she replied, her face set in determination as she returned to sit next to Sam.

"What a mess!" he exclaimed. "I don't want to abandon Sam. Of course I don't. But it is all so complicated." He slumped onto the bed on the other side of Sam and held his head in his hands.

Sam rested a hand on Jon's knee causing Jon to look up, his eyes wide.

Nan had never seen Sam look so intent, so alive, so present. The boy's lips moved, struggling, his face tense with effort. One sole word squeezed between his lips, "Jon," followed by a sigh of relief.

Jon's hand flew to his mouth.

Never had Sam spoken. At best he grunted and groaned. Of all the words he could have said, it was Jon's name he had chosen. No wonder tears welled up in Jon's eyes. Nan felt her own eyes glistening.

Sam's struggle to speak was not over. His lips quivered, his brow furrowed, his nose flared. "All," he finally said. Gaining confidence as he went on, the words came a little easier. "... is .... not ... lost."

Nan was overjoyed at Sam speaking and she expected Jon to be, but he looked on with dread. She sensed his muscles poised to pounce as if he feared another violent outburst. And sure enough the boy's fingers began to twitch. Nan prepared to catch his arms should Sam lash out, but the boy clasped his hands so tight his knuckles turned white. No anger twisted his face though. Instead she saw only intense concentration, as if some unearthly battle raged inside him. Then, Sam let out a long sigh, unclasped his hands and smiled.

That smile, like a sun bursting through storm clouds, so open, so relaxed, so rich in meaning, had Nan hoping that her wildest dreams were about to come true. Jon however looked unnerved. Surely he could not have wished for more. Had he not spent years with a boy who had been inaccessible, barricaded behind a mental wall, dumb and disoriented?

"I ... need ... to explain," Sam continued.

"Take your time," she said.

"Words come with ... difficulty," Sam began, brushing sweat from his brow. "I must ... be brief. Sam and I are a ... chimera."

"Sam and I?" Jon asked and barked with laughter as if the idea was absurd. He glanced at her. Ignoring his call for complicity, she leant forward, a glow in her eyes.

"What makes you say that, Sam?" she asked.

"Because there are two of us."

"Two?" Jon said, incredulous. "I see only one."

"If Sam is what he says, you would only see one person," Nan replied. "A chimera manifests itself as two very distinct personalities in a single body."

Jon returned her smile with a soured-faced look, as if she were siding with Sam in some battle of wits. "You only make things worse," he muttered.

"Sam is the boy you know," Sam continued, articulating the words with more ease. "New things terrify him. He can't speak … out loud. He stumbles. He falls." Sam paused to catch his breath. "I am a girl. I play piano. I talk. I walk. That violence you saw was Sam trying to kick me out."

Nan thought she would burst with joy at this news. At last. After so much waiting. She grinned at Jon, but he looked away, his fists clenched so tight, his knuckles were white. His face had taken on a sickly pallor.

"Why only now?" Jon asked, shaking his head.

"I just awoke."

"This is preposterous," Jon burst out, unable to contain his anger.

"No it's not," Nan said. "Just as the second set of genes can lie dormant for generations, so the second person can remain veiled till it is time to emerge."

"You make it sound like this is all part of some grand scheme," he said. He paused as if realising something, then went on, "Quit dreaming. Sam is not your long-awaited saviour."

10.

:: bah! - twelve years effort wiped out by four ill-chosen words - all is not lost - what rubbish - of course it is - thanks to your intrusion the world is in ruins - why can't you follow my example and hold your blasted tongue - admit it - you want to strut about like a princess, to have people admire you, to think you are so much better than a cripple like me - the new girl who can walk and talk, the girl who plays the piano so sweetly - ha! you shied away from telling them you are a girl - this is my body, a boy's body, you don't belong - you burst in uninvited - you stomp about fouling everywhere with your bitter memories - because of you I have hurt myself and others too - you have angered Jon and set him against me - the one person who really cared now wants to abandon me to those nasty food-mongers - you have breached my walls, you have bridged the gap between here and there, letting in an inquisitive, confusing rabble - how am I to protect myself from the unholy muddle - you have left me nowhere to hide - while you are here I will always be exposed - don't try that saviour codswallop on me - it is not me that is deluded, it's you - you couldn't save a fly, let-alone protect those drowning children - goodness knows how you convinced anyone you could save them - everything you touch turns to evil

Oh Sam. That is so unfair. His words cut straight to my heart. *I know you are angry and confused, but I am doing my best in an impossible situation, just like you. You are right on one count: I am no saviour. I do not wish that for myself. I would not wish it on anybody. I have no idea*

where those visions of children come from. But the suffering is terrible. I feel the pain and fear of each of them. It is unbearable. The thought brings tears to our eyes.

"Now you've upset Sam," Jon says, raising his voice.

"Me? How can you be so sure? It might be something quite different. Sam, what are you crying about?"

:: don't you dare reply - the question is for me

Reply yourself then.

:: never - I am not here to answer - give them but one word and they'll drag your soul out screaming

They can't take your soul, Sam. I know he won't believe me, but I try. *Your soul is yours. It can't leave your body.*

"You see," Jon says. "Your precious other Sam has no answer for you."

"Why are you fighting me, Jon?" Nan asks.

"Fighting? I'm not fighting. It is you that are stirring things up. It is you encouraging Sam's delirium. All because you desperately want your dream to come true. If we are in for wild ideas, why not see him as possessed."

"This is not possession." Nan sighs. "People are possessed by evil. Sam couldn't walk. Now he can. Sam couldn't talk. Now he can. Do you call that evil?"

:: yes yes yes - she is evil - she is taking control of me - summon the exorcist - chase her out

They can't hear you Sam. Only I can. You'll have to try harder if you want them to know what you think.

:: filthy temptress - you think you're clever - you won't catch me like that

"All I know is that every time Sam beguiles us with some wonderful new number, a catastrophe lurks in the wings. He urgently needs specialist help."

"Be serious, Jon. We are on the run in a ruined city, chased by the food police. Even if your worries were founded, and I am sure they are not, the type of psychiatric help you are talking about was dismantled shortly after the Disaster."

"This can't go on." Jon pulls at his hair. "Who knows what

damage this is doing to Sam? I prefer to return to town, rather than let this continue."

:: see what you've done - my father is going to hand me over to the very people he has protected me from all these years

Nan gets to her feet and plants herself between Jon and us. "I won't let you."

"Afraid you'll lose your precious saviour?" Jon says, his tone spiteful, his body shaking with anger as he gets up to face her.

"Now who is possessed?" Nan says, her fists clenched.

Jon feints but Nan blocks his attempt to get round her. Their fingers interlock and they grapple. From behind Nan, I reach out to grab their clenched fists, but their movements are wild and unpredictable. I duck, their flailing arms narrowly missing my head. Each struggles to push the other back, their chests heaving, locked together, their faces only inches apart, eyes blazing, lips quivering. I take advantage of the stalemate to grasp their hands and send out calming thoughts. To my relief, they cease pushing and their arms sink to their sides.

When they draw back, I shift between them and take hold of their hands. Jon stares down at his hand in mine, his free hand cupped over his mouth in dismay. I throw myself wholeheartedly into sending wave after wave of peaceful throughs till the tight lines around Jon's mouth and eyes fade. Glancing at Nan, I see she is about to cry.

"I'm so sorry," she says, brushing tears from her cheeks. "I don't know what got over me."

A soft knock comes at the door and Ralph steps in. He halts a moment, his eyebrows arching as he sees Nan in tears, then he hurries closer. "Time to leave," he whispers. "There's a squad of police massing outside. Grab your things and follow me."

11.

Jon shook his head. It was unthinkable. He'd just had a flaming row with Nan. Thank heavens he was the last of their group as they hurried down the tunnel. No one wold see the shame on his face. Whatever had come over him? It wasn't just Sam that was unpredictable and destructive.

Distant shouts rang out above. The police were looking for a way in. No one spoke. Ahead, Nan held Sam's hand. The boy had wanted to hold Jon's, but he had refused, much to Sam's disappointment. He needed time alone to mull over what had happened.

For years he'd dodged prying government eyes, constantly at risk that some dutiful citizen would report Sam's condition. Now look at him. The police had broken into his flat. He was fleeing with members of an illegal sect. For goodness sake! They practised healing. They ate natural food. Above all they welcomed the advent of a saviour come to overthrow the police regime. He would never be able to return to his quiet life. He had always seen himself as a mild person. How had he become such a hothead? His chances of survival were slim what with Sam's outbursts and his own anger?

Ralph paused to light a lamp, then hurried them along a series of narrow, twisting tunnels. As they plunged ever deeper, the sound of pursuit faded, leaving only their own footfalls, the occasional drip of water and their laboured breathing.

They had been walking for ages, when Ralph halted. They

had reached a major crossing. "We are under Baxter," he said, "but we are far too deep. There is no direct access. We will have to go on till the tunnel returns to the surface. Then we can track back."

"Where are we headed?" Jon asked, wary. All three admitted they belonged to some sort of sect. He was afraid he and Sam would end up captives of their saviour-seeking group.

"There's a centre for refugees. They will know where to go."

Jon was unhappy. The last thing he wanted was to wander disease-infested ruins. But he kept quiet. The time come, he would flee with his son.

Nan had picked up Sam, clutching him against her chest. The boy was whispering in her ear. It was easy to imagine they were plotting to get rid of a troublesome father.

Jon plodded on. The tunnel had been sloping upwards for a while. Surely they'd surface soon.

As they rounded a tight bend, Ralph halted mid-stride and waved them back, extinguishing the lamp. Footsteps could be heard ahead. Nan stumbled several times as they retraced their steps, forcing her to put Sam down.

They had barely gone fifty yards when footsteps came from ahead. Blast. They were surrounded. "Follow me," Ralph whispered, pushing past only to halt a few yards further on.

"Go that way," he said, pointing down a tunnel. "We'll lead them off."

"Be careful," Nan said over her shoulder as she plunged into the dark.

Jon hurried after, having no wish to be left behind. Nan walked fast making it difficult to keep up. He stretched out and placed a hand on her shoulder, only to feel a warm hand settle on his. The moment the boy's fingers touched him, a strange calmness flowed over him, as if his senses were being numbed. He snatched his hand away, letting out a hiss as he did.

"What's the matter?" Nan asked.

Jon pressed his lips together and refused to speak, fearing another tirade. The sound of running boots thudded close by.

"Take this, Sam," Nan said, handing him the flask containing the potion. "Drink a few drops once a day. Now run." She
pushed the boy down a low side-tunnel. "Go to the fence. Crawl
under. Look for the square at the centre. We'll meet you there."

"You can't send Sam off like that," Jon said as Sam crawed
inside.

"We need to stall the police," Nan replied, "to give him a
chance."

Jon had no intention of hanging around. Let her do so if she
wanted. "I'm going with Sam," Jon said. "If you don't want to
help him, I sure do."

Nan huffed but kept a tight hold on her annoyance. "You
won't be able to get out," she said.

"Why ever not?"

"The entrance is far too tiny."

Jon clenched his teeth in a effort not to shout. She must have
known all along. Her life might mean nothing to her, provided
her little saviour was saved, but he wanted to live just as much as
he wanted Sam to live. Her saviour could go to hell, but not with
his son.

"Sam?" Jon called out. "Sam?" He got no answer.

Down the tunnel, the thunder of boots grew ever louder.

"Run!" Nan said and set off away from the tunnel Sam had
used.

Jon hesitated. Should he crawl after Sam? They might hide
in the folds of the earth. The thunder of boots and a foul smell
of chemicals made up his mind. He broke into a run, stumbling
after Nan.

12.

A rosy glow heralds a new day as I struggle from the dark tunnel into the clinging arms of an air thick with the smell of chemicals. Dull forms lurch around, taking shape as the light grows. A wide expanse of upturned bricks, jagged slates and broken beams; the memory of happy homes. Slant-wise across this wasteland runs a high fence a dozen yards away. I shiver as a gust of wind catches a tangle of waste paper and chases it against the fence.

:: world's end - life's end - a boundary crossed only once

Ignoring Sam's warning, I pick my way across the treacherous terrain and am about to get down on my hands and knees and crawl under the fence, when the ring of heavy boots startles me. Where are they? I see no one. Then a tight squad of Food Police surges round a curve in the fence, not more than fifty yards to my left.

"Hey! You! Stop!" an angry voice shouts as the men break into a run.

I fling myself to the ground and wriggle through the hole, snagging my trousers and cutting my leg on the barbed wire as I do.

:: now you are condemned to limp like a door-to-door saleswoman pedalling death

You're delirious, Sam. Let me think.

The first rays of sun slink over the horizon, braving the smoky haze. I scramble to my feet, hastily brushing soot and dust from my hands. I hurry across the corridor of flattened rubble, an exposed no-man's-land some twenty yards wide. Despite the urgency, I am careful not to catch my foot in the holes.

:: you are a dead duck, blasted usurper, stuffed and basted over a hot fire, and me with you - would that I could sever the cord that links us

Ahead, deeper into Baxter, a jumble of charred ruins juts upwards, a grotesque blackened forest casting long, harsh shadows. The pervasive smell of burning and the ever-present chemicals are so strong they catch in my throat making it hard to breathe.

:: don't you recognise the smell? - you are going up in smoke

Nothing stirs behind me. No immediate sounds break the silence. Have they given up, scared off by the fear of disease? In the distance I make out a hint of bird song. Strange, incongruous but beautiful. There are no birds where Jon and Sam live. Jon said they'd been sprayed out of existence.

I reach the far side when renewed shouts explode behind me; the police are still in pursuit. Where should I go? There are no clear paths, but between tumbled walls and the remains of roofs I catch sight of a road. I head for that.

I wind my way as fast as I dare through the debris. My leg hurts, making me limp. Rusted girders stab sideways, slanting into the air, shored up by slabs of stone and heaps of dust and dirt. Withered flowers clutter the way, their crinkled leaves sprayed white, victims of toxic ill-will. Reaching the remains of the road, I hobble forward, heading ever deeper into the ruins. I would like to examine my leg. It hurts more and more, but the police are close behind.

:: stop - now - throw yourself off a cliff for all I care, but whatever you are doing to my leg hurts terrible - it makes me feel woozy - I wish dad were here to stop you

I feel as woozy as you, Sam. There's nothing I can do about it.

Several times I clamber treacherous piles of bricks fallen from a wall. They roll beneath my feet and I sink painfully to my hands and knees. Reaching a fork in the road, I hesitate then opt for the narrowest path, hoping the police will follow the wider one. No such luck. The steady sound of footfalls follows which-ever way I turn. Somehow they know where to go.

Passing ruins that loom above me, I come into a circular clearing. Could this be the centre Nan mentioned? What am I supposed to find here? An ornate fountain stands in the middle, intact but devoid of water.

:: a pulled-down built-up desert - I'm no camel - find me an oasis

Sam is right, thirst is going to be a problem. My throat is parched and irritated by the dust and the smell of smoke, but first I have to get away. I hobble across the open space and hide amongst the ruins of a once majestic building.

Silent and unmoving, I observe the police fan out and search the surrounding ruins. They are far too thorough. Making as little noise as possible, I edge backwards deeper into the ruins.

The building is made of stone and some rooms remain in-tact. Here and there on smoke-darkened walls, I spy fragments of frescoes. They intrigue me, but now is not the time.

:: and they say I am blighted by distraction! - Why don't you stop and admire the washed-out colours while the police kill us

What have you got against art, Sam?

Before he can reply, the inevitable happens. A wall has caved in, blocking the passage. I try to push past, causing bricks and rocks the roll noisily to the floor, but there is no way by.

:: the line's end

13.

I am about to retrace my steps when I hear a sharp "Psst!"
Startled, I freeze.

:: run!

I should. But where to go?

A second urgent "Psst!" hails me.

Low on a wall, through a metal grating, I spot movement.
I take a hesitant step closer. "Through here," a forced whisper
says. The grating shifts revealing a passageway just large enough
to crawl through. Should I trust the person? The shouts of the
police are only a stone's throw way. I have no choice.

:: I'm not going in that filthy hole with a dark murderer

Sam tries to tear back control, but I keep a firm grip.

Stop that, Sam. You'll get us killed.

I sit on the floor and edge feet-first into the hole. In the
pitch dark I can't make out my rescuer, but whoever it is helps
me to my feet and pulls me away from the grate. "We can't stay
here." It sounds like a boy, but I can't be sure. "They've got a
sniffer."

"A sniffer?"

"A man who tracks like a dog, with his nose."

Gripping my hand, the boy pulls me forward. I try to shake
free, not wanting to be dragged without my consent, but the boy
insists. "You'll never find your way alone." He leads me through
the dark, down narrow passageways till we reach what must once
have been a sewerage system. The stink is unbearable. "This'll

throw them," he says, chuckling quietly.

:: phew! - I am going to throw up those bitter memories you filled my head with

No. You're not. Despite my insistence, I fear he's right. The smell is revolting. I clench my teeth, but there is little I can do. We follow the stench, on and on and on, till I wonder if I will ever smell anything else.

:: stench - pickled stench - it is a good name for you - people will say, here comes the stench

You forget you will stink too, Sam.

Turning a corner, daylight beckons in the distance. The promise of fresh air has me hastening my pace. But instead of continuing, the boy takes a side turning and enters a small room.

I make out a low table, several chairs and a rough bed. "We'll wait here, till it's safe. They'll get tired of searching. They always do."

The boy is a few inches taller than me and probably several years older. He is solidly built and surprisingly muscular. He wears a dirty t-shirt and his shorts are just as filthy. Both his legs and arms are tanned as if he spends a lot of time outdoors.

:: stop that immediately - don't think I can't feel you warming to him - you are not using my body for any nonsense like that - yuck!

You really are delirious, Sam.

"My name's Mart," the boy says.

Before I can reply a wave of weariness rolls over me and I sit heavily on the edge of the bed, feeling dizzy. My leg aches. I roll up my trousers. The cut is small and the blood has already dried, but it hurts as if it were far worse. The skin is swollen and feels unnaturally hot. Not good. It must have got infected.

The boy kneels down and examines the wound. "Does it hurt?" he asks.

I wince as he presses lightly. Apologising, he lays the flat of his hand over the cut. His fingers are cool and soothing. When he pulls away, I wish he hadn't.

Sam wrenches control from me in my moment of weakness

and is about to lash out at Mart, when I manage to wrest back control. Just in time. Fortunately, Mart is so intent on my leg he notices nothing.

"Not good." He stares at the tiny gash for a long moment. "We won't be able to wait it out," he says. "We need to get you to a healer. Fast."

When he gets to his feet, I do likewise and almost keel over. Luckily he catches me. Sliding my arm over his shoulder, he takes some of my weight and helps me to the door.

:: any excuse to get in his arms - girls are sickening

Not sickening, Sam, sick. I can't manage more. Most of my remaining energy goes in preventing Sam grabbing control. Luckily as I weaken, so does he.

We move outside and follow a narrow alleyway between two buildings. Little by little the growing fire in my leg creeps up to my knee and then edges ever higher till my whole body is ablaze.

:: give me cupboards any day, a legion of comfy cupboards, full of sweet velvet darkness and the caress of silk scented scarves smoothly slipping over my skin so soft so sweet so soothing so

Long rocky beaches surge around me and waves crash amid the sights and sounds of the surrounding ruins. I fight against the fear that I might see children's bodies floating in the water. Finally, I close my eyes and try to concentrate on staying upright and in control, but I drift.

When I come back to myself, I realise the boy is carrying me, my head lolling on his shoulder. I hear his laboured breathing close to my ear. It is that sound that accompanies me as I drift off again.

14.

Jon slumped on the cold stone floor, his back to the wall. His head ached, a foul taste filled his mouth and his stomach heaved uselessly, but he, at least, had been spared. In front of him, stretched out on the flagstones lay Nan, unmoving, her clothes torn, her face bloody.

What had he done?

He held his head in his hands and stared at the grey-speckled floor. He would willingly have cried, if he could. Everything had gone terribly wrong. He had been so angry. It had flared the moment the food police laid harsh hands on them. Was it not her fault he was there? Had she not plotted this in the name of her saviour? Had she not encouraged Sam in his delirium? She was probably even the cause of his violent outbreaks. The list of accusations was unending.

Telling the police the whole story had seemed the only option. Anger and righteous indignation had spurred him on. And fear, above all, gut wrenching fear. His imagination had run amok at what the police might do. Never in all his wildest imaginings had he thought they would force him to watch them systematically brake Nan.

He closed his eyes, but the images persisted, no matter how tight he squeezed. How could anyone be so methodically inhuman? He had seen it on their faces, cold and calculating, not the slightest feeling, not even a spark of twisted pleasure. And through it all, he had been a flinching accomplice, the one that had pointed the accusing finger.

He got down on his hands and knees and crawled the short distance to her lifeless form. Why ever had they locked him in with her corpse? Was it part of some elaborate, long drawn-out torture? He tried not to look at her bloated face, convinced it would haunt him for ever. Instead he closed his eyes and placed his hand on hers, as if that might bring pardon. He expected her skin to be cold, but it was surprisingly warm, too warm for a dead body.

He opened his eyes to find her staring at him from under swollen eyebrows. Thank heavens. She was alive. A rush of relief shivered through him, quickly followed by guilt. "I'm so sorry," was all he could blurt out. He didn't expect an answer and he got none.

Instead the cell door burst open and two guards strode in pushing a stretcher on wheels. Surely they weren't going to punish her any more. He didn't have the courage to protest.

The two men heaved Nan's limp body off the floor and placed it cautiously on the stretcher with a care that surprised, if not alarmed him. What could they be planning? Turning to the door, they motioned for him to follow and wheeled Nan out. He trudged after, dreading every step. How often was he to witness their mindless cruelty?

In his resignation, he was unsurprised when they walked past the lifts that led to the torture chambers. Surely there could be no place worse than those white tiled rooms.

The corridor ended in a metallic door. So this was it. The guards unlocked the door, pushed him through then wheeled the stretcher cautiously after. To his surprise they left, locking him in what appeared to be an ill-lit tunnel.

"Hey! What's going on?" he called out. No one answered. He tried the door. It was locked. He hammered on it. No one came. He hammered again and again. Nothing. He peered down the tunnel, but it curved away leaving no idea where it led.

A groan had him turning back to Nan. They couldn't stay there. The young woman needed urgent care. He grasped the stretcher and wheeled it away, halting every few paces to listen. With his luck, there'd be guards in ambush round the next bend. The further they went, the more he hoped they might escape. The idea was absurd. Why ever would police hunt them down and torture them at length, only to let them go. There hadn't been the slightest hint of explanation.

Unlike the tunnels they had fled in, these were solidly shored up with periodic pillars and the floor was dustless and mostly even. The way sloped steadily upwards, forcing him to pause frequently to catch his breath. Each time he did, he checked on Nan. Her breathing was laboured and her lips in a sorry state. His own lips were cracking. If only they had some water. Had there been a puddle, he would willingly have got down on all fours and lapped it up, but the tunnel was as dry as his mouth.

He was both surprised and relieved to step out into fading daylight. Partly concealed under a rocky overhang, the entrance opened onto a narrow path that wound across a narrow expanse of wasteland to a high metallic fence topped by barbed wire.

Baxter. He hadn't wanted to go there, but now he saw it with relief. If Nan was right, many healers had taken refuge there. They might save her. Unfortunately, there was no way he could transport her. He eased his hands under her shoulders and legs to see if he could carry her.

"I wouldn't do that, if I were you," a voice said from the shadows.

Jon almost knocked over the stretcher in his surprise. Before Nan could pitch to the ground, a man stepped out and steadied her.

"The stretcher is loaded with a bomb. The moment you lift her off, it will explode."

Jon took a hasty step away. "Why should I believe you? Who are you?"

"I'm Chris. From Baxter." Nodding to the stretcher, he added, "We've seen it all before."

"But that's terrible. What can we do?"

"Tricky." Chris glanced around as if in search of something.

"We need to slowly lift her, placing rocks in her place."

They collected small rocks and arranged them around the wheels of the stretcher. Chris lifted Nan little by little and Jon placed rocks on the stretcher. They both held their breaths as Chris finally raised Nan free, but no brilliant blast blew them to smithereens.

"Let's send this where it came from," Chris suggested. He wheeled the stretcher to the tunnel and let it roll down the slope. Then together they carried Nan to the fence. Just as they were struggling to get the stretcher under the barrier, a distant explosion rang out and a dense cloud of black smoke belched from the tunnel.

15.

Where am I?

A raging gale howls off the sea, scattering squawking gulls...

No. That's not right. It can't be.

... Man-high waves crash onto the beach driving sand and sea-life towards the scrub that borders the beach.

Run, you fool!

On hands and knees, I struggle up the beach, clasping at a dwarf bush as a wave rolls over me, wrenching me back. The bush comes away in my hands, roots and all, and I am washed halfway to the next crashing wave. I claw at the sand and dig in my toes. I rage at the elements; a torrent of words in an ancient tongue.

The wave slams into me, sweeping me forward, buoying me up and over the waiting scrub, almost to the first line of pines. I fling myself at a tree, flesh from my hands torn by the rough bark as I fight to hold on.

The wind abruptly dies, the waves are gone, and silence crashes down like a door slamming shut. Only the occasional chorus of loud-mouthed crickets braves its hold. I lie heaped in a sand-covered clearing, surrounded by an army of twisted oaks. I spit sand from my mouth and struggle to get up. My hands are bloody, my eyes smart and my limbs ache to the bone. Above, the sun blazes, scorching exposed skin, leaving me parched.

I wipe the sweat from my eyes with painful fingers and peer between gnarled branches. I am alone. There's a purpose to this. There must be. I heave myself to my knees only to tumble onto the sand. But what? Rolling on my back, I shade my eyes from the glaring sun. This won't do. My brain is withering in the heat.

I slide and slither through the sand, like a dying snake, weak and worthless, inch by inch, towards the shade of the oaks... I am not going to make it.

A squad of soldiers bursts amongst the trees and hauls me to my feet, their rough hands gripping my arms, their nails digging into my flesh. Unable to stand, they half lug, half drag me away, my feet in tow, gouging a deep gash in the sand.

"You," a voice booms, "are found guilty." I force my eyes open.

"What have I done?" I croak, looking at seven cloaked elders in purple robes, seated in a row above me, their faces stern and unforgiving. The room is majestic, adorned with flowing drapes and sombre tapestries. It could be a courtroom, or a throne room. Compared to the furnace outside, it is refreshingly cool. Silence hangs in the room, but in the distance, I hear muffled screams and shouts and the sound of metal on metal.

"You dare ask!" the man in the middle cries out, veins bulging on his forehead. "You have whipped our people into a frenzy with your insinuations. You know full well it is a lie. Admit it."

Instinctively I reach for my power, but it is gone, drained, leaving just an empty husk.

"Have you nothing to say?"

"May you be forgiven," I say haltingly, but with conviction. To my alarm, I have no control over the words that tumble from my lips. It's as if I were repeating someone else's lines.

Seven stony faces stare at me, unblinking, their minds untouchable, their expressions impassive, condemning not only me and everything I stand for, but all the people who live on this age-old island, including themselves.

"You are sentenced to death. You will be executed tomorrow. At sunrise."

I could well cry out, "You too!" But I have no desire to have the last word. I have no desire for anything. I have failed. Failed. My knees buckle and I crumble to the floor.

The heavy tread of soldiers resounds across the court. A studded boot kicks me full-force in the ribs sending pain searing through my lungs before I am hoisted upright and dragged away.

My cell contains a single window, set high in a curve of the wall. From it, a finger of sunlight falls on my spread-eagled form, hands and feet bound by leather thongs to rings anchored in the floor.

The walls are sandstone yellow, like all buildings on the island, dug as they are from the rock. The floor and ceiling are golden too. Only the door is a darker colour, teak most likely. My prison has been hewn from the very fabric of the island. Surrounding and engulfing me, the land calls. I can feel its pulse, a long-drawn-out beat, far longer than that of the trees, stately, steady and reliable, but for how much longer?

I could tug at the bindings, but it would be futile. I have no will to struggle. The elders are stronger. They have beaten me into submission. How could I ever dream of opposing them? I think of all those who will perish and remorse overwhelms me. The children so bright with hope and those women who gave their bodies to make a future for this world. They will be snuffed out because I failed. Tears well in my eyes, not for me but for them. A shudder rips through my bruised body, and I let out an anguished cry fraught with frustration and despair.

Little by little the tears dry up, the sobs sink to a moan only to die away and stillness settles over me. My eyes flutter closed and I drop ever deeper into the earth, merging with the throb of its pulse.

I am boiling up, caught by a desperate fever that rattles my bones and muddies my mind. Somewhere, in the distance, a damp cloth cools my forehead. Oh bliss. Drops of moisture fall on my cracked lips and trickle into my parched mouth, bringing sweet relief.

"It's going to be all right," a voice whispers, almost to itself.

Moistened anew, the cloth roves my temples, sets off down my cheeks and crosses my jaw bone till it settles around my neck. A cool breeze fans my moistened skin, bringing with it a medley of scents of life and hope.

I struggle to crack open my eyes, eager to make the most of this short reprieve, but they are glued shut.

"Wait," the soft voice says. The moist cloth caress my eyelids, once, twice, ... uncountable times, gentle but insistent, till, released, my eyes flick open.

"Mart?" I croak, recognising my young saviour, his face lit by a broad smile.

"You've been ill, very ill," he tells me.

"I failed," I say, tears springing to my eyes.

"Shhh," he replies, placing a hand on mine.

I long to say more, to unburden myself, to be done with it, but tiredness weighs so heavy that I close my eyes and succumb to sleep.

16.

A long beat booms in my blood... then falters and halts, leaving me suspended, terrified I will fall, only to start again, louder, stronger, sending a violent shudder through the rocks. The walls of my cell groan and the door shatters showering me with shards of wood. Outside I hear shouts and running feet that fade rapidly. Then nothing. Just the heightened throb of the earth, closer, more urgent. Coming.

The earth shudders. Cracks streak across the ceiling and down the walls. A section of the roof breaks away and crashes to the floor close to my head, covering me with yellow dust and sharp splinters of rock. I struggle with my bonds, but they hold fast. I twist my body as best I can, narrowly missed by another chunk plummeting to the ground.

Hardly has the dust settled, than the ground buckles and my arms and legs are wrenched in opposing directions, sending searing pain down my legs and arms and up my spine. I scream as the floor heaves higher, digging into the small of my back. Cracks criss-cross the ground. One of my hands flies free. I reach across, scrambling to unleash the other as lumps of the ceiling crash around me. Dust gets up my nose and fills my lungs. I cough and splutter. My fingers are numb and the thongs are lashed tight, but I wriggle free.

Turning to the door dangling loose on its hinges, I take a

step towards freedom, when a giant slab falls from the ceiling blocking the path. My eyes rove the ruins in search of a way out. Below the window a large gash has opened through which stabs a brilliant shaft of light. It's far too narrow, but I manage to squeeze halfway through. Twisting and turning are no use. If the next seism closes the gap, my efforts will be over.

The ground trembles beneath my feet and I push forward in desperation. The whole wall shifts, groaning as it does, and abruptly I break through, stumbling away as the cell collapses inwards and is engulfed in a chasm that opens in the floor.

I have to flee the ruins. The beach? No! There's to be a tidal wave. Such was my vision. People will be trapped between the raging earth and a wall of waves.

I clamber over a giant slab of sandstone and slither down a heap of rubble, jarring my damaged ribs and bruising my backside, till my sliding carries me out of the remains. Gathering what little strength I have, I straddle a snake-like gash, my legs giving way as I land, and I fall flat on my face in a patch of grass. I lie struggling to regain my breath, as several violent shakes shoot through the ground. There is nowhere to go, no escape.

Hearing children wailing nearby, I struggle to my feet and stagger towards them. Beyond a giant pine, miraculously intact, I find five little girls huddled around a huge boulder, keening beyond solace, tears streaming down their cheeks. Moving closer, I spot a tiny arm reaching out from under the boulder, the hand clenched tight, grey and lifeless.

"Come," I say, chocking back tears. "It is too late for her. But you, you must get away."

I pick up the smallest who clings to my neck, sobbing. I take the hand of a second girl and pull till she turns away and follows. The other three heave themselves to their feet, and reluctantly come after us, sniffing back tears, hands held, heads bowed.

We thread our way through what was once the sumptuous palace gardens. They resemble a lunar landscape with the occasional exotic plant perched on a rift in the ground. There is nowhere to go, no way to escape, but these girls need hope and a destination. I lead them along the spiralling path, weaving round and over obstacles, ever upwards to the palace summer house built at the highest point. The path is deserted. The distant screams are the sole sounds. Those who have survived must be fleeing for the beach and boats. If only they knew.

The summer house is a jumble of rubble, but the wide stairway that leads up to it is intact. We sit, catching our breaths, as we look over the island to the giant expanse of water beyond. A telltale white line divides the sea just below the horizon.

"What's that?" A girl asks, pointing to the approaching line.

"It's a giant wave."

"Are we going to drown?" one of littlest asks, her anxious face turned to me.

I shake my head, unable to answer.

The wave hits the coastline far below and rushes on, its roar audible.

The girls huddle close and I put my arms around them. Their trembling sets me trembling too.

An immense wall of water sweeps through the town, arrogantly brushing aside all in its way. On it comes, lower now, less fast, but still immense. Maybe. I let myself hope.

The girls are crying and I cry with them. Through tear-filled eyes, I see the wave towering above, suspend a brief moment before it crashes down and engulfs us, ripping us from each other, swirling us around. I am flung high above the waves only to fall back into their watery embrace.

In desperation, I crack open my eyes and discover Mart leaning over me, concern creasing his face. I failed. I failed them all. I can still feel the wall of water pursuing me and I begin to tremble. I feel its immense weight crushing the life from me and I pray it will end. Mart takes me in his arms, cradling me, and I burst into sobs.

17.

Jon awoke with a crick in his neck and an unpleasant taste in his mouth. His legs, which were folded under him, had become numb. The slightest movement set off a pain like needles jabbing him. Cracking open his eyes, he discovered he was curled up in an armchair close to an open window over which a lace curtain fluttered. On closer inspection he realised it was no window; just an oblong hole in the wall.

Next to his armchair, a glass of water and a bowl of fruit sat on a small table. He gulped the water, trying to wash away the bitterness, but it didn't work. Picking up an apple, he sniffed it's red skin and bit into it sending juice squirting into his mouth. Chewing was hard work, he'd got out of the habit. He swallowed the chunk whole and returned the remains to the table.

Where was he? And how had he got there? Several armchairs were scattered around the small room, but he was alone. He struggled to his feet and hopped around till his legs let him walk properly.

Pushing aside the lace curtain, he found an inner court with row after row of potatoes, carrots, salads and radishes. He could even smell flowers, the scents of which contrasted starkly with the odour of chemicals that permeated the rest of town.

He half expected the door to be locked, but it wasn't. Outside an empty corridor stretched away in both directions. Where was everybody? He was about to set off when an old woman emerged from a nearby door. Dressed like an escapee from another age, she wore a long, colourful skirt that reached to her ankles and a bright yellow blouse, over which she'd slung a shawl. Most striking was her long silvery hair bunched up in a pony tail.

"Ah, Mr. Neufeld. I am Dr Swinton," she said, holding out a hand for him to shake. Who were these people that didn't know touching was dangerous? "Feeling better?" she asked, unperturbed by his refusal to shake hands.

He wasn't sure if he felt better, but he nodded all the same, and asked, "Where am I?"

"At the refugee centre in Baxter."

Baxter? The plagued ruins. He remembered that was where he had been heading, but he couldn't remember why. "How did I get here?"

"Our people brought you in when you collapsed. There was nothing wrong with you that a good meal, some water and a little sleep couldn't cure."

Dr Swinton, who continued to study him closely, seemed to expect a question. Jon felt his face warming. He couldn't possibly admit he had no idea why he was there.

"You had a question?" she asked.

"To be honest, I have no idea why I am here. I can't remember what happened."

"You've had a shock. That can cause temporary amnesia. Don't worry. Everything will come rushing back soon enough."

He suspected he wouldn't be very happy when it did.

"I'd like to show you something," the doctor said. The woman led him down the corridor past the room he'd been in only to halt several doors further on. Straining her ears to hear, she turned the handle and pushed open the door.

Jon had no idea what she wanted to show him, but followed. This room evoked distant memories of hospital bedrooms, although there were none of the electronic gadgets they used back then. Close to the window was a white metal bed with white sheets and covers in which someone was sleeping. A solitary chair sat next to the bed and a small table sported various bottles and jars.

"Take a seat," Dr Swinton said.

Jon was hesitant. He couldn't make out who was in the bed, but he was unwilling to move closer. Dr. Swinton half helped, half pushed him towards the chair. As he sat down, he deliberately looked out the window at the mass of flowers.

"I'll leave you a while, Mr. Neufeld. If you need me, I'm just down the corridor. My name is on the door."

The sheets rustled as whoever was in the bed shifted and Jon smelt some kind of ointment. He continued to stare out the window although all his other senses were turned towards the bed.

"Jon," a familiar voice said.

Very slowly he turned to look, bracing himself for a blow. At first he couldn't make out what he was seeing. The person had a bandage around her head and there was a thick layer of cream smeared over her lips and nose. Then she turned and he recognised her. Nan.

Tears sprang to his eyes. The whole nightmare came rushing back: the accusations, the betrayal, the screams, the blood, the foul stench and him standing there, unspeaking, unmoving, unhinged. He burst into sobs, his chest heaving violently. he would have keeled over had he not gripped the chair.

"Jon," Nan said again. "Don't blame yourself. These things happen."

Anger flared in him. How could he not blame himself? He was the one who had given her away. It was his fault she had been tortured. He wanted to lash out, to shout at her. But he remembered it was his anger that had caused the catastrophe in the first place. Despite his wild ideas, he realised she had done nothing to deserve the horrors.

He wiped his nose on his sleeve and ran the back of his hand over his eyes. "I'm so sorry," he said, "so, so sorry."

18.

Jon sneaked a peak at Nan, wincing at the sight of her bruised and battered face.

"It's not as bad as it looks," she said. "I was lucky you were there. They were more interested in scaring you than hurting me."

Well they succeeded. Her appearance continued to alarm him.

Jon ate his meal in silence, hunched over a tray in his lap. Nan was propped up with several pillows squeezed behind her back as she sipped a drink. He was glad not to have to speak. His mind ran over what had happened like an obsessive finger prodding a wound. He groaned, but when she looked at him, he just shrugged.

A young woman, dressed as extravagantly as Dr Swinton, came to collect his tray. "Sorry I took so long," she said. "There was an alert. A squad of food police marched into Baxter."

Jon sprang to his feet, his hands trembling as he looked out the door and through the window, making sure they were not about to burst into the room.

"Don't worry," the woman said, "we chased them away."

The idea of a crowd of hippies fighting off well-armed, well-trained police was hardly reassuring. He slumped into the chair, staring at the floor.

When they were alone, Nan asked, "Is there news of Sam?"

Sam! It wasn't that he'd forgotten his son, but he had been

so engrossed in what had happened to Nan he hadn't given the boy a thought. A second wave of guilt and self-recrimination washed over him. He got to his feet in an effort to shake the dark pall that enveloped him.

"I've heard nothing," he said, turning to her. Her face was a mess. "Surely it must hurt?" he asked

She looked surprised.

"Your face, I mean."

"Not if you don't make me laugh." She tried to smile, but it clearly hurt. Her attempt at humour only made him feel worse.

"I'll go and ask Dr Swinton," he said.

"No need." She waved a button on the end of a long wire. "I can call her."

Unlike the young helper, Dr Swinton came immediately. "Is something the matter?" she asked.

"I'm fine," Nan said.

Jon glanced at Nan, who nodded. "We just wanted to know if you had news of my son Sam?" Jon asked.

"A twelve year old, with short straight brown hair and fine, almost feminine features?" the woman asked.

The description didn't please Jon at all, but he held his annoyance in check, saying, "That's him."

Dr Swinton sighed. "He's been very ill. We weren't sure he'd pull through, but he's surprising resilient and is on the mend."

"Ill?" he asked.

"He was very lucky," Dr. Swinton said. "He fell ill in the only place people are capable of healing him."

Jon must have looked confused because she added, "Most of the surviving healers live in Baxter. We have considerable experience handling what you folk call the Disaster."

The Disaster. Jon felt an icy cold grip him. No one survived the Disaster.

"Don't worry. It's curable."

Jon shook his head.

"Ask Nan here," Dr Swinton said. "She knows something about surviving that plague."

Jon stared at Nan in disbelief.

"I caught it in the early days, before Baxter was destroyed, but late enough that groups of vigilantes were already shooting people suspected of having the disease. I was lucky. A very good healer took me in, hid me and cared for me. I recovered, but she was burnt for her troubles."

Jon looked at her aghast. His son had been looked after by someone who had had the dreadful sickness. She had even shaken his hand and come to his house. Indignation flared and he could feel anger kindling again, but one look at Nan's face was enough to quell his ire.

"With the right treatment, it can be cured," Dr Swinton said. "But your Sam took some time to reach us and the illness had progressed to a stage where healing is more difficult."

"Can we see him?" Nan asked.

"You had better get more rest, Nan. You never know when you might need your strength. But Mr Neufeld, you can go, if you don't stay too long."

Jon hesitated, afraid the question would sound terrible, but he had to know. "Is there…?"

"Don't worry Mr Neufeld. You will not be infected. It is only in the early stages that the illness is contagious."

Jon glanced at Nan who looked disappointed. She wanted to see Sam as much as he did. He smiled at her, even though it felt odd. "I'll come right back and tell you how he is."

On the way to Sam's room, Jon asked Dr Swinton where everyone had gone.

"Very few live here," she said. "Baxter is increasingly dangerous. The Food Police have become more adventurous, as if their fear of the illness is no longer a deterrent. Each time they penetrate deeper into the ruins. Earlier today, one of their squads almost reached this centre. We have set up traps, but they are stubborn and vengeful."

"This place seems built for many more people. Where have they gone?"

"We have another centre, hidden in the Wilds. Many have

gone there. In some ways it is safer than here."

He would hardly call the jungle around the town safe. It had been left to grow wild. Rumour had it dangerous animals and bands of barbaric men prowled there.

Dr Swinton opened a door and invited Jon inside. Once he entered she left.

Bathed in the warm light from yet another garden full of vegetables, Sam's room was smaller than Nan's, barely big enough for the bed, a small table and a chair. On the chair sat a young boy, his expression grave as he stared at the bed. Jon was shocked to see how dirty he was. Hardly the best person to accompany someone so ill. The boy's t-shirt and shorts were filthy and his tanned skin looked none too clean either.

Jon took a step towards the bed. There, pale and unmoving, his body covered by a sheet out of which peeked only his face, swollen and sweating profusely, lay Sam.

19.

Sewers!

Jon clamped a hand over his mouth and nose to ward off the smell. After the bright scents of flowers, the stench was all the more repulsive. Remaining close to the door, he shifted his head, attempting to locate the source. It was all around, as if a broken sewerage pipe ran through the room. There were even several flies buzzing lazily between him and the bed. He took a half-hearted swipe at one that settled on his hand.

The rest of the city had long been rid of such carriers of disease. Hygiene was of the utmost importance in the battle to stave off another disaster. No wonder people in the city were convinced Baxter was dangerous. Those who lived there apparently did so in the most primitive conditions.

The boy sitting next to Sam's bed stretched and shifted causing his chair to creak. Jon didn't want to talk to him. He wanted to see Sam, alone. He turned to go, but must have made a noise because the boy looked up. Getting to his feet, the youth greeted him with a grin.

"Hallo. I'm Martin. But most people call me Mart."

As the filthy boy approached, the stench grew worse. With a shock, Jon realised it was the boy that stank. He wrinkled his nose and took a step back shying away from the boy's hand offered in greeting. How dare he bring such filth near Sam when he was so gravely ill?

Surprised at Jon's refusal to greet him, the boy looked confused then shrugged before returning to his vigil by the bed.

"I think you should leave," Jon said, unable to conceal his anger.

Mart paid him no further attention, much to Jon's irritation. Instead, the boy took hold of Sam's hand and pressed it to his cheek.

"Don't touch!" Jon exclaimed.

"Why ever not?"

"You'll make things worse with all your filth."

The boy shook his head. "If it weren't for that filth, as you call it, we wouldn't be here."

"What nonsense."

"How do you know? You weren't there."

"OK, Mr. Know-it-all, explain."

At first Mart clenched his fists, thrusting them deep into his pockets and said nothing. He stared out the window apparently lost in thought, before turning to Jon. "Sam and I were cornered by a squad of Food Police and they had a sniffer. I imagine you know what that is. Well, the only way to escape was to use a sewer and its smell to conceal us."

Ok, his virulence had been unjustified, but the presence of the kid, and above all his self-assurance, annoyed him. "Could you leave me alone with my son?" he asked, adding as an after thought, "Please."

Jon wondered why the boy looked so perplexed. Surely his request had been simple enough. Finally Mart rose unwillingly and headed for the door.

"You might want to have a wash," Jon said as Mart stepped around him. "I imagine you no longer need to hide behind that smell."

"You haven't been here very long, have you?" Mart said with a chuckle. "Water is scarce. I'll see what I can do."

Finally alone with Sam, Jon moved to the bedside and sat down. Around the boy's eyes the skin was puffy, his lips were visibly swollen and a sheen of sweat covered his face. Jon shuddered. He wasn't dupe. Dr. Swinton said Sam was recovering, but he'd seen people in the throws of the disease. So many had perished during the Disaster. Dying or living had ceased to make sense.

Apart from the rasping of Sam's breath and the faint rustle of the breeze in the leaves outside, the room was completely silent. Jon got to his feet, moved to the door and peered out. The corridor stretched away in both directions with not a single person in sight. He strained, but could hear no sign of life.

Sam groaned and tossed in his sleep, causing the covers to fall to the floor. Jon picked them up and replaced them over the boy's feverish form. As he did, Sam groaned a second time and his eyes cracked open, only to close tight, then open again.

"How do you feel?" Jon asked.

Sam stared at Jon, uncomprehending.

"You caught an illness," Jon said. The boy's face creased in alarm. Jon hastily added, "But it is going away."

Jon sincerely hoped he was right. He had no idea how the sickness evolved. That wasn't surprising; everyone had shunned those who caught it. Could he trust Dr. Swinton? Maybe a brief period of calm in the symptoms might be a reprieve that announced the end.

"Here," a voice said behind them. Jon spun round to see Mart standing in the open doorway, grinning, a pitcher of water in one hand, a glass in the other. "I thought you might need this."

Mart ventured into the room and poured a little water into the glass. Jon was relieved to note the boy no longer smelt so badly, but he still felt a deep dislike towards him.

Mart was about to offer the water when Sam shied away, as if terrified. Startled at Sam's reaction, Mart took a step back, slopping water onto the floor. Jon wrested the glass from his hand, saying, "It's alright Sam. I'm here. Everything is going to be OK. I've got a drink for you."

Behind him he heard Mart snort, but ignored it. He brought the glass to Sam's lips and let him sip. When the boy tried to gulp down more, Jon pulled the glass away, saying, "Easy does it."

"They've managed to chase away the Food Police," Mart said. "But several people were wounded."

Sam's head swivelled round to look for who was speaking. When he spied Mart, he began keening, a dreadful sound that had Jon wanting to clap his hands over his ears. He tried to soothe the boy, but he was unconsolable.

"Leave!" Jon spat the word, the vehemence of his reaction surprising him. Mart took a step towards the door, but did not do as he was told.

A flash of irritation flared in Jon, but he took a deep breath and turned back to Sam. He was surprised to find the keening had ceased and the twisted lines of terror were gone, only to be replaced by a look of understanding and intelligence.

"Don't be too hard on Mart," Sam said. "He saved my life."

20.

"Where'd he go?" Mart asks. I have to smile when he peers under the bed as if Jon might be concealed there.

"Back to Nan. The teacher I told you about. She's been ill."

When I break into a fit of coughing, Mart crosses the room, pours a glass of water and hands it to me.

Sitting down by the bed, he faces me, his forehead furrowing in thought. "Your father said something that puzzled me."

As he says no more, it is my turn to be puzzled. I sip the water and wait.

"Why did he say you were his son?" he blurts out, only to pause a long moment, his cheeks colouring. "I thought you were a girl."

I set down the glass on a table next to the bed. I need to have my hands free to figure this one out. It is not going to be easy. "I am a girl," I reply.

Mart's forehead creases. He has heard the unspoken 'but'.

"But we are more than that."

"We?" He jumps up, casting about for the other person.

:: blinking boy - I hate him - he does not see me or hear me or care about me - he sees only you - and the look in his eyes is enough to give anyone the willies

"Sit down. This is going to take some explaining."

Mart takes a deep breath, but remains standing, leaning on the back of the chair.

"You must have noticed I sometimes get clumsy. Even walking or talking become extremely difficult."

"I have," Mart nods. "It is really odd."

:: odd! - you should look at yourself mate - with those pro-truding ears and that rash of silly freckles you look ridiculous

"That's because inside this body you see," I tap my chest, "there is not just one, but two people."

Mart shakes his head. "How can that be? Surely there can only be one person in each body."

I pick up the glass and take a sip. My mouth has gone dry and my throat is still sore from the illness. "Normally, yes. But from time to time, instead of having one set of genes, a person is born with two. Nan said it was called a chimera."

:: yeah tell him about the monster - frighten the wits out of the bugger

Mart's eyes are fixed on me as if trying to pry into my head. "So the other part of you is a boy?"

"Yes. The original Sam has difficulty getting around in the world. Till I came along he muddled his way through life walled up in his head."

:: muddle me up - muddle me down - muddle me all around - but do not let the cat into the castle

Pulling the chair a few paces away from the bed, Mart sits down, holding his head in his hands. "What a nightmare!"

:: nightmare!!! - you couldn't be more right mate - a filthy evil female lies heavily on her victim and suffocates him

It is hard to ignore Sam's gibberish, especially when he's daz-zling me with his wit. "For you or for me?" I ask.

Mart looks up, catching my eye. "For you." He looks away, his face colouring. "I can't imagine how it could be. My body is my refuge; the place where I am alone with myself."

"Sam would agree with you. He calls it his castle."

:: stuff his freckled face in the muddy moat with the croco-diles or push him off the topmost turret and see if his flapping ears can save him from splattering on the cobblestones below

"So he talks to you?"

"All the time." I can't help smiling.

"I thought you said he couldn't talk."

"He may not be able to talk to anyone else, but in his head he is a real poet."

:: that's me - the gibbering idiot full of fleas - the noisy nonsense wordsmith - the thrice useless creator of countless conundrums - the ultimate maker of pointless peccadillos

I smile again. *Stop that Sam. You are hilarious.*

"He's talking to you now, isn't he?"

"I'm not sure he's talking to me, but he is talking."

A strident whistle interrupts our conversation.

Sam dives into the deepest recesses of our mind, his hands mentally over his ears. I have to struggle not to follow suit.

"What's that?" I ask as the whistle abruptly stops.

"The food police have invaded Baxter. That's the second time today."

"Shouldn't we hide?"

"They won't get far..."

A second whistle blasts loud and urgent.

"Stay here," Mart says, calling over his shoulder, "I'll be back in a second."

A loud crash has me swinging my feet to the floor in alarm, but the moment I try to stand, my head begins to spin. I sink onto the bed, short of breath. Another crash echoes from outside followed by the sound of running feet. The door bursts open and I brace myself for the worst.

Mart dashes in pushing a wheelchair and skids to a halt just short of the bed. Taking hold of my arm, he helps me up and into the chair. "We need to get you into hiding," he says as he wheels me out into corridor. "It may be nothing, but ..."

I am surprised to see we are not alone. People emerge from doors, their arms full of boxes, and sprint past. I clutch the armrests of the wheelchair as Mart veers down a side corridor. It ends abruptly in a dark chamber where people are waiting. The moment we enter, a man pulls a cord hanging from the roof and a metal door slides shut with a dull thud, plunging us in utter darkness.

:: he's going to kill us - they are stark raving mad, madder than a load of hatters inside out

Someone turns on a tiny torch and I make out a man labouring to turn a gigantic crank. The lift, for it must be that we are in, shudders then begins to descend. Over the creak of the mechanism I hear shouts and gun shots.

The lift sinks ever deeper, but not fast enough for me. The shots are far too close.

:: help! - help! - help! - this is no game you fool - you will get us killed - let me out

If I relinquished control of our body, it will tremble violently. It is hard to shut out Sam's continuous keening. *It's going to be all right, Sam.* To my despair, I have little sway over his emotions,

Finally the lift bumps to a halt, the sliding doors spring open and the passengers hurry down a dimly lit corridor. Some thirty feet from the lift entrance, Mart has to ask for help to carry the wheelchair through an airlock. Once on the other side, he slows his pace.

Pointing to the airlock, he says, "They may try to use gas."

"How often does this happen?"

"This is the first time they've dared mount a full scale raid."

We enter a large, low-roofed hall off which I spot many tiny cubicles. Each has bunk beds. Mart halts the wheelchair by one of the rows of trestle tables and benches that fill the room.

"There's a kitchen and storerooms down there," Mart says, pointing to the far end of the hall.

Suddenly I remember Nan and Jon. I peer in search of them, but they are nowhere to be seen. "Where are Jon and Nan?"

"They may be in another shelter." He doesn't sound hopeful.

All of a sudden the hall resonates with what sounds like a giant gong. Heads turn in the direction of the airlock. "They are trying to break through," someone whispers in horror.

"It should hold," another says.

A second giant blow sends looks of alarm careering round the hall.

Sam screams.

21.

:: this is hell's mess - listen to that infernal hammering - smell the panic in the air - the stink of ill-cooked food and poor-ly-washed bodies - look at the seething mass of mindless people scurrying about - running from their fear in this dank warren
I have to agree, Sam.

Row upon row of trestle tables flanked by benches stretch the length of the low-roofed hall. Many tiny rooms, most with-out doors, some housing bunk beds, others store rooms, are dotted around the walls. There are even several kitchens. People weave their way between tables shifting boxes to cupboards while others stagger under the weight of armfuls of vegetables. A few people offload their meagre belongings as they claim a bed.

I turn the wheelchair to face the sass on which the food po-lice pound with renewed vigour. The air vibrates with the shock of their blows. A lump of rock breaks from the ceiling above the metal door and falls with a thud to the floor. All movement ceas-es as anxious faces turn to scan the walls. Mart lays a reassuring hand on my shoulder and I feel the muscles in my neck tense as Sam reacts. Then abruptly the hammering stops.

When the ringing in my head finally dies down, I hear the muffled sound of voices beyond the door and the screech of metal on metal. What now? Let's hope they don't have some device to cut their way through.

A shudder ripples through Sam and I feel his mounting terror. He cringes at the thought of the Food Police bursting in. I pull Nan's little flask from my pocket with trembling fingers and lift it clumsily to my lips. *Just a nip*, she'd said. *It's going to be all right*, Sam, I say as I savour the taste of the sweet liquor.

"They're blocking the entrance," a tall man whispers.

"How d'you know?" a man carrying vegetables asks.

"Seen it on the monitors."

"As if that would stop us getting out," a chubby woman replies, chuckling. She dons an apron, takes the vegetables and heads for a smaller room to the side of the main canteen.

The man in the white coat shakes his head. "Most tunnels surface not far from here. They'll just wait for us to come out. The tunnels that range further afield are more risky. They've been less well tended and could easily cave in."

The discussion roves backwards and forwards between advocates of the best escape. Mart sighs and wheels us to a quieter corner. "I'll get you something to eat," he says. "Then you should rest. You need to get your strength back if we are to escape."

Should I be annoyed at him mothering us? He means well. The tension in the nape of my neck is easing and the trembling has ceased. Nan's potion is having its effect. *Feeling better, Sam?*

:: wonderful - with the food police about to break in and a usurper inside my head about to break out I feel really great

I smile. *And where would I go Sam, if I were to break out?*

:: to hell and good riddance

But you said we're already in hell…

"Here," Mart says, balancing a tray of food in one hand and grasping a couple of mugs in the other. Setting the tray on a table, he places a slice of vegetable tart in front of us. "It's not as good as those I make, but it will do."

I look up to see him watching me, a sparkle in his eyes.

"You cook?" I ask, blushing.

"Yup," he replies, wolfing down a piece of tart. "Learnt at the same time I learnt healing."

"You'll have to cook for us one day."

:: a crook, a devious cook, a shady character always brewing, hatching, cooking the books

Stop babbling, Sam, and enjoy the food.

:: it is surely laced with poison

We eat in silence. The tart is delicious and we wash it down with fruit juice. Once we have finished and Mart has returned the tray to the kitchen, he says, "Would you like to go for a walk?"

I nod and he helps me to my feet. Linking arms, he walks me away from the sass. Many people greet him and a lot ask questions or have things to discuss. Each halt brings a welcome rest. My knees will give out at any moment and the small of my back aches. When I rub it with my free hand, Mart says, "You should drink more. I'll brew you a herbal tea when we get back."

We are about to return to the wheelchair, when a young girl runs up, her long, blond hair streaming behind her. "Mart," she says, pushing the hair from her face as she catches her breath. She glances briefly at us, her eyes a startling blue, sizing us up. Then her gaze returns to Mart. "Mother needs your help."

"Her lungs again?" he asks.

The girl nods and tugs at Mart's sleeve. "Hurry."

:: she's pretty, isn't she? - I bet you're jealous

Are you interested in her? Sam shudders. *One round to me.*

"Sam, this is Jenny. Jenny meet Sam."

"Hallo," I say, wondering if I should hold out my hand to greet the girl, but she crosses her arms and looks at Mart.

"I'm going to have to leave for a while." Mart says, casting about for someone to help me. When he spots a woman in a white coat stepping out of a nearby storeroom he calls her over. "Jean, could you walk Sam back to her wheelchair? I have to go look at Jenny's mum. Her lungs are playing her up again."

Jean is a short, thin woman with a mop of red hair and an expressive face. "Sure," she replies with a grin, looking from the girl to Mart to me. Mart gives me an apologetic smile and hurries off with the girl still clinging to his sleeve.

"Where is your wheelchair?" Jean asks.

I point to the far corner of the canteen and we set off slowly in that direction.

"You are recovering very quickly," she says, patting my hand. "Most people take longer."

"It must be Mart's tender care," I say, knowing that will annoy Sam.

:: what rubbish - that meddling boy has nothing to do with our recovery - you can thank my great resilience - I've spent years cultivating mechanisms against all manner of attacks

I don't want to disillusion you, Sam, but you are hardly resilient. Without Nan's potion you would be prey to the slightest change.

"He's an excellent healer and a wonderful cook."

Having two conversations at once is a bit like juggling; it would be so easy to get in a muddle and snatch the wrong ball out of the air. "But he's so young," I say, thinking out loud.

"His parents died during the Disaster and he was taken in by our best healer. Despite his very young age, she taught him everything. She used to say he was a gifted child. What's more, he's naturally resistant to that plague people called the Disaster."

We have walked most of the way across the canteen and I am exhausted. My head is beginning to spin, so I halt for a moment and lean on a table. "So this healer is like a mother to him?"

"She would have been, but the Food Police executed her." She rolls her eyes in exasperation. "How stupid can you get? They slaughter the only people who could ever save the world if another epidemic were to break out?"

To think Mart had not only lost his parents, but also his teacher and guardian. "That's dreadful. Yet he is so cheerful and easy-going."

"I'm not so sure he's that happy. The loss hit him very hard. I reckon the healing saved him. He threw himself into the work. Many people around here have him to thank for their lives."

"So he has no family?"

"I wouldn't say that. In a way, the whole community has adopted him."

:: you see - if ever we get away you can't possibly take lover boy with you, that would be far too selfish for a saint like you - everyone here needs him - ha! that's got you stumped - one round to me

22.

Nan would have collapsed from fatigue, had Jon not had an arm slung round her waist. He hurried her as fast as her legs would carry. Shouts erupted all around. People pushed past in a desperate dash for shelter. In the distance she could hear gun fire. By the time they reached Sam's room the corridor was deserted, but shots rang out ever closer. Jon pushed open the door and helped her inside. The room was empty.

"Mart must have got her to safety," she said. A scream rang out and heavy boots pounded along the corridor. "We must do the same."

To her alarm, Jon refused to budge. "What if Sam just stepped out for a moment?"

What nonsense! She grabbed his arm, trying to shake reason into him. "We can't stay here." When he took a step towards the door, she pulled him back. "Don't be daft!" she said indicating the window.

He shuddered, as if breaking free of a spell, and helped her to the window.

He scrambled out, tumbling into a flowerbed. Righting himself, he came to help her. She had no strength left, but with him tugging, she managed to clamber out. They crossed the inner courtyard and were about to climb through one of the gaping windows on the far side when crashes from within had them turning away.

She glanced around. The courtyard ran some twenty yards between two wings of the building and was blocked at each end by corridors running between the two parts. In the corner closest to them a dense thicket of wisteria intertwined with several other climbing plants.

A shot rang out and a bullet crossed the courtyard embedding itself in the wall opposite. They flung themselves to the ground, half concealed behind a clump of roses.

"There," she whispered pointing to the thicket. Jon was about to crawl towards the wisteria when she stopped him. "Not through the flower bed. It'll leave a telltale trace. Use the path."

She'd called it a path, but it was little more than a lazy curve of stones at irregular intervals. She got down on her hands and knees to follow him, trembling as she did. The stones were often far apart and her trousers did little to protect her knees.

Jon glanced back, halting for her to catch up. But renewed shouts from inside had her waving him on.

The wisteria had twisted and turned forming a tiny hiding place just large enough for them to huddle out of sight. She could feel his laboured breath warm on her ear and his knee was wedged against her. His closeness should have been reassuring, had he been relaxed, but she was acutely aware how tense he was.

Hoards of Food Police were scouring the rooms around the courtyard. They weren't searching for people so much as venting their anger on the installations. The courtyard was inundated with the din of furniture being smashed and a flurry of objects were hurled through the windows. You'd have thought Baxter was a personal affront to the men's ordered world.

Their hiding place was squashed against the wall of the corridor between the two wings. Twisting awkwardly to look over Jon's shoulder, she was horrified to see they were crouched in full view of anyone walking inside. When he saw what she was looking at, he helped her clamber through the window. She hobbled across the corridor and he part lifted, part shoved her out the window on the other side.

The courtyard they entered was identical to the previous one, although there were no searching police in the surrounding rooms.

"Let's make a run for it," Jon whispered.

She shook her head. Running was out of the question, her legs would never hold. She stumbled forward with his arm laced around her waist. They had not reached the far side when crashing came from the rooms behind. The Food Police were catching up. The two reached the next corridor that divided the inner courtyard without being seen and climbed in only to be confronted by a policeman.

The sight of a gun levelled at them was terrifying. As the man pulled the trigger back, she felt a calm spread over her. Jon, in comparison was trembling.

"I wouldn't do that if I were you," she said, her voice calm and distant, almost as if it were not her own.

"Shut up!" the man shouted, waving the muzzle of his gun at her.

"You don't believe me. But when that gun behind you goes off, you'll have only a brief moment to regret not listening."

It was a desperate ploy. The man was tense and wary. Surely he wouldn't fall for such an obvious ruse. She struggled not to show her fear and doubt.

When the man wavered and snatched a hasty glance over his shoulder, she pushed Jon to the floor and flung herself forward rolling past the man. As she did, she swung out her leg sending the policeman sprawling. Several shots went off, smashing into the nearby wall.

Glancing round, she found Jon cowering on the floor, his head covered with trembling arms. "You can get up," she said and leant her back on the wall, her chest heaving as she struggled to regain her breath. At her feet lay the policeman, a red patch staining the back of his uniform jacket. She wiped the blood from the knife clasped in her hand.

Jon stared at her as she sheathed the knife. "Where did that come from?

Instead of answering, she said, "Help me up." He got to his feet and held out a hand. They climbed out the window and surveyed the scene in front of them. Unlike the other courtyards, this one had a low brick construction in the centre from which radiated narrow pathways.

"Great," Nan said, pleased. "We might be in luck. It looks like the head of the waste shoot."

Ducking, they hastened across the opening to the small building. She skirted it in search of the entrance, leaving Jon to crouch with his back to the brick wall, concealed by a laurel bush.

Pleased her memory hadn't been wrong, she returned. "I was right," she told him. "We are near the kitchens. The shoot is used to dispense of waste. It piles up underground and then gets shovelled away to be used as compost."

"Let's go," he said, getting to his feet.

"The only problem is the locked door."

They tried forcing it with her knife, to no avail. They pushed as hard as they could, but it wouldn't budge. When the Food Police stormed adjacent rooms, making a dreadful racket, Jon and Nan took a run at the door and it finally burst open with a dreadful crash. They fell forward almost slipping into the hole that lay at the centre.

A shout went up and she could hear the pounding of boots.

"Get in!" she ordered. "Feet first."

He did and she followed. She let go of the rim of the shoot with some trepidation. The passage was pitch black and an ugly smell rose from below. The shoot angled away steeply, turning as it did. She flew out the end and landed with a sickening thud atop Jon in the middle of a slimy heap.

23.

The shock of landing was lessened both by the stinking mess and Jon who hadn't managed to get out of the way. Her arrival drove him deeper into the decaying heap and his struggling showered them with gunge. She put out a hand to push herself up, but it sank into the rotting food.

When she managed to roll free and clambered to her feet, she had only one wish: to be rid of the sticky muck that clung to her. Her hands were plastered with the stuff. She couldn't even wipe her face clean. Then she remembered where they were and what had happened. "Run!" she cried. "They'll try to gas us."

She halted almost immediately, shivering in the dark. He hadn't followed. Barked orders spewed down the shoot. "Jon?" she whispered. "Here," his voice came back. She groped towards him till she felt a grimy hand grasp hers. Yanking him away, a sinister hissing spread behind them. They broke into a stumbling run, terror driving them on.

"Stop!" she said minutes later. "Can't ... go ... on." They halted. When she managed to get her breath back, she could hear Jon sniffing the air. She sniffed too, but there was no telltale whiff of gas. The stench of rubbish was all she could smell.

She tried to remember a map she'd seen of the tunnels. "There must be a room nearby," she said. "A resting place for those working the compost."

She pulled away, meaning to slip off and find the room, but he hung on to her hand, saying, "I'll come too."

She'd find it better alone. She'd need all her senses to feel her way. "I won't be long," she said. But he clung to her hand like a child terrified of being abandoned. What with the dark and the stench and the Food Police roaming around, there was enough to terrify anyone. Had he been a child, she would have taken him in her arms. But he wasn't and both were covered in stinking scraps of food. The thought disgusted her.

"Come on," she said and felt her way along the wall with her free hand. It couldn't be far. The rough map had the room close to the shoot. She was beginning to wonder if she'd been mistaken when she felt the wood of a door frame.

"Found it," she said, pushing open the door and stepping inside. Once he joined her, she closed the door and searched for a switch. It would be a miracle if the police hadn't destroyed the generators, but she tried all the same.

With a click, a dim light came on, its glowing filament clearly visible. "Batteries," she said, explaining it more to herself than Jon.

They were in a tiny underground room with a couple of chairs, a small table and a bunk bed. She glanced at Jon. He stood shivering with potato peelings in his hair and traces of squashed tomatoes and egg plants on his face and shoulders. His clothes were caked with apple skins and carrot peelings and unsavoury mould not to mention a persistent slime.

She wanted to laugh, but the pleading expression on his face begged her not to. She shivered instead. To her relief there was a bucket of fresh water. As he splashed the liquid on his face, she went in search of a cloth. There were two towels hanging behind the door. When it was her turn to wash, it was like shedding a monstrous skin and becoming human again.

Once they were washed, they explored the room. A second door stood across from the entrance. She tried it. It was locked. She rattled the handle in frustration. "There's probably a stock of food inside," she told him, but she had no strength to force it. While Jon put his shoulder against the door and struggled unsuccessfully, Nan rummaged through the draw in the table and found a torch. It worked and the batteries were charged.

Shining the light, she peered into the furthest recesses of the drawer and saw something glint. Easing her hand cautiously inside, afraid some long forgotten bug might bite her, she grasped a metallic object. A key. She found it hard to resist a triumphant smile as he turned to Jon and said "Try this."

"Where the…?" Jon began, and took the key.

It fit and the lock clicked as the mechanism slipped into place, but the door was stiff and they had difficulty opening it. When they finally managed, they discovered not a cupboard, but a narrow passage winding off into darkness.

"Where does that go? he asked.

She shook her head. "No idea." It hadn't shown on the makeshift map. "The foundations of Baxter are riddled with tunnels."

Once inside, she locked the door and pocketed the key. She handed Jon the torch and let him take the lead.

Every now and then a tunnel joined theirs. They paused to rest sore muscles and catch their breath before continuing straight on. After some hundred yards of oppressive, brick-lined tunnels, they came to another locked door. Disappointed, Jon was about to turn back, but she insisted he try the key. Against all odds, it worked. Cracking open the door, a shaft of light probed the darkened tunnel.

Half blinded by the sudden surge of light, she squinted over his shoulder trying to get a glimpse of what lay beyond. When she finally managed to make out the scene, her mouth fell open and she only just managed to stifle a gasp.

24.

The sound of footsteps wakes me. Keeping my eyes closed, I stretch my legs. I haven't felt so rested in ages. When I do open my eyes, I am lying on a bunkbed fully dressed, with a blanket over me. Goodness knows how I got there.

"Time to wake up, sleepy head," Mart says.

I turn to see him leaning against the wall across the little room, watching me. "How long have I been asleep?"

"Nearly twelve hours," he says, breaking into a broad grin as he pushes away from the wall. "I was beginning to wonder if I shouldn't concot a remedy for sleeping sickness."

:: thanks heavens he didn't get it into his sun-baked head to squash up next to you in this narrow bed

I can't imagine him trying that. I know Sam is just taunting me, but all the same, his suggestion leaves me troubled. I avoid looking at Mart, tending an ear ostentatiously towards the canteen The place is remarkably quiet. "So the food police have left us in peace?"

"For the moment."

Pushing aside the blanket, I swing my legs off the bed and get cautiously to my feet. I feel shaky, but, after a few steps, I gain confidence and follow Mart out of the room into the canteen. It was full the day before, but now it is deserted.

"Where is everyone?" I ask.

"Most have gone to our settlement in the Wilds."

"But …" The ease with which he talks of leaving surprises me. "This is your home. How can you abandon it so easily?"

"We have no choice. We can't stay for ever. Sooner or later food will run out. Besides, we've known for ages this was only a temporary home. The moment the police got over their fear of the plague, they were sure to march in."

While Mart fetches breakfast, I watch several small groups, backpacks slung over their shoulders, heading for the shadows at the back of hideaway.

"There's not much food left," he says laying a loaf on the table with a couple of mugs of steaming tea. "Almost everything has been removed. No point in leaving anything for the food police, they don't eat such things."

:: leave them a tasty plate laced with rat poisoning, they might be tempted - give them a taste of their own medicine.

With Sam chattering about revenge, it takes me a moment to realise why Mart is laughing, but I am in no mood for jokes.

"So we have to go?"

He nods, then breaks off a hunk of bread and offers it to me.

Turning the bread over in my fingers I ask, "Why didn't you leave earlier?"

"I wanted to give you as much time as possible to recover. The journey through the tunnels is not going to be easy." Pulling off a chunk of bread, he bites into it and chews vigorously, glancing around the room as he does. Another small group is heading out, leaving behind a feeling of desolation and despondency. "We are going to be the last to leave. We'll go as soon as we have finished eating."

We eat in silence. Gulps of hot tea help wash down the bread, at the cost of a burnt mouth.

"Can you carry this stuff to the kitchen?" He points to a room off the side of the hall. "I'll get my backpack."

Half way back from the kitchen I hear an explosion from the far end of the hall followed by a piercing scream. A wave of dust and debris billows into the canteen, settling on the tables and benches. That is exactly direction the groups had taken to leave. I feel Sam tense and I quickly reach for Nan's little bottle and place a drop on my tongue.

:: we are trapped like sardines squashed in a tin - like lobsters simmering in the pot - like a stuffed pig on the spity spit - like - like

Take it easy Sam. It's going to be all right.

"Quick!" Mart calls out as he runs across the hall with his pack jiggling on his back. "They are breaking in." He grabs my hand and tugs me after him.

"But I thought we were to go that way," I say pointing in the direction of the noise.

"Too late for that."

Just as he pulls me into a store cupboard, a squad of police surges into the underground canteen, a terrifying mob, wearing protective clothing, their faces concealed behind gas masks. The pounding of their boots is accompanied by a sinister hissing.

:: gas - they are trying to kill us - run - get out - I don't wanna die

Mart pushes aside a pile of boxes to reveal a tiny door. He pulls it open, shoves me inside and follows, drawing the boxes back in place. When the door is closed we stand in pitch dark. I hear him fumbling in his pack. "Where did I put the torch? Ah here it is."

By the light I see we are in a narrow tunnel. Mart squeezes past and leads the way down a steep slope. The floor is slick and I have to hold on to the side of the tunnel not to go skidding down after him. Water trickles down the walls which are as slippery as the floor.

Mart is getting ahead and I speed up, struggling to stay close, but my feet slip from under me and I slide, careening on my backside down the slope, till my feet tangle with his, and he falls too, tumbling on top of me, his backpack crushing the wind from my lungs and his torch flies up in the air, snapping out the moment it hits the ground and is gone with a clatter somewhere behind us and I fling out my arms, trying to grab the slimy wall, to keep from slithering further, but my hands find no holds, it only hurts, and I cry out in pain, and we slew down the tunnel gaining speed as we go, each bump in the floor a shock jarring my spine, we are thrown from side to side, bouncing backwards and forwards off the walls with each twist in the tunnel, shoulders, arms, hips, knees, heads, all battered as we go, till abruptly Mart's feet ram into a wall, his pack slams into me and I am crushed against him, sliding up over his back till I am lying on top of him, my shoulders pressed against the wall which gives way in a shower of bricks and we tumble forward onto damp earth, our helter-skelter at an end.

In a heap, our bodies a hopeless muddle, we lie still for a long moment. Then Mart turns, groaning as he does, and I feel his hands on my face, exploring. "Are you all right?" he asks.

"Yes." My voice trembles. Then I feel his arms lace around my waist pulling me close. I cling to him and burst into tears.

25.

I grasp a twisted root that juts from the side of the tunnel and snakes to the earth below, disappearing in a dense knot of smaller roots at my feet. I grit my teeth and hold on tight. If I let go, I will fall. My legs are trembling and my lungs heave in a desperate effort to breathe. Moist and heavy with earthy odours, the air is suffocating.

"Stop, Mart. I can't go on."

Mart turns back and as he does, the pack on his back scrapes the wall, causing several clods of earth to tumble to the ground with an ominous thud. He places his torch in the middle of the tunnel and steps gingerly round it so he can kneel at my feet. Heaving the pack from his shoulders, he opens it and rummages inside. From the very bottom he pulls out a little packet and un-wraps it, handing me a cake. "Eat. It's full of of good things."

I am not hungry and my mouth is dry, but I take a bite only to gasp in surprise. Rather than dry, it is succulent, filled with fruit and spices and grains.

"Chew it well," Mart instructs, pulling out a second cake. "Mmmm," he mumbles as he munches. "One of my best."

"You made this?"

"Sure. It's normally meant for people recovering from severe illness. I make several batches for the hospital every week. You're lucky, I just made these."

:: there is no way he could have made such a delight, its far too good for a knock-kneed, bony-elbowed kid like him to have anything to do with

Sam's comments halt abruptly and he pretends to sulk, but he can't conceal his embarrassment. His praise must have caught him by surprise. *I'm glad you like it Sam.* His response is like a mental tongue being stuck out.

Now that Sam has ceased his chattering and I am no longer breathing so noisily, the silence is oppressive. From time to time, it is broken by a dull thud as a further clod falls from the walls or roof.

"Is this safe?" I ask pointing to a lump of earth that just broke from the roof.

His face twists in a grimace. "Safer than on the surface."

Sure. From what I heard in the shelter, the Food Police are on the rampage throughout Baxter spraying anything that moves with bullets and anything else with poisonous gas. I just hope Jon and Nan found refuge, though that seems unlikely. Even our underground stronghold was breeched.

"Another cake?"

"No thanks." I couldn't possibly eat more. It was so rich and my stomach seems to have lost the habit.

I peer down the tunnel as far as I can see in the meagre torchlight. Apart from the occasional roots that it skirts, the tunnel makes its way in one straight, unstopping line. It's difficult to judge the passing of time, but I reckon we've been following it for about thirty minutes.

"How much further?"

"I don't know. I've never explored this tunnel."

"But you know where it goes?"

"Outside the city."

I wonder if we will be any safer in the Wilds. I know so little about this place.

:: don't get your hopes up usurper - only squalid disorder awaits us in their foul jungle - it is inhabited by savage pigmies that swell your head till it falls from your shoulders then wayward children play football with it

You're in a good mood, Sam.

Mart shoulders the backpack and gets to his feet. "Ready for more?"

Although Mart's cake has lifted my spirits, I am not sure I can walk far, but I get to my feet and stumble on.

:: we will turn into worms grubbing around, then you won't need to gripe about walking

Thanks, Sam. I do believe he's getting used to having me around.

Ten minutes later I can go no further. I reach out and grab Mart's hand, planning to tell him how exhausted I am when some feet along the tunnel several larger clumps of earth fall to the floor. Both of us skip back in alarm. Just in time! With a thud, a section of the roof collapses where we had been standing, blocking the passage.

Mart curses and leads me back a safe distance, examining the walls and ceiling as we go. "Have a rest," he says opening his backpack and fishing out a small shovel.

No wonder that pack seemed so heavy.

:: he's got a model railway in there, a spare pair of slippers, a cat's bowl, an old telephone directory and one of those signs that people use to flag down trains not to mention

Enough Sam. You don't need to go to such lengths to express your appreciation. My remark is greeted by a mental blush.

"I will try to dig through," Mart says.

"Isn't that dangerous?"

"Sure. But staying here is even more dangerous."

I slump on a clump of roots, lean my back cautiously again the wall and close my eyes. I wish I could sleep but I'm too exhausted and above all too worried. What would I have done had I been alone? I'd never have made it this far. I'd be lying dead in the ruins of Baxter. I didn't used to worry. But I can't seem to stop. I hope the Food Police don't pump the tunnel full of gas.

:: another mess! - now you have got us buried underground

That's unfair. And before you say it, it isn't Mart's fault.

:: why ever not? - he dragged us down here - all he can do is worm around in the mud - wouldn't surprise me if he got stuck in that hole he's digging

I glance nervously towards the torch placed in the centre of the tunnel a short distance from the cave-in. All I can see of Mart is his feet dangling from a hole in the earth at waist height. From time to time, he scuttles back dragging a heap of earth and roots with him. His hands and arms are caked in mud and his face is smattered with it.

He grins at me, his teeth a line of white in the black. "I've got nothing to shore up the earth," he calls out in a forced whisper. "Bits keep falling in..." His last words are lost as he plunges back into the hole.

I must have fallen asleep because when I look up again he is pushing his sack through the hole. "You made it?"

"Yes," he says turning back to me. "I'll go first, then you crawl after."

Getting to my feet, I shuffle to the makeshift entrance. It is barely big enough to crawl inside. Pushing my hands first followed by my head and body, I ease my way into the black hole and slither worm-like forward. Every time I brush the sides of the tunnel, small clumps of earth break away and roll round my body to the ground beneath. I am not yet half-way through and my breath is coming ever harder.

Putting all my remaining force into pushing forward, I snag the roof of the tiny passage. A larger lump of earth falls on my back. Flattened, the air explodes from my lungs and I gasp for breath. I can't move. With my hands stretched out in front of me, there is no way I can free my body. I dig my fingers into the earth and try to heave myself forward. To no avail. Panic seizes me. I am going to suffocate in this muddy hole.

"Mart," I call out. "I'm stuck."

26.

:: I told you we'd get buried alive, but you wouldn't listen - after all, why should a saviour listen to a cripple? - you only have ears for your beau

Oh Sam. That's unfair.

A scuffling in front of me is the only answer I get to my calls for help. Then I feel Mart grip my hands. He tugs, but both our hands are slick and they slip apart. Then I hear him slithering away. Surely he hasn't given up so easily. I lie still, eyes closed, finding it hard to breath. Every time I manage to move a little, the earth renews its grip on me, weighing ever more on my spine.

When I feel his hands again, he has a cloth and is wiping my fingers. Strong hands grip mine and I hear him grunt as he pulls. My arms and shoulders ache, but I am no closer to the exit.

He tugs again and I stifle a scream as my arms are almost wrenched from their sockets, but, to my relief, I inch forward. Lumps of earth shift around me as Mart pulls again and I shift further and more easily.

As I finally emerge and fall, exhausted into Mart's arms, I hear a resounding thud as the passage collapses. He slings an arm under mine, holding me up, and helps me stagger on.

Despite our efforts, we stumble, our feet catching on half hidden roots. Clods of earth tumble around us. We press on, labouring against the aches and pains. My brow is slick with sweat and I frequently wipe the wet from my eyes. Mart's breathing is coming as hard and fast as mine as we reach another place where the tunnel has collapsed blocking the passage.

A wave of despondency crashes over me. I sink defeated to the ground, paying no heed to the dampness of the mud seeping through my clothes. My mouth hangs open as I pant, my lungs complaining bitterly. I lean forward and rest my head on my knees, tears mingling with sweat. Mart remains standing, his legs spread-eagled, his hands on his knees, his head hung loose, panting. Neither of us speak.

Finally he lowers himself to the ground next to me, slides an arm around my shoulder and pulls me closer. In slow motion, I lay my head on his shoulder and give in to the sobs that surge unchecked. As my body is wracked with despair, I feel his fingers raking through my mud-caked hair.

"What a mess," I say, unsure if I mean my hair or the situation. His fingers cease their combing and I regret having spoken. "Don't stop," I whisper.

:: stop that immediately - it is downright disgusting - he is supposed to be saving us, not dallying with you

But instead of continuing, Mart struggles to his feet and moves closer to the cave-in.

"What's up?"

"Shhh," is all he says as he strains on tiptoe, peering at the ceiling. To my surprise, he stretches up and holds one hand close to the muddy ceiling as if in search of something. "There's a draught. We must be close to the surface. Maybe we can dig out."

"But what if we come up in the middle of the Food Police?"

"I'm pretty sure we've gone beyond Baxter." He offers me a hand. Every bone aches as I heave myself to my feet and join him. He's right, a tiny breeze is blowing into the tunnel. I feel it cool and refreshing on my cheeks.

"Stand back. This whole thing might collapse."

He pulls on a tiny root projecting from the ceiling. Nothing happens. He shakes the root and the roof shudders, but remains in place.

"Careful," I say.

He grins, his face caked in mud, and yanks on the root. A large clump of earth breaks away and tumbles to his feet. It is followed in quick succession by several other clumps leaving a gaping hole in the ceiling through which I can see only darkness. Stepping onto the fallen earth, Mart clambers up and peers out.

When he says nothing, I scramble up next to him, my arm slung around his waist for support. His body gives off such welcome warmth in the biting night air, I huddle close, peering out through a forest of blades of grass. As my eyes adjust to the light of the moon, I see a tangled mass of leaves and branches writhing in the wind. Here and there, shifting patches of colour catch the moonlight like willowy dancers weaving their way across a darkened stage.

The sight is extraordinary, but the surrounding soundscape enthrals me more. Against a backdrop of groans of age-old branches struggling against the wind and the accompanying complaint of leaves, the shrieks of nightbirds, the high-pitched cries of bats and the throaty calls of animals on the prowl set the scene for a nighttime drama that is both enticing and menacing. Nearby, a creature moves unseen through the grass, only the rustle revealing its presence.

A sharp hiss to my right has my head swivelling in that direction. I freeze. Only a foot from my nose, a cobra surges from the grass, its hood spread wide in defiance, its tiny eyes bulging, its tongue flicking in and out.

"Don't move," Mart whispers.

As if I could. Fear paralyses me. I can only stare at the forked tongue and the beady eyes. Then, abruptly, I feel a rush of air as its head plunges at my face. It moves so fast I have no time to dodge. I close my eyes, steeling myself against the blow. But none comes. My heart is beating furiously as I cautiously open my eyes. The cobra has shifted back to its erect pose as if nothing had happened.

The second time it feints an attack, I am no less startled. My heart almost jumps out of my chest. The snake is so rapid I would stand no chance if it struck. But it doesn't. Instead I sense the tension subside as if the beast has deflated and then it lowers its head and slithers away.

27.

Jon held his breath. The dazzling light came from the middle of a room in which Food Police milled around, rolling out wires, lugging monitors, installing foldable tables, plugging in gadgets. Almost within touching distance, two officers sat with their backs to Jon and Nan, their heads together, deep in conversation.

Had it not been for the insistent throb of the generator, opening the door would have alerted the men. What's more, the pungent smell of oil and exhaust from the generator covered the stench of rotten food that clung to them.

"... Is that a risk?" One of the officers asked, raising his voice to be heard over the bustle and noise.

"It's been a long time. I doubt an illness could..." The second officer's words were drowned out by a group of men carting in a crate overflowing with protection suits and masks.

"Good," the first one said, nodding to the suits. "No point in trying to ferret out the remaining rebels. They'll be well hidden. All we need is to spray this godforsaken place."

"That'll finish the blighters off!"

"Not directly. It'll kill the plants so they'll have nothing to eat. But above all, it'll poison their water. That'll drive them out."

"I just hope it doesn't get into our water."

"No danger. We have powerful filters."

"We are not supposed to stay, I hope?"

"You can if you want." He chuckled. "No. We'll have a couple of men kit up and keep an eye on things."

They got to their feet and were about to move to the monitors when a young orderly ran into the room and halted in front of them. Saluting, he said, "Message, Sir."

"Go ahead."

"The Commander said it was private," the orderly said.

All three of them drew closer to the door. Jon felt Nan's warning hand on his shoulder. He didn't dare breathe for fear they'd be discovered. Luckily the men were so engrossed in their conversation they paid no attention to their surroundings.

"What?" one of them exclaimed.

"The doc says he probably got it from a cut," the orderly explained. "The Commander says you're to retreat, immediately."

"But what about the spraying?" the first officer asked.

"No. Definitely not. The Commander says it will only increases the risk."

"What about our observers?" the second officer asked.

"Call them back. No one is to stay."

They dismissed the orderly and glanced at the monitors before rounding up the men and exiting as fast as they could. The monitors continued to paint phantom pictures of Baxter, the generator coughed and spluttered and the protection suits slouched over the side of the crate like deflated dummies.

"That's useful," Jon said after they'd waited five minutes and no Food Police had returned. "Or at least those suits would be if ever they decide to spray."

"Sure," Nan said, sounding distracted. "What worries me is that some have probably caught the disease. In Baxter that would not be a catastrophe. We have the skills and the remedies needed. But the pharma and their police have murdered or outlawed the only people who could help them. They have no answer to the disease but death and destruction."

Jon had visions of the city once again engulfed in a pall of sickly smoke as people set fire to their neighbours in a desperate bid to escape the illness. "Is there nothing we can do?"

"Survive," Nan replied bitterly. "Later, we might help a few, if they let us. Last time, a healer offering help was a target for people's anger and frustration, not to mention their guns."

Ten minutes later they emerged into the harsh light of day to be greeted by a nauseating stench. Baxter's hospital was a scene of utter desolation. Doors had been ripped from their hinges, furniture had been flung out of windows, carefully tended flower beds had been trampled by an army of boots, shrubs had been hacked to pieces, papers were scattered everywhere, but worst of all were the bodies. They lay strewn amid the chaos, the ailing and the healthy alike, men, women and children, abandoned with their limbs at awkward angles, their sightless eyes staring, their clothes torn, stained blood red, a feast for swarms of flies.

Jon's hand flew to his mouth, a clenched fist pressed against his lips, unable to stifle a cry of despair. The world swam as his eyes clouded over with tears. No. No. No. How could they?

Nan laid an arm around his shoulders and he let himself be pulled gently into her arms. His head sank heavily onto her shoulder. What was the point? He could not oppose such all-encompassing evil. It was too immense.

A groan nearby had Nan pulling away. Without her for support, he slumped to his knees, his head sagging forward till his forehead touched the ground.

"Jon. Help me," Nan called out.

He crouched, unable to respond, eyes closed, mind blank.

"Jon! I know it's hard... terribly hard, but these people need help, and helping others is the best thing you can do right now."

He cracked open his eyes, looking up at her tear-smeared face, and took her outstretched hand. Struggling to his feet, he trudged after her. She crouched by the remnants of a clump of lavender. There, sprawled on her back, lay a young girl, hardly a few years older than Sam, her t-shirt ripped apart revealing a bloody gash. She lay unmoving, her face pinched in pain, but her eyes were open and sought him out, following his every move.

"It looks bad and it must hurt terribly," Nan said, taking the girl's hand in hers, "but I think the bullet only grazed you." Turning to Jon, she asked, "Fetch some water. There's a well by the entrance."

28.

Jon stepped over several bodies to reach the well. He avoided looking at the corpses, afraid he might stumble on Sam. But these were all adults.

The head of the well had been smashed and, peering inside, he could make out a body tossed down the shaft. If the water wasn't polluted, it soon would be. He trudged back bearing his bad news.

"Keep watch over the girl," Nan said. "I'll go and fetch a stretcher... If I can find one intact."

He squatted by the girl, but the position hurt too much. Dragging over a large wooden tub of flowers that had miraculously escaped, he sat with his back against it.

Seeing the girl looking, he asked, "What's your name?"

"June," she said, speaking so softly he had to strain to hear.

"Well, June, we're going to get you out of here and take you to a safe place." So many empty promises. It made him sick. Who was he to promise safety? He couldn't even guarantee his own.

"Why?" the girl asked in a wheezy whisper.

He guessed she meant the violence. He couldn't help her there. Visions of trying to reassure Sam sprang to mind. But he didn't have it in him to play that game.

He shook his head. "I don't understand either."

"They were so angry."

"I know. Maybe discovering life flourishing in Baxter was too much for them. Like being forced to stay in a grey world and being told colour is bad only to discover your neighbours live happily in a paradise of colours."

"But the killing?" The girl shuddered and tears flowed down her cheeks. "Snuffing people out without a thought."

Seeing her cry made tears well in his own eyes. "It makes no sense," he said, his voice sunk to a whisper like hers.

Nan returned at that moment, a rucksack on her back and a stretcher under her arm. She glanced from him to the girl and back. "I see you have been cheering each other up." Both stared at the ground, neither replying.

"Her name's June," Jon finally said.

"Well June, you are a lucky girl. It doesn't look like anyone else survived."

Laying out the stretcher next to June, she added, "Let's lift you onto this and get away."

Between them they shifted June onto the stretcher, not before the girl blacked out.

"Where now?" Jon asked once they had made their way around the hospital grounds.

"I'm not sure. A lot of people must have escaped, judging from the few bodies. I guess they went to the Wilds. People from Baxter fled there a long time ago and a small colony has grown up in the jungle."

"Yes, they did," a tiny voice said. June had regained consciousness.

"Do you know where it is?" Nan asked.

"I went there once..." Her voice trailed off.

They had reached the limits of Baxter. Bulldozers had long since flattened a wide corridor of rubble around the city marking the frontier with the Wilds. They paused in the shelter of some bushes, laying June and her stretcher on a patch of grass. Nan pulled a small parcel from her backpack and unwrapped it. "Cakes," she said and handed one to Jon.

"Can you mange to eat by yourself?" she asked Jane. "Or would you like me to feed you?"

The girl held out her hand for the cake, wincing as she did.

"Mmm. This is delicious," Jon said, munching the mixture of

pastry and dried fruits.

"Mart makes them," Nan said. The mention of the boy caused Jon a surge of irritation. His displeasure was short-lived. How could he be so petty after all he'd been through? He just hoped the boy had survived and managed to guide Sam to safety.

On their feet again, with June suspended between them, Nan was about to venture out into the open no-man's-land, when a piercing whistle rang out from the jungle opposite; one single blast. Nan faltered and waved Jon back. From the shadow of a bush, they peered across at the jungle trying to identify the source of the warning, for warning it clearly was.

"There," Nan whispered, pointing to a clearer patch in the tight knot of foliage.

A man in the shadows waved wildly for them to move back and get down. Then he was gone. The appearance had been so brief, he wondered if he'd imagined it, but Nan had seen it too. She turned from the open causeway and led them, stumbling in their haste, to a thicket some thirty yards back.

They had still ten yards to go when they heard a growing roar echoing off the jungle like a hoard of savage beasts in rut, kicking up rocks as they went. Jon glanced over his shoulder, tripped and fell. While he scrambled forward on all fours, Nan dragged June and the stretcher amongst the trees.

A gigantic vehicle, the likes he had never seen, surged into view. Perched above immense wheels bigger than a tall man, was a glass cabin in which four Food Police scanned the jungle and Baxter with what looked like binoculars. A fifth man wrestled with an oversized driving wheel, wrenching it left and right to compensate for the ruts in the terrain. Each time the monster hit a loose stone, it stuck to the tread and was then flung out behind the vehicle.

29.

Mart heaves me out of the hole and wraps his arms around me. No matter how much he tries to soothe me, I can't stop shaking. I imagine the cobra darting forward and every sharp noise makes me jump.

"It's alright," he says. "It's gone. It was as frightened as you. It didn't want to hurt, just scare you away."

Away? I wish I could get away. My knees feel weak and my legs are trembling. I cling to Mart. The thought of forcing our way through the jungle with its wild beasts and noxious plants terrifies me. I can't face this any more. All I want is a quiet corner to curl up and sleep.

"I can't go on," I say. The odds are so heavily stacked against me something inside snaps. No! No! No more! Deep down, in the recesses of my mind, Sam mutters.

:: snakes kill - snakes kill - snakes kill

"Sure you can," Mart insists, pulling away and looking around.

He is curious and rises readily to a challenge. Am I that different? Surely if he can, so can I. Taking a deep breath, I calm my wayward nerves. Despite my efforts, shudders continue to ripple through my body and I am unable to quieten my foreboding. Maybe if I get acquainted with the place, I will be less afraid. In the moonlight, the hole at my feet does seem less spectacular. It lies in the middle of a clearing around which tower enormous trees, densely interwoven with creepers and other climbing plants.

"We should get away," Mart says.

"We can't possibly fight our way through that," I say pointing at the impenetrable forest.

:: beware the fidgeting jungle - it tosses and turns - branch rubbing against branch - sharpening poisonous thorns

Don't Sam. You are only making things worse.

Mart grins. "No we can't. But we could take the path." He points behind me.

Turning, I discover a narrow path. What a relief to discover order in this disorder, but I am still unwilling to venture away.

Mart takes my hand and pulls me towards the path. "Time to go."

"Time indeed," a voice says behind us.

We both spin round to find an old woman standing there, a wicker basket over her forearm. Where did she come from? The jungle is impassable. Her apparition has me frozen in astonishment, but Mart tugs me away.

"If you are thinking of running," she chuckles, "that wouldn't be a good idea. You'll get lost. This place is a maze."

"Who are you?" Mart asks.

"Wrong question."

Mart and I stare at her amazed. What an odd thing to say.

"What you need to know is what I am?"

:: a crone, a hag, a bouncing old bag

What an extraordinary woman. She is alone and unarmed in the jungle at night. Judging from the deep folds around her mouth and eyes she must be at least eighty, maybe that's why Sam called her a hag, yet her back is as straight as any young person and she looks spritely. In comparison, I feel old and weary.

"So what are you?" Mart asks, his tone condescending.

"There's no single word. I might once have been called a witch, but that word now fills people with horror. You might say wise woman, but the criminals who run your city have outlawed such people. I collect flowers, I listen to the wind, I talk to animals, I concoct remedies from the bark of trees, and I know my way around this wonderful chaos you call the Wild."

"I've heard about people like you," Mart says. "They live in a forest and lure young people into their house and poison them with irresistible food."

:: lulling us with her sweet words then up into the soup with us and bubbling nicely amid the carrots and turnips thank you

The woman bursts out laughing. Her voice is not so full and rich as that of a young woman, but her laugh still rings out like delightful music. "I love those old stories. They remind me of when I was little. But I have no intention of doing you harm. My task is to heal, to set things right, not to lay waste."

"What are you doing out at night with your basket?" I ask, half expecting some crazy answer.

"I will tell you willingly. But we should get away before those who are following you arrive. If you trust me enough to follow, I will take you to a place to hide and rest."

I sense she means no harm, but Mart is reticent.

"It's alright, Mart. She's OK."

:: you are hopeless, a naive wooly-nilly with mashed turnips for a brain - I side with your beau

Mart remains unconvinced, but distant noises from the tunnel leave him no choice. The woman strides away along the path and we hurry after.

"Keep close behind or you'll get lost," she calls over her shoulder and veers to the right down a new path.

I stumble several times. Mart offers me a hand, but the path is narrow and we have to walk single file. When my breathing becomes laboured and I stumble again, Mart calls out, "Stop. Sam can't go on."

The woman stops and retraces her steps till she stands in front of me. She takes my face in her boney fingers and pulling it forward she peers into my eyes. "You caught that pesky plague those pharmaceutical companies conjured up, didn't you? How long ago was that?"

"Less than a week. I got up yesterday."

She grasps my wrist and presses her thumb against the vein, her face intense with concentration. When she finally removes her hand, she grunts.

"So?" I ask.

"The sickness hasn't left you. All this walking is doing you no good." She rummages in her coat and pulls out a handful of leaves. She selects a couple and hands them to me. "Chew. They don't taste good, but they will help. We won't be able to go where I planned. It's too far. I'll take you somewhere nearer till you recover."

30.

"Here we are," the old woman says, halting abruptly.

She must be pulling our leg. Despite the growing daylight, I see nothing but an outcrop of rock amongst the ever-present trees. When she does move forward, she doesn't disappear behind the outcrop as I expect. Instead she pushes aside a mass of creepers and slips between two trunks. I hasten to follow, worried we might lose her. Mart hurries after.

What we discover is breath-taking. We are inside an immense hanger, the superstructure of which can just be made out through the many plants and bushes that have taken up residence. Here and there, rusted machines rise above the vegetation as if trying to break free of a stifling embrace.

Leaving us no time to marvel, she weaves her way through the bushes and we hasten after.

"Keep close," she insists. "This place is littered with traps."

The news alarms me and the trembling begins again. I have no time to pull out Nan's potion. Instead, I breath deeply and try to calm our joint nerves.

"Here. Hold on to my belt," she offers, no doubt sensing my distress.

I shuffle behind her, clutching her belt with trembling fingers. Up close, I am surrounded by the odours of flowers. Maybe that is what is in her basket. Whatever it is, it has a calming effect and the trembling recedes.

To my surprise she begins softly singing a high-flung song, the words of which make no sense. When I hear a sharp hissing coming from the undergrowth around me I grind to a halt, forcing the woman to stop too. My body trembles violently and there's nothing I can do to stop it.

She tries to reassure me, but when that fails she takes hold of my hands and stares into my eyes, whispering strange words till I feel my body relax. It is as if I join Sam in a woollen cocoon far removed from the world. Sounds are muffled and my other senses are numbed.

Snapping her fingers in front of my nose brings me back to myself. I look around, surprised to find I am sitting in a wicker armchair in a charming little room, the walls of which are hung with brightly embroidered cloth. There's a low bed in one corner, covered in thick woollen blankets. The sight is inviting.

"You can sleep in a moment," she says, "but first you must eat. My soup will help you recover."

:: You see - your beau was right - she's going to poison us with her soup

I thought we were to be the soup, I say wearily. I spoon warm soup into my mouth, surprised how hungry I am. The taste is unfamiliar but nourishing. Once I have finished, she helps me to the bed and I fall asleep the moment she pulls the covers over me.

I sit on one of the slabs of stone that line the port, watching the water lap against the islanders' painted longboats. The sun is low over the ocean tingeing the crests red and orange and yellow. The colours are so intense they resonate in my chest. The sky too is majestic. It leaves me feeling elated, but that elation is short lived. The gravity of my situation leaves no place for joy.

I am glad to be free of my followers. Their constant stream of questions drains me. I need to be alone to collect my thoughts. What I must do is so daunting I doubt I will succeed. How can I possibly save these people when the elders are bent on stopping me?

"Miss," a voice calls out from the entrance to the port. "Miss, the army are chasing away your followers."

I get wearily to my feet and join the young girl. "Where are they?" I ask, taking hold of her hand.

"At the gate to the city."

"... how have you survived so long?" I hear Mart ask as I drift from sleep, still tense at the confrontation on the island.

"I have lived here all my life. When that plague broke out, I was intent on helping. But so many healers were slaughtered I had no choice but to flee."

"Are there other people like you living here?"

She chuckles. "There's no one like me." Mart laughs too. She seems to have charmed him or at least overcome his reticence.

"There are other people. Many fled the city and its rulers, but few survived. Those who did, banded together. You don't want to bump into them, they've become more savage than the wildest of beasts."

I lie awake, my eyes closed, listening to her describe the Wild and its inhabitants. A grim place. We have been lucky to meet her. We could so easily have fallen into the hands of a wild group. The island in my dreams was hostile, but this place is far worse.

:: Oh no! - give me the hag any day - not flea-infested apes sporting tomahawks - does this nightmare have no end?

"I only rarely come here," the woman explains, "It is too near a camp of one of those groups. As soon as your friend has recovered, we'll go somewhere safer."

"How close?" I ask, leaning on my elbow as I turn to look at her. Then I scream! And I keep screaming. Curled up in the woman's lap is a brightly coloured snake, its head raised, staring intently at me.

"Stop!" the woman says. "You'll have that band of no-goods knocking at the door."

I clamp my mouth shut, swallowing my terror, and almost choke.

:: run! run! filthy slithering beast, harbinger of death - look at those fangs dripping with venom - look at the insane desire in its eyes

"Yes. It's a snake. So what? It is completely harmless…"

:: harmless - what claptrap!

A shrill cry interrupts her. She immediately gets to her feet, placing the snake in the chair. "Help her up," she orders Mart.

"What's going on?" he asks as he helps me stand.

The woman hands Mart a shawl. "Wrap it round her shoulders."

Another shrill call shakes us all.

"It's the Guzzo," she says, grabbing a long staff.

"The Guzzo?" Mart asks.

"A dreadful gang of thugs who have been trying to catch me for years."

When a violent crash rings out from the other side of the hangar, the woman barks, "Follow me."

31.

"That was a close shave," the young man said, a broad smile on his lips as he emerged from the foliage. "My name's Tim." Realising they were struggling to carry June, he hurried to help. When Jon mumbled, "I'm OK," he took Nan's end of the stretcher, which Nan willing relinquished. "We need to get out of sight," Tim said. "They'll be back in twenty minutes."

Pulling aside a giant leaf revealed a narrow path between the trees. "Let me go first," Tim said, exchanging places with Jon. Nan brought up the rear. Jon began sweating the moment they were engulfed in the jungle. His senses were assaulted by all manner of smells, some of them sweet and cloying, others fine and delicate and then there was the foul smell of mould and decay. Worse than the onslaught of odours were the noises, each relating a different tale of horror. The jungle chirped and cracked and groaned and growled and even snapped and slithered; the whole damn world seething with dangerous life. Several times he could have sworn he saw movement out of the corner of his eye, but each time he checked, only swaying leaves were to be seen.

After ten minutes winding their way along the narrow path they reached a clearing that backed onto an outcrop. "There's a cave," Tim explained. "We can hole up for a while. But we won't be able to carry the stretcher in."

June made a vain attempt to get to her feet, but collapsed into Tim's arms with a groan. "Don't fret," he said. "I'll carry you." He promptly cradled her in his arms, swung her into the air with surprising ease and disappeared behind one of the rocks.

The cave was larger than Jon expected. Along three sides ran low cots, little more than an odd assortment of rough planks hastily nailed together. In the farthest corner someone had built an open hearth, formed by an irregular circle of stones. A trail of soot snaked up the wall and disappeared through a narrow crack in the roof. Jon lowered himself gingerly onto a cot, his legs trembling, a dull pain in his chest oppressing him.

Laying the girl on one of the cots, Tim turned to Nan saying, "Can you give me a hand to prepare something to eat?"

Nan followed the young man, her steps weary as he led her to a door at the back and the two disappeared inside.

When June groaned, Jon stood and shuffled to her side. Beads of sweat pearled on her forehead and her eyes were bright with fever. "Where are we?" she asked, her voice frail.

"In a safe place. We are on our way to a settlement of people from Baxter."

She shut her eyes as if to digest his words. "It hurts," she said.

Jon was no healer. Had he been a healer he would probably be dead. There was nothing he could do. He didn't even have water. But her pleading look obliged him to do something. He pulled aside her torn t-shirt and looked at the wound. It was swollen and the flesh had turned bright red.

"Nan," he called out.

Nan came hurrying back carrying a tray piled with exotic fruit and a pitcher of water. "What's up?" she asked. He didn't need to reply. She'd spotted the wound. Placing a hand on the girl's forehead, she quickly withdrew it. "You're burning up." Turning to Tim, she asked, "Have you got medicinal herbs?"

"Just the basics." He hurried away and returned with several small cloth bags, a pestle and a mortar. Nan pulled a pinch of dried leaves from a bag, sniffed them and placed them in the mortar. Asking for a clean cloth, she began grinding.

She tended to June's wound and then they ate the fruit. It tasted as strange as it looked, but Jon found it refreshing. Once the meal was over, the girl closed her eyes and slept. Jon closed his eyes too, but couldn't sleep. He listened to Nan and Tim.

"How far do we have to go?" she asked.

"About an hour's walk."

"We can't hang about. June needs remedies we haven't got."

"There are several healers in the settlement. They will have what you need."

"Have many people fled Baxter?"

"Several hundred. Maybe more. A number of us have been guiding refugees back to the settlement."

"Can you house so many?"

"We'll have to extend the walls..."

"Walls?"

"The settlement is barricaded behind high wooden barriers, partly to keep out wild animals, but mostly to keep out marauding gangs of humans."

"Is it that bad?"

"There are several gangs in the area, but the worst call themselves the Guzzo. They are human only in form. In all else they are worse than animals."

Nan whistled between her teeth. "Are we safe?"

"You are OK. But the rest of the journey is going to be tricky. We have to travel close to their camp."

Jon was alarmed. There seemed to be no safe haven left. How ever had he managed to live in ignorance of these dangers? Of course, he was well aware of the Food Police, but for a long time they'd left him and his son in peace.

"I'm wondering if I should fetch reinforcements," Tim said.

"Isn't that risky?"

"Not half as risky as taking you three along. You're worn out and the girl is seriously ill."

"How long will it take?"

"A couple of hours there and back. But I have to round up a group to protect you and that might take time."

"When will you leave?"

"The sooner the better."

Jon was worried about being stuck in the cave. "Are we safe

here?"

"Normally, yes. But, whatever you do, don't venture out. And talk only in whispers."

"How much food and water is there?" Jon asked, unable to silence his anxiety.

"Don't worry about that," Nan told him. "There's enough for several days."

32.

When Jon opened his eyes, judging from the light that fil-
tered through the entrance, it was still daytime. The passage of
time was hard to tell, but he had the impression he'd slept a good
number of hours. He felt rested and refreshed. Tim must have
been gone a long time.

The sound of Nan rummaging through her backpack had
him turning to greet her. To his alarm, instead of Nan he discovered a monkey, the contents of the pack scattered at its feet.
It was fingering the torch. When Jon got to his feet, the monkey
jumped back, baring its teeth and chittering angrily, the torch still
clutched in its fingers. Afraid the animal would make a run for it,
Jon shifted in slow motion towards the entrance.

Seeing him move, the monkey dashed to escape, bowling
into him as it did. Both of them were sent flying and in the fray,
Jon grappled with the furry beast trying to get hold of the torch.
The monkey bared its teeth and snapped, narrowly missing his
face. Terrified at such naked fury, he pushed the monkey away
and it pelted out the entrance.

Jon sat on the ground breathing heavily. He ran a trembling
hand over his face to reassure himself. Apart from the stubble on
his chin, nothing was amiss. When he turned to the cots, he saw
Nan grinning at him.

"I didn't know you were so passionate about monkeys," she
said.

"Not monkeys," he said, trying to conceal his irritation at her
obvious amusement. "Torches. It stole your torch."

"Blast. Did it get anything else?"

Nan finished returning her things to her pack when sounds of scuffling outside had them wondering if Tim was back. Jon was about to go to greet him, when Nan raised a warning finger.

The scuffling, which had grown louder, was now accompanied by a snuffling, as if a large animal were sniffing around the entrance in search of food. Bar taking refuge behind the door to the food supplies, they had nowhere to hide. And there were no weapons at hand.

Nan planted herself between June and the entrance, her fists clenched, readying to confront whatever was now scratching frantically at the narrow passageway. Jon swallowed with difficulty, his mouth suddenly dry. How could Nan possibly remain so calm?

The scratching abruptly ceased and the animal let out a roar of frustration. The hairs on Jon's neck stood on end. Then the footfalls moved away, the animal off in search of easier prey.

Jon slumped onto a cot and let out a sigh of relief.

Nan turned to June who couldn't stop trembling. "Don't worry," she said, grinning. "It was far too fat to get in here."

Her playful grin made him aware of the immense distance that separated them. All he could do was grit his teeth. He no longer had the strength to stave off such vicissitudes and smile. He felt old and weary.

"Jon," Nan called out. She was seated on June's cot, the girl's head cradled in her lap.

"Yes?" he managed, letting his head hang as he looked away, his eyes set on the ground.

"I think you need some care and attention too."

Her words sparked a burst of anger. He didn't need to be mollycoddled. He was not one of her charges.

He heard the cot creak as Nan shifted, but he refused to look up. He heard her footsteps as she crossed the cave and he stiffened in anticipation. When her hand ran down the back of his head and settled on his neck, he shifted along the cot, muttering, "Don't."

She sat next to him and took his hands in hers. "You are worth far more than you think," she said, lifting his fingers to her lips and kissing the tips of them. "Life has suddenly become very hard for you. You lost your son. You underwent the worst form of torture." He groaned. "And now you are shipwrecked on wild and dangerous shores with a couple of women. Who wouldn't feel downtrodden and exhausted in such circumstances?"

The more she talked, the longer she held his hands, the less he wanted to pull away. When she put her arms around his shoulders and pulled him into a hug he no longer resisted. His head fit snugly into the hallow between her neck and shoulders. He let it lie there and closed his eyes. He felt engulfed in her warmth, soaking it up like a parched tree. After a while, Nan shifted so his head lay in her lap and she could lean against the wall. As he drifted off to sleep he wondered if she would feel drained after all he'd taken from her.

The sound of boots in the cave awoke him with a start. Had the Food Police discovered them? Or was it that band of wild men who camped nearby? One glance was enough to reassure him. Tim had returned with people to accompany them.

33.

Harriet trots ahead, weaving through the ruins of long dead factories. I struggle to stay apace, afraid I'll get lost if I don't. Mart is hard on my heals, catching me whenever I trip.

Several times he offers to carry me. "I've done it before," he insists. I decline, annoyed at myself. I'm hardly more agile than my clumsy other half. Thank heavens he's not around for this nightmare. Stop that, I tell myself. The last thing you want is to awake him and have him facing this.

:: you won't get rid of me that easily, body-snatcher - you are way more clumsy than you imagine and you have no excuse - graceless, ungainly fumbler, what a bumbling clod you are

You can talk! I battle to contain my annoyance. Fighting Sam is not going to solve our problems.

Somewhere, not so far away, I hear the crashing of careless feet blundering between overgrown machines. Blood-curdling growls and cries of enthusiasm are punctuated by half-articulated oaths as someone stumbles on unseen obstacles. Every loud noise has Sam cringing. Why go to such lengths? It doesn't make sense. Even if they have a long standing vendetta against Harriet, it is hardly worth their pains.

I look up just in time to glimpse Harriet disappearing between two towering chimneys. I hasten after, slipping through the narrow space that still smells of soot, into another of those giant halls littered with disarticulated machines doing battle with creepers and stunted trees.

:: can't you dream up a landscape that is less gothic, usurper?

- what a miserable nightmare you've dragged us into

Instead of crossing the space as we did earlier, Harriet veers to the left and elbows a passage past a dense knot of ferns, dislodging screeching birds. When I struggle after, I discover a flight of stairs plunging into darkness.

"Take my hand," she whispers. "And give a hand to your friend." I turn to Mart who offers his hand. "Don't let go. It's dark." With which she sets off down the stairs, me and Mart in tow.

:: what a wonderful opportunity to ditch your admirer - just let his fingers slip from yours, an accident of course, a moment of distraction, and he'll fade into the dark, for ever

Shut up, Sam. That won't work on me. All the same, I clutch Mart's hand tighter.

When we reach level ground, Harriet continues without a pause across what sounds like a vast expanse. Our footfalls bounce back, distant echoes from chance meetings with a host of sounds, none reassuring. The air is ripe with all manner of odours that shift and evolve as we move forward.

After barely a minute, I stumble and fall almost dragging Mart down with me. Harriet stops. I hear her rummaging in the dark. Then I feel her hands on my waist. Groping, I discover a cord wrapped around me, one end reaching forward to Harriet, the other going back to Mart. "You afraid I'll run away?" I ask, but it's not funny. Nobody laughs.

I feel the presence of a nearby wall, a ghostly pressure on my mind. It's as if being unable to see heightens other senses. Holding out my hand confirms my intuition, although I wish I hadn't. My fingers land in a slimy nastiness that clings to me. My stomach strains to reach my mouth and it is all I can do not to retch.

:: Revolting icky mess - why don't you just roll in the appalling ooze while you are at it?

I ignore Sam as I try to wipe the muck on my trousers.

After interminably edging forward in the dark, Harriet orders, "Come closer and hold on to my belt. We are crossing a field of pitfalls. One false step and you'll break a leg... Or worse."

I force myself to follow, trying to anticipate when Harriet abruptly sidesteps. I have nothing to guide me but the shifting of her hips and the tension in her back. For all her apparent confidence, I sense her apprehension. I clench my fists in concentration and my knees, weak from the walking, start to tremble.

When she suddenly halts, I can't help bumping into her. Mart is more agile and avoids colliding with us. "We'll be alright now. But we still need to stay quiet," she whispers then pushes open a door and we enter a long corridor that is dimly lit by tiny openings in the ceiling.

Once freed of the rope our pace quickens. The corridor curves to the right before straightening out. It is littered with tattered sheets of paper covered in washed out diagrams, no doubt the remains of machine operators' manuals. Some are propped against the walls in precarious stacks. I'm sure to be the one to upset such a pile and, sure enough, I do, sending an alarming crash echoing along the passage.

:: well done, gawky nit - the assembled company has decided to award you a medal, a thistle pinned to your backside

Your backside too, Sam!

"Nearly there," Harriet whispers as we pass through another door and climb a narrow set of windowless stairs lit only by light from below. They go up so high we must be well above ground. Panting, I stop several times to catch my breath. Untroubled by the effort, Harriet waits patiently till I'm ready.

The climb turns out to be well worth it. When Harriet unlocks a door at the very top we step through into a spacious room, much bigger than Jon's flat. There are windowless windows on all sides, but most are obscured by the branches of trees growing outside. Mart goes to a window and leans out. I join him. No one can possibly see in unless they scale the trees. I look down. The drop is at least thirty feet.

:: now's your chance - a little friendly push and your dandy will end up dangling from the branches of one of those dastardly trees

I am about to snap at Sam, fed up with his insistent, gloomy opposition, when Harriet hails us. "I wouldn't stay too long at the window if I were you," she warns as she empties the contents of her backpack onto a table.

Hurrying back to the door, I turn on my heals to take in the scene. Plants have sprung up and grow abundantly despite our height above ground, but between the plants are tables and chairs surrounded by long, low cupboards in one part and several inviting beds in another, each draped with what looks like heavy-duty mosquito netting.

Seeing my interest, Harriet says, "To stop the creepy-crawlies from keeping you awake at night." I remember the snake and shudder. I doubt the netting would be enough. Suddenly the beds are less appealing.

34.

What with the size of Harriet's aerial hideout and the obstacles littering it, I can barely see across the room, but I can make out workbenches and various glass containers.

"I make healing mixtures," she explains. "But for now, a hearty meal would be our best remedy."

Harriet clears bunches of dried herbs from a table, sorting them into various wicker baskets and pulls up chairs. I sit across from Mart, both our heads cradled in our hands like weary chicks. Neither of us have the energy to talk. He looks pale and there are dark shadows under his eyes. In contrast, his hands are large and strong. I'm surprised I hadn't notice before. They are still stained from clawing a passage through the earth.

"Here. Eat this," Harriet says handing us a handful of dried fruit. "Wild apricots. They will tide you over till the meal is ready and they're good for muscle cramps."

Sucking on the apricots that are refreshingly sour, we watch Harriet kindle a fire in the hearth and hang a large kettle over the flames. Little by little I feel some of my strength return.

"Marinated veg," she explains. "Made before I left. Cooked enough for a week. Must have known I'd have company."

:: can't understand what you nuts see in this messy food - think of the risks, and the filthy work preparing it - those things grow in the ground - yuck! - and then you have to chew them till your jaw aches - most likely the stuff will give you a stomach ache if it doesn't poison you - and when it's all over you still have to clear up the mess - what's wrong with those clean, tasty, energy-saving pills?

Come off it, those pills are disgusting. And cooking is a real pleasure.

:: what do you know about cooking? - you only just popped out of your dark hole, usurper - you have never cooked

There are other lives, Sam.

:: wild fantasies and wishful thinking, stewed up in your addled brain

Why am I arguing with him? Well at least he's acknowledging me. *I can't spend all day talking to you. There are things we need to know.*

"Why are those thugs after you?" I ask as Harriet dishes up steaming bowls of vegetables steeped in a thick brown sauce and hands us some unleavened bread. The question has been bothering me.

"It's not me they are after," she says, taking a seat at the end of the table between us. "It's you."

"That doesn't make sense," Mart says, looking up wearily from his bowl. "Their grudge is against you."

"Their feud with me is more of a game we've been playing for years. But chasing you is deadly serious." She takes a spoonful of vegetables, sniffs appreciatively and makes approving noises as she tastes it. "Deep in the jungle there's a school; more like a prison if you ask me. They call it the Centre and it pays good money for kids like you. Well not you," she says to Mart. "Her," she says prodding a thumb in my direction. "They only take girls. Intelligent ones."

"So that is what you are up to," Mart challenges.

Harriet sighs. "There's no dispelling your distrust, is there?"

Mart shrugs. "I was asked to protect Sam by people who will never forgive me if harm comes to her. I take my task seriously."

Maybe I ought to be flattered, but being tailed by a guardian angel irritates me, even if he does have attractive hands and a delicious mouth. I glance across the table at him to make sure he isn't pulling my leg, but the tender way he catches my eye before looking away is clear enough. Irritation subsides as I feel my face colour and I look away too.

:: told you you should have shoved your smeary dandy out

the window when you had a chance

Sam's snide remarks only spark my irritation.

"It probably won't change your mind," Harriet added, "but those people who call themselves educators are no more my friends than the Guzzo."

"Why would they collect girls?" Mart asks, shaking his head. "Sounds more like a zoo than a school."

"They don't seem to have the common good at heart," I add.

"Rumour has it," Harriet begins, mopping up the sauce with a hunk of bread, "they are searching for a particular girl… "

"A prize specimen," Mart says, spitting out the words.

This conversation leaves me perplexed. Why would people go to such lengths to get one girl? It would make sense if the girl was heir to the throne or had some influential or rich parents.

:: maybe they collect girls like some collect prize bulls, so when there are none left, they have a good stock for future use

Sam's wild idea sparks visions of horror, as I imagine a breeding farm for future citizens.

"What are they after, a ransom?" Mart asks, only to reply himself. "No. That can't be. Why bother to pay for the others?"

"Power," I say, the answer popping into my head. "Whoever they are looking for is a source of power."

"Power?" Mart asks, echoing Sam's question.

"Imagine someone has the potential to be a future leader…"

:: or saviour

Cut it out, Sam. I know you have been shut in your head all this time, but not everyone is as self-centred as you.

"OK. But that doesn't explain why they take so many?" Mart asks.

"They don't know who she is. That's why they have to catch as many as they can," I blurt out as the idea comes to me.

"I think you are right," Harriet says as she gathers bowls and spoons. "What worries me is what they do to those who aren't what they are looking for."

35.

I shudder in horror as I think of that training camp, hidden in the depths of the jungle, where girls are schooled as instruments for ill at the service of the rich and powerful.

:: yeah - moulding, shaping, forming till the little blighters have no will of their own - the ultimate school for thought - drilling the minds out of them - spare me from that fate, sister

Sister? Are you becoming over familiar, Sam?

:: There are horrors that even I will not poke fun at, little girl

Turning my attention back to Harriet, I hasten to change the subject. "How long have you been living up here?"

"I've been coming for years," Harriet says as she shifts the soup bowls to a bucket on the floor. "But this is only one of the places I use. I move around. Makes me more difficult to trace."

Mart has laid his head on his arms that are folded on the table. His eyes are closed.

"You two should go to bed," Harriet says.

Mart yawns and gets to his feet, rubbing his eyes as he looks around. I feel less tired, but make for the bed the farthest from the windows. I survey the covers cautiously before lifting the netting. Best to be sure. Mart seems to have less qualms. He lets himself collapse on a bed near the window and starts snoring almost immediately.

Sitting on the edge of the bed, I watch Harriet pick up the bucket of dishes and sling a cloth over her shoulder.

"I'll be back in a short while," she says.

"Can I come?" I ask, getting to my feet and letting the net

drop back.

"You should sleep. You've been ill."

"I'd rather talk."

She hesitates then nods. I follow her to the door.

"Here, take this," she says, handing me the cloth and we descend the stairs.

I hear the water long before we reach the basement, but it is only when we walk into a small room at the foot of the stairs that I see its source: a fractured pipe with water cascading over a large table then onto the floor and across into the next room. An array of algae and aquatic plants form a flourishing carpet around the table. Harriet rolls up her sleeves and places the bucket under the tiny waterfall, letting it fill.

:: all that water gives me the widdles - I hope she's got a toilet stashed away

You are right, Sam. "Harriet, is there a toilet?"

"Use the room after next. The water will wash everything away."

I splash my way through the next room into the one beyond, enjoying the way the water cascades around my ankles. When we are out of sight, I say, *I'll let you do the honours, Sam,* and I relinquish control, mentally looking the other way.

How odd this business of being a girl in a boy's body. For all its oddness, the situation recalls distant memories. Sam is embarrassed too and is taking time getting his act together. *Need help?* He splutters mentally, his fingers in a knot. So I take back control and do it for him.

Back in the adjacent room, Harriet has scrubbed our bowls and they await in a neat row for me to dry.

"Do you know anything about dreams?" I ask, washing my hands before setting about drying the dishes.

"Why? You having nightmares?"

"Not exactly."

I have finished drying the dishes. I expect Harriet to lead us back to her place, but instead she takes the bucket and beckons. Instead of taking the tunnel we arrived by, she leads me along a narrow passage in the opposite direction.

After a short walk, we emerge in an open space where the floor and roof have caved in. Two trees have pushed there way between the jagged ruins till they break free and deploy their canopies in the air above. Shafts of sunlight stream through gaps in the leaves, casting dappled light on the vegetation.

Harriet winds her way between the bushes, pushing aside vines and creepers till we reach a large flat stone between the two trees.

"We can talk freely here. No one will disturb us. So what do you want to know?"

:: who you are.

OK, wise guy, why don't you ask the questions?

:: I know who I am

Apparently not. If I am part of you.

Tearing myself from the discussion with Sam, I look up at Harriet. Her head is cocked to one side, appraising me.

"Where do you go when you are not here?" she asks.

I frown.

"I get the impression you are not always here."

:: she thinks you are on the verge of madness, lost to the world in your nightmares

"Do you know what a chimera is?" I ask.

Her head snaps back to me, her gaze piercing. After a long, hard look, she nods.

"Well…" I pause, hesitating to say more. "… That's what I am."

"Two people in one," she says, her brow furrowing, almost as if she is talking to herself. "So when you appear absent…"

"I am talking to Sam, my other half."

"Sam? And what's your name."

Relief washes over me. At last someone who accepts what we are and might just understand.

"I don't really have one. Sami, maybe."

"Sami?" The corners of her mouth twitch up in the beginning of a smile.

"That's one of the problems. Sam was here first. He's a boy in a boy's body. I came more recently. And I am a girl."

"Tricky. And does Sam talk?"

"No. At least not with words."

"You mean he stopped talking when you arrived?"

"No. From what I can gather, he never talked, except to me."

"And what does he talk about?"

"He doesn't so much talk to me as around me. Doing so would mean acknowledging me and he'd be stuck with me." I shift, uncomfortable at the memory. "He was furious, at first."

:: wouldn't you be?

"He called me a usurper and wanted to kill me."

"Understandable. Must've been quite a shock."

:: you bet - almost scared me out of my skin - those bloody big eyes staring at me!

My body shudders in response to Sam's memory.

"He says it terrified him."

"And is he still terrified?" Harriet asks, picking a handful of ivy leaves growing around the base of the rock. She pulls a small pouch from her pocket and places them inside.

I pause by a way of a question to Sam. He doesn't immediately respond.

:: I'm still cheesed off - I resent not having this body to myself - but I've kind of got used to you - not that I would miss you if you were gone

"He's still annoyed, but no longer as much as before."

:: That's not what I said

"He would still like to get rid of me."

Harriet gets to her feet and paces the small space around the rock we are sitting on, running her hands along the bark of the two trees that tower over us. "You say you arrived. Where were you before?"

: on an island covered with water trying to save every one

"Sam says I was on an island. That's why I wanted to talk of dreams, but more of that later. In Sam's life time, I think I must have been asleep."

36.

Jon stumbled along the winding path, trying to avoid the roots that forced their way up through the hardened earth. Nan walked ahead. Judging from the way her shoulders slumped and her head hung, she was exhausted. Some feet in front two men carried the stretcher bearing June. She had sunk into a feverish sleep as the growing infection took its toll. The sooner they got her to healers, the more chance she'd have of surviving. Tim led the group, moving forward with caution, a stout stave grasped in his hand. On either side five men marched, some touting sticks, others brandishing clubs. All were on edge, constantly scanning the jungle, alert for signs of the Guzzo.

When their convoy reached a towering rock that overhung the path, Tim signalled a halt. He peered around the rock to ensure no ambush awaited them and was about to take a step further when he jumped back. Several creatures stalked out. They might once have been men, but looked more like apes. Their hair was long and matted, their beards splayed around their faces, a filthy, twisted mass, but what made them appear inhuman was their bulging eyes that darted here and there like a cornered animal. Tattered remnants of shirts and jackets were all they had for clothes, bound together by lengths of string.

In their filthy claws they grasped knotted tree roots they swung threateningly, forcing Tim to retreat. Several guards moved to flank him, their clubs at the ready. A powerful stench behind him had Jon glancing over his shoulder. Five wild men stood there brandishing lumps of wood.

Weapons at the ready, both guards and wild men faced off in tense silence. When a dozen more wild men arrived, Tim must have decided it was time to act. "What do you want?"

One of the wild men, a massive brute with a ring threaded through his nose, stepped forward and pointed at Nan.

"No!" Tim said. "You can't have her."

Jon took a protective step in Nan's direction.

The man growled and raised his club as if preparing to strike. Tim took a step back and brandished his stave.

"Stop!" Nan shouted. She strode to Tim's side and asked. "What do you want from me?"

Jon thought the answer was obvious, although he hoped he was wrong.

The brute grunted. Could they even talk?

"You come," the man said gesturing towards the jungle.

"Why?" Nan insisted.

"Woman ill. You help."

"And if I help, will you let me go?"

The man nodded causing the ring in his nose to bounce up and down.

"I must talk to my friends first," Nan said, turning her back on the wild men. She walked to Jon and Tim followed.

"You can't trust them," Jon whispered. "Look at the state they're in. They must live in filthy conditions. What happens if this woman dies, despite your help?"

"Jon's right," Tim said. "You'd be taking an enormous risk. Maybe they would accept if you said you'd come back later."

"No. I will go, but only if they promise me safe conduct."

"You can't possibly trust them," Jon said.

"I will judge that from his answer," Nan insisted, looking over her shoulder at the leader.

"We will all come with you," Tim offered. "You'll be safer."

"No," was Nan's reply. "If June doesn't get help soon she'll die. You must take her to the settlement."

Tim nodded. "Then the others will accompany June and Jon to the settlement and I will come with you. At least then you will find the way to our place."

Jon wasn't feeling very brave. He would much rather run for safety, but he said, "I will come too."

"That's good of you, Jon. But you don't need to put yourself at risk," Nan said, a tired smile on her lips.

"Last time I should have helped you, I didn't, I couldn't and I will always regret it. Now I can help and I will."

Nan marched back to the wild man, stopping dangerously close. "I will come," she said. "But only if you promise safe conduct to myself and these two men." She pointed to Jon and Tim. "They will accompany me. Also you will not harm any of the others. They will leave immediately and will not attack you."

Tim came to join Nan and Jon stood on her other side. He was so close to the wild man he could see the grime ingrained in the lines on the man's face, but above all he could smell the vile odour. It took a considerable effort not to show his revulsion.

"Yes," the man said.

Nan held out her hand. He looked at it, perplexed. Then, as if an age-old reflex kicked in, he tended his hand hesitantly and Nan grasped it. The man looked pleased and he signalled to his men to follow. Nan walked next to him with Jon and Tim behind. They rounded the large rock and headed off down a narrow path that led into the thickest part of the jungle.

37.

A muffled moan greeted Nan as she pushed aside the tent flap. Inside, on a makeshift cot, a huddled woman lay shivering despite the pile of rags that covered her. The chief of the wild men, whose name she had learnt was Borg, hung back refusing to enter.

"When did the woman last have a drink?" she asked.

The brute shrugged and bobbed his head, causing the ring in his nose to jiggle ludicrously. Out of the corner of her eye she saw Jon place a hand over his mouth to conceal a grin. She scowled at him and turned away.

"Could you get some water, Tim? Make sure it is as clean as possible. Have it boiled and then bring it to me."

"How much?"

"Enough for a drink and washing wounds."

She strode to the bedside and peered down at the woman's face. Nan felt anger blaze. The girl couldn't have been more than sixteen. She would have been pretty had it not been for the filth and the dark bags beneath her eyes.

Cautiously pulling the bed clothes aside, Nan drew in a breath as she saw the battleground of lacerations on the girl's back, many of which were festering. She heard Jon let out a gasp as he peered over her shoulder.

Shrugging off her backpack, she handed it to Jon. "There's a cloth bag at the bottom," she said, her voice tense. "Give it me."

Jon untied the cords that held the bag closed. As he did, Tim bustled in bearing a jug of steaming water and an empty bowl.

"I washed the bowl with boiled water," he told her. Catching sight of the woman's back it was Tim's turn to gasp. "However did that happen?"

"Ask the wild men," she snapped, burying a clenched fist in her pocket. Seeing Jon fumbling to extract her bag from the backpack, she said, "Give me that."

She snatched it from him, her lips drawn in a tight line, and began rifling through its contents. Not finding what she wanted, she pulled the scarf from around her neck, spread it on the bed and upended the bag, emptying a series of small packets onto the scarf. A refreshing whiff of flowers wafted up.

"Give her some water," she told Jon, before returning to her packets. "Make sure it's not too hot," she added, "and only a few drops at a time."

Tim poured a little water into the bowl and swilled it around to cool before handing it to Jon who knelt by the bedside.

Having found what she was looking for, Nan watched Jon free the rags around the girl's face. He moved the bowl closer to the girl's lips, but seemed uncertain how to get her to drink. She saw him cringe then he pressed the rim of the bowl against her lips. The moment the bowl brushed the girl's mouth, her eyes flew open, wide with terror, and she screamed, her arms windmilling wildly. Jon was knocked backwards and the bowl was sent flying, showering water over them before it hit one of the tent poles and smashed to the ground. Borg hooted with laughter, undeterred by the filthy look Nan gave him.

She pushed Jon aside and ordered Tim to find a new bowl. Meanwhile, Jon shuffled to a corner of the tent where he stood, head bowed, jaws clenched. Tim returned with a bowl which he cleaned as best he could and then Nan gave the girl a drink. "I'm going to clean the wounds on your back," she told the girl once she'd drunk. "It will hurt. But if I don't do it, you won't survive."

The girl closed her eyes and moaned. Nan picked up her little bags which had been knocked to the floor in the scuffle. Emptying a selection of crushed herbs onto a cloth, she knotted it and plunged the bundle in the hot water. "I'm using thyme and lavender and violet," she said to no one in particular. "That should help cleanse the wheals and encourage the healing."

Judging the tight bundle had soaked enough, she pulled it from the water, squeezed it, letting the droplets fall back into the bowl, and used it to dab the wounds. The girl winced then fell silent.

When Nan had finished, she unscrewed a small jar that lay amongst the many packets emptied from her bag, sniffed it then began applying it to the lacerations. Blasted men. Either they blundered through people's lives completely insensitive to those around them, causing pain and havoc. Or they were ineffectual, doing nothing or all the wrong things till they caused as much damage as the blunderers.

Interrupting her mutterings, she sent Tim to find a clean cloth to cover the girl's back. Once a cloth had been found and placed over the wounds, Nan got wearily to her feet and turned to face Borg. Crossing the space between them she stood in front of him and, taking a deep breath, slapped him with all her force. He staggered backwards, his hand flying to his face to cover his reddening cheeks. No doubt he could have avoided her blow had she not taken him by surprise. It had surprised her too, but she wasn't going to show him that. Instead, she stood there looking at him belligerently.

"Why d'yer do that?" Borg asked, rubbing his jaw.

"Even if you didn't whip this girl yourself, you are responsible. You should have stopped it. Are you not head of this tribe? Look at you. No animal would let itself go the way you have. You should be ashamed. Go wash and get some order in your life. If you are the head here, you need to set an example."

With which she turned her back on him and began shoving her things into her bag. "We're finished. Let's go."

"Don't forget to give her water," Nan told Borg on her way out. "And for god sake, find some clean blankets to cover her."

38.

I scoot across the rock, intending to lean against one of the trees, but the bark is so rough, I return to the front lip and perch on it. The muscles in my neck are tense and a headache is coming on. I clamp a hand over my forehead while I massage the nape of my neck. It seems to calm me, a little.

"So what's this about an island?" Harriet asks, picking up a piece of bark. She sniffs it then breaks off a piece and hands it to me. "Chew," she says. "It will help the headache." The rest of the bark she places in her pouch.

:: you are not going to eat that filthy stuff - it has been lying on the ground

I steel myself against Sam's disgust and my own, nibble off a piece and begin chewing. "I'm not sure. When I was ill I had a dream. Well it was more than a dream. It seemed so real. More like a memory than a dream."

"You can spit that out," Harriet tells me. I let the soggy lump fall to the ground. "So what did you dream?"

"The island was under threat, but I couldn't get the authorities to heed my warnings."

"Sounds a bit like Cassandra."

"Who was she?"

"She had the gift of prophecy, but was cursed. No one would believe her. It drove her mad."

:: that better not be your case - I don't want to be holed up with a nutter - I would go bonkers

"I don't think I was cursed," I say, "and the situation didn't drive me mad, but it did drive me to distraction. I say 'me', because I suppose it was me in those memories. They were so vivid. The distress of those children as the tsunami was about to carry them away was unbearable." I break off, submerged by a wave of intense sadness.

"People in authority can be so pig-headed," Harriet says. "Just look at this lot here. How stupid can you get? You have a plague and what do you do? You kill the only people who can deal with it."

"That's a little different. On the island, the threat was yet to come. Here, the threat has come and gone."

"That is only partly true." Harriet pulls a couple of apples from a pocket and hands me one. "They misjudge the situation. It would only take a bad bout of flu or, worse, the outbreak of an epidemic and they would be submerged like your children by a wave of destruction. So many people have been driven over the brink of precariousness and are vulnerable."

She bites off a chunk of her apple and chews, her brow furrowed. "There is nothing worse than unquestioned convictions. Blindly believing you are right can be devastating. What's more, enforced or self-imposed conformity kills as much as any plague. Anyone that strays from their limited definition of what is right and acceptable, like your self..."

"You too," I say, tossing the core of my apple into the dense undergrowth, causing a stir as an unseen creature claims its prize. I hastily draw my feet onto the rock and hug my knees.

Harriet nods. "Such people are ruthlessly eliminated or driven out to fend for themselves in the Wild."

:: hmpf! - that sounds familiar - am I not driven back into the inner wilds?

"Isn't it human nature to be convinced that what you see is how it is?"

Harriet chuckles. "Yes. We need to believe in what we see, but we confuse our thoughts with our perceptions and we forget that thoughts need not be true to reality."

"But surely the world will set you right. The first time you stub your toe on some difference, surely that will change your mind."

"You'd be surprised how much energy people expend twisting the world as they think it is or should be."

I think of Sam. Maybe he can talk or walk normally, if he wants.

:: now who is dreaming of another reality?

What would it take to have you see things differently?

:: there you go trying to impose your reality on me

How do you explain that I can walk normally with the same body you find so difficult to manage?

Harriet taps me lightly on the arm. "You are having one of those conversations," she says. "You are no longer here."

I nod. "Sam refuses to accept he might be able to talk as easily as I do."

"Who knows why he is as he is? I understand you want him to be 'normal', but I wouldn't be so sure he can do what you can."

:: see - even your crazy wild woman agrees with me

"Don't say that. He's bad enough without telling him he's right."

"Tell him I'm not taking sides."

"I don't need to. He understands everything you say."

"Ah. There you are," a distant voice says. Harriet and I look up to see Mart peering down, a broad smile on his lips.

"Shhh!" Harriet said in a whisper. "We are on our way up."

"He sees himself as my guardian," I tell Harriet as she leads the way.

"Does he know?" she asks over her shoulder.

"Yes."

39.

Harriet unhitches the pouch from her waist, unclamps the leather strap that holds it closed and upturns the contents onto the table causing lumps of bark and half-dried flowers and leaves to tumble out. "I have to search for food," she says as she sorts her treasures into heaps.

"Can I come?" I ask, buoyed up by the prospect of learning more.

"Not this time." She sniffs one of the flowers, then discards it on a growing pile under the table. "You need rest."

I open my mouth to protest, but am obliged to stifle a yawn. She's right. Sam has been asleep for a while.

:: knock it off chatterbox and let me sleep

He turns over mentally and falls asleep again.

"I'm rested," Mart says, stretching. "Surely I can come."

Damn him! If Sam were awake he'd have used more colourful words. But I am not Sam and anyway I am too tired to bother.

Harriet hands Mart a wicker basket and straps her pouch around her waist.

"We'll be back in a couple of hours," she says and they head for the exit. "I'll lock the door. Whatever you do, do not open it."

I don't fancy sleeping alone above a ruined factory, even if there is a comfortable bed awaiting me, but I turn my back on them, not wishing to appear petty or cowardly.

Once they are gone, I double check the door. It is securely locked. I tour the bedroom cum workshop cum kitchen in search of errant creatures. Not that I have any idea what to do if I find one. The very thought makes me shudder, but I find nothing. Retreating to my bed, I clamber in and pull the netting tight behind me. I crawl under the blankets, pulling them up around my neck, and lie on my back staring at the light flitting across the ceiling.

As I drift between sleep and waking I brace myself for a return to the island. What will it be this time? Surely I have already seen the worst.

All is dark. Night must have fallen. Odd. I hear no sound of waves breaking on the shore. Pricking my ears, I detect a faint scratching like claws on wood. Every muscle in my body tenses. I am not alone.

:: you're creepy - cut it out

Sam's fear makes the hairs stand on my neck.

The scratching grows louder, coming closer, then stops. Listening hard, I make out laboured breathing. A dull thud sounds nearby, followed by a second, then a third and several more. Footsteps. Someone, several someones are padding around me in the dark.

:: this isn't your island - it's a hoard of savages come to drag us away - hide under the covers you idiot

Too late. A heavy hand grabs my arm and yanks me from the bed, pulling a knot of covers and netting after me. This is no dream! The netting rips free and falls over me as my feet thud to the floor. I gasp for breath, preparing to scream, when a filthy hand fumbles across my face in search of my mouth. I bite, my teeth sinking into flesh only to spit out blood and grime. The man mutters a curse and hoists me into the air, flinging me over his shoulder as he heads for a window.

:: not the window - I hate heights

Responding to Sam's fear, I kick out with my feet and hammer on the small of the man's back. To no avail. As the man prepares to climb out the window, I twist my hips and, to my surprise, manage to jerk free. Tumbling sideways, my legs get caught in his coat slowing my fall. To my dismay, he topples after me. I stretch out my hands to break the fall. When he lands on top of me, my head jerks forward hitting the floor with a sickening crunch.

:: at last you're awake - I shouted till I was hoarse - I called you a mighty heap of names, but I couldn't rouse you - did you have to knock yourself out? - just when those rabid men were going to drag us off and sell us as slaves

I want to object. It wasn't my fault. But my head throbs as if Sam were hammering to get out. His voice pounds inside my skull. All I want is quiet. My neck is so stiff, I can't move without a searing pain shooting down my back. I try opening my eyes but see only blurred masses. From the little I make out, I must still be in the loft. How can that be? *What happened to the men?*

:: they scarpered - at least I think they did - it was hard to tell - they made such a racket - maybe they thought they'd killed you - couldn't sell a corpse, could they?

Charming! I crack open my eyes, but my vision is still blurred. When I shake my head to free my sight, I groan as a the pain rips down my spine.

"Don't move," a male voice says. So some of the men are still here.

:: that's no wild man - that's your sweetheart - how can you not recognise him

Mart? It doesn't sound like him. Have my ears gone funny with the blow?

"That's better," the voice says. "Stay still."

Sam is right. It is Mart. Relief floods over me and tears well in my eyes.

"Harriet will be back in a moment. She went to fetch plants and tree bark to treat your head and neck. She insisted you should not move." He chuckles. "She said I should hold you down if you tried to get up."

:: see - what did I tell you? - loverboy has got you in his grips

That's not funny, I say, unable to conceal my pleasure at the idea of being held in Mart's arms.

"You gave us a real fright," Mart continues, oblivious to

our silent conversation. "There we were chatting away, never dreaming anything had happened to you. After all, the door was locked and we are high above ground. And what did we find, you lying face down on the floor, groaning. I hurried to your side and could see you had a big bump on your forehead. I wanted to turn you over, to make sure nothing else was wrong, but Harriet stopped me. She said we had to be careful. You might have damaged your neck or spine. So she examined you then left in search of remedies."

"And remedies is what I found," Harriet says, kneeling down next to me. "How do you feel?"

I am afraid to speak for fear I've lost my voice too.

:: I can't believe that a chatterbox like you could possibly lose her voice

"Shaken," I venture and the word trembles as I speak it. "My head hurts." I go on to tell them about my neck and back.

"Well there'll be no moving for a while," Harriet says.

"But what if those men come back?" Mart asks.

"It can't be helped. We'll just have to keep them away."

40.

Jon sat alone by the fire warming his outstretched hands. Despite the closeness of the cheerful blaze and a blanket pulled tight around his shoulders, he shivered. The flames did nothing to alleviate his gloom. Instead their flickering brought back sinister memories of another fire in which the food police had plunged their torture irons. As if set on making himself feel worse, he recalled the young woman who had been so savagely whipped by the wild men and his mind went over and over his ineffectiveness.

Forcing himself to look away, he glanced around. He was in a log cabin in New Baxter. It was furnished with rows of wooden tables and an odd assortment of chairs; a canteen he'd been told. Sure enough, a smell of food lingered. The high-set windows were small and barred, proof against attack Tim had said.

The fortified village had turned out much bigger than he'd expected, with line after line of long, low log cabins. Tim explained that the original village had been built by early settlers from Baxter wanting to make a new start beyond the reach of the Food Police. Now it was home to the families who'd recently been forced to flee. Jon had seen many people moving about the compound, stopping from time to time to chat, seemingly unaffected by the chaos outside. Near the centre of the settlement, a group of children dressed in ill fitting clothes trouped into a school talking quietly. There was also an infirmary, although he hadn't seen it. Nan had gone to enquire about June and, above all, Sam.

Jon went to a window, where, standing on tiptoes, he could just see out. Sheltered under the awnings of the cabin across the way, Nan was deep in conversation with an old man dressed in long flowing robes. He looked like a priest. The sight reminded him that Nan was part of a sect who revered Luminaries. Could these people be part of that movement? Now that Sam was probably amongst them, would they persist in their absurd belief he was their much-awaited saviour? Sam couldn't even look after himself.

Jon turned away from the window when the door opened and Nan walked in accompanied by the priest.

"Jon, meet Axel," she said, nodding towards the priest. "Axel, this is the father of Sami I talked about."

Sami! Of course. The girl, not the boy. For people who professed an all encompassing view of the world, they were very narrow minded. "Any news?" he asked.

"I am sorry to say your child and her friend never turned up here," Axel said, "and none of our guides have seen or heard of them."

"There is one good piece of news," Nan added, clasping Jon by the arm. "Scouts slipped into the ruins of Baxter, earlier today, and no trace was found of either Sami or Mart."

"It's Sam," Jon muttered, pulling free of Nan.

"I'm sorry…" she began when shouts outside interrupted her.

All three hurried to the door. People were running in different directions. Some carrying bags, others dragging children after them. Many calling out. The priest stopped one of the men.

"What's going on?" he asked.

"Food police!" the man replied between gasps for breath.

"Where?" Nan asked.

"Entering the Wilds," the man said as he moved off. "Heading this way," he called out over his shoulder.

"They've never ventured into the Wilds before," the priest said to no one in particular.

"So what are you going to do?" Jon asked.

"Fight," the priest and Nan said together.

From the little Jon had seen of the settlement, there seemed to be no defence, lest it be the barricade surrounding the encampment. That would hardly resist an attack from the Food Police. He hastened after Nan who had left the priest and was heading for the centre of the compound. He caught up with her as she reached the school.

"We've got to get the children to safety," she said, pushing open the front door.

Inside children were lined up in silence, quietly climbing a ladder into what must have been an underground passage. He was amazed at their self-possession. Any normal child would have been frozen in panic or screaming at the thought of the Food Police coming.

Nan helped the smaller children descend while Jon watched on, feeling useless.

"My bag," a little girl exclaimed. "I've forgotten my bag."

Jon went in search of her bag, glad to have something to do. It was exactly where the girl had said. Before returning, he glanced out the window. All was quiet now. No one was in sight.

When he returned to the room with the ladder, he found that only he and Nan remained. She signalled for him to go down and followed, pulling the trap door closed behind her. A dim light lit a narrow passage along which he could just make out the children filing away. He set out after them with Nan close behind.

They had gone only fifty yards when an explosion rang out behind them. The ground shook and he would have fallen had he not braced himself against the walls of the tunnel.

"First line of defence," Nan said. He wanted to know what she meant, but she pushed him forward. Ahead, the children had not faltered and were now a good way away.

A second explosion rang out a few minutes later, less violent this time, and further away. "Second line," Nan said as they continued. He didn't understand, but whatever was happening, it was clearly going as planned.

Feeling less threatened, he took a moment to examine the tunnel walls. They were carved out of earth and rock and were shored up by timbers at regular intervals. Thinking back over the evacuation, it had been carefully planned. Even the children knew what to do.

The tunnel ended abruptly in a door, through which the children had gone. He followed and found himself in a large, low room that resembled one of the log cabins in the settlement, except the walls were made of bricks and there were no windows. The children didn't stop, but went across the room and through another door at the far end. Peering inside, he found row upon row of bunk beds lining the walls of another large room. It was then that the little girl came to fetch her bag and thanked him.

Nan stepped past, navigated her way between the children who laid out their things next to their beds, and, reaching the far side of the room, opened a door. Beckoning for him to follow, she moved out of sight.

He'd expected another room, but instead he was at the foot of a winding stairway that wove steeply upwards. Nan was already climbing. He followed, despite his aching legs. Reaching the top, she turned to him and held an outstretched finger in front of her lips. Then she eased open a door and light flooded in. They were not outside, as he had first thought, but in some form of hide.

He moved cautiously close to one of the narrow slits that served as lookouts and peered in search of the settlement. To his alarm the whole area below was shroud in smoke. He clamped a hand over his mouth to stop himself from crying out. New Baxter was no more. The police had already destroyed it.

41.

Life is dull when you can't move your neck. I stare at the ceiling and listen to the occasional tales told by Mart and Harriet, not to mention Sam chattering to me. Much of the time I sleep. Harriet's massage before she trusses up my neck is the best moment of the day. Not only does she know how to soothe my damaged muscles, but those circular movements send shivers down my spine.

:: how can you possibly get pleasure out of someone's dirty fingers wandering over your body, prodding you?

"Lie still," says Harriet as she binds the cloth around my neck, blocking it to a pole that runs from the top of my head to my waist. Every time she has to lift my head, a sharp pain shoots down my spine, but it is not so dire as when I first fell. "There's more movement in it," Harriet adds, "but you should still not put weight on your neck."

Mart helps me eat and drink. I am grateful, but I wish he didn't enjoy looking after me so much. It's going to be a problem. Of course, there are some things no one can help me with. At those moments Harriet binds my neck as she has done now. I hate it. It feels like I am locked in a straight jacket and am going to suffocate.

Bright light gives me a headache, so I keep my eyes closed. Then I don't have to bother with my vision being blurred. The fuzziness irritates me. It's as if I can't get a grasp on the world. To make matters worse, I see strange filaments moving across my vision. Harriet says they are normal after such an accident. I am less sure. These filaments don't float free as if they were inside my eye. They congregate around Mart and Harriet, connecting them and me in a dense, moving web. I try to ignore them and at times I do forget they are there. But the moment I think of them, there they are weaving a web through the world.

Harriet helps me to my feet and I walk to a curtained off corner of the loft where she has installed a chamber pot. Once I have finished, the first time without her help me, I shuffle around the loft. Mart has cleared a circuit just wide enough for the two of us side by side. It's good to move, even if the upper part of my body is bound to a pole and my arm is firmly in the grips of Mart.

We have just reached the row of windows facing out over the Wilds, when an explosion rocks the building sending cups and cutlery scuttling across the table and onto the floor. I cry out, afraid I will be flung to the ground, but Mart holds on to me.

:: flaming howitzers - not again - are these people bent on snuffing us out?

"What the hell was that?" Mart asks, turning towards the window.

"Get back, you fool," Harriet shouts, hurrying to my side. "There might be more."

As if prompted by her words, a second explosion, much stronger and closer, has a whole section of the outer wall fall away, leaving a gapping hole and a five storey drop.

With Harriet on one side and Mart on the other, they march me to the centre of the room. I see Mart glance at the ceiling, a worried look on his face. If only we could crawl under the table, we might be protected from falling masonry.

"Lay me under the table," I say.

"Too dangerous," Harriet replies, still holding my arm.

A small part of the ceiling over the missing wall crumbles and falls to the floor with a crash sending up a cloud of dust. I cannot raise my hand to ward off the dust. I struggle desperately not to cough, fearful that it will shake my neck and send stabs of pain down my spine. To my relief Harriet holds a handkerchief over my mouth and nose. Mart is doing less well. He sneezes several times. No more explosions are to be heard.

"We should leave," Mart says, after a long silence.

Harriet glances at me and shakes her head.

If I were brave I'd tell them to leave me, but I am not. I'm scared. With my neck as it is, I cannot fend for myself and the thought of them abandoning me makes me miserable.

In the distance a shout sears through the silence as if declaring the end of a truce. Then a snarl erupts much closer, inarticulate and almost animal like in its savagery, followed by several urgent shrieks, some nearby, others more remote. Soon there's a chorus of yells ringing throughout the jungle. A sinister rumbling rolls through the Wilds and the building trembles around us making us huddle together for fear the walls will collapse. The clamour of voices transforms into screams followed by more explosions, many of them, smaller this time and more distant. An uneasy calm returns punctuated only by the occasional moan. We are the unwilling witnesses to an intense but short-lived war which we can only follow with our ears, leaving our imagination free to conjure up visions of horror.

:: a requiem for a shouting male choir and unaccompanied human screams set in a minor mode announcing the end of the world - a miserable piece of work that should never have been composed let alone performed

The walls and ceilings around us hold good, but I am shaken to the core. The savagery of what must have happened leaves me moaning in distress. Tears spring to my eyes and overflow down my cheeks. My whole body trembles beyond control. Mart and Harriet put their arms around me in an effort to comfort me, but they cannot ward off the distress I feel.

42.

Jon sank to his knees nursing his head in his hands. A series of smaller explosions rang out across the jungle punctuated by piercing screams. He pulled at his hair in anguish. The children were now orphans. A shudder shook his body as distress tore through him.

"What's the matter?" Nan asked as she pulled him to his feet. "Are you hurt?"

"How dare they do such a thing?" he muttered, anger seizing him.

"There was no choice," was Nan's reply. Her calmness and determination shocked him, making him even more angry.

"But think of the children."

"They're OK."

Were human lives so inconsequential? "Ok? How could they possibly be OK? They've lost their parents."

She looked perplexed. "What are you talking about?"

The more he thought about it, the more he trembled with rage. "Those bastards just killed their parents."

Nan looked confused then grinned.

Jon was furious. "How can you be so callous?"

"There's a misunderstanding," she began, trying but failing to look serious. "It's not the people of the settlement that have died, but the Food Police. The folks of New Baxter set traps for just such an attack."

Anger flared again as Jon realised he'd made a fool of himself. He turned away to hide his confusion and moved to the slit in the wall. Below smoke was clearing, driven away by a stiff breeze. The settlement with its high wooden walls and its rows of log cabins stood intact. Beyond the village, he could make out two gaping holes in the vegetation partly masked by smoke. Here and there bushes had caught fire, but he spotted movement as people lugged what must have been water to dowse the flames.

"Feeling better?" she asked, coming to stand next to him.

"I thought …" He shook his head, feeling such a fool. "I couldn't see how all those gentle people could possibly fend off several squads of Food Police."

"They are far tougher than you think, but it might not do to let it be known."

"Well whoever sent the police will soon find out, even if no one survived. This is war, you realise. Next time they won't get caught so easily."

"You are right," she said, her expression grim. "The moment we get word that all is safe, we should return. I want to take part in discussions about what to do next."

"But what about the children? Shouldn't they stay here, just in case?"

"We can't leave them on their own."

Jon didn't fancy being cooped up with a hoard of children - he was not a school teacher or a nursemaid - but he couldn't face the thought of interminable discussions about war and tactics. "Go," he said, waving her away. "I will stay with the children, but send someone to help me."

"Are you sure?" She cocked her head, sizing him up.

"I'm no good with children," he admitted, with a wry smile, "but I am even less good with war mongers."

She clasped his shoulders and pulled him into her arms. He let himself be hugged, but did not return the gesture. "Let's get this over with," he said, meaning her parting, but blushed when he realised she might think he meant her hug. "The children will be wondering what is going on."

When they pushed open the door and stepped into the dormitory, all heads snapped in their direction. Jon had wondered if the children might panic, but they seemed calm. Seeing the two adults arrive, several children got to their feet and hurried to meet them, others joined, till all the children were grouped around Nan and Jon.

"The attack has been defeated," Nan announced.

To his surprise none of the children cheered or clapped, a few grinned but most welcomed the news almost as if it didn't concern them. Despite their apparent restraint, the children's relief was palpable. Jon wondered what education had left them so disciplined.

"We must plan what to do next," Nan explained. "I am going to return to the settlement, but you will stay here with Jon until we are sure it is safe."

Glancing at the upturned faces that stared expectantly at him, he couldn't help noticing several doubtful looks. He wasn't surprised. He was a complete stranger and some of the kids were very young. At least no one seemed outwardly hostile.

"I will send someone from the settlement to give Jon a hand," Nan said. "Be kind to him." She grinned. "He's had a hard time recently and might be a little fragile."

Nan nodded to him then turned and left.

Jon eyed the children who seemed to expect something from him. He had no idea what to do. He thought of Sam. Hadn't he looked after the boy all those years? It hadn't been easy, but this was completely different.

"Are you hungry?" he asked, realising that he himself felt hungry after all the emotion. "Is there any food?" The moment he asked, he feared he'd made a mistake. What if there was nothing?

"Yes," one of the older girls told him, her plaited hair bobbing up and down as she spoke. "We always keep a stock here in case this sort of thing happens."

The children set about preparing a meal. They were well organised and Jon had little to do, bar pushing a couple of heavy tables together in the middle of the dormitory. There were dried wafers, a cross between biscuits and bread, and cheese and tins of pickles. Several pitchers of water were brought in and everybody sat down to eat. It was frugal, but it would do.

He was about to tuck in when the older girl, whose name was Mary, turned to him and asked, "Will you say grace?"

He'd never said such a thing in his life. Neither he nor his parents had been religious. In fact in a world ruled by terror few people were practising believers. Any churches that survived the Disaster had been requisitioned for lodgings. He had no idea what he should say. Afraid it might shock the children, he didn't want to admit his ignorance, so he said, "Maybe you can say grace, Mary. I'm sure you will do so much better than I could."

She placed her two hands together, bowed her head and closed her eyes. "For what we are about to eat and drink may the Divine make us truly thankful." In chorus, the other children added, "Amen."

"Amen," Jon said.

43.

The meal was over, the remains of the food stocked away and the tables cleaned, but still no one had come to assist Jon. The children sat looking at him, as if waiting for a signal. He was at a loss what to do. An uneasy silence settled over the group. If only he could take them outside, they could go for a walk, but that was out of the question.

"What did you do before all this?" Mary asked, waving an arm to encompass the whole room and beyond.

He could have hugged her for coming to his rescue. "I played piano. I was a concert pianist." Many faces around the table remained blank. "Have you ever heard a piano play?"

They shook their heads. He wasn't surprised. There were few pianos left and even less people capable of playing them.

"There are various different types, but mine was like a large flat box, wide at one end and narrower at the other, on spindly legs with a series of keys at the wider end that you pressed down to make music."

It struck him these children might rarely have heard music, let alone a grand piano. As if to confirm his suspicions, one of the youngest girls asked, "I don't understand. What do you mean by music?"

Her question startled him. Surely they must have heard music. "Don't you ever sing?"

"We've been told singing is a waste of time," an older boy said.

"We are very busy, you know," a little girl chimed in.

"Music making is a frivolous pursuit…" Mary added, as if echoing words she'd heard.

He'd been thinking of singing for them, but he hesitated. Maybe music was not allowed. Surely not. How could a group of healers ignore music? There must be some misunderstanding.

"I can't imitate a piano," he said. "But I can sing some of the music."

He'd never been good at singing, but at least he had a good ear and could pitch the notes correctly. He wondered what to choose. He could sing the opening of a piano piece, but without words that might sound odd. He struggled to recall a song, but he'd never paid much attention to popular music. Then he remembered a lullaby Jane had sung to Sam when he was little.

He glanced at the children who were silently waiting. Some frowned. A couple looked frankly hostile. Their attitude was unnerving. To be honest, they looked like a club of pinch-faced senior citizens with indigestion. The sight made him wonder how they lived. Whatever did they learn? But enough procrastination. He drew in a deep breath and began to sing, quietly at first, then with more strength as he gained confidence.

Once he had finished he looked at the children's faces. They were transfixed. Some had tears in their eyes, others looked dreamy and distant. None seemed to know what to do. If they had never heard music, no wonder they didn't know how to applaud. He wasn't fool enough to believe it was the quality of his singing that moved them. It was the music itself.

"Have none of you ever sung?" he asked. As one they shook their heads. "Would you like to?" His question drew some enthusiastic nods. Others looked sceptical.

"It must be difficult," a little boy said.

"Well let's find out," Jon replied. He pushed back his chair and got to his feet. "It will probably be easier if you stand up."

With a scraping of chairs, but very little chatter, the children stood. They looked apprehensive, which didn't encourage him. He wasn't sure how to proceed, never having taught anyone to sing, especially not a group who hadn't heard any music in their lives. In a way they were like Sam. The boy had been so little interested in music, it was as if it didn't exist.

"I will sing the first few notes of the lullaby." He did while the children listened. "Now sing along with me." He could barely hear their voices which sounded strangled. "Ok. That's a start. But we are going to have to encourage your voices. Help me push back the tables and chairs. We need more room."

Once they'd cleared the middle of the room, he had them walking around. At first they followed each other in a giant circle. He obliged them to move at random. "Flap your arms as if you were birds," he told them, doing the same himself. From the cautious way they moved, Jon suspected they were embarrassed. He certainly was. He hoped no one walked in.

"When you raise your arms, breathe in. When you lower them, breath out." He was pleased to see that, with time, the children became less self-conscious. Judging from the energy some threw into the exercise, they were enjoying themselves.

"Good. Now make a sound each time you move your arms. It doesn't matter what." From timid singing they went to growls and squeaks and cries. Judging from their startled expressions, the sounds surprised them.

He raised a hand and the noise stopped, although not without a look of disappointment on many faces. "Maybe we need to be careful how much noise we make," he said, concerned they might be heard.

"That's no worry," Mary said, her face flushed from the exercise. "This place is sound-proofed, provided the doors are shut."

"What has all this grunting and groaning got to do with singing?" a very serious-faced little girl asked.

"We need to free up your singing voices," Jon told them. "This pacing and making noise is designed to wake them up."

He called them closer together. "Do you know what humming is?" None of them had ever heard of it. "You sing through your nose." He demonstrated. "Try." They did. "Now listen carefully, I am going to hum a note and I want you to hum the same note."

The moment they had to sing in chorus, their voices died away to whisper.

"Whatever happened to those wild animals?" he asked. "Come closer, much closer." When they formed a tight knot around him, he continued. "Let's hum that note again, but very, very quietly." They did and to his surprise everyone was more or less on the right note. "Good. Now try again, but a little louder." Progressively he got them to hum louder.

"Now I am going to hum three different notes, one after another. I want you to imitate me." After a few tries they managed. "Excellent. Now let's take a step further. We'll all begin on the same note then little by little you can explore other notes tracing out your own path up and down. As you do, listen to the notes of others and be aware of how yours fit with theirs. Do they sound good together or do they clash. Remember, there is no right or wrong. Just the sounds we make. Now close your eyes."

He set the first note which they held for quite a while until he hummed something different. Little by little the more adventurous strayed from the base note until almost all the children's voices were shifting amongst each other in a surprising counterpoint that rose and expanded till the whole room was vibrating to the sound of it.

When the last voice fell silent and everyone had opened his or her eyes, they stood amazed, their faces aglow, their eyes sparkling as they looked at each other.

The magic of the moment was broken by a sharp voice from the far end of the room. "What are you doing? I have never heard such a racket in all my life." All turned to see the priest standing in the doorway, his features twisted in disgust. "It seems like I did well to come and check on you."

44.

I am back lying on my bed, Mart having removed the many stones and pieces of cement scattered on the covers. Harriet says I can turn my head from time to time, so I now peer right to watch the two struggling with a large bookcase to block the gaping hole.

:: the world is full of holes, some big, some small, but most dark and deadly - stick you nose or your neck or your hand or your foot or even just a little finger in one and fortune will bite it off

The poet is back. For all his dark humour, his presence is reassuring.

Outside, birds and insects chatter again as if they hadn't just been silenced by terror. Whatever happened, it was quick and deadly.

Having shoved the bookcase into place, Harriet and Mart wash their hands and sit at the table with a glass of water and a pile of apples.

Mart polishes one on his sleeve and offers it me. I refuse. I'm not hungry. He looks disappointed.

"What was that explosion?" I ask.

"There's a settlement near by," Harriet said. "Sounded like it came from there."

"Settlement?" Mart asks.

"People who fled Baxter."

"How come we saw no sign of it? Surely we came that way," Mart asks, his tone accusatory.

"It is well concealed and you were busy with other things. Anyway, I chose to skirt it."

"Why do that?" Mart asks, draining his glass only to slam it down on the table. Such behaviour is so unlike him.

"Careful with my glasses," Harriet said. "They are difficult to come by."

"But why avoid them. They might have been able to help."

"The few people who know I am here the better."

"But there may be people I know…" Mart says, getting to his feet. "I should go and see. If any are hurt I might be able to help."

So much for me worrying about him spending too much time looking after me.

:: that's love for you, fickle as the wind, a lot of noisy flapping that gets your heart beating and then it's gone, leaving you deflated, wondering where the love went

I bow to your superior expertise. When he bows mentally back, I realise I'm wasting my time. Irony doesn't have any effect on him. *Don't you get tired of twittering about love?* I certainly do.

:: I'm constantly on the lookout for dangers - I shadow your every move - I echo your every thought - I unknot all your knots and undo all your blunders

I burst out laughing, startling Mart and Harriet.

:: they'll be thinking you are delirious or gone hatters

Hatters?

:: mad like the hatter - all hatters are said to be strange in the head - it's the brim - stems the flow of blood to the brain

"Are you alright?" Harriet asks.

"Just Sam playing the fool," I reply.

Mart snorts in disgust and moves away from the table, pulling his jacket around his shoulders.

"Sit down, Mart," Harriet orders. "We have no idea what happened. For all we know, the jungle may be swarming with armed police. Or perhaps the people of Baxter have planted bombs. Anyway, you are needed here."

Mart glances at me, shrugging his shoulders, then looks back at Harriet, his jaw set. "You don't decide what I do."

"No. I don't," she replies, crushing dried leaves. "But I can and will advise you. Don't go at the moment. Apart from the possibility that this building is more damaged and risky than we think and the likelihood that there are dangers lurking outside, it is certain that you'll get lost on your own."

Mart shoves back a chair, slings his jacket over the back and plops down almost toppling over backwards as he does.

Sam sniggers in my head.

You wouldn't like someone bossing you around.

:: anything that gets on the nerves of that pesky boy has my vote

Harriet pushes a pile of dried leaves across the table and hands the pestle and mortar to Mart. "Take your frustration out on this."

Mart grabs the pestle and begins pounding the leaves.

"Grind," Harriet says. "No need to smash the life out of the poor things. You'll destroy any properties they might have and Sami's neck will be all the worse for it. I thought you knew how to do such things. Weren't you taught by a healer?"

Mart scowls and begins grinding.

Harriet gets to her feet and goes to stand behind him, placing her hands on his shoulders. He shrugs as if to shake her off, but she continues her massage.

I am fascinated by what I see. The swirling filaments are back. A dense beam descends and enters Harriet's head where it travels down into her arms and through her hands into Mart's shoulders. How on earth can I see such things?

I observe Mart or rather the strange dance within him. A dense knot of filaments is lodged in his chest and spins rapidly like an angry whirlwind. I get the impression it is trying to fight off Harriet, but she is much stronger. Little by little the whirling slows and the ball unravels till it flows in various directions, including towards me.

Did you see that?

:: what? - are you complaining that she has her hands on your beloved? - I would be wary of her if I were you - how can you know what they do when they go off together in the jungle?

I give Sam a mental shove, saying: *You're impossible.*

Apparently only I can see these filaments. How strange. I can't be inventing them. I have no control over them. They've probably always been there but I had to fall on my head to see them. Shame I can't observe the field around myself. I wonder what that would be like.

45.

"What a disaster," the priest muttered, shaking his head.

Caught up in the delights of their singing, Jon was shocked at the man's abrupt manner and lack of respect. Were all priests as insensitive as him?

"You've done enough damage," the man said, pointing an accusing finger. "Go back to New Baxter. You're needed there."

Jon sneaked a glance at the children. Some looked apologetic, but most were still aglow with the music.

"I'm a musician," Jon said, pulling himself up to his full height. He felt he owed it to the children. He certainly owed it to himself. "Making music requires skill and practice. Making music and listening to it can be one of the most uplifting experiences in life. I refuse to let you belittle what these children have done. It was beautiful and touching and I thank them for it."

The moment he had spoken, he regretted it. He'd never been one to defy the established order, at least, not openly. And anyway, who was he to speak out? He was just a passer-by, an escaped criminal on the run. Tomorrow he could well be gone. And these children's lives would continue without him.

"You have no idea how we live or what values we go by," the priest accused. "You come blundering in here with your high-flown ideas and your petty self-satisfaction. Maybe you believe you are helping these children. Well you are not. Each of them has a route traced out and your little contribution can only bring distraction at best and confusion at worst. Leave, before you do any more damage."

Jon toyed with idea of insisting, but doing so would be pointless, if not puerile. Turning to the children he said, "Good bye children. I have enjoyed singing with you. I had hoped we would do so again but apparently that is not possible." Heading for the door, he whistled the lullaby.

All the way back to New Baxter, Jon mulled over what had happened. How could a society turn its back on music? And at what price? No wonder the children were so taciturn. In his angry imaginings he conjured up a Luminary who was a gifted musician, just to spite these people. He made a mental note to teach Sam to sing, if ever he caught up with his son.

The moment he found Nan, she greeted him with a worried look. He imagined the fight had gone worse than they'd thought, but she drew him apart and asked: "You look unhappy. What happened?"

"Your priest told me what he thought about music and kicked me out."

Nan took several further steps away from the group, drawing him by the arm. "Why on earth did he do that?" she whispered. "He's normally quite level-headed."

"Because I taught the children to sing."

"Ah! I should have warned you."

He was glad she hadn't. At least the children had got to sing. "You never seemed opposed to music," he said. "I got the impression you enjoyed it. And that couple living in the ruins, they came from Baxter, but he was a piano tuner."

"I know. But those who live outside Baxter for any length of time are more open."

She looked over her shoulder at the group milling around the central table and said, "People here have survived by putting a fence around their way of life. It pre-dates the Disaster. It's partly due to our being in service to the luminary and the fact that we have to wait so very long. It is also the importance given to practical knowledge and its transmission to the children. Each has to learn a trade."

"But music? How could you refuse music? Are you not healers? Surely you are aware of the impact of music on health."

"It wasn't always so. It has to do with the role of popular music. The elders saw it as a distraction if not a threat to children's education. It was seen as part of the mindless innovation our age-old lifestyle seeks to combat...."

"Nan," a voice called out from the group around the table. "Can you give us a hand."

Nan led him over to the table. "This is Jon," she said. "He's the father of Sam and Sami. He escaped the Food Police when I did."

"We are trying to anticipate their next move," a tall, austere man explained. "How will they react now we've blown up fifty of their men?"

Fifty. What terrible news. Yet the man mentioned it as if discussing the weather. Even if life didn't mean much to the Food Police, they'd surely retaliate. If fifty had been killed, they would want to multiply that toll by ten, at least. The police had hardly been subtle in their cruelty to Nan and him. He'd expect a very heavy-handed response.

The whole group stood awaiting Jon's response as if he were an expert. Well maybe he did have first-hand experience of the Food Police.

"They will hit back hard and fast. They won't send men this time. It'll be bombs or fire or their patented poisoned gas." As he spoke, he realised that his absurd, off-hand ideas were most likely an accurate guess. "Yes. They'll seek to annihilate you and soon. If I were you, I'd flee as far and as fast as possible."

46.

The door to the loft bursts open and a young girl rushes in, panting, her clothes torn, her hair dishevelled.

:: good lord, a girl straight from an adventure - yum - lay the table and hand me a fork and spoon

Come off it, Sam. I thought you hated adventures.

:: not when a pretty thing like that has had them

I shake my head mentally. *You have strange tastes.*

:: not half as strange as yours

Glancing around, the girl gives a shocked look at the hole in the wall and the roof then turns to Harriet. "I thought you might be here," she says, struggling to catch her breath. "You have to leave. Now!"

"Calm down, Priscilla," Harriet replies, taking hold of the girl's hand. "Breath. Deeply. Like I taught you." The girl's chest heaves up and down, a look of intense concentration on her face. "Good. Now what's going on."

"It's the Food Police. They attacked the settlement. We blew them up."

Mart whistles between his teeth.

The girl notices him and makes a face. "You here? I've got a score to settle with you."

"The Food Police," Harriet reminds the girl.

"Fifty dead. Now they are going to attack again. We expect bad things. Very bad things. I came to warn you. You need to leave. Immediately."

:: that's torn it - fifty - those blood suckers will stop at nothing to get revenge

"Are you sure?" Harriet asks Priscilla, glancing at me.

"Yes. Everyone is falling over themselves to pack and leave. Even the wild men have been warned."

"Thanks, Pricilla. Now run back to the settlement. You need to catch them before they leave."

"I'm not going back," Priscilla says, pouting. "The priest told me if I run to you, I might as well stay with you."

"He kicked you out?" Mart asks.

"None of them like me seeing Harriet. They think she's strange. They'd be quite happy to get rid of me."

"That's terrible," I say.

"Who are you?" the girl asks, her tone none too friendly. "What are you doing here?"

"She's a very special guest," Mart says.

The girl makes a rude noise. "Special, my arse."

"What did I tell you about using such words?" Harriet says.

"Sorry, Miss," the girl says, although she doesn't sound contrite.

"Priscilla was kidnapped by the wild men," Harriet explains. "She's a fast learner, so she picked up a lot of their foul language and a good deal of their bad habits."

The girl scratches her head, unsure how to take Harriet's words.

"We can't leave," Mart says, coming to the stand by me.

"Why ever not?" Priscilla asks, latching onto his sleeve.

:: competition - I like her - a bit rough around the edges, not at all like those polished girls

As if you know anything about girls.

"Sami can't travel," Mart says, shaking himself free.

The girl turns to look at me, a sneer on her face. "Leave her behind. She's not one of us."

"Now, now, Priscilla. You know better than that," Harriet says. "Help me pack some food."

"Should we bind Sami's neck?" Mart asks.

"Oh goodie. I'll help you wring it," the girl says delighted.

Mart sighs. "Not wring, Priscilla, bind." He enunciates each word with exaggerated precision. "Sami had an accident."

"No need," Harriet replies. "We'll just wrap a bandage round it for support and carry her on a stretcher."

"Do you have one?" Mart asks.

"No. But two poles and some netting will do the trick."

We have been navigating a narrow path through the jungle for ten minutes, when Priscilla chirps up, "Aren't we going the wrong way? The others headed for the mountains." She lets go with one hand to point, causing the stretcher to sway to one side almost throwing me to the ground. My neck must be getting better because I brace myself but no pain comes.

"Careful," Mart cries out, taking much of my weight alone.

As she catches hold of the stretcher she makes a point of shaking me before apologising.

:: there's spirit for you!

Wait till she throws us to the ground.

"We are going this way on purpose. If those food madmen follow the folks from New Baxter they'd be sure to catch us."

"So where are you taking us?" the girl asks.

"That's to be a surprise."

Judging from Harriet's frequent hesitations I'm not sure she knows.

We set out again, but Priscilla keeps looking around as if expecting someone to jump out. Her steps slow and we get ever further behind.

Harriet calls out, "Wait for me. I have to check the path." She disappears into the undergrowth and for a while we hear her thrashing through the jungle, then the sound fades.

Now that we are alone, Priscilla is constantly running her fingers through her hair as she glances urgently at the surrounding jungle.

:: maybe the charming little creature is just worried we'll be waylaid by bandits or wild men

Creature? For once he is not teasing. That's a surprise. He's genuinely interested. Whatever happened to being locked away in his castle?

My amazed wonderings cease as does all conversation when a whooshing fills the air and a net falls over us. Under its weight, Mart and Priscilla sink to their knees and I go down with them. Mart struggles to get free, battling with a seething mass of hands that grab him. Priscilla offers no resistance and is quickly led away. Mart fights to keep the wild men away, but there are too many and they are stronger. He won't hold out long.

As I lie unmoving under the net, my eyesight flickers from normal to that filament-filled vision. The last thing I need is distraction. Aping the wild-men's movements, squirming host of filaments lunge at Mart, whose tight bundle of threads manages to repel some of the attacks. But there are too many and he is suffocating under their combined assault. Another minute and he'll be overwhelmed.

Desperate and furious I lash out mentally at those sickeningly numerous filaments and to my amazement my efforts send them scattering. As normal sight returns I see the whole crowd of wild thugs fall over backwards like a bunch of clowns in a circus. They sit, scratching their heads, no doubt wondering what happened to them.

47.

The wild men plop down where they stand, several landing on the edge of the netting, keeping Mart and I prisoner. Priscilla is nowhere to be seen.

Mart struggles to break free, but his efforts are hampered by the net. The men are scotched like unresponsive lumps of blubber, staring blankly in front of them.

:: what dim wits - you've blown away what brains they had

I did nothing. I insist, but, with a rising sense of guilt, I have to admit I did something, although I have no idea what.

"Try there," I say, pointing from where I lie under the net. "There are no men on that corner of the netting. Maybe you can crawl out."

He gets on all fours and inches forward. The closer he gets to the edge, the tighter the netting becomes. He is forced to snake on his belly till he is disentangled. The wild men sit like zombies, making not the slightest move to stop him.

"Well done," I say, keeping a constant eye on the wild men.

"Now your turn," he says.

:: handicapped as we are, I doubt we'll do much worming

"If you drag the stretcher, maybe I can hold the net up."

He shakes his head, looking sceptical. "I can only get in and out lying on my stomach and I wouldn't have the strength to pull you after me. If only I could shift these lumps."

"Don't you have a rope in your bag?"

He shakes his head. "I can't move them. They are too heavy."

"Not them. Me. Use the rope to pull the stretcher out."

It is not easy to crawl under the net. It takes a good deal of sweating and cursing till Mart has tied the rope to my stretcher.

"That won't work," I tell him. "The moment the stretcher moves, I'll be pulled off. You need to tie me to the stretcher."

Having done so, he eases out. As for the men, they stay frozen in their forlorn positions, their faces blank. Will they be like that for ever? I shudder. What have I done?

Mart heaves on the rope. The stretcher sticks on uneven ground then jerks forward. Thank heavens I'm lashed on.

Using my hands to push up the net, my movements keeping time with Mart's tugs, I jerk and jar my way to freedom.

Mart unlashes me, but he cannot carry me on his own.

"Help me to my feet," I say.

He shakes his head. "Harriet said you shouldn't."

"It's that or wait till the men recover and carry me away."

Mart gets behind me to support my head and neck and eases me up till I am standing unsteadily with his arms around me.

"What a pretty sight." The sneer in Priscilla's voice is evident. "Shame we can't leave you like that. We could lash you to a tree together. A peace offering to the wild animals. But she's got an urgent appointment and you can't go with her."

Mart shifts so I can see Priscilla. She is surrounded by an impressive guard of wild men all armed with clubs. Judging from her behaviour she is not their captive. Rather she is their leader.

A grin spreads across her face at my dismay. "You won't wheedle out of this one with your fine words. My friends here will pack you off to where you belong."

"And where would that be, you useless…" Mart begins. He is so furious, I feel him trembling. I grip his hand in an attempt to calm him and whisper, "Let it go."

"A special place for brats like her." Priscilla jerks a thumb at me. "She won't smile once they've finished setting her right."

"What about Mart?" I ask.

She smirks at my concern. "They don't want the likes of him. He's not good enough. Besides, I have plans for him."

She comes closer and sounds out his arm muscles, prodding them with the tip of her index finger. Mart can do nothing to ward her off as he clings to me for fear I will fall. When she pinches his buttocks, he squeals and tries to squirm away. The girl barks a throaty laugh, saying "You'll do."

The men who were stunned have recuperated and are the brunt of jokes of their colleagues

Priscilla claps her hands to get their attention. "Take her to the Centre," she says, "and bring him with us."

As a group of thugs move towards us, Mart holds out a hand for them to stop. "The people in Centre won't be happy if Sami is seriously injured. Her neck is badly damaged and if she tries to walk, she may well end up paralysed."

:: Smart boy you've got there

Sam's begrudging praise surprises me. He's right, although Mart's gambit is a gamble, but it works. The men halt, unsure.

"Carry her on the stretcher," Priscilla snaps. "Now let's get out of here before the Food Police put an end to our plans."

Mart helps them lay me on the stretcher then Priscilla drags him off before he can say goodbye.

Two wild men heave up the stretcher and we set off at a brisk pace along the path. As we pass the place where Harriet pushed into the jungle I wonder what happened to her. Could she be watching, waiting for a chance to rescue me? Or did the wild men catch her and tie her up or dispose of her? Somehow I can't believe she would get caught. She's far too wily.

The heat and the swaying of the stretcher leave me in a daze and I doze off only to awake when the movement halts. The light is failing. We have stopped before a metal gate, a good fifteen feet high. There's an electrified fence on either side that stretches away as a far as I can see. Just inside the gate I spot a small hut that looks deserted. The wild men lay my stretcher on a rise close to the gate and ring a bell.

Beyond the gate, at the end of a long drive I make out a sprawling house in the middle of a grassy meadow with the occasional towering oak. The jungle presses in on the fence from all sides, making the sight incongruous. The house is a mass of windows ablaze with light, underscored by balconies and terraces. The roof catches my attention, dotted with chimneys of all sizes and shapes. The place seems peacefully sleepy when a door creaks open and light streams down the drive. Then silence falls again. So this is the Centre.

48.

The toddler clutched Jon's coat with determined fingers as if he expected to be abandoned at any moment. Nan had placed him in Jon's arms along with an already sodden handkerchief, saying the boy's name was Wenslas. The child's nose was constantly running and his eyes were red from crying. With her hands free, Nan was able to lead a couple of slightly older children from amongst those that clustered around her. Most of them had lost their parents at the hands of Food Police. Motioning for Jon to follow, they set out in pursuit of the other settlers along a path snaking away towards the hills and mountains beyond.

He had been surprised at the speed and efficiency with which the settlers evacuated their home. "They knew it would happen sooner or later," Nan told him. But that didn't explain the calm with which they gathered up their meagre belongings and removed anything that might help the police locate them.

He was relieved the priest had taken the head of the cortege, as far away as possible. The man had made no remark at seeing Jon reunited with the children, but the look of disgust on his face spoke more than words. The hold the man had over the settlers remained an enigma. He strutted like a cock leading his hens. Why would a group of people who were mostly healers and scientists submit to the influence of a man whose world view was based on narrow beliefs?

To calm Wenslas, who continued crying between sniffles, Jon began humming the lullaby. To his surprise and delight, several youngsters hummed with him, but they quickly stopped at a sharp reprimand from an older child. Jon stopped too and peered over the heads to check on the priest. Maybe humming was not wise. It might attract unwanted ears. He needn't have worried, the jungle made so much noise, there was little chance anyone would hear.

"It's all right," he whispered as if the children were part of a conspiracy. "No one will hear." He motioned with his head to the front of the column of refugees. "Not even your priest." Some children smiled, but the older ones looked at each other, troubled.

Looking down at Wenslas, who thankfully had quietened, Jon found the child staring at him wide-eyed. "More," the boy said.

Jon took up his humming, alone.

Wary that an attack might come at any moment, he kept a constant eye on the jungle and the path behind. Through a narrow opening, he spotted jagged shapes peeking above the jungle. The sight intrigued him. He paused to make sense of what he saw. It was as if the jungle was swallowing up the last of the past. Then he saw it. A clock tower, almost obscured by creepers. Only the minutes hand and a part of the dial were visible.

He shook his head in disbelief. These fantastic ruins were that of a village, or maybe a town that had long since been abandoned. He knew there were many such places reclaimed by the jungle. But he had never seen any.

His attention snapped back when Wenslas tugged at his shirt collar. Nan and the children had paused when he did, no doubt welcoming a chance to rest. The remainder of their group was no longer in sight. He urged the children on.

Ahead the jungle would soon give way to more rocky terrain that curved upwards till it reached the base of the mountains. He hoped they wouldn't go far into the mountains, the peaks and slopes of which were white with snow. Neither the children, nor himself were dressed for such cold and his arms were beginning to ache from carrying the boy.

The moment they left the lush vegetation the temperature plummeted and the chatter of the jungle gave way to a howling wind coursing between the rocks. Jon soon welcomed the merger warmth that came from the child cuddled in his arms. Their little group came to a halt in a clearing offering some shelter from the wind. The children huddled around Nan and Jon, stamping their feet and rubbing their hands. Why ever had they not brought blankets? Surely the adults must have known it would get cold.

"How much further?" he asked Nan over the top of the children's heads.

"Don't know," she replied. "I've never been this way. I'll catch the others up and ask."

As she set off, Jon crouched down, settling Wenslas on his lap. "Come as close as you can," he said to the children.

"I'm cold," a child said.

"Me too," another echoed.

"I'm hungry," a little girl complained.

He was thinking of getting them to sing - at least that might keep their minds off the cold - when a deafening roar like two giants doing battle came from along the path. A dense cloud of dust rose in the air. Several children were so alarmed they began to cry.

He was torn between reassuring them and running in search of Nan. It was then she staggered into the clearing, her face haggard, her whole body covered in dust.

The children moved to join her, but Jon stopped them. "Let me go. She's had a shock." He handed Wenslas to one of the older girls and eased his way between the children to join Nan. "I'll be back in a moment."

Her eyes were wide in horror and tears streamed down her face, making streaks in the dust. She looked like she might collapse. He threaded an arm around her waist and led her across the clearing away from the children.

"What happened?"

"There's been a landslide," she said between sobs.

A feeling of dread stole over him. He wanted to ask if anyone was hurt, but dared not.

"It happened so quickly," she said.

She began trembling. He wanted to comfort her, but something held him back. When a sob broke from her, he let his instinct guide him and wrapped his arms around her, pulling her into a hug. She laid her head on his shoulder and broke down, her breasts heaving against his chest as she sobbed.

Glancing over her head he saw the children growing restless. Many were looking in their direction and some were inching towards them.

"I know it's hard, but tell me what happened."

She shook herself, wiping a hand across her face and pulled away, her jaw set. "It was a massive rock slide." Her breath caught in a sob. "They were buried alive." Tears brimmed in her eyes. "They had no chance."

The thought of being buried beneath a mass of rocks had him shuddering with horror, but he was relieved that the two of them and the young ones had escaped.

Nan turned to look at the children. "We are all alone," she said. "We are stuck between a rock slide and the Food Police."

He glanced in the direction of the children who were huddled in a tight group as if they sensed the worst. They would need food and shelter and warmth as soon as possible. "Is there nowhere we can go?" he asked. "What about the wild men?" He didn't like the idea, what with their filth and their violent habits, but he had no other solution.

She shook her head.

She was right. They could never take the children there. Then he remembered the ruins he'd seen. It might at least provide shelter. Surely that was a start. "I may have a solution," he said.

49.

The square was dotted with indistinct blocks covered with lichen and moss. Jon halted his pacing and stared at the mass of foliage for the tenth time. The jungle watched jealously over the former city, refusing to relinquish its hold. No matter which way they approached, they uncovered no path in. If ever they were to get beyond this natural wall, at least they would be well hidden.

Jon looked around the overgrown square. The children had laid out their meagre rations and were picnicking. He cursed. The adults had been so sure they would reach their destination.

When Nan had broken the news of the landslide, he had been shocked at the children's lack of reaction. Even if many were already orphans, he'd expected them to be hard hit. Instead none had cried and few had spoken. Were they numbed by what they heard? Or were they already deadened by earlier losses?

In contrast, Wenslas skipped around the square, a grin on his face. If anything, as the others sank into mournfulness, he overflowed with life, humming the tune Jon had sung earlier.

When the child let out a sharp cry and disappeared, Jon rushed to the spot, quickly joined by Nan. They could see no sign of him. As others gathered, Jon used a staff he'd fashioned from bamboo and began prodding the dense mop of leaves that formed a wall along that side of the square. To his surprise, he chanced on an empty space. Pushing aside the branches, he uncovered a series of steps sinking into the dark, but Wenslas was nowhere to be seen. Blast the boy!

"Can you hold this up?" he asked Nan, shaking the foliage

as he did. "Any light would be welcome down there." He didn't relish venturing into the hole, but somebody had to. The steps were littered with leaves which might be slippery, but the rain, had there been any, had not penetrated so far.

After a dozen steps, the stairs gave onto a wide tunnel stretching away into the distance. In the welcoming leafy light from skylights, Wenslas sat playing contentedly with a large snail. It had left traces of slime all over his hands. Jon scooped up the boy and carried him and his slimy friend up the stairs and left him in the care of Jenna, one of the oldest Baxter girls.

"Who would have thought the entrance would be underground?" Jon said, eyeing the tunnel.

"What makes you think that dingy hole will come to our rescue?" Nan asked. "I'm not taking the children down there. The place is probably crawling with creatures that will not take kindly to being disturbed."

"On the contrary. It is surprisingly clean." Now he thought of it, the absence of rubbish or wild animals was surprising. "Come and have a look."

"We can't leave the children alone."

"Jenna," Jon called out. "Keep an eye on the children. We'll only be a moment."

As Nan still hesitated, he took her by the arm and led her to the stairs. They were about to climb down, when a distant rumble had them halt. She glanced at him, frowning. He shook his head. Was it thunder? Or another landslide? Probably not. The rumbling persisted, getting closer and louder. His eyes met Nan's in horror as they both realised what it was: marching feet.

They ran around the square gathering up the children and herded then down the stairs, silencing those who grumbled. Before pulling the dense foliage behind him, Jon shot a last look around. There, in plain sight, lay Wenslas' bag, bright yellow with all its contents scattered around it. The footsteps were so close he ought to abandon the bag and flee. But it stood out like a signpost screaming: We are here. Come and get us. He dashed into the open, grabbed the bag, shovelled its contents inside and sprinted for the passage which Nan was holding open. As the wall of leaves fell into place, he caught sight of row upon row of boots marching into the square.

At the bottom of the stairs Nan halted and looked quizzically at him, then whispered, "Take the lead. I'll bring up the rear."

Jon put a warning finger to his lips and waved the children to follow. The tunnel continued its twisty way for quite a distant. The further they went, the more relieved he felt.

The soft, green light made their slow progress seem unreal. For more than ten minutes they came across neither side tunnel nor exit. Jon had taken to carrying Wenslas again as the boy started crying. He'd lost his snail. The younger children dragged their feet, scuffing up leaves as they did. Jon glanced over his shoulder at Nan who was also carrying a little one. They would need food and shelter soon.

He called a halt, listening for signs of pursuit, but all was quiet. Putting down Wenslas to rest his aching arms, Jon turned to Nan who had joined him. "Do you think this place has a good hotel?"

She smiled wearily. "With a big bath and hot water."

Jon bent down to pick up Wenslas only to discover the boy had disappeared. Looking around, he was nowhere to be seen. "Wait here," Jon told the group as he hurried back down the tunnel but found no Wenslas. Hastening back, he beckoned for the others to follow and strode round the bend in the tunnel.

He expected to stumble on Wenslas seated in the middle of the passage, fascinated by some trinket he'd discovered. Instead the empty passageway came to an abrupt halt at double doors. He imagined the food police on the other side with their deadly spray at the ready.

"Keep the children out of sight while I have a look," he said.

"Don't you go stealing my bath," she said, not even smiling.

Watching the group retreat, he took hold of the door handle. It could well be locked or rusted. Who knew how long it had remained unopened? To his surprise it turned easily and he cracked open the door. What he saw had him burst out laughing.

50.

"Can you walk?" Despite the question, the female voice strikes me as devoid of concern.

I look up from my stretcher to see a tall, slender girl dressed in a deep blue skirt that reaches to her ankles and a matching blazer, under which she is wearing a white blouse fastened around her neck by a blue tie emblazoned with what looks like a splay of gold stars. There's a similar coat of arms on the breast pocket of her jacket. Her face is stern and unsmiling as she stares down at me.

:: zero marks for human warmth

"Yes," I reply, as I push myself up on an elbow. "If I walk slowly."

She offers me a hand and hauls me to my feet then lets go as if I had the plague. If only she knew. I sway unsteadily, but she pays no attention and marches along the drive towards the house. I follow with shaky steps, falling further and further behind. Apart from the occasional tall oaks, the expanse around the house is given over to the greenest and smoothest lawn I have ever seen.

:: it must be synthetic - how else could they keep it so green in the middle of a jungle? - that or they have a powerful wizard

The girl halts on the top step in front of the entrance and stands tapping her hip with the flat of one hand. When I reach the stairs, I stop to catch my breath before climbing to the door. She pushes it open and ushers me in. A pungent smell of floor polish greets me as I step forward cautiously onto the wooden parquet.

"You are lucky," she says, letting the door swing closed behind me.

:: maybe that's why her clothes are splattered with stars
You are making no sense.

:: lucky stars

"Why lucky?" I ask.

She looks down her nose at me. "Because only the best come here."

:: there must have been an error if you are here

I catch sight of sturdy double doors standing slightly ajar. Inside I make out row upon row of chairs.

Stepping forward, she pulls the doors closed. "Follow me." She turns on her heals and heads down a corridor to the left, only to halt at a door labelled Waiting Room. Pulling out a bunch of keys, she unlocks the door and indicates I should enter.

Peppermints! After the floor polish in the entrance, the smell takes me by surprise. The room is tiny. The only furniture being a number of chairs dotted here and there with no apparent order. A large window looks over the lawns. The other walls are fitted from floor to ceiling with shelves, brimming with books.

"Wait," she says as she closes the door and leaves.

:: they sit in the antechamber of the court awaiting judgement while outside woodworkers hammer at the gallows
You are grim this evening, Sam.

I move to the window and look out. *No carpenters at work.* As night falls, the scene seems harmless enough. In the distance, across the lawn, between the oaks, I make out the high electric fence ringing the centre.

:: a pretty prison

I turn back to the room. The short walk has tired me and my head is pounding. I drag a chair to the window and sit down, relieved to get the weight off my legs. Gazing distractedly out, I massage my neck and shoulders. After a while, bored with watching the play of the house lights on the leaves, I lean my head against the window frame and close my eyes.

When I open them night has fallen. I can hardly make out the silhouette of the trees that merge with the sky and lawn. I must have slept several hours. I get to my feet and pace the room. How long am I supposed to wait?

:: they have forgotten us - or maybe it is deliberate - try the door - I am sure it is locked

Grasping the handle, I turn and, to my surprise, it opens.

Venturing into the corridor, I am almost driven back into the room by a group of girls pushing past, all dressed in blue and white like that first girl. They chat, paying me no attention.

:: don't let them get away - I smell food

Sam's right. I'm famished. I follow them. Several other girls, alone or in pairs join us, but none seem to notice me. Reaching a translucent glass door, they step inside and I catch a glimpse of tables and benches were many girls are eating. A delicious odour of spiced food wafts out. Then the door swings closed.

I go to push it open when a hand grabs my wrist. A girl steps in front of me blocking the way.

"Not dressed like that!"

She is taller than me and stockily built. No way could I push past her.

"But I'm hungry."

She shakes her head.

Every single girl I have seen in the Centre is dressed with the same long, dark blue skirt and blazer with a blue tie.

"Where?" I ask

She points back down the corridor, her lips pursed.

: a load of blue-armoured zombies - do you think they still have brains?

Sure! Remember, they are the best.

I walk down the corridor, but have to flatten myself against the wall not to be swept away by girls heading for the refectory. They talk excitedly in a language I've never heard.

All along the corridor doors open onto small rooms, each with a few armchairs, an occasional low table and the ever-present book-filled shelves. Every door has a number painted on it, but there is no logic to it. None contain clothes.

I trace my way back to the Waiting Room.

:: this could take all night - they are trying to starve us

About to reply, I spot the word: Uniforms on the next door.

:: I could not imagine a more appropriate word for this lot

The door is unlocked. Inside I am greeted by a smell of new clothes. Row upon row of blazers are suspended from hangers on a bar that stretches the length of the long room. Beneath, on a second bar, are skirts. Separated by a narrow corridor a multitude of white blouses hang from a bar running parallel to the opposite wall. At the end of the row, I discover a cupboard big enough for me to step inside. Pile upon pile of white underwear has been arranged on shelves with numbers indicating sizes.

At the sight of so much female attire, I feel Sam recoil.

: no way - I'm no girl - you will not catch me wearing this stuff - I'd die

You have no choice. This is an all-girls school. I say school, but I am not sure. I've seen no classrooms. And where are the teachers? Where is the principal? I've seen no adults at all.

Come on Sam. Let's get this over with. I'm hungry. I pick out underwear that looks to fit me.

He struggles to wrest control from me, making my fingers fumble as I undress. My clothes are so filthy from days of travelling, I am glad to be rid of them. *Quit doing that, Sam. You'll make me put my pants on back to front.*

My joke makes him so furious he manages to fling the pants across the room where they catch on a hook near the ceiling.

I take another pair and finish dressing. I even find a suitable set of sandals. Just to annoy Sam, I twirl round, making my skirt flair out then stride between the rows of clothes swaying my hips.

:: cut that out and get something to eat before I die of hunger if not shame

51.

I enter the refectory without any rough hands waylaying me.

:: thanks to your disguise

Not disguise, Sam, uniform.

Despite this sign of belonging, the girls, both big and small, continue to ignore me. Their behaviour makes me feel empty, as if I am becoming a ghost from the inside out. Maybe part of that feeling stems from Sam cringing at being dressed as a girl.

I lean against a wall and watch, not wanting to blunder in and make a silly mistake that will have me thrown out before I get a chance to eat.

:: wait much longer and we'll be in time for the next meal, if we don't die of starvation before

Sam's right. I need to act. Few new girls have entered since I arrived. But I get the impression I still lack important information. Like wearing the uniform, there is an order to life concealed in the folds of their careful movements and their hushed conversations.

Every new girl who enters heads for a hatch in one wall and collects a plate of food that she places on a tray with cutlery and a glass before joining a group at one of the tables. I take a tentative step towards the hatch expecting to be accosted, but I make it to the opening where a plate of food awaits me. Potatoes dribbled with butter and sprinkled with chopped chives, tiny carrots and tender slices of beef. I run the back of my hand over my mouth to ensure I am not dribbling.

:: well at least they are not in league with the Food Police

I lift the plate onto a tray and crane forward in the hope of seeing who is preparing meals, but no one is visible.

Turning to face the room, I hesitate, my heart pounding. Although not a single pair of eyes is turned in my direction, I get the impression everyone is watching. Almost all the tables are taken by quietly chatting groups and I can't imagine walking up to one and asking to join them.

:: eat while you can before they decide you are no longer allowed to

I move to one of the few free tables and sit down. The moment I lift a forkful of potato to my mouth, a bell rings making me jump. With a din of scraping of chairs, the girls get to their feet, jostle to leave their trays at the hatch and file out. I stuff food into my mouth, convinced someone will come and snatch the tray from me.

Sure enough, I feel a presence at my side. Looking up I see the same girl who took me to the waiting room, her face twisted in disdain.

"The meal is over. Leave your things at the hatch and go to study period."

I hurry to the hatch, snatching a last forkful of beef before abandoning the tray. I turn to ask where to go, but I am alone.

:: let's go find a place to study

I can't imagine that will be easy.

The corridor is deserted. The girls must be at 'study'. But where?

:: let's skip it - no need to go messing with books or preparing tests and all that school nonsense

We've got to live with these girls. We can't just shut ourselves away in a cupboard. I suspect we are safe here from the wild men and the Food Police.

I open the first door and peer in. Girls are sprawled in armchairs, several lie on the floor, one is leaning against the window frame, all engrossed in books. I retreat and close the door quietly. In the second room, the girls are gathered around a blackboard arguing about incomprehensible hieroglyphs written there.

:: mathematics

I am intrigued, but I have nothing to contribute. In none of the rooms do I find the slightest chance of fitting in. If this last room is no better, I will go and sit under a tree and stare at the night sky. A map has been pinned to a wall and girls my age stare at it. On the map is a sizeable island surrounded by an immense expanse of water. The form of the island is familiar as is the town situated up the hill from the small port. Atlantis!

"It says here a volcano took the islanders by surprise and sank the place," one girl says, waving a book above her head.

"A volcano would never make it sink," another girl counters.

"I read they angered their gods who drowned everyone as punishment," a third girl says.

A shudder runs down my back.

"There was no divine retribution," I say, stepping amongst them. A number of girls shy away. "But everyone did drown," I say, tapping the harbour with my index finger.

The girls stare at me. Some size me up, a couple look defiant, but most are intrigued. I detect no surprise in their eyes. They were well aware of my presence. Do they play this game with every newcomer?

:: you are the bait of the week

"How can you be so sure," the girl who waved the book asks.

"I was there," I reply causing several girls to titter.

"You don't look that old," the book girl says, grinning.

I ignore her. "It was a tidal wave. The elders refused to believe in the danger." I feel anger rising in me at the memory and clench my fists. "No one escaped."

Several girls are no longer smiling, but the book-girl smirks. "So how did you get away?"

"I didn't." The memory of the drowned children brings tears to my eyes.

"What an actress!" the girl exclaims. "You should join the theatre group … if they'll have you." Turning to the other girls, she adds, "You can't possibly believe this nonsense?"

"The wave hit here," I say making a sweeping motion from the sea to the port. "When the earthquake shook the island, most people hurried there to escape. They were the first to die." I run my finger inland and up towards the town. "The wave was so high and so strong, it pushed its way to the town carrying away everything in its path. I can still hear the temple bells ringing and the screams in the town."

"And where were you?" the smallest girl asks, pulling at her shock of black hair.

"I had rounded up a group of small children and led them through the gardens to the summer palace at the top of the island." I tap on the very centre of the island. "The earthquake that preceded the tidal wave had left it in ruins, but we sat on a flight of steps that was still intact. There was nowhere to go. We watched the water coming ever closer." I choke back a sob at the memory. "Even when it towered over us, I hoped we would be spared, but nothing could quell its anger."

Several girls were staring at me aghast, amongst them the black-haired girl, her eyes bright with tears. The book-girl was still smirking.

"Nice try," she says. "But I don't believe a word of it."

"Well I do," the little girl says and she steps forward and takes hold of my hand.

"You always were easily influenced, Tia," the book-girl says. "Maybe it has something to do with your size." I feel Tia flinch. Turning to me, the book girl says, "And what is the moral of your little story?"

:: so full of distain - does she realise how much she belittles the people around her? how much they must hate her for it?

I smile at Sam's silent words. "The moral?" I repeat. "That some people in positions of power are so caught up in being powerful that they can't hear the warnings of the small and less powerful."

52.

The moment the bell rings, the girls hurry out leaving me alone with Atlantis. However did they get their hands on such a map? Maybe it's not so surprising. Even if the population perished in the tidal wave and the island sank, there was no lack of traders. They would have known what the island looked like.

:: forget your Atlantis - we are back at square one - where now?

Find a place to sleep, I suppose.

I get to my feet, but rather than head for the door I scoop up a book. The cover is worn and frayed. The Secret History of Atlantis. I open it at random. Page 34. And read. The general council was composed of five men picked from the best families. They made all the major decisions about the island. I shiver. How could I forget? I snap the book shut and toss it to the floor where it lands with a dull thud.

A book on the selves catches my eye. The title is embossed in white letters: The Unknown Saviour. Smaller than most books, it fits in the palm of my hand. I flip it open. On each page is one short phrase printed in the centre. I read: A saviour raises as many hopes as he does hates.

:: now there's profound thinking for you

Don't be so cynical.

:: who? me? - never - it's just that being a saviour is not a very popular profession

I slip the book in the inner pocket of my blazer where it snuggles next to my chest and open the door. The corridor is deserted. I can't help sighing. This game is getting tiresome. Do all newcomers get such preferential treatment or is it just me?

:: anyone can see you are a monster, it doesn't surprise me

Don't start that again.

"It's not funny, is it?" a voice says.

I spin round to find Tia leaning against the wall, her face twisted in a grimace. Has she been listening to my thoughts? She pushes off the wall like a dancer about to launch into a choreography and proffers an outstretched hand. I hang back, unsure how to respond.

"Funny?" I ask to cover my confusion.

"Tormenting you," she says, letting her hand fall to her side. "They did the same to me. I hated it."

"How long have you been here?"

"Two months. But we can talk about that later," she says, grasping my hand and pulling me down the corridor. "Let's find you a bed."

We cross the main entrance. "That's the meeting hall," she says, nodding towards the double doors I noticed earlier. "You'll see tomorrow." At the end of a long corridor flanked by many doors, no doubt leading to rooms similar to those I was just in, we reach a spiral staircase.

"My name's Tia, by the way," she says, pausing at the foot of the stairs. "What's yours?"

"Sami."

:: don't worry about me! - just cast me into oblivion

I'm not sure she'd take kindly to knowing they have a boy in their midst.

:: how can you be so sure?

The stairs are steep and I have to pause to catch my breath and rest my trembling legs at each landing. Tia waits patiently. At the top, we step into a narrow corridor under a sloping roof with skylights here and there opening onto the night sky. Behind many doors, I hear hushed voices. Halfway down the corridor, a glass door opens onto a tiny balcony. The air is stuffy and I am seized by a desire to get out in the fresh air.

"May I?" I ask, pointing to the balcony.

"Sure." She pushes open the door and we step into the night only to be greeted by a cool breeze. I sit on a bench and she squeezes next to me. Taking a deep, liberating breath, I sigh with pleasure. Above the night sky is ablaze with stars. No light from the ground mars their splendour. I trace the meandering Milky Way across the heavens till I reach Venus, proud and stately. "Beautiful," I whisper. An involuntary shiver runs down my spine. I am unsure if it is the emotion or that I am growing cold. Tia must have sensed me shudder because she slides an arm round my shoulder and pulls me closer, bringing welcome warmth. I lean into her embrace.

"It was hard at first, very hard," she begins, her voice so close to my ear her breath tickles. "I missed my parents terribly. Even if life with them was not easy. When I arrived I cried a lot. The other girls were not always very kind. Nobody offered help. That's the idea, so they say. You've got to make it on your own."

I wonder who 'they' are, but instead I ask. "How come you came here?"

"My parents couldn't cope."

I turn to her, my face only inches from hers. I can't imagine her being difficult. "Why was that?"

"I got impatient. So impatient I could scream. They thought so slowly. Like brainless snails. It got on my nerves. I was always kicking up a stink. Shouting. Smashing things..."

"So your parents sent you here?"

"No. One night there was a knock at the door. It was late and my parents were scared. When they opened a woman stood on the doorstep. She wore a long black dress. I remember it well. It was so unusual. Her hair was straight and black and her piercing eyes made her look severe. They didn't want to let her in, but she insisted, saying that I was in danger. I saw it all. My door was ajar. Once inside, she told them the Food Police were coming. I think my parents were expecting it. Everyone has heard the police remove difficult or unhealthy children."

:: that's why Jon kept me a secret all those years - he did a good job - nobody ever came to fetch me before you forced your way into my life

"My parents called me and had me shake hands with the woman. I didn't like the way she held onto my hand as if I belonged to her. When I tried to pull away, she wouldn't let go. The only problem with me, she said, was that I was gifted and needed special education. She insisted the Centre was the only place for me, but my parents had to decide quickly. I had to leave if I wanted to survive. I didn't want to go, but I was given no choice. My parents agreed. They looked relieved, though I'm not sure if that was because I would escape the police or they would be rid of me."

"So the woman brought you here?"

"Not straight away. We were hurrying down a street when two food police jumped out and grabbed us. I was terrified. I was sure they'd take me away and kill me. But the woman pulled out a shiny metal object and pointed it at them. I put my hands over my ears, expecting a bang, like a gun, but there was just a faint crackling and the two men's eyes rolled back and they crumpled to the ground. What frightened me more than the police turning up was the calm way she slid the metal pointer back in her pocket and stepped round the men as if nothing had happened."

:: I wouldn't argue with her - goodness knows what other smart weapons she's got up her sleeve

I shiver at the thought.

:: well at least they are not in league with the food police - though she could be worse

"We will catch a cold if we stay here," Tia says. "Let's go in."

:: do you think that woman could be hiding here?

"Before we go, tell me, why are there no grown ups here? Where's that woman?"

"She left me at the gate. One of the girls came to fetch me. There are no adults here. Just us."

"But why?"

"I'm not sure." She gets to her feet and peers out over the starlit grasses that surround the Centre, then turning back to me, she continues, "Since I've been here, I've never seen an adult. Like me and you, new girls are left at the gate. I was told being on our own was the best way to learn." She shakes her head. "Apparently we are to be an elite. The new leaders."

"You certainly seem to have managed to organise life well enough. Are there never any squabbles?"

Tia makes a strange spluttering sound, midway between laughing and choking. "No one would dare. We are too afraid of the punishment."

"Punishment? You punish yourselves?" I can't keep the surprise and alarm from my voice.

"Hardly. No. There are three girls who run the show. They've been here since the beginning. They mete out the punishment."

:: a school with its own child gorillas - gruesome - mind if I sit this one out?

Tia's face turns pale and she clenches her fists. "They decide everything."

"Then maybe I should meet them," I say, getting to my feet.

"You don't want to do that." Her voice trembles, her hands too as she grabs me by the shoulder.

"I hear you," I say, placing a hand on hers. "But how could I go on if I begin by being afraid of them?"

She lets go of me and her shoulders slump. "OK," she says, shaking her head. "I'll take you to them. I just hope your courage holds out."

:: she's the one who has courage

"You don't have to come," I say. "Just show me the way."

"Sure I do. If you can't go on without confronting them, what would I feel like if I let you go alone?"

Inside Tia halts in front of a door and is about to open it when a burst of laughter explodes within.

53.

Jon's laughter had a host of colourful birds surge into the air and dart backwards and forwards through a weird muddle of a five-star hotel foyer and a giant hothouse overflowing with tropical plants. The reception desk was still in place as were a set of armchairs and low tables, but vines and creepers had crawled over everything lending grotesque shapes to each object. To cap it all, Wenslas was perched on a high stool behind the desk with a creeper around his neck and shoulders. The boy ginned. Jon checked to be sure no one was waiting in ambush, but he could hear only the songs of birds and a breeze rustling the leaves.

He beckoned for the others to join him then stepped out cautiously and frayed a path to the desk. As they emerged, several children gasped at the sight, but most just trudged out and stood silently staring around, their hands in their pockets.

"If we are lucky," Nan said, joining him, a grin on her face, "this might be the answer to our prayers. Or a part of it at least."

Jon skirted the reception desk and lifted Wenslas into his arms. "You should be careful," he said as he unwound the slender stem from around the boy's neck. "Some vines can do harm."

"We should find a place to stay," Nan said.

"And some food," Jenna added joining them.

"If we want our presence to remain a secret, we should not leave traces behind," Nan said, tugging gently on one of the creepers covering the reception desk. "Better not to use the ground floor if we can help it."

"OK," Jon said, hoisting the boy onto his shoulders. "Wenslas and I will go find a place to sleep."

"Can I come too?" Jenna asked, her look pleading.

"I thought you wanted to search for food," Jon said.

"The others can do that. When we get back they will have a meal ready."

Jon hoped her optimism was justified, but he doubted it. The hotel had been deserted for years. "Ok."

Jenna let out a yup of delight and headed for what looked like a flight of stairs. Jon might not have recognised it, such was the profusion of plants tumbling down the incline, had it not been for the lift door hanging open next to it.

"We can't go that way," he told Jenna, who was about to scramble up amongst the vines. "Anyone entering will see someone has been here. We need to find another route. And anyway, most of the children could never climb that." He wasn't sure he'd manage, even without Wenslas in his arms.

He peered into the shaft wondering if there might be a way to climb up, but the lift was stuck above head-height, blocking access to the upper floors. They turned back and picked their way amongst the growth round the foyer in search of another exit.

The hotel must have been impressive in its heyday judging from the size of the reception. Their task was hard work. The walls were concealed behind a mass of creeping plants that were so dense any door, if there was one, would be completely hidden.

It was Jenna that found the first door, which, once they had prised it open, led only to a tiny office that had been spared the green invasion. It was no use to them. They took to working their way inch by inch around the foyer, pushing aside leaves in an attempt to peer behind the creepers. They found several more doors, most leading to store rooms. Jon made a mental note of the different tools they found, thinking they might come in useful later. Other openings led to rooms on the same floor. He pointed them out to Nan who explored with a group of girls.

They made their way around the whole reception area without finding the exit and came to a halt next to the lift. Wenslas kicked at the creepers, putting increasing force into his efforts.

Jon was a afraid the noise would attract attention. "Stop that," he said. "You'll hurt yourself."

The boy obeyed, swaying backwards and forwards, a sullen look on his face. Then he bumped into Jenna, pushing her against the vines. She countered and the two tussled close to the gaping lift shaft, much to Jon's alarm.

"Look out!" he said.

Jenna pushed the boy away from the hole expecting him to rebound off the creepers but instead he disappeared. Jenna burst into tears, no doubt convinced she'd sent him to his death. Jon hurried forward, sure the boy hadn't fallen down the shaft, but he made a show of peering in to reassure her. All he could see was a mass of plants vying for room in the narrow opening.

Then Jenna squealed.

"What happened?" Jon asked.

"Something attacked me."

This time, when the hand darted out from amongst the creepers, Jon saw why Jenna had squealed. Moving closer, he positioned himself to catch the hand next time it attacked and when it did, he caught it and tugged. Out popped Wenslas, a grin on his face. Jenna was furious. She raised a hand to hit the boy, but Jon shielded Wenslas with his outstretched arm.

"That wasn't very nice, Wenslas," he said, shaking the boy's arm. Keeping a tight hold on both children, Jon pushed Wenslas back between the creepers, forcing open a hidden door and followed, pulling Jenna after. All three tumbled on the dirt-ridden floor of a narrow hallway. In the struggle that followed, as he tried to get up while keeping the two apart, Jon received one of the punches intended for Wenslas. Luckily it landed on his hip causing Jenna to cry out in pain and cease her fighting.

Once his eyes adjusted to the dim light he found himself in a stairwell that wound upwards. It was largely free of plants. He was so delighted he pulled both Wenslas and Jenna into a hug. The girl drew back, a questioning look on her face. "We've found it," Jon said. "Let's go and explore." At his explanation, Jenna flung her arms around him and returned his hug.

54.

As they climbed, Jon had a hard time restraining Wenslas who pushed ahead in his urge to explore. "The floor might not be safe," he warned. "We don't want you falling to the ground." He regretted his words the moment he said them because Wenslas laughed at the idea of landing amongst the others. The thought that he might hurt himself didn't cross his mind.

They had to climb to the third floor before finding one free of plants. Luckily the roof held good and, after a few tentative steps, Jon decided the floor was solid. Even the windows were intact. Had he been able to open them he would willingly have let in fresh air.

Before Jon could stop him, Wenslas cantered down a corridor that curved away in both directions, kicking up a cloud of dust, only to reappear a minute later by the other corridor a dusty fantom fast on his heels. Not satisfied, the boy dodged Jon's outstretched arms and continued to gallop round his new-found circuit. Taking Jenna with him, Jon set off after Wenslas. There were rooms on both sides, all the doors of which stood open as if awaiting visitors. The electronic mechanisms that had once held them shut must have failed over the years.

They peered into the first. The bed had been made and looked ready to receive its next guest. When Jenna saw the eiderdown, she dived onto the bed with a shout of glee only to be engulfed in a dense cloud of dust. Rolling onto the floor, she crawled away, a hand over her nose as she coughed violently.

There was a small basin in one corner. He turned the tap,

giving up a silent prayer for water, but only an earwig fell out and scuttled away. Moving to the window, he was relieved to see a curtain of trees shielded the hotel.

Mid way round the circuit, they discovered a large meeting room that might serve as a canteen, although they would need to find a place to cook, not to mention water and food.

"Is there no end to your energy," he asked the boy as he stopped him running once more around the floor. "Let's go and tell the others what we've found."

Back on the ground floor, not only were Nan and the children nowhere to be seen, but there was an eerie silence that set Jon's nerves on edge. He took the two children and searched down one corridor but the indoor jungle grew so thick it was impassable. In the other direction they discovered the kitchens. Someone had forced their way in, but no one was inside. Back in the corridor, he tried to push further from the reception, but a wall had collapsed and trees and plants blocked the passage.

He retraced his steps, convinced Nan couldn't have gone that way. It was then he noticed Wenslas wasn't with them. He glanced at Jenna questioningly. She shrugged.

"The kitchens?" he asked.

"Maybe."

In the kitchens they found no trace of the boy. They were about to leave when Jenna asked, "What's that?"

"What?"

"That thudding."

He heard nothing. Surely she couldn't be imagining it. He moved in the direction she indicated, then paused and cupped a hand behind his ear. "You are right." She shrugged as if to say, "of course". The dull thudding was coming from the far side of the kitchens, but there was nothing there apart from rampant plants swallowing kitchen utensils.

Jenna pushed past him and shook the vines that clung to the wall, to no avail, but the thudding persisted.

"Somebody is in there," Jon said, shifting backwards and forwards trying to locate the origin of the noise. He halted at a bulge in the foliage. When he tried to tug on the branches, to his surprise, a whole pan of the greenery swung away in his hand like a leafy screen revealing a giant door that reminded him of those massive fridges in butchers' shops and hotels. He pulled on the handle which hinged down and the door creaked open.

The thudding stopped immediately and a small head peered round the door, eyes wide and tearful. It was one of the young girls who sometimes played with Wenslas. As she stepped out, she was followed by a gaggle of boys and girls with Nan bringing up the rear. When she saw Jon she flung her arms around his neck and hugged him, her body trembling.

"I thought we would never get out," she said, a shudder in her voice.

"However did you get shut in there?"

"I jammed the door open with a stool, but someone tripped over it and door sprang shut before I could stop it. We searched everywhere for a way to open it. There had to be a safety mechanism, but if there is it doesn't work any more."

"So what is in there, that you all went inside?"

"Food. Lots of food."

"But surely it has gone off."

"No. I don't know how. It has remained cool in there. Maybe it's the door. Much of the food is more recent. As if someone were keeping a stock."

Jon shuddered. "I hope not."

55.

Three girls huddle together on the floor flanked by their beds, their foreheads inches apart, their faces bright with laughter as they whisper of meals and clothes and hopes and dreams. Could these really be the three Tia warned about?

We stand by the half open door, watching, unnoticed. Tia is tense, ready to flee, while I lean back, silent, gauging them.

:: they continue to ignore you, even when you stand in the heart of their intimacy - they don't seem so dangerous to me

No. Not ignore. Wrapped up in each other, unaware of the rest of the world.

The girl who greeted me at the gate is amongst them. Despite the intense look on her slender face, she appears different. Maybe it's the tie and blazer she's discarded. Or is it the smile on her usually unsmiling face? The book girl sits opposite, a book clasped in her hand, her other hand gesticulating.

Tia leans close and whispers in my ear, "These are the three that reign over us."

The book girl looks up, as if she has sensed Tia's words, and spots us. A sneer forms on her lips as she snaps her book shut. "Girls. We have company."

The others turn to look, their smiles hanging suspended. Strange how you can tell a smile is not meant for you.

"Who gave you permission to bring her here?" the book girl asks Tia.

"This shunning of new girls is not right, Gwen," Tia says, her voice trembling.

:: your new friend is courageous or very foolish

"Oh! Lovely," a ginger haired girl says, a sparkle in her eyes. "A revolution. Will there be demonstrations? And parades? And people padlocked to the school gate? Bring on the revolting girls. I'd love to put down a revolt."

:: why ever did she brings us here? - is she suicidal? - get out before it is too late

"Cut it out, Marge" the book girl says. "This is serious."

"You are always so earnest, Gwen," Marge retorts, giving the book girl a friendly shove. "Why not let this one play itself out? A real social experiment. Wouldn't be the first time."

:: what makes me sure the only experimenting she'll be doing is hurting younger children?

Turning to Tia, Marge asks, "So what do you plan to do? Hand out leaflets? Hold secret meetings? Set traps for us leaders? Have us assassinated?"

Tia stands there silent, at a loss.

:: they are so sure of themselves - maybe someone needs to shake their confidence

You are wrong, Sam. Shaking them up would only make things worse. They'd get angry and aggressive, more so than they are now. At the moment it is only a game. Imagine if they seriously set out to hurt others through spite.

:: I suspect that is exactly what they already do

"There will be no revolution," I say, convinced by my exchange with Sam. "People get hurt in revolutions. Both those who instigate them and those whose ideas are overthrown, not to mention those who stand by and watch."

"Listen to her," Gwen sneers. "She's so cock sure. Were you in a revolution like you were on Atlantis?"

"No," I reply, aware that I have probably made things worse.

"What's this about Atlantis?" Marge asks, her eyes bright.

"She spun some yarn in study hour about having been on Atlantis," Gwen replies.

"Sami is extremely well informed," Tia says, moving forward to stand at my side.

"Nobody asked your opinion," the gate girl says, not even bothering to look at Tia.

:: punch her on the nose for me - she's an insufferable prig

"You weren't there, Celine. She knew all about …" Tia retorts only to be interrupted by Gwen.

"Nothing she couldn't have read in a book."

"Not everyone gets their knowledge from books," Tia replies, her fists clenched.

:: this is going to turn into a fight - I don't like fights - it's always me that gets hurt

It was you that wanted to punch her.

:: only in my imagination

"I'm fed up with this," Celine says, turning her back on us. "Why are we wasting time on these dunces. I say we punish them and get back to our own business."

"Yes," Gwen says. "A spell outside the fence would do them good."

Tia shudders next to me. Being shut outside with the wild animals must be a real nightmare.

"You could, of course," I say.

:: are you mad?

"Sami!" Tia says, spinning round to look at me aghast.

Gwen chuckles. "Your new-found friend has no idea what she's getting herself into."

"But you would be wasting a good opportunity," I insist.

Gwen blows out an explosive breath. "I can't believe it. She's only just arrived and she is already trying to wheedle her way out of punishment."

"No. Hold on," Marge says, clearly intrigued. "What do you mean?"

"You could hold a trial in front of the assembled girls," I say.

Tia gasps. I wish I could explain. I take hold of her hand hoping to reassure her, but she flinches and pulls away.

:: let's just hope she doesn't do anything stupid - I hate pain

"Interesting," Marge says, running the tip of her tongue over her lips. "I like the idea of staging a trial."

"And you complain about my books," Gwen says. "Your un-ending show is far worse. Not everything has to be on a stage."

:: divide and reign

Maybe. I certainly seem to have hit lucky.

Marge turns to Celine. "Just imagine. The girls assembled. The hall packed. And her," she points to me, "dragged in. A pitiful specimen. After a few days in the wilds. To wear her down. And us announcing her punishment. A sentence so terrible the girls will tremble with fear."

"You have forgotten something," I say. "You have to accuse before you pass sentence."

:: I am amazed they haven't twigged - your casual attitude should give it away - surely they must spot the trap

Marge looks delighted. "Oh yes. The act of accusation. You two nailed to a board. Each one of our accusations a nail holding you down."

:: I wouldn't like to be caught alone with her - she's terrifying

"Not two," I say. "Just one. Me. No one else has conspired with me." I look at Tia who frowns.

:: she realises something is going on - she's not sure what

Jabbing Tia with an outstretched finger, Gwen says, "True. I doubt this one understands what is going on."

:: neither does she

"So you agree?" Marge asks. Celine nods. Gwen pulls a face. "But what are we going to do with her?" she asks, pointing to Tia. "We can't just let her get off."

"I say we lock them both outside the gate," Marge says with evident delight.

"No. Please don't," Tia says, tears streaming down her face.

I put an arm around her to comfort her. She doesn't push me away, but remains stiff and unyielding.

"Can you manage?" Gwen asks. "Or do you need help?"

"I can manage," Celine replies.

56.

Tia howls, her scream so piercing, it rattles my brain. I wedge my fingers in my ears and try to step back, but she grabs my arm and clings on. Her whole body is trembling and I tremble with her. When I unplug my ears, apart from the rustle of the breeze in the leaves, silence has fallen. It is short-lived. The hoots and growls return, punctuating the steady click of cicadas.

"What happened?" I whisper.

"A thing slithered over my foot. It was all thick and cold and slimy."

"Is it still there?" I ask, unable to keep my voice steady.

"No. It slipped away the moment I screamed."

Relieved, I pull free of her grip and shake the long chain that binds our ankles to the gate. "If ever we get free, we need to find a place to shelter," I say. One that we can close against snakes and the like. "Do you know where we can go?"

"No. We never come out here. Except rarely … as punishment."

The moon is breasting the jungle and is almost full. The trees and creepers sway in its silvery light. To my alarm glowing eyes peer from amongst the foliage.

I tear my eyes away and look at the gate house, a squat outline in the moonlight just inside the fence. It is no use to us. Celine padlocked us to the gate by two long chains then locked us outside and walked off with the keys in her blazer pocket. As I look into the distance trying to make out the lights of the centre, something cold and smooth slides over my foot. I scream. Tia screams. And we clutch at each other shaking in terror.

:: for god's sake get a grip - breathe - you are scaring the hell out of me

I take a deep breath, but to no avail, the shuddering is beyond my control. Together we form a tight knot of terror that feeds itself. A thump in the nearby undergrowth has us frozen. Laboured breathing follows amid the cracks of branches and the scratch of leaves as a heavy weight is dragged along the ground. We skitter away, but the chains pull us up short. A dark form backs out onto the path, its legs straining as it drags its prey after it. A sharp twist of its muzzle shakes its catch free of a root and it disappears into the jungle opposite.

I stuff my fist in my mouth to stop from screaming and when I feel Tia is about to scream, I clamp my other hand over her mouth. Misunderstanding, she bites me. Hard. Her teeth hitting bone. I cry out with pain. Bringing my hand to my mouth, I try to staunch the blood by sucking it.

"I'm so sorry," she mumbles and breaks into sobs, her body sinking to a heap on the ground.

:: it takes so little to push someone over the brink

I spit a mouthful of blood onto the ground and lick the wounds. They sting. I look down at Tia grovelling. Sam is right. She is beyond help. It's not her fault. But part of me wants to kick her till she gets up or bleeds like I do.

:: time to pull back from the edge - if you want to go through with your plan - now is not the moment to go mad

I sigh. *You are right Sam.* I place a cautious hand on Tia's shoulder and when she doesn't bite, I kneel next to her and take her in my arms. She is shivering. Fright probably. And cold. We are dressed for fire-lit studies and rosy warm dinning halls, not the bitting air of the jungle night.

From time to time, the world heaves about us as a host of animals shifts in a cacophony of grunts and growls. Then an edgy hush falls, till the next upheaval. Beyond caring, we sit in the middle of the chaos, clinging to each other, silent and exhausted. My thoughts waver then wander. Where could Jon be? And Nan?

Still running from the Food Police. No doubt. In another world. And Tia. Her heart. Beating. Beating fast. Close by. Her hands sweaty. Feverish. And my hand pulsing. Sore. A long way away. Getting further. And I drift.

Tia lurches to her feet tossing me to the ground. Her breath coming in short bursts, a strangled scream in her throat. Winded, I lie on my back staring up at the sky when the moon, which has reached the zenith, is blotted out by a large furry head. The animal's fetid breath envelops me as it nuzzles my nose and mouth. I almost retch, My nerves screech, as I strain not to scream. A rough tongue darts out and licks my cheek. Then the animal curls up on its legs and plops down next to me, its head resting heavy on my chest.

:: you chose the strangest friends

I dare not move for fear I switch from friend to feast. Let's hope Tia doesn't try something stupid. Hearing her settle onto the ground some distance away I'm reassured. After a while the animal lets out what sounds like a sigh and its head becomes heavier.

Inching my good hand up I place it on the animal's head being careful to apply only the slightest of pressure. It shifts, pushing up against my hand. At first I think it wants to drive me away. But as it repeatedly nudges my hand I have to smile as I am convinced it is trying to encourage me. I bury my fingers in its rough fur and slide them down its muscular neck. It sighs again and rests its head back on my chest.

Feeling warm and safe for the first time in ages, I relax and drift to sleep.

57.

I am not alone when I awake, although it is not a large furry beast cuddled up next to me but Tia. The sleeping girl looks frail and defenceless, her skirt caught up around her thighs revealing scratches and bruises along her slender legs. Could the animal have been a mere dream? Bringing my hand to my nose, I sniff. The unmistakable whiff of a large dog or wolf leaves no doubt.

:: lucky it chose to befriend you - I can't imagine why

Because it knew you were hidden there somewhere.

No reply is necessary. Sam's disbelief is palpable.

The sun has not yet risen, but the sky in the East is tinged red and birds dart amongst the branches singing their joy at a new day. I ease free of Tia who groans, turns over and goes back to sleep. My every muscle complains as I stretch and brush dust from my skirt and blazer. In doing so I hit my hand against a jacket button causing a sharp pain. I examine my wounds. The flesh around the bites is fiery red and swollen. I place a fearful finger over one, not daring to touch. It is on fire.

A sharp rustle of leaves catches my attention. I turn to see my fury friend emerge from behind a boulder and lope to my side. He nudges my hand and I splay my fingers in the hair on his neck, massaging the bulging muscles. He is impressive. Seated, his head reaches my shoulders. He pants, his tongue lolling out, revealing a set of viciously sharp teeth behind tense lips.

His nose quivers in the fresh air sniffing the scents. Then his muzzle seeks out my hand. I plunge it in my pocket, afraid the blood will spark less civilised drives, but he grabs my forearm in his jaws and pulls my hand from my pocket. I am relieved when he just licks my hand and whines, then bounds off.

:: he's gone to find others to share you as breakfast

Sam jokes, but his mental voice is none too steady.

As if to belie him, the dog returns, bounding along the path with something grasped in his jaws. He nudges me several times till I realise he wants me to take the sprigs. I recognise the clusters of tiny white flowers and the strange almost furry-like leaves. Yarrow. Harriet showed it to me. What did she say about it?

:: that it was the best remedy for wounds

I glance at the dog astonished. His eyes meet mine, a deep intelligence staring out "How clever," I say, patting him on the back with my good hand. "Just what I need."

If only I remembered what to use and how to prepare it.

:: the flowers and leaves - Harriet said use a pestle and mortar

Just let me look in my medicine bag. Sam scoffs, mentally. *It's not my fault if you don't appreciate my humour.*

I pull off a bunch of flowers and a couple of leaves. I could apply them to the wound but that doesn't sound right and would probably hurt. I sniff the flowers. They give off a strong, sweet odour. Bringing one leaf tentatively to my lips, I bite into it. Not bad. A bit bitter. I stuff the flowers and the leaves into my mouth and chew. When they turn to a sticky paste I apply it to the wounds. The animal sits back on its haunches and watches me. I have no bandage to hold the compress in place. I'll just have to hold my hand steady till the paste dries.

The throbbing eases the moment the wounds are covered. I sit between the dogs front paws, cradling my hand and lean my head on its chest. He rests his jaw on the top of my head. "We need a name for you," I say.

:: why not call him yarrow?

What a good idea. "What do you think?" I ask the dog.

:: he can't hear me

Who knows what he can hear? "So we will call you Yarrow."

He licks my ear. I laugh, even though my face is wet.

My laughter awakens Tia who cries out and jumps to her

feet. When she sees the dog she skitters away, her mouth fallen open in fright.

"It's alright," I say. "Yarrow won't hurt you. He's a friend."

She keeps her distance, her eyes fixed on the dog. When she does look at me she asks, "What's that on your hand?"

I explain, although I steer clear of saying who bit me.

"How did you get bitten?"

:: tell her the grim truth

"You bit me. Don't you remember?"

She looks aghast. "I would never do that."

I shrug. No point in arguing.

Behind us I hear keys rattle and I turn to see Celine unlocking the gate. Yarrow gets to his feet and growls, baring his teeth, then slinks away into the undergrowth and disappears. "Yarrow," I call out, feeling abandoned.

:: let him go - she will take fright if she sees him and we will be left here for ever

Celine strides towards us swinging her keys on their chain, a broad grin on her face. "You girls sleep well?" she asks as she unlocks the shackles around our ankles. The pressure of the metal has left a red weal where the skin has been chaffed. "Shame you missed breakfast. It was particularly good this morning. And I doubt you'll have time for lunch, what with the trial and everything."

:: what a nasty specimen - will you let me take over so I can flatten that pretty little nose of hers

"Follow me," Celine says, paying us no more attention.

Tia limps then stumbles. I manage to catch her before she falls but wrench her arm as I do, making her cry out. Celine waits for us at the gate, peering off towards the centre as if nothing was happening. Threading an arm around Tia's waist, I take some of her weight and help her struggle inside the grounds. Behind us the gate clanks shut.

58.

Jon popped the last morsel into his mouth and chewed with tired jaws. He was out of practice. Juices from the grilled meat had dribbled down his fingers and now dripped into his other hand cupped beneath. He licked his fingers then slurped up the greasy puddle from the palm of his hand.

With the help of the older children they had carted a sack of potatoes and a box of frozen pork chops along with a large jar of pickles to the uppermost floor where they had discovered a penthouse suite with an open fireplace, a tiny kitchenette, a separate office, a white tiled bathroom and a balcony that ran the length of the building. The suite was big enough to house them all.

When night had fallen, they tore up prospectus about the hotel hauled from the reception and smashed a broken, wooden chair they found in a cupboard. Laying the paper and wood in the grate, Jon set about kindling a fire. Smoke billowed into the room causing everyone to cough. They sent the children into the corridor, telling them to keep quiet.

With a handkerchief over his nose he peered up the chimney, but it was too dark to see anything. He wondered if it was blocked, but once the fire blazed, the hot air rose and sucked the smoke out of the room.

Roasting the meat and potatoes was a challenge. He hadn't wanted to return downstairs. The presence of so much fresh food in a deserted building troubled him. He was afraid they might stumble on someone. Finally they fetched a grill from the kitchens and found a few bricks in the tunnel they had arrived by.

Licking his lips, Jon leaned against the bed with a sigh and looked at the children scattered about the room finishing off their meal. Most were sprawled on the thick rugs, gathered around trays that served as tables. Despite their hunger, few were able to finish. Too tired maybe. Or unused to so much meat. The younger ones were already curled up, sleeping on the double bed. Wenslas lay with his head in Jenna's lap, fast asleep. When she saw him looking, the girl grinned. He smiled back. Wenslas wasn't alone.

Nan gave him a weary smile as she tugged herself to her feet using an armchair as a lever. Going into bathroom, she returned with a wet flannel which she used to wipe the mouths and fingers of the sleeping children. When she reached Wenslas, she lifted him off Jenna and lay him on the big bed amongst the infants.

"Your turn now," she told the older children. "Hands and face." He heard groans, but all got to their feet and headed for a wash.

There was no running water, but they had discovered a tap that worked in a cleaner's cupboard. Must have been a different circuit. Several buckets had been requisitioned and were now full in the bathroom, in the kitchenette and in the toilet.

Jon picked up all the trays and leftovers and piled them up in the kitchenette. Then he pulled out a pile of eiderdowns. The children had taken them out on the balcony earlier and shaken out most of the dust. As they did, Nan had had to silence them several times as the shaking and shoving took on the allure of a wild game.

Jon spread the eiderdowns over the rugs, leaving a safe distance from the fire. Then he washed the trays as best he could with a cloth and cold water and put them out on the balcony to dry. While he was out, he flung the remains of the food over the side, watching it sail into the trees and disappear amongst the foliage. An answering growl came from below followed by the sound of a scuffle. Someone, or something would eat well that night.

Waiting for Nan to finish getting the children into bed, Jon followed the balcony one step at a time, making sure that it was solid enough to hold his weight. At the far corner, a metal staircase wound down the outside of the building. A fire escape. He tried to make out if and where it reached the ground, but it was swallowed up by the jungle.

He was returning to the sliding penthouse door when Nan stepped out. Taking him by the arm, she led him back the way he'd come and sat with her back to the wall out of earshot of the children. Jon sat next to her.

Both stared off into the distance. They were just high enough to see over the crowns of the tallest trees. "Somewhere, in that haze on the horizon is the city with its food police and its torture and its dreadful illness," Jon said, keeping his voice to a whisper.

"We were lucky to find this hotel," she replied.

"I'm not so sure," Jon said, chewing on a fingernail that he'd broken making the fire. "I'm worried about all that food. Someone must have stocked the place. What if they come back?"

"Tomorrow we should explore the surroundings. See if there is any trace of movement. Transporting that food would need a vehicle."

Who could possibly afford to run such vehicles and procure all that food? It certainly wasn't the food police. They had vehicles, it was true, but no food as far as he knew. That would be a twisted joke: the food police stocking real food while forcing the population to eat pills. He almost choked on the idea.

His thoughts were interrupted by Nan grabbing his arm. She looked alarmed. His questioning expression had her nodding over the balcony and down to the left, at the opposite end of the building to the fire escape. He strained to hear. Over the racket of the jungle, he could hear the roar of an engine. No. Not one. Several.

59.

Jon and Nan crept to the edge of the balcony and peered over. What with the moonlight and the jungle canopy they could see little more than the occasional ray of headlights, but they could hear the whir of engines and the screech of brakes.

"Get the material inside," a male voice snapped. "Then we'll meet in the penthouse."

Jon and Nan shot each other a glance and dashed back to the children. The room reeked of smoke and roast meat. Food stains spotted the bed and rugs. There was no way they could conceal their presence.

"Find something to block the door," Nan said. "I'll wake the children."

He opened the door and peered down the corridor. No one. There was only one other suite. If they were very lucky, the men would use that. He opened the service cupboard and pulled out several brooms. Maybe he could wedge the door closed. Back in the suite, he rammed several brooms under the door handle. It might give the impression the door was locked, but would not hold if someone shoved hard.

The children were awake, although bleary eyed. The older ones readied the infants to take them onto the balcony. If the worst came to the worst they would have to climb down the fire escape. With the help of Jenna and several other children they carried a heavy table from the study and pushed it against the door.

"We could use the bed too," Jenna suggested.

"No time," Nan said, ushering everyone outside.

Jon was the last to leave. Pulling the curtains tightly closed behind him, he clicked the door shut. If ever someone stepped out onto the balcony from the other suite, that might stop them seeing signs of their passage.

Outside the children were huddled about Nan near the metal staircase. Jon turned in the other direction. Below, he could hear men offloading heavy objects, complaining as they did. He tiptoed to the windows of the other penthouse suite. It was identical to the one they had used. The sliding glass door to the balcony was slightly ajar. He examined the mechanism, wondering if he could block the lock.

"You coming?" Nan whispered close behind him.

"If only we could block this…" he said, rapping the door with his knuckles.

"Try this," she said, handing him a hair clip.

He took the pin, but was at a loss what to do with it.

She took it back and wedged it into the locking mechanism, then slid the door to. At first it wouldn't close, but then it snapped shut with a metallic crunch.

The moment he heard the sound, he could have kicked himself for being so stupid. How were they supposed to know if it was blocked? They couldn't open it to check. Seeing the way she shrugged, he guessed she realised too.

"We should go," she said.

"I would like to stay and listen."

"Let's get the children to safety first."

Jon picked up Wenslas who was sprawled on the balcony fast asleep. "I'll go first," he whispered. "Nan, you bring up the rear. No noise," he said to the children. "Not a wink."

The metal stairway wound down in tight, steep curves, leaving little room for Jon with the boy in his arms. Unable to see where he was setting his feet, he examined each step with his toes before putting any weight on it.

When they reached the floor below, he halted and peered around to make sure nobody was about. The men were still busy below, but he heard several car doors slam making him think they must have finished. Glancing up to see if the children were following, he set off down the next leg of the descent.

The going got difficult the moment they entered the jungle. Vines and creepers had wound around the stairs making every step a risk. At one point, just below the first floor, a dense knot of leaves and branches completely blocked the passage. Pushing aside the leaves he could make out the stairs continuing to the ground.

He signalled to Jenna, who was some steps higher, and she squeezed past the children to join him. "Hold Wenslas," he whispered. "I'm going to try to climb round this obstacle."

Unclasping Wenslas's arms that were threaded about his neck, he handed Jenna the sleeping boy and turned to examine the tree. A thick branch had grown between two steps, splaying smaller branches in every direction. He wondered if he could climb out along the branch, but there was too little light to see where it went.

"Why don't you climb down the outside?" Jenna whispered.

He wasn't sure what she meant. He stuck his head out between the railings and looked at the stairs from the outside. She was right. He might climb down that way if he clung to the railing. The ground was not so far away if he fell, but he couldn't be sure what he'd land on. Now was not the time to break a leg.

"Let me try," she said, handing him the boy.

He was going to say it would be dangerous, but she had already slipped between the railings and clinging to the metal, scaled below the branch before clambering back onto the staircase.

"Hand me Wenslas," she whispered, pushing her arms between the branches. The sleeping boy was heavy, but he did as she said and the boy disappeared safely through the branches into her arms.

"Your turn," she said.

He was far too big to slide between the railings. He would have to climb over. The uppermost bar reached his waist. He climbed onto the first railing, using the rungs above for support. Then, balancing on one leg he lifted the other over the top railing and brought it down on the far side. The rusted metal dug into his fingers as he clung to it. His heart hammered in his chest and his hands were slick with sweat.

Taking a deep breath, he repeated the move, till he had both feet on the outside. Shifting his grip to the upper railing he felt downwards with one foot till he reached the end of the step and he was able to lower his whole body. On a level with his eyes, a group of children were anxiously watching his exploits.

"Hold on to the branch to get under it," Jenna suggested.

He glanced round and saw Jenna standing several steps further down. If he swung from the branch as she said, he might be able to get his feet on the next rung. He never suffered from heights, but his arms and legs began to tremble and he felt unable to move.

"It'll be all right," Jenna said. "I'll catch your feet and guide them."

It was now or never. He gripped the bough and, letting it take his weight, he shifted off the edge of the stairs and lowered himself into nothingness. He was relieved to feel Jenna's hand grab his feet and place then on a railing. Once he was sure it would hold, he shifted his hands till he was able to clamber over and join Jenna.

The older children climbed down, finding it considerably easier than him. As for the younger ones, Nan handed them through the branches to Jon.

Once everyone had rounded the obstacle, Jon took the lead on the short distance to the ground. The fire escape didn't stop there. It twisted under ground like a corkscrew digging its roots. He looked around as the children and Nan joined him, wondering which way they should go. The jungle was dense and there were no natural paths.

"Maybe we should go on down," Nan suggested.

The idea filled him with misgiving. The metal had been eaten away by rust and the entrance was barred by a mass of tightly knit creepers and vines. What's more, there might be wild animals down there. But then there would be wild animals where ever they went.

He set about pulling the vines to one side with the help of a couple of children. To his surprise, a large pan of foliage and branches lifted up, revealing a passage. Rather like the one masking the cool room door, he had the uncomfortable feeling this too had been done deliberately. The passage might be frequently used. He glanced around, but found no trace of people entering or leaving the stairs.

"Let's go," he said. He stepped on the first rung only to feel it tremble as if someone were climbing up.

"Hurry up. We are late," a voice rang out below.

Jon turned and waved the children back into the jungle. The group scattered amongst trees and vines. Jon hurried after them and crouched behind a spiky bush with Jenna and Wenslas.

Several men emerged from the stairs and continued on up the fire escape without a pause. Judging from their size and ease of movement the men were fit. That didn't stop them cursing when they encountered the branch. He was afraid they would retrace their steps, but the men rounded the obstacle in no time and were soon out of sight.

60.

The underground corridor was clammy and the smell of
male sweat was unpleasant. Jon should at least have been pleased
he could see where they were going, but the existence of floor
level electric lights made him uneasy. Other people might be
about or those climbing the fire escape could come back. He
came to an abrupt halt and hit himself on the forehead with the
flat of his hand. Several children bumped into him, startled at his
antics. How stupid! By blocking the sliding doors to the pent-
houses they'd locked the men out. They might well already be on
their way down.

"We must hurry," he said over his shoulder and hastened off
down the corridor. What they needed was the cover of darkness.
When an unlit corridor branched off to the right, he took it,
feeling his way with outstretched hands. The walls were slimy,
making him cringe. He wished they hadn't lost Nan's torch. "Has
anyone got a torch?" he asked, more out of disgust and despair
than hopefulness.

"We all have," a little girl replied. "In our bags."

He wasn't sure if he should hug her or strangle her. Why had
no one said? "Can you loan me yours?" he asked.

He heard her riffling inside her backpack, muttering under
her breath as she did. "Here," she said, prodding him with the
torch.

Turning it on, he looked where they were going. A large expanse of water filled a dip in the tunnel floor. Floating on it were
disgusting looking weeds. Here and there a bubble rose to the

surface and popped letting off a stench.

Nan shifted forward to look. "Wrong tunnel," he said with a groan. A wave of despondency washed over him. They would never have time to look for another.

Wenslas had found a large pole which he used as a walking stick. "Can you lend me that?" Nan asked. He handed it over reluctantly. Grasping the pole at its extremity, she sounded the nearest water. It was not deep.

"Carry the little ones," she told the children, "and follow me. Do not stray from my path." Turning to Jon she said, "I'll take the lead. Can you keep an eye on the rear?"

"Come on Wenslas," he said, stretching out his hands.

The boy crossed his arms and pouted. "Want my stick."

"Nan will give it back, later."

Behind him, he could hear the tramp of feet and the muffled sound of voices. "No more time," he muttered as he whisked the boy off his feet and hurried after Nan.

The water was truly disgusting. Covered in a thick coat of slime, it belched gas every time he moved. To his alarm the tunnel slopped down. Not much, but enough to make the water ever deeper. He wanted to warn Nan, but she was too far away. If he didn't hurry, he'd lose them. "Do you have a torch?" he asked Wenslas.

"Not giving it." There was a pout in the boy's voice.

"Take mine," Jenna said. He hadn't realised she was just in front.

Switching it on, he searched the walls in the hope that Nan might have missed a turning. Nothing.

"There," Jenna said. He followed her out-stretched finger and saw a wide tube branching off to the left at chest height. Moving closer, he found it was dry and sloped upwards. "Nan" he called, trying not to be too loud. She couldn't have heard because her light continued to move on.

"I'll fetch her," Jenna said and splashed after the others.

Some minutes later, Nan's light halted and turned back "We can't continue," he told her. "The water is getting deeper."

"Maybe the path will go up," she replied.

"You can't be sure." He pointed to the tube they had found. He was about to say it went up and caught himself. How could he be sure it didn't curve back down further on?

Wenslas, who was still in Jon's arms struggled to get up and peer into the tunnel. Distracted, Jon was caught off guard when the boy gasped the rim of the tube, pulled himself inside and skittered off on all fours till he was out of reach.

"Blast!" Jon said as he struggled to reach the boy.

"Looks like he has made up our minds for us," Nan chuckled and gave Jenna a leg up. Jon in turn cupped his hands so Nan could climb up. Her boots were covered in disgusting slime that clung to his fingers. He tried rub it off on his trouser, but quickly gave up and began handing Nan the smaller children.

The tube did continue to curve upwards till it came out in a thicket with tiny branches sporting long, sharp thorns. As if that wasn't enough, through the tight mesh of branches he spotted three vehicles, the sort designed to cover all types of terrain. With their engines ticking over, they were ready to leave. Several men lounged against the bonnets.

Sticking his head back into the tube he whispered, "Silence. Men are out there." He ducked back outside hoping to catch what was said.

"... Could have been those wild men. We've already had problems with them."

"They wouldn't bother to block the doors."

The clatter of heavy objects falling blotted out the reply.

"Be careful, you idiot," the first man shouted. "That could explode."

"And what about the Centre?

"No problems there. The girls are faring well enough."

"How have they reacted to the new girl?"

Jon thought of Sam, wondering where he could be. He chided himself for not thinking of his son more often. Then, like an unwelcome visitor, that girl crept into his mind, the one who had taken over Sam. Surely she couldn't be one of those girls. Sam could never be mistaken for a girl.

"According to our informant, there's to be a trial."

"A trial?"

A trial! Jon shuddered at the thought. He had witnessed enough summary trials conducted by the Food Police to know what horrors were possible. He strained to hear more, but the words were smashed to smithereens by the slamming of doors and the revving of engines. The men had no qualms about being heard. Anyone for miles around would know they were there. When the cars finally sped off, they left behind a stunned silence and a swathe of questions.

61.

Someone must have waxed the floor. Not only does it give off a comforting golden glow in the early morning light, but the smell of beeswax hangs sweet in the air. Row upon row of empty benches await the trial, with me, alone, on a stool facing them. My ankles are bound by chains just below a platform on which a table and three chairs are set.

I close my eyes, rest my elbows on my knees and cradle my head on my hands. I would willingly drift off, but my hand hurts and my back aches. I wish I could lean against a wall.

"We could make this easier for you," a voice says.

I open my eyes to find Gwen standing in front of me, her feet apart, her hands on her hips. The smile on her lips is meant to appear friendly, but it is frankly predatory, like a wild animal baring its teeth.

"I'm sure you don't intend to cause trouble," she continues, taking a step closer, too close. She cups a hand under my chin, forcing me to look into her grey eyes.

:: if she thinks she can intimidate you, she's got it wrong

She is frightening. Look at those tense lines to either side of her mouth. Can't you see the will to do harm? And what of that glow of pleasure around her eyes? She is probably imagining inflicting pain.

:: sure - but in the depth of her eyes there is fear and denial

I hold her stare till she digs her fingernails in my skin and I yelp.

She shoves my head to one side saying, "All you have to do is say you were mistaken and you will obey us in the future."

:: it is as easy as that - bow down to the queen and kiss her painted toenails

"That would make sense," I say, not wanting to provoke. "And what would happen then?"

"You would still be punished. Of course. But not so much."

"I see."

"I knew we'd come to an understanding." She turns as if to leave.

"The only problem," I say, "is that I have done nothing wrong."

Halting, she grins at me, a grin that is midway to a sneer. "You exist. That's wrong enough." I cringe. There is a wildness in her twisted face that is alarming.

:: she's completely bonkers

Shh, Sam. I need to think.

"I am who and what I am, just like you are all you are."

She hangs suspended a moment, maybe unsure how to react.

"And I don't like who you are," she says, sending a spray of spittle over my face as she forces out each word.

"You don't like who you are," I reply, emphasising the word 'you' as I wipe my face dry.

Her hand flies so fast I have no time to duck. Her whole weight is behind the blow. It connects with my face making a terrible scrunching sound that rattles my teeth and resonates through my head. I cry out as I fly off the stool and smash into the podium.

I lie in a heap, sobbing, as I fade in an out of consciousness to the pattering of feet and the scraping of benches. The girls have arrived. Muted conversations peter out, leaving way to a collective in-held breath.

"Girls," Gwen says, raising her voice as if that were necessary. "We are here because something serious has happened."

"A new girl," Marge continues. There's a pause while I suppose she points at me. "She has not been properly received amongst us, yet she has already been plotting to disrupt our life. You don't want that, do you?"

A feeble chorus of noes echoes around the room.

"Sorry? Did someone say something?" Marge asks, her tone threatening.

There's an embarrassed silence as if no one knows what to answer. Marge repeats her question. "We don't want someone like her disrupting our life, do we?"

"No, Marge," the girls reply as one.

:: this is disgusting - there will be no real trial - no accusation - no defence - just a judgement and above all a sentence

There's a taste of blood in my mouth. I must have bitten myself when she hit me. I'm lucky she didn't break my teeth. My head is throbbing where it smashed into the podium and I ache all over. I can't go through with this. It was a silly idea. What was I thinking?

:: if you don't stand up and defend yourself, I will wrench control from you and do it for you

You're sweet, Sam, but you know you can't. I wish Yarrow were here to defend me.

:: he's not - you've got to do this on your own

I spit a mouthful of blood onto the floor, take a deep breath and heave myself up onto all fours.

"This miserable specimen," Celine goes on, "this apology for a girl, needs to be punished severely for what she has done."

Using the stool for lever, I stagger to my feet and sway trying to focus my eyes. Out of the blur I see row upon row of girls. As my sight clears, some have tears in their eyes, others look terrified, some look stern and unforgiving.

"I have done nothing," I say, my voice sounding weak. I cough, hoping to clear my throat. "Since I came here…"

"We are not interested in what you have to say," Gwen says. "I say we lash her to a post in the jungle and leave her there for good."

One of the girls gasps. I search for the source and find Tia, her hand over her mouth. Several other girls look shocked.

"I am not afraid of the jungle," I say, hoping Yarrow will be there to protect me.

"Defiant words," Gwen says, grinning as if she is about to win first prize in a beauty contest. "Or stupid ones."

"It is not your judgement that counts," I begin. "But that of all the girls in this room."

"Silence!" Gwen calls out.

"Let her speak," Marge counters. "This could be interesting."

This is the opening I need. I take a deep breath and look at the girls closest to me on the benches. Their eyes are all fixed on me. But what should I say. I have no idea. I stand silent for a long moment, my mind blank.

"She's got nothing to say," Gwen taunts.

"Shhh," Marge says.

"What is the most important thing in life?" I ask, no idea where this is leading.

:: being true to yourself

"Being true to yourself," I echo.

"What does that mean?" Marge asks.

:: speaking out when things are not right - not being cowered by other people's opinions

I echo Sam's words, adding, "When a new girl arrives here, do you really want to ignore her? Maybe she brings news from the outside world. Maybe she knows things you do not. Who knows, maybe she is destined to be your friend, to help you in a difficult moment."

"Enough of this rubbish," Gwen says, taking a step in my direction, her hand raised. Marge holds her back, forcing her to be seated again.

"When a new girl arrives, do you think it is right to lock her out in the jungle at night? Do you think it is right to hit her and knock her to the ground when she cannot defend herself? Do you think it is right to chain her up and put her on trial for wanting life to be better? Yes I want change. I admit it. Is that a crime? If life here is like I have lived it these last hours, then of course I want it to change. Wouldn't you?"

I pause to look at the girls. I am far from convincing all of them, but a few are on my side or at least are having doubts.

"This place could be a real chance for each of us." I think of Tia and how she was at her parents' home and the promises that woman made. "We all have our talents just as we all have our difficulties. What we need is a place where we can count on each other. We don't need fear. We don't need judgement and even less punishment."

I glance at Gwen whose face is dark with rage. She looks ready for murder. "Even those people who try to get their way by violence have talents that are worth developing just as much as they have difficulties with which they need help."

She jumps to her feet and, staving off Marge's attempts to restrain her, flings herself at me with a blood curdling cry, her fists clenched. I brace myself for the blow, but it never comes. Several of the larger girls in the front row move to protect me. Others grab Gwen by the shoulders and are obliged to tackle her to the ground as she sets about anybody within range. She continues to shout abuse even with several girls sitting on top of her and others holding her arms down, not all of them very kindly.

"Don't hurt her," I say. "We all have our problems."

"You upstart bastard!" she shouts at me. "I'll get you yet."

Her tirade only stops when someone shoves a handkerchief in her mouth.

:: so much for book learners being civilised

Not all who read avidly are like her, Sam.

62.

Who would have thought a voice in my head could wake me up?
:: let me remind you this is my body and you are the voice
Let's not start that again. You still woke me.
:: and about time - you've been asleep for over twenty four hours
Amazing. No wonder my stomach feels like it has shrivelled up.
"Ah. You're awake," Tia says, removing the hand she had laid on my shoulder. "I was beginning to worry you might never wake." She offers me a glass of water which I gulp down.
"You hungry?" she asks.
"Bring on the food before I gobble you up."
She giggles, making a show of shifting further away.
"You got the strength to come down to the canteen?" she asks, getting to her feet.
I swing my legs out of bed and place my feet on the ground. I have been sleeping in my uniform which is all scrunched up and doesn't smell so good.
:: be thankful no one got the clever idea of undressing you - pretty pickle that would have been
Sam is right. Imagine Tia discovering my boyish body. She would be horrified or possibly disgusted. Or maybe she would be furious, feeling I'd cheated her. How could I possibly explain I am a girl despite the boy's body? It's not a problem I've been confronted with before.
"Don't you have another uniform for me?" I ask, wrinkling up my nose, "I can't go down dressed like this."

"Sure you can. You look sweet whatever you wear." Tia blushes and looks away.

:: maybe if she finds out you are really a boy that would suit her fine

Shut up, Sam. I feel my face heating and run a hand over my cheeks, hoping she doesn't notice. The last thing I need is to have her misconstrue my embarassment as interest.

I get to my feet, meaning to fetch a new uniform, but my legs buckle under me and I plop down on the bed.

"How thoughtless of me," Tia says, straightening my pillow and helping me lie down. "I'll fetch you a tray of food. Would breakfast do?"

"Maybe you should bring two," I say, grinning.

Tia bursts out laughing and heads for the door.

:: you've made a conquest - she is completely besotted

You love exaggerating. I cup my sore hand in the palm of my good hand. The swelling has gone down, but the skin is still bright red around the bites. Yarrow will have to bring me some more of his magic. I close my eyes and drift off to sleep, imagining my fingers running through his fur.

I am awoken by a clatter announcing Tia's arrival. Sounds like she has dropped a knife or a fork. She enters backwards, pushing the door open with her hip, then turns to reveal a tray on which she carries a plate of bacon and eggs and grilled tomatoes. There's buttered toast too, and jam. And a cup of tea. It all smells so good, I think I might be dribbling. Folded under her arm, she is also carrying a clean blouse and skirt.

"Everyone wants to talk to you," she says as she places the tray at the end of my bed. "I told them you're still exhausted."

I look longingly at the food, but Tia has other plans. She unfolds the blouse and holds it up for me to see. "Let me take your jacket off," she says. Not waiting for permission, she undoes the buttons and pulls the sleeves over my hands. Her fingers brush my chest, leaving Sam deeply disturbed. It troubles me too. Shaking out the jacket she hangs it over the back of the chair and returns for the blouse.

:: for godsake, stop her before she has me completely naked

"I don't like people seeing my body," I say, half choking on the words. "Turn round and don't peek."

"Whatever for? We are both girls. It's not as if I were a boy." My face must be bright red. "Please. Humour me."

She turns her back with a huff and grumbles about how unbearably prude I am.

I make the most of her turned back to slip out of the skirt and pull on the new one.

"Finished," I say, fumbling to button up the skirt.

I see her move to help, but I hold up an imperative hand to stop her causing her to scowl.

"Can I eat now?" I ask. "Or am I to be punished for being, what was it, prude?"

She hands me the tray, a faint smile on her lips.

I fork a rasher of bacon into my mouth and chew. It's delicious, I shovel a whole fried egg in before I've finished chewing.

"Take it easy," she says.

I put down my fork which is already loaded up with two bacon rashers and finish munching. "Tell me," I ask, before my mouth is completely empty, "who cooks all this delicious food?"

"We do."

"How does that work?"

"We have a roster. One of the older girls is in charge."

I scoop up the two rashers of bacon and fold them into my mouth with a little push of my finger which I suck clean. As I chew Tia explains that working in the kitchen taught her to cook. Where she had been slouching on the bedside, she now sits up, proud of her achievements. "All the girls know how to cook."

"But where does the food come from?"

"We leave a written shopping list in the gate house and a few days later, most of what we asked for is waiting for us."

I remain silent a long moment wondering who supplies the food. My mind turns to the girls who ran this place. "What will happen to Gwen?" I ask.

"She locked in her room. We wanted to talk to you before

deciding what to do."

:: you're the boss
Cut it out, Sam.
"What do you think?" I ask.

"She tried to kill you" she replies, tapping her curved index finger on her head. "Surely she should be punished or at least locked away."

"But if we punish her, doesn't that make us like her?"

Tia frowns. "How else can we stop her doing it again?"

Indeed. I have no idea.

There's a knock at the door and tall, slim girl I've never seen before comes inside. She nods to me by way of greeting and blurts out, "Gwen has escaped."

"How did she manage that?" Tia asks. "Her door was locked."

"Climbed out her window onto the roof."

"Have you searched the grounds?" I ask.

The girl looks at me, surprised, as if she hadn't expected me to talk.

"Someone saw her get in a car by the gate house. Marge and Celine were with her. They drove off."

:: how could they possibly know she wanted to get away?
I know far too little, Sam. Things don't make sense.
"What's your name?" I ask.

"Rachel."

"We need to talk, Rachel," I say. "It is probably too soon to talk to all the girls. Maybe you and Tia can get together a smaller group of girls, those you think are important."

"Where should we meet?" Tia asks.

I glance about the room. At some time there must have been several beds judging from the marks on the floor. Mine is the only one left. That and a dresser and a chair is all the furniture there is. With a few extra chairs we could easily accommodate such a group around my bed. "Couldn't we meet here?" I ask, not feeling up to moving.

The pair look doubtful. "Bring in some chairs," I suggest.

While they hurry off to fetch people, I set about finishing my breakfast. It is cold and I have a sinking feeling in my stomach. I'm not sure if it is Gwen escaping or me having eaten too much. Whatever, I'm still hungry.

I'm licking my fingers when a knock comes at the door and a stream of girls enter, some carrying chairs, others blankets. All nod in greeting, but keep a timid distance, settling as far away as possible. Their silence is unnerving. Why are they so intimidated? As more and more enter, the late arrivals have no choice but to sit on the floor around my bed.

When Tia and Rachel return, taking up the only remaining place in the room on the bed next to me, there must be over twenty girls packed in the room. All eyes are fixed on me, expectant.

:: now what, Saviour girl?

63.

The girls sit in their immaculate uniforms, shoulder pressed against shoulder, hip against hip, here a head leaned on a shoulder, there an arm draped over a knee. Some are seated on chairs, leaning forward, expectant, others lounge on the floor, while Tia and Rachel are next to me on my bed, vigilant, their backs against the wall.

A timid knock sounds at the door and all heads turn to look as a tiny face peers in.

"Can I come too," a little girl asks.

"Not now, Pri," one of the girls near the door says. "We'll tell you all about it later."

The girl, who looks crest fallen, glances pleadingly in my direction.

"Come in Pri," I say. "We've saved a small place next to me."

A bright smile lights up Pri's face as she threads her way amid complaints from those who have to squash aside to let her by. When she is settled, I turn to the assembled girls and look round the room wondering where to start. All eyes are focussed on me.

"Let's begin from the beginning. How did all this start?"

Many eyes turn to a tall bespectacled girl who rakes her long slender fingers through a mop of brown hair. Older than most, she is sitting on the floor, squashed in a corner, half hidden by two girls her age that flank her.

:: she cringes - I bet she hates being the centre of attention

"What's your name?" I ask.

"Rebecca." She speaks so quietly, I have to strain to hear. "But most people call me Becky."

"You know the answer to my question, Becky?"

"Because I was here at the beginning."

"Tell us."

"I may have been here at the beginning, but I wasn't the first. Three girls were already here."

:: I bet I know who they were

"Marge, Gwen and Celine were waiting for me."

A murmur ripples through the room at the mention of their names. Becky cringes, so much so that one of the girls next to her puts an arm round her shoulder to comfort her.

"What happened, Becky?"

"They were terrible," she says, tears in her eyes. "They knew that other girls would follow, so they tried their ideas on me. They were not so sure of themselves back then and rather clumsy. I have the marks of their doubts and mistakes on my back."

She breaks down and begins to sob. Several girls hug her.

"So what happened then?" I ask everyone.

"We started arriving," a chubby girl says, her round face red as if she has seen too much sun.

:: she looks like she was roasted in an oven

"What's your name?" I ask.

"Eileen, but most people call me Cook."

"So you are responsible for all this delicious food?"

"Not just me. All the girls help." She waves a podgy hand over the assembled group.

"So Eileen, what happened when more girls came?"

"The Terrible Three divided us into rooms and gave us tasks. I was lucky in the kitchens. They wanted nothing to do with cooking. It was below them. Others were not so lucky. They decided everything. I suspect whoever put us here made them change, because later they let us have more say in what happened. Although that didn't stop them hurting those they didn't like."

"But why are you all here?" I ask. "Tia told me she had difficulties with her parents. What about you?"

As several start talking at once, I point to one indicating she should speak. Most have had problems with their parents, with other children or with teachers at school. They have all been promised the Centre is where they can flourish. Despite complaints about the violence of the Terrible Three, almost all say they have learnt a lot and enjoy working with other girls on projects.

"So who are these men that fetched Marge and the others?" A sea of blank faces stares back at me.

"Presumably Marge and company knew," I say, thinking out loud. "Those girls seemed to have been in contact with these men. How else would the men know to come and fetch them?"

:: it's odd that no one knew anything about these men and what they were up to

"I heard them talking," Pri says. "I think they had a telephone or a radio."

"Has anyone searched their room?" I ask. "Or anywhere else they used to meet."

Judging from the embarrassed looks, nobody had thought of it.

:: I doubt they'll have left any evidence behind

"Who will go?" I ask.

Rachel stands, saying "I'll go, but not alone. That place gives me the creeps." Eileen volunteers. "I'll come," Pri says, patting my knee by way of farewell as she scrambles off the bed.

:: another follower there

One of the best.

"Now the three have gone, are those men going to march in?" a girl with her hair in pigtails asks.

"What's your name?" I ask.

"Hanna."

"Well Hanna, I have no idea." Maybe we should plan to get the girls to shelter. "Are there secret ways out of here?"

"If there are," Hanna says, "I bet those men know about them."

"Not all of them," Tia says. Everyone turns to look at her.

Shifting forward to the edge of the bed, she adds, "Rachel and I, and a couple of other girls, had a project about a man called Guy Fawkes. He dug his way under parliament in the hope of blowing it up. Well we dug our own tunnel, in secret…"

"Amazing!" someone says.

"However did you get away with that," another girl asks.

"We did most of the work when the Three were plotting."

:: these girls are really amazing - who would have thought they could do such things

I want to remind Sam how resourceful girls are, but now is not the time.

"How far did you get?" I ask.

"We were lucky. Our tunnel met up with a much older one that had collapsed. We were able to shore it up. We haven't had time to explore it very far, but I reckon it goes well beyond the limits of the grounds."

Rachel, Eileen and Pri return. Once they squeeze back into the room and shut the door, Rachel says, "They have taken everything with them."

"Not everything," Pri says. "I found this under a bed." She hands me a small metal box. There is a dial on the front, a cluster of small holes on one side and a couple of buttons on the other side. I hand it to Tia who then passes it on and it makes the rounds of the room.

:: it's a two-way radio - the sort soldiers and the police use

All of a sudden there's a crackling sound and a male voice says, "Yes. Who's there?"

Silence fills the room. I motion for the girls to hand it to me, wondering how we can turn it off. "Answer, goddamnit!"

:: the red button - press it

I do as Sam says and the crackling ceases.

"Well now we know," Tia.

:: and they know too

64.

Jon shivered and pulled his jacket collar tight about his neck. A stiff breeze had got up sending dried leaves swirling around their feet. Several of the younger children were huddled in the arms of older children, whining despite the girls' efforts to placate them. To think they'd locked themselves out of the penthouse. It had never occurred to him they might want to return.

The jungle bristled with unseen life. The undergrowth stirred, branches cracked amid grunts and growls, there were even distant howls and the shrieks of night birds. Despite the children's torches, the thought of travelling in the dark made him shudder. But they couldn't stay outside with so many children. He took a hesitant step forward, unsure where to start.

He turned to Nan and said, "I'm going to look for a place to sleep."

"I'd prefer us to stick together," she replied. "Why don't we follow the track. This was probably once a road and there are sure to be buildings. It would be easier going. I can't see us forcing a passage through the jungle."

The road had long since given up its fight. The asphalt had been wrenched apart by knotted roots and grasses and creepers forced their way through the many cracks, pushing upwards and outwards till the road had almost slipped from memory. Had it not been for the recent passage of vehicles, Jon and kids would have made little headway. As it was, guided by a couple of torches, they wended their way along the narrow tyre tracks, keeping a constant eye out for returning vehicles.

Here and there the tip of a crumbling wall surged from the jungle, a gaunt reminder that all manner of ordinary people had once walked those streets oblivious to what would soon befall them. It was astounding the hotel had survived so well. Presumably the men made sure that parts remained intact. Jon had spotted no other building that had been so lucky.

Pushing forward along the two parallel channels between the grasses, they were forced to pause whenever one of the children could go no further. Nan frequently had to tend to cuts or stings. After nearly an hour, they came to a crossroads, discernible only by a widening of the ways.

Nan looked questioningly at him, the lines of her face distorted by the dancing torch light. He and Nan scoured the ground, moving in ever increasing circles, but the tracks gave no indication which way to chose. They pointed their torches down each track, but the feeble beams met only darkness.

"If we flattened the grass, maybe we could stay here," Jenna said, when they returned. She began stomping on a tuft of grass with the help of Wenslas. Jon had to silence the boy who let out a whop of delight.

"There is no food or water here," Jon said. "The supplies we brought from the hotel won't last very long." He was going to suggest they pause to snack, but what if creatures were attracted by the smell of food.

Nan came to his side and laid a head a moment on his shoulder. "I'm tired," she whispered.

So was he, but he didn't want to admit to it. "Where now?" he asked, pulling free of her.

"There," Nan said, pointing along a vague trail to the right.

He wonder why she chose that way. What did it matter? The further they went, the more spaced out the buildings were. He had to admit, although it made little sense when all was jungle, they were clearly heading out into the countryside.

"Look," she continued, waving her torch beam in that direction. "It's wilder. Maybe there's less chance of bumping into a vehicle."

He didn't have the heart to say that there was also less chance of finding a place to stay.

Gathering up the children, they prepared to set off. Jon circled the clearing, probing the grasses with his torch to make sure no one was left behind. Half concealed by a small bush at the very limit of the flattened area, he discovered Wenslas fast asleep curled up in the arms of Jenna who was also asleep.

He patted her on the shoulder, hoping not to startle her, but she just turned over and cuddled closer to the little boy. Jon had to shake the girl for her to wake.

"What?" was all she said as she rubbed her eyes.

"Time to go," he replied, lifting the boy into his arms and offering Jenna his free hand to help her up.

Wild, Nan had said. She was right. The track proved to be largely overgrown and Jon was forced to hand Wenslas to Jenna and go up front to fray a path between the grasses and bushes. Clearly vehicles went that way much less often. In the back of his mind he had visions of the path petering out. He tried to push the idea away, but it prodded him with stubborn insistence.

The children had long since gone beyond their limits. Several stumbled and fell and Nan had no remedies left to treat the minor cuts and stings that became more frequent. They wouldn't be able to travel much further. The whole endeavour had been absurd. The jungle could continue unabated and untamed for miles. Who were they to challenge it?

At one point the creepers had surged forward, forming a dense wall across the whole path. He had to force them apart to make any progress. The branches clawed at his clothes as he squeezed through narrow gaps. Several times he felt the sharp sting of a thorn digging into his skin, leaving a bloody gash as it did. He struggled on, beyond caring. It was then that he stumbled out onto a neatly kept road lined with round stones painted white. It was like stepping into another world. The sight was so incongruous he sank to his knees, unable to bear the thought. Behind him, their whole group popped out of the jungle as if rejected. They hung suspended, mouths open, staring at the road and the high gate that stood in front of them.

Nan helped him to his feet and they edged towards the gate. Just beyond the fence, which ran into the dark to either side, there was a small gatehouse that appeared empty. On the gate and at several places along the fence were signs depicting a jagged piece of lightening.

"It's electric," he called out. "Don't anyone touch the fence or the gate."

In the distance he could just make out lights. There must be a house inside the grounds, but it seemed a long way off. As he looked, several lights flickered on, indicating a wide avenue that curved through a plush lawn to the house. He thought he saw someone move out onto a porch, but it was difficult to tell.

A rattling sound brought his attention back to the gate where he saw Wenslas shaking the metal structure with all his little force. Jon's heart skipped a beat, expecting to see the boy jerk away, electrocuted.

65.

A young girl bursts into the room, her hair awry, her chest heaving as she struggles to catch her breath. Several seated close to the door swear as she looses her balance and topples on top of them. "Watch what you are doing, idiot!" Several swipe at her.

"Stop that," I say, getting to my feet, only to sit down my head spinning, as Tia's waiting arms catch me.

"What the matter, Saskia?" Tia asks.

Saskia rights herself and blurts out, "People at the gate." Several girls gasp.

"It's those men," Becky cries out, struggling to her feet.

Panic ripples through the room as girls strive to get up.

:: do something before they stampede - someone will get hurt and I don't want it to be me

"Sit down," I say, putting power behind my words. Most people halt and turn to look at me, uncertain what to do, but Becky continues to battle towards the door.

"Becky," I say, my voice sharp. "Becky, listen."

She halts, but only because those people around her heed my words and grab her by the arm, none too kindly. Some of the fight must have gone out of her, because she struggles only half-heartedly to get free.

"Becky, we do not know who this is. If it is who you fear, we will make sure that everyone gets to the tunnels and safety…" I say, not at all sure it would be feasible. I have terrible visions of a tangle of girls desperately struggling to force their way into an ever narrowing tunnel.

"It's not men in cars," Saskia says, raising her voice to be heard. "It's a crowd. Children mostly. They rattled the gates."

"Nobody got electrocuted?" Rachel asks, alarmed.

"No. The moment I saw children I turned the gate off."

"Are you sure there are no men with them?" Eileen asks.

"There might have been one," Saskia says. "I dunno. It's night and hard to see, even with the lights of the Centre."

Looking to Tia for support, I get to my feet. "Let's go and welcome these people." The girls, who are now standing, squeeze to the side, leaving me a narrow path between them. With Tia holding my arm and Pri's arm about my waist I head in measured paces for the door.

:: you'd make a successful career as a handicapped princess

You are always so helpful, Sam.

News must have spread, or maybe the other girls were already massing in the corridor awaiting the end of our meeting, for the whole school greets me and falls in behind as I make my way along the corridor to the main entrance.

:: your court is assembled

I'm not sure if Sam is ironic or taken aback by my success. I am certainly surprised. That everyone should look up to me makes me uncomfortable

"Has anyone got the keys?" I ask, remembering how Celine locked us out.

"I have," Saskia says, rattling a bunch as proof.

How different the main hall looks through its half open door now that I have the whole school following me and not in front about to judge me. Saskia holds the front door open and Tia and Pri help me down the steps. My legs are trembling and I am not sure I can make it. I could send a delegation and wait in the comfort of the house, but it seems important to go.

I pause at the foot of the steps to gather my strength, leaning on Tia's shoulder. I glance over her shoulder to see the girls streaming out. The younger ones look tired, but most are alight with excitement.

The scrunch of wheels on gravel has everyone turning to see

Saskia pushing a wheelchair at breakneck speed. With a flourish she brings it to a halt and bows like a prince to her queen. Some girls, who are slowly coming down the steps, laugh, while others cheer.

It is a relief to have the weight off my legs. I let Saskia push me, flanked by Tia and Pri. The other girls form a joyous procession, spreading out to fill the width of the drive as they flow along behind. Their chatter and the crunch of their feet on the gravel are strangely reassuring. Now that I no longer have to concentrate on avoiding falling, I look ahead, making out a group of people clustered on the far side of the gate.

The closer we get, the more perplexed I get. Almost all the group are children and many are very young. What could such a group be doing at night wandering in the jungle? There do seem to be a couple of adults accompanying them, but they are bent over a child and I can't see them properly.

:: maybe they are trying to hide and will jump out when we open the gate

That seems unlikely, Sam.

When we are within a short distance of the gate, Saskia pulls on the brake of the wheelchair and I get to my feet with Pri and Tia holding my arms.

"What do you want?" I ask, raising my voice.

"Shelter and help," a woman, one of the two adults, calls out. I am wary about letting them in as long as the adults remain concealed.

"Why don't you show yourself?"

"We are not hiding. It is just that one of the children is gravely ill," she replies. Her voice is familiar, but I can't place it.

:: it's a trap - don't let them in

I take a step forward with my two helpers accompanying me. "What's the matter with it?"

"A bite. A snake or a spider probably," the woman says, sounding annoyed at the delay. "For god-sake, let us in. We have no antidote and he's going to die."

She sounds exhausted and at her wits' end. As she speaks, I

remember who that voice belongs to. "Nan?" I ask, hesitating. Could it really be her?

The woman stands and faces me. "Sami?" she asks, the name spoken with joy and disbelief.

I hurry forward, calling out to Saskia. "Open the gate and get them inside."

As Saskia unlocks the gate, I ask Tia, "Have we got any medical supplies?"

"Yes. In the infirmary," she replies. "Should I run and fetch something?"

"No. We'll put the boy in the wheelchair and hurry him to the house."

Looking up I see the gate is open and a tall man is moving forward, a young boy in his arms. In a flash, both Sam and I recognise him at the same moment.

:: dad - my daddy

Sam's cry is so poignant that tears spring to my eyes.

"Jon," both Sam and I cry out together.

Hearing his name, Jon halts mid-stride, a perplexed look on his face. What must he think discovering his son dressed as a girl, surrounded by a crowd of girls?

"Sam?" he asks, his voice trembling and uncertain.

"Sami," I reply then send Tia, Pri and some of the elder girls to help the little ones. I make my way in Jon's direction, moving amongst the children, laying a hand on each to welcome and reassure them. As I do, a strange feeling comes over me. My legs no longer tremble and I feel my strength flowing back. When I reach Jon, who has settled the boy in the wheelchair, I feel like I could run back to the Centre.

"Welcome to our school, Jon," I say and stretch forward to lay a hand on his arm. I sense him hesitate. It is as if he can't decide whether to give in or to cringe and pull back. Finally, unmoving, he lets my hand come to rest on his forearm. When I pull him into a hug, he doesn't resist, but remains stiff, despite a sigh that escapes his lips.

66.

"I'm Pri," the little girl said with a self-assurance Nan found admirable in one so young. "Follow me. I'll show you where your group will sleep."

They were standing in the entrance hall of the building the girls called the Centre. It was a sprawling construction that must once have been a manor belonging to a rich family, but, judging from what she could see, subsequent occupants had made many changes and additions, leaving it a muddle of conflicting styles. There was a time when she would have sounded out its growth and development to understand the successive groups that had lived there. But what intrigued her most was what this group of girls, all spick and span in their uniforms, was doing in such an enclave of order in the middle of the wilderness.

Off down a side corridor heading away from the entrance, a cluster of girls were balancing piles of bedclothes in their arms. Pri beckoned Nan to follow. Having reached the end of the corridor, the girls laboured up a spiral staircase under their burdens. Nan followed, her group of refugees traipsing after. Laughter and giggling greeted them as they stepped out onto the landing at the top. Other girls were dragging mattresses across a narrow corridor into an unused dormitory. Such merriment had Nan wondering how these girls managed to create this haven of good humour when all around was hate and disease and killing.

"Sleeping quarters for the new arrivals," Pri said, shooing away one of the boys that stepped forward to offer help with the mattresses.

Pri then linked arms with two of the younger Baxter girls and led them off down the corridor. Returning with towels, flannels and soap, she handed them to Jenna, who glanced at Nan, as if to ask, who is this girl? Is she real?

"You lot can't have eaten for ages," Pri said. "Eileen, our head cook, has gone to round up her aides. I heard she's making vegetable broth. I hope so. She makes the best soup I've ever tasted." She ran her tongue over her lips. "I'm ravenous after all these adventures. Bet you are too, Saskia.

"You're always hungry," Saskia said. Nan recognised her as the one who had unlocked the gate. "I'm borrowing a couple of your girls," she said. "We'll get you some nightshirts sorted out." She paused and scratched her head. "Not sure what we'll do about them, though," she added, pointing to the group of boys huddled in a corner.

An animated conversation broke out between the girls of the Centre about what to do with the boys. Although they were standing nearby, looking intimidated by so many unknown girls, no one thought to involve them in the discussion. Glancing frequently in their direction, several girls were in favour of putting them in a separate room, especially those boys who were older. Some even suggested locking them in. Nan had to laugh.

"I don't think they'll do you any harm," she said, grinning. "Anyway, they have been living together for years," she said. "I don't see why they should be separated just because this is an all girls school."

She glanced around, suddenly aware of something she hadn't noticed before. Where were the adults? How odd. She hadn't seen a single one. Only girls. Surely there had to be teachers or a matron or a nurse or a cleaning lady. Pri had mentioned one of the girls doing the cooking. Another question to ask Sami. Nan was eager to be at the girl's side again. She hadn't realised how much she missed Sami. And she wanted to learn how Sami had ended up in such a place, but first she had to make sure the Baxter refugees were settled in.

A bell rang out from below, dull and mellow, an inviting

sound. Pri grinned. "Food," she said, dropping the pile of pillows she was carrying. So much for order and discipline. "Come on everybody," Pri called out over her shoulder as she made a beeline for the stairs. "We can finish that later."

The dining hall was large enough to house all the girls as well as the children from Baxter. Uniformed girls were standing in an orderly queue at a hatch waiting to collect their soup. They chattered quietly amongst themselves. The moment they saw the Baxter children arrive, several girls broke away and came to greet them. The children were ushered to a couple of tables, then the girls went to fetch them soup. Bread and cheese had been laid out in neat rows of tables. Nan could see no trace of dust or dirt. The reaction of the girls and the orderliness of the whole scene had Nan wondering again about the absence of adults. Was this some strange pedagogical experiment in which children were forced to govern themselves?

Nan caught sight of Sami sitting at a table on the far side of the room, surrounded by a group of girls who were talking animatedly to her. She seemed a lot thinner and there were dark shadows under her eyes, but despite her weariness she listened attentively to each girl. Seeing Nan arrive, Sami beckoned.

As she wove her way between the tables, Nan glanced around for Jon. He was nowhere to be seen. She had been so caught up looking after the children she hadn't once thought about Wenslas.

"Where's Jon? And how is Wenslas?" she asked as one of the girls shifted to free her a place next to Sami. Nan straddled the bench and sat down. Sami slid an arm round her waist and laid her head a moment on Nan's shoulder before pulling away and returning to the conversation.

"Jon is with the boy in the infirmary," a girl replied.

"Meet Rachel," Sami said, nodding to the tall, slim girl.

"The boy will be fine," Rachel added. "We found a suitable antidote and he's looking much better already."

"Has Jon had anything to eat?" she asked, getting to her feet.

Sami grasped her sleeve and tugged her back onto the bench.

"Don't worry. That has been taken care of."

A bowl of soup appeared in front of Nan and when she turned to see who had brought it, she discovered Pri. "Thanks," Nan said. "Not eaten yet?"

Pri grinned. "I can wait."

"Hey, Pri. There's a place for you here," a girl said across the table from Nan as she and her neighbour shifted to make room. "Come and eat before you bite someone."

Pri laughed. "I don't bite. What will our guests think? See," she said nodding to Nan, "she's already moving away."

"Only a little," Nan replied with a grin. "But tell me," she began, turning to Sami, "where have all the adults gone?"

67.

Sami frowned. "I don't know," she said, turning her spoon in what little remained of her soup. "I'm not sure anybody knows." She looked around the table, inviting suggestions.

"They just parked us here because they didn't know what to do with us," Saskia, the gatekeeper, said, grinning. She tore off a piece bread and handed it to Sami saying, "For the soup."

Sami dunked the chunk in her soup and spooned it into her mouth.

"I can't believe that," Pri said. "The Food Police never lacked imagination when it came to being nasty. Surely it would have been easier to get rid of us."

The calm with which she envisaged being eliminated had Nan shuddering. The girl was so young. Nan wondered if she really understood what she was talking about. Young children sometimes talked of death as if it could be reversed.

"They have no qualms about making people disappear," Pri added. "My father and my brother were dragged away in the middle of the night, never to return."

"But the people who put us here are not on the side of the Food Police," Tia said. "When that woman came to fetch me, the one who was so strangely dressed, we were attacked by the Food Police and she left them lying unconscious."

"That might have been for show," Pri said, mopping up the last of her soup with a piece of bread.

"Why do that?" Tia asked. "There would be no point."

"So you'd spread false rumours," Pri insisted.

"I heard they were looking for a particular girl," Rachel said. Nan looked up, alert, eager to know what the girls knew.

"Where did you hear that?" Saskia asked.

"Just before I came here, several girls disappeared from my school. Everyone was afraid, but we talked about it, amongst ourselves. The teacher swore it wasn't the police. She should know. All teachers were employed by the police."

Nan thought of her little private school, the one Sam had gone to. The police hadn't employed her, that was for sure. Although they probably kept an eye on her. She studied Sami, trying to gauge whether the girl realised it was probably her they were looking for.

"... Rumour had it that they have been searching for quite a while," Rachel said.

"Why would they want to find a girl?" Jenna asked, causing all heads to turn in her direction. She must have been standing behind Nan for a while, but they were so engrossed nobody noticed. "Surely they had a good reason. It must take a lot of money and effort to create a place like this."

"Meet Jenna," Nan said. Jenna nodded. A couple of girls smiled, others narrowed their eyes, sizing her up as if she might be a potential rival.

"Maybe she was a threat," Rachel mused.

"Yeah. Sure. Can you see any of us being a threat?" Saskia asked. Turning to Pri, she grabbed the little girl and twisted her in a headlock. "Are you a threat, Pri?" she asked the struggling girl as she made a show of pummelling the crown of her head.

"Let go, you brute," Pri spluttered and wriggled free. She got to her feet and shifted out of reach, but not before she punched the older girl on the shoulder saying, "Not with thugs like you around." Her indignation set off a chorus of laughter.

Nan turned to see that all the girls as well as many of the Baxter children were now crowding round their table, forming a tight cordon of captivated faces.

Pri straightened her blazer and raked her fingers through her hair, then, drawing herself up straight, she asked, "Why collect so many if they are only looking for one?"

"Maybe they don't know who she is," was Rachel's answer.

"That would make sense," Pri said. "Like casting your net wide then sifting through what comes up."

"Lots of little fish like you Pri," Saskia said.

Pri shrugged as if Saskia was a desperate case they had to put up with.

Nan had to smile at their antics. There was a rough fondness between the two that was endearing.

"It is not difficult to imagine the Food Police feeling threatened," Sami said. "They are terrified by an old man growing a carrot." There was nervous laughter at Sami's words. "But if they are not the Food Police," Sami said, "who are they? And why would they feel threatened?"

"Maybe it's not the same people," Jenna said.

Once again all heads turned to look at her as if everyone was surprised an outsider had something to say.

"What do you mean?" Pri asked.

"Well maybe those who are looking for this girl are not the same people who put you here."

Faces were thoughtful. It made sense in a twisted sort of way. Putting the girls there would be uncharacteristic of the Food Police, whereas hunting down a possible threat was very much like them.

"Anyone for desert?" a chubby girl with a ruddy, round face asked.

"Oh, yes please, Eileen," Pri said. Everyone burst out laughing and Pri pouted.

Once the slices of chocolate cake had been handed out and the noise died down as they ate, Nan spoke, "Jenna may be right. Those who set you up here don't seem afraid of you. They would never leave you alone if they were. The jungle would be no deterrent if you wanted to escape."

Several girls nodded in agreement, but all were still busy with the chocolate. Some of the younger Baxter kids had the stuff smeared around their mouths. Nan was about to pull out a handkerchief when Eileen produced a wad of paper tissues and handed them around. How thoughtful.

"That makes sense," Pri said licking her fingers clean.

"Your cake was wonderful, Eileen," Sami said. "Your soup too."

"Here, here!" Pri said.

A wave of muffled appreciation rippled around the room which Eileen dismissed with a toss of her hand as she headed back to the kitchens.

"But what will we do when they come?" a tall, bespectacled girl asked, her voice trembling. Nan hadn't noticed her before. The girl, who was biting her nails, was older than most.

"That's a good question, Becky," Sami said, getting to her feet. The girls shifted to make room for her as she walked round the table till she reached Becky's side. Taking one of Becky's hands, she asked, "Why do you think they will come?"

All attention was on Becky, who looked like she prayed she could slink away.

"Not why," Becky said, her voice barely audible despite the silence. "When?"

Sami opened her mouth to answer when a bell rang out in the distance. Sami looked as surprised by the noise as Nan felt. The girl turned to Saskia.

"It's the gate," Saskia said. "The alarm goes off if anyone tampers with it."

The girls at the table got to their feet. Those grouped around the table retreated.

"But I thought it was electrified," Sami said, her face creased with concern.

"It is," Saskia said. "But someone must be trying to get in despite that."

68.

Jon took a deep breath and, leaning his hands on the back of the chair by the Wenslas' bed, shifted some of the weight off his aching legs.

"Why don't you sit down," the girl suggested. Her voice was soft and pleasant. If he closed his eyes he could imagine her as a nurse, except she couldn't be more than twelve or thirteen and she was dressed as a schoolgirl. "This could take a while and you must be tired after carrying him all that way."

Jon sank onto the wooden chair and fixed Wenslas' face, looking for any sign of degradation, a vigil that made him tense. He forced himself to look away. The curtains had been pulled over the single window. Not that there was anything to see. It was night.

His attention turned to the girl who was mixing a poultice on a work surface that ran the length of the wall across from the bed. Above the surface a number of glass fronted cabinets displayed a surprising variety of bottles and jars of all sizes and colours, each carefully labelled in neat script.

"My name's Cilla, by the way," she said as she pulled open one of the cabinets and lifted down a dark brown jar which she unscrewed. Spooning out a dollop of thick yellow cream, she added it to the substances already in the bowl in front of her and mixed with slow movements of her spatula. At the far end of the narrow expanse was a sink and a small, corrugated draining area on which several beakers and a flask lay upturned.

"I'm Jon," he said and turned back to the unconscious

figure. "And this is Wenslas." The boy's face was deathly pale, his breathing shallow and laboured. Despite Cilla's reassuring voice and her quiet, self-assured manner, Jon wonder if he wasn't crazy relinquishing Wenslas to her. She was barely a child. Not that he knew much about healing. That had always been the province of his wife. He'd shied away from it, all the more so since it was her insistence on healing that got her killed.

"Here," Cilla said, proffering him the spatula and a porcelain bowl. "Spread a thin layer around the bites on his leg."

A wave of lassitude swept over him as he took the material, almost as if it sapped his energy. What's more, he was afraid he would do something wrong. He began applying the unguent with trembling fingers. At the smell of the thick gooey mixture, a flood of memories came back. Jane had been quite secretive about her work as if she realised he didn't want to get involved, but he had often seen her mixing potions and ointments in their kitchen.

"My wife was a healer," he said, half to himself. The moment he said it, he wished he hadn't. Why should he share such things with this girl?

"You'll be used to this, then."

"On the contrary. I avoided having anything to do with her work."

"How so?"

"I'm not sure." He'd always told himself he disliked healing because it had got her killed, but his hesitation stemmed from earlier. Much earlier.

"What with the plague, maybe you were afraid of contagion."

Jon wondered what the girl knew of the plague. She could only have been a few years old when it burnt its way through the city. "No. My hesitation goes back before that."

She took the spatula from him and placed it with the bowl in the sink. "Let me bandage that up."

He stood and held up Wenslas' foot so she could wrap the bandage round his leg. Her every gesture was precise. "Where did you learn to heal?"

"I'm not a healer," she said, laughing. "But I'd like to become one, when I'm older. But I didn't answer your question. I learn from books, from practice and by talking to the other girls. And I listen to my instinct."

"Aren't you afraid it will mislead you?" he asked, thinking of several occasions when he had hesitated over an impulse. He dared not follow instinct for fear he'd make a mistake.

She frowned, puzzled at his question. "Instinct is always right," she replied. "It wouldn't be instinct if it weren't."

Her words were like the sun's rays bursting through a cloud. They could have brought him long sought comfort, but instead he felt as if he were seated on another planet and didn't know how to bridge the immense gap between them.

"How long have you lived here?" he asked, seeking refuge in a different topic.

"A couple of years," she said, pulling a face.

"You don't look very happy about it. I would have expected you to be delighted. Where else could you learn so much about healing so young?" He thought of the witch hunt that raged against healers in the city and the ruthless way they were eliminated.

"The Centre wasn't always so welcoming." She grimaced. "There were days when I'd have preferred a nightmare to what happened here. Being in the infirmary shielded me from the worst," she said, waving her arm to encompass the small room and all it contained. "You couldn't begin to imagine the exactions that took place, in the name of education and leadership training, often on a mere whim."

Her words were so full of vitriol that he looked towards the door as if expecting a monster to burst in.

"Don't worry. That's over now. Quite suddenly," she said with a shudder. "It was that new girl Sami that ended it. A real miracle. None of us could have done it. May she be blessed."

Jon cringed. It was as if he spent his time running from one painful subject to another.

"What did she do?" He had to ask, even if he didn't want to know.

"There may not be any adults here." This was news to him. He hadn't noticed. "But this place was run by an iron fist. Three pairs of them in fact. Celine, Gwen, and worst of all, Marge."

"Girls?"

She nodded. "They had been here from the beginning and reigned over this place like it was their realm and we were their serfs. No one dared contradict them." She unbuttoned her shirt sleeve and pulled it up revealing a burn mark on her lower arm.

Jon gasped. "Another girl did that to you?"

"Marge. It was one of her little 'experiments' to see how good a healer I was."

Jon was so engrossed in Cilla's tale, that the sound of a distant bell had him jump. "What's that?" he asked.

"Trouble," Cilla said. "Someone is trying to get into the grounds."

69.

"What do you plan to do?" Nan asks, placing a hand on my arm so I heed her words. The news of people at the gate has thrown the room into turmoil and conversation is difficult over the din. "Somebody has got to harness all this wasted energy," I say close to her ear.

I clap my hands loudly and raise my voice to get everybody's attention. "Listen!" I say. I have to shout the word several times before the girls fall silent. "I will go down with a small group to see who is at the gate. We need to get the rest of you to safety." Turning to Eileen who has removed her apron, I ask, "You know where this tunnel is and where it goes?"

She nods.

"Good. Help Becky round up the girls and show them to the entrance. But don't go in till I give the signal. Nan, you should see that all the Baxter children get to the tunnel. Make sure everyone keeps quiet."

Nan shakes her head. "I would prefer to go with you. Jenna is quite capable of shepherding the children to the tunnel. They will listen to her."

There is no time to argue. "Ok." Turning to Pri, I say, "Go tell Cilla what is happening and see if the boy can be moved to the tunnels."

"And if he can't?"

"Try carrying him on a stretcher."

:: what's going on? - sounds like you are preparing for a siege
Could be. You slept through the excitement. There are people at the gate

and we are going to meet them and see what they want.

"Tia, Rachel, Saskia and Nan come with me. Everyone else go with Becky, Eileen and Jenna." I get up and head for the door, but pause. "Pri?"

"Yes."

"Once everyone is at the tunnel entrance, hurry to join us at the gate. You will be our messenger."

Pri grins then hurries off to the infirmary.

"Should we bring weapons?" Tia asks as we set off down the corridor for the main entrance.

"Weapons?" I ask, wondering what kind of weapons school-girls could possibly have and whether they would be of any use against whoever is at the gate.

:: we've fallen in with a bunch of amazons - I'm glad you are here to protect me

I smile at the idea of protecting Sam. *Of course I will.*

"Several of us are quite good at archery," Tia says.

I hesitate. Weapons might give the wrong signal. If whoever is at the gate is armed they might fire if they see the girls carrying bows and arrows.

:: they are more likely to burst out laughing

"Ok. But hurry." To my surprise all three girls head off in search of their bows and arrows leaving me alone with Nan.

"Good to have you back Nan. You still squabbling with Jon?"

She looks taken aback then laughs. "We've been too busy to argue."

"Is he still mad at me for stealing his Sam?"

:: hey you didn't steal me, you invaded me

"He doesn't talk about it much. I don't know."

"What don't you know?" Jon asks arriving at that moment.

I feel a surge of emotions from Sam at the sight of his Dad. As for me, I feel embarrassed at discussing him behind his back. "How's the boy," I ask.

"Still unconscious. Cilla is organising a stretcher with that little girl."

"Pri," I say.

"Yes, Pri. I promised to accompany them, but I just wanted to check with you first."

He glances at Nan. It is with her that he is checking, not me. I see both respect and complicity in his eyes. I would let her answer, but she turns to me. "That's a good idea, Jon," I say.

He looks at me, although I get the impression he would rather not. Mistrust is etched in his features, but his eyes also betray hurt and longing.

"I don't think we will need to use the tunnel," I say, "but just in case, it would be good if you were there to help. From the little I've seen these girls are well disciplined. But, who knows, maybe the voice of an adult, a man at that, would calm them in a moment of panic."

His face screws up as if I have said something distasteful then he nods and heads off to the infirmary without a word.

"Don't let his reaction bother you," Nan says. "You unwittingly touched a sore spot." She shakes her head as if unsure what to think. "He's been mulling over his uselessness as a man."

:: you women are enough to drive a man nuts - no wonder Dad doesn't know where he is or what he is

Tia and the others arrive at that moment sporting quivers on their backs and a crossbow in their hands.

"Crossbows are better than long bows if we are under attack," Tia says as we head for the main door.

Outside, a cool breeze brings the sweet scents of night flowers from the jungle. The scene would be idyllic if it weren't for the clatter coming from the gate. An occasional spark shoots up as someone triggers the electric fence. Saskia has extinguished the lights on the drive so we can approach unseen. Footsteps on the gravel would give us away, so we walk on the grassy verge.

As we get closer I make out a considerable group milling in front of the gate. By the light of an electric spark I see men throwing branches at the gate. A second spark reveals the haggard nature of them, their filthy clothes, their unkempt beards. "It's the wild men," I whisper.

"Are they armed?" Tia asked.

"Clubs are all I see," I say.

"I know these people," Nan says. "I healed one of their women. Let me talk to them."

I am relieved it is not the men in the cars who drove the three girls away. They are likely to be more formidable foes.

"Are they liable to attack us?" I ask.

Nan hesitates. "I'm not sure."

The moment our little group steps out in full view, a throaty roar goes up and the men surge closer to the fence. Too close for one as a spark arcs from the fence to his outstretched hand. He screams and falls to the ground writhing.

"Stand back!" Nan shouts. "We don't have enough healers to heal you all if you are electrocuted." When the men quieten , Nan calls out, "Borg!" Nothing happens at first, but when she calls the name a second time, a massive brute with a ring threaded through his nose steps forward.

"What do you want disturbing us in our sleep?" Nan asks.

"We got orders to turf you out," the brute replies.

"And who gave you orders?" she asks.

"That ain't none of your business."

70.

A scuffle breaks out behind the wild men, but there are too many massing near the gate to see what is going on. Then the scrum of men parts and a girl elbows her way through dragging a boy after her. Even in the dim light I can see the boy is in a sorry state. His chin and cheeks are covered with an ugly stubble, his clothes are in shreds and he is filthy. How could anyone let themselves go so much?

:: the wild men are hardly a good example

The girl drags him forward by a chain round his waist. With a savage "Whoop", she draws a jagged knife from her belt and holds it under boy's neck.

"If you don't let us in," she shouts, "I'll slit your pretty boy's throat."

I recognise that voice. Where have I heard it before? An image of Harriet springs to mind, the old wise woman seated at her table with sprigs of herbs hanging from the ceiling around her. But this isn't her. The girl can't be much older than me.

:: no but you saw her at Harriet's place - her name is Priscilla

Priscilla. Then the boy must be… Surely not.

:: Mart

"I'll count to ten," Priscilla shouts. Her face twisted into a savage mask, her eyes rove from side to side.

:: she's bonkers - there's no way you can reason with her

"Borg," Nan calls out, "you can't let this girl kill him." She sounds desperate.

Borg shrugs. "Ain't got no sway over her," he says. "She does what she wants."

"You're flippin' right, I do," Priscilla says, tightening her hold on Mart. His head lolls to one side as if he is barely conscious. If the girl lets go, he'll fall to the ground in a heap.

Sam's right. No point in trying to reason with her. I turn to Tia and nod. I hope she understands. "Saskia," I say, "let's open the gate like Priscilla asks."

Saskia lowers her crossbow. Her eyes are full of doubt, but I nod for her to go ahead and she moves towards the gatehouse. "I have to turn the electricity off before I can open the gate," she explains to the girl.

"Turn on the flood lights," I tell her. "So everyone can see."

She throws the switch and lights flicker on around the gate and grow in intensity till we can see almost as well as in daylight.

"Put down that knife," I order.

"Not until the gate is open," Priscilla says. "I don't trust you lot." As she speaks she takes a step forward. Mart must be unconscious because she struggles to hold up his dead weight with just one arm. We move to the gate and Saskia pulls out her bunch of keys.

Priscilla is still a good fifteen feet away as she stumbles and puts out her knife hand to steady herself.

"Now!" I shout.

I hear the twang of bows as Saskia and I scramble back to the gate house. There is a piercing scream as we dive behind the little house for shelter. Then all is silent.

Peering round the wall, I try to make out what is happening. The wild man are standing like zombies, frozen to the spot. By the gate two filthy mounds lie on the road. One is Priscilla, an arrow sticking out of her forehead, another in her chest. The second is Mart, unmoving. And between the two sits a giant dog, eyes ablaze, daring any to come near. My heart leaps for joy as I recognise Yarrow.

"Get the gate open," I scream. Seeing Saskia dropping her crossbow to open the gate, I have visions of the wild men rampaging in and slitting out throats. "No," I call out. "Get your arm ready. You too Tia and Rachel. Let Nan open."

Once the gate is open, I rush to Mart and kneel at his side, cupping a hand over my mouth and nose to ward off the stench. With my other hand, I absently stroke Yarrow who nuzzles my hand away as if to say, you have other things to do. Mart's neck is red with blood. I place a wary hand on his chest and am relieved to feel the gentle rise and fall of his lungs. I run a tentative finger through the blood on his neck, but there is no gapping gash, just a thin line, barely a scratch.

I look through tear-filled eyes to see Nan wary of the dog.

"Yarrow," I say, "this is Nan. She's a friend."

The dog pays her no attention.

Nan kneels next to me as far from Yarrow as possible. "Mart'll be alright," she says, brushing a tear from my cheek. "He just needs a bath and some loving care."

My face heats and I jerk my hand from Mart's chest.

:: I should think so - you're not going to start that again

Sam, please, not now.

"I'm going to see if I can deal with these wild men," Nan says getting to her feet. Every line on her face speaks of tiredness, if not exhaustion.

I scrub my eyes with the back of my hand and look around. Tia, Rachel and Saskia stand by the gate side by side their crossbows trained on the wild men. They make an impressive sight and I am proud of them. But when I look closer I see their features are drawn and their jaws set. Tia looks close to tears.

As for the wild men they stare into space, their mouths fallen open, at a loss what to do. Despite their wild appearance and their churlish ways, the death of Priscilla has shocked them.

Nan is talking to Borg, but I can't hear. It is difficult to gauge his reaction. One minute he cringes, looking frightened, the next he brandishes a fist, defiant. He shakes his head often, causing the ring in his nose to jiggle and his matted hair to flop from side to side, like a crazed puppet losing its stuffing.

Throughout it all, Nan remains calm, her eyes fixed on him. Finally she holds out her hand. Borg looks at it, indecision and wariness written all over his face, then raising a hand he takes hold of hers and shakes it up and down with such awkwardness as if the gesture were long forgotten.

Nan turns to me and beckons. I join her, with Yarrow at my heals. The wild men shy away.

"Borg has agreed to leave us in peace. But there is a problem. He is terrified the men who ordered him to attack us will not only come after us but them too and their wives and children."

I look around. There must be some thirty men. We can't possibly house them in the Centre. The thought of these filthy creatures mixing with the girls has me shuddering.

:: they could build a shanty town down here - surely you can find material for that

I'm not sure we have enough food for everyone.

:: they could forage for food and help protect you

Yarrow bounds off into the jungle as I join Tia and the girls and ask in a whisper, "Do you agree we offer them and their families asylum in return for them helping to protect us?"

All three look frightened, but agree.

"Here's what I suggest," I say returning to Borg. "Some of you fetch your wives and children as quickly as possible. The others stay here and we will help build shelters under the trees. The fence will help protect you and in return we expect you to forage for food and help protect us and the Centre. Do you agree?"

Borg looks at his men before staring off at the Centre, then nods, a broad grin on his face. He stretches out a hand for me to shake, which I do, trying not to retch at the stink that follows him around, then he hurries off to talk to his men.

I turn to Tia and the others. "You can lower your bows." As Tia rests her crossbow on the ground she begins to tremble. I take her in my arms and she burst into tears. "I killed her," she says, her voice strangled. "I killed her."

Glancing over Tia's shoulder I see Rachel on the verge of tears. "Come," I say. All three of us huddled, our arms around each other, our heads pressed together, as we dissolve into tears.

71.

"It's in the pit," Eileen said as she unlocked the garage door and pushed it open. "Be careful. I don't think we left it open. But you never know."

Eileen entered followed by several girls carrying trestle tables. The rest filed in with arms full of blankets and boxes of food. Behind came the Baxter children carrying their backpacks. Jon and Cilla brought up the rear with Wenslas unconscious on a stretcher. Pri accompanied them carrying medicine for the boy.

Without missing a beat, Eileen roped in several Baxter boys and, with their help, strung up blankets over the windows. When she was sure no light seeped out, she switched on two small bulbs casting a feeble light over the scene.

The space was big enough to house three or four cars. Judging from the dust, it hadn't been used in years, although the place still smelt of oil. Several drums stood in one corner next to a heap of tyres. A collection of wrenches and spanners hung on the wall from nails, each according to its size.

The stretcher was laid on two adjacent benches and Cilla sat next to Wenslas, redoing his bandages. Having checked she didn't need his help, Jon stood and looked around.

A small group of children set up a trestle table against a wall at the back of the garage. They then sorted out and lined up all those torches that were in working order. In the middle they put a box containing an assortment of batteries. The dud batteries and the broken torches were placed in a box under the table. The sight had Jon wondering where these girls got their supplies.

Many torches came from the Baxter children, but Becky had also carried over a considerable stock from the house.

In the middle of the garage was the inspection pit. With help from Jenna and the older Baxter boys, Eileen removed several of the oil stained planks that covered it and placed a ladder in the hole. She found several portable wooden barriers and set them up around the hole.

Once she was sure it was safe, she said, "I'm going to check the beginning of the tunnel. It's been a few weeks since we last went down there."

"Don't go too far," Jon said. "We might have urgent need of you."

Taking Jenna with her - the two had got chatting on their way to the garage - Eileen climbed down. Their voices came back more and more muffled as they moved deeper under the earth.

Several trestle tables had been set up on the far side of the garage on which a large collection of rucksacks had been lined up and, under Becky's supervision, children, mostly those from Baxter, were busy filling them with blankets and food. "Blankets first Martine. That is your name, isn't it?" Becky said to a little girl. "We need to be able to get to the food easily."

Pri enlisted those who had nothing to do to fetch benches from the main hall and set them up in rows around the walls so those waiting had somewhere to sit. She accompanied them on their first trip, planning to go from the house to the gate and join Sami.

A cluster of girls that had been setting up benches were chatting quietly. Jon heard one of then giggle. "The girls don't seem so unhappy," he said to Cilla, resuming their earlier conversation.

She glanced at the group and smiled. "I think we'd all have been quite content, had it not been for those three tyrants." Wenslas groaned. She turned to him saying "There, there," and wiped his sweaty face with a damp cloth. "Our problem is what the people who planted those three will do next."

Various reasons for locking a group of girls away from civilisation sprang to mind, most of them reprehensible. He preferred not to consider them. He thought of Cilla and her healing. He had to admit these girls would never have developed such skills in town. They certainly would not have been so capable of running their lives. The regime of terror maintained by the Food Police discouraged people from being resourceful and independent, especially girls and women. Had not the vast majority of healers been women? Were they not blamed for the Disaster by the police?

"I believe Marge, Gwen and Celine were their underhanded way of keeping control," Cilla went on. "Those three always said their discipline was designed to make us strong, dynamic forces in society, but they did everything to make that goal unattainable. I have no idea if those who planned this place intended it so, or if they completely misjudged the three girls."

"I get the impression those three did succeed," I said.

She frowned, suspecting I was poking fun at her. "How so?"

"Look," I said waving my arm to indicate the garage. "You are in the throws of a major crisis. Men are massing at the gate trying to break in. Unknown forces are plotting against you. Yet look how calmly you plan your escape."

Cilla grinned . "Well, yes. I see what you mean. But you will never hear me saying those three should sign up for a new period of tyranny."

A muffled burst of laughter drew our attention to the pit. Jenna's head emerged from the dark, closely followed by Eileen.

"See. I told you so," Eileen said, giving Jenna a friendly punch on the shoulder.

"But can I have one of your uniforms?" Jenna asked.

"That depends if you pass the test," Eileen said, a sly smile on her face.

"What test?" Jenna asked, her hands on her hips. "You never mentioned a test."

"You have to spend a night in the jungle."

Jenna burst out laughing.

"Shhh!" several girls said in chorus.

"I've already done that," whispered Jenna, slinging an arm

around Eileen's shoulder, pulling the girl into a hug. "So? Will you accept me?"

"Let me go, brute." Eileen laughed as she shoved Jenna away. "You won't get your way by force."

"So how am I to get what I want?"

Pri came bursting into the garage at that moment, her chest heaving as she struggled to get her breath back.

"You can return to the house," Pri said. "All is OK. Nan and Sami negotiated a peace treaty."

Several girls cheered. When others told them to be quiet, one replied, "Why? There's no need to be careful any more."

"Eileen, Sami needs you down by the gate," Pri said.

Eileen grabbed hold of Jenna's hand and pulled her towards the door, saying, "Let's go see what she wants."

Jenna looked over her shoulder at Jon for approval. "Go," he said, wondering how he was going to cope with all the Baxter children on his own.

Letting out a cry of delight, Jenna and Eileen hurried out.

"Oh. And you too Cilla," Pri said. "We have another wounded boy on our hands."

Jon groaned.

72.

Seeing Eileen walk down the drive hand in hand with a girl from Baxter, I get to my feet. The two are deep in conversation, oblivious to the world around them.

:: they make a cute pair - love at first sight

"Eileen," I say, annoyed at his remark. "Who is your friend?"

Letting go of the girl's hand she says, "Meet Jenna."

"Uniform," the girl whispers in her ear.

"Is it alright if I give Jenna a uniform?" Eileen asks.

"Why are you asking me?"

:: who's the big boss now?

"Yes. Er…" She shifts uncomfortably from one foot to another. "Sorry. Old habits die hard. You sent for me?"

I had indeed. When did I start giving orders?

"Yes. Can you rustle up food for these men?" I point to the group of wild men squatting beneath a cluster of trees. "I don't think they've had a proper meal in ages. Nothing fancy."

A worried look flits across her face. "I'm concerned about our stock," she says. "Who knows if we'll get any more."

We'll have to talk about that. I have no idea where all the supplies come from. If those men decide to cut them off, we'll be in trouble. "The wild men have agreed to help forage. But tonight, for them and their colleagues who have gone to fetch wives and children, we need to provide a meal."

"Soup?" she asks.

"That would be fine. Check with them for numbers." Then a thought crosses my mind. "Have you got some way of carrying the stuff down here. It wouldn't be good to have them in the Centre. Certainly not until they have washed and are wearing decent clothes."

:: all the girls will be scratching themselves wild because of the wild men's lice

"The trolley won't work on the gravel," she muses.

"Have you got a wheel barrow?" Jenna asks. Eileen nods.

"If Jenna is to be your assistant, you'd better see she is properly dressed," I say.

Jenna lets out a whoop of joy and the two hurry away.

I turn to see Pri helping Cilla carry a bag of medical supplies.

"I doubt you'll need all that," I say, kneeling next to Mart's unconscious form.

:: soap, a stiff brush and several gallons of perfume would be a good start

I smile.

Cilla and Pri kneel next to me.

"Phew! He stinks," Pri says, holding her nose. "Is there anything wrong with him that a good wash won't cure?"

Cilla examines the cut on his neck, then his arms and legs. "Nothing serious," she announces. She examines his chest and stomach, having no qualms about touching the boy. I look away, saying to Pri, "I agreed to let these men and their families take refuge within the fence. In return they are to forage for food and help protect us. It would be good if we could build a shelter for them down under the trees, but for tonight we need blankets..."

"Any blankets they use will need to be burnt afterwards," Pri says. "It would be a real waste, especially if we are not sure we will get any more."

"You are right," I say.

"What's the problem?" Tia asks, joining us.

"How to clean up and dress these men and their families when they arrive," I say.

"Well I might have a solution for the cleaning part," Tia says. "But I've no idea how we could find clothes for all these men unless we dress them in our uniforms.

:: yeah - like me

Pri giggles. "I'd like to see that." She designs exaggerated female curves with her hands as she traces the lines of her body.

"Don't kid yourself," Tia says.

Pia runs her hands through her short hair. "No sense of humour," she mutters. "So, how do you suggest getting enough water to wash them, a rain dance?"

"Sure," Tia said wiggling her hips. On which Pri whistles and cheers. Several of the men who were dozing nearby look up alarmed. "Cut it out," one complains. "I wanna sleep."

"I discovered a hot spring on the other side of the grounds," Tia says. When Pri screws up her face in disbelief, Tia replies, "I stumble on it when I was running away from Marge last week."

"Ok. Let's check it out tomorrow," I say. It must be way past midnight. "We should get to bed."

"Who will man the gate so the others can get in?" Tia asks.

"I will stay with Saskia a while," I say, hoping to get a moment alone with Mart if ever he comes round.

"It's that boy," Pri says, almost accusatory. "You know him."

:: she's sharp that one

"True," I say. "But that is not why I will stay."

"Come off it. I saw how you reacted when you thought his throat had been cut."

Images of the moment flash through my mind and my stomach lurches. "I was worried." Hoping to sound nonchalant, my voice comes out strangled.

"I think we should stay and keep an eye on her," Pri says to Tia. "For her own good."

"Don't be mean, Pri. Sami doesn't need us torturing her. She's got enough to think about without us messing with her. Let her have her moment alone," Tia says, slinging an arm around the girl's shoulders and leading her up the drive towards the house.

To my surprise, Pri breaks free and runs back. Taking both my hands in hers she looks me in the eyes and says, "I hope he's alright." Then, giving me a hasty kiss on the cheek she races back to Tia and the two fade into the dark.

I turn back to Mart. Cilla is still kneeling by his side, pressing gently here and there on his stomach. "There really is nothing serious," she says. "But he has many cuts and bruises and is filthy. If we don't clean him up, many will get infected."

"Can't we move him to the house?" I ask, looking around for something to carry him. "There are baths up there…"

"But I thought you said no wild men in the house."

"I did. But he's not a wild man. He was a prisoner of that girl, as was I before they brought me here."

"Who will wash him?" she asks, her look piercing. "You?"

:: no way - I'm not touching that - he's filthy and he's a boy

I too shudder at the thought, but not for the same reasons as Sam. Do I fancy him? I like to be with him and when he isn't so filthy I enjoy looking at him. I feel my face heating.

:: how can you possibly think such a thing - do I need to remind you that you are in a boy's body - that you are at the head of a group of beleaguered girls in a world of terror fuelled by a crazed Food Police - that you just adopted a tribe of filthy individuals who will probably eat the hand that feeds them

"Nan could do it," I say. "She's a healer."

I look round for Nan and see Yarrow loping in the gate. Somebody will have to close it. The dog bounds up to me and licks my hand. I stroke his head as I continue searching for Nan. I find her listening to a group of wild men. I get up and join her. When I arrive, I hang back, not wanting to interrupt. Seeing the dog, the wild men break off and shy away. "He won't hurt you," I say, finding it hard not to be exasperated by their subservience.

"You should get some sleep," Nan says with a tired smile.

"So should you," I reply. "But first I have a service to ask."

She takes leave of the wild men and I wish them good night. Once out of ear shot, she turns to me. "So what can I do?"

"Mart is still unconscious. He is injured, but not badly. The trouble is, he is filthy and his wounds will get infected if he isn't throughly washed. I wondered if …"

"If I would wash him for you," she says, grinning and pats me on the hand. "Of course. No problem."

73.

Jon scowled. With Jenna and Cilla gone, he'd have to find someone to help him cart Wenslas back to the house. He looked around for what remained of the Baxter kids. All the older kids, both boys and girls, had teamed up with the girls from the Centre and left. So much for the girls' reticence about boys. He rounded up the little ones but couldn't be bothered to check if all were there. It was highly unlikely any would be missing. Looking back at the stretcher he realised none of them were big enough to help him carry it.

He glanced around the garage, but it was deserted. He would have to leave Wenslas unattended while he fetched help. He didn't like doing so, but if he shut the door Wenslas would be safe, provided he didn't awake. As Jon pushed open the garage door and ushered the children out, he had visions of Wenslas climbing into the pit and wandering through the tunnels. That would be just like him.

Outside, seated with her back against the garage wall, was a tall lanky girl, her head in her hands. He remember her. She was the one wearing glasses. She'd been helping Baxter children fill the backpacks. "Are you alright?" he asked.

She wiped a hand across her face and rubbed her eyes.

"I can't take it any more," she said, her voice shuddery as tears rolled down her cheeks.

This was neither the time nor the place for heart-rending discussions. He had enough problems. Maybe having something to do might tide her over. "Can you give me a hand? I have no one to help carry the stretcher. Wenslas is still unconscious."

She scrambled to her feet, surprising him by her willingness. She blew her nose then peered inside the garage, only to turn back, saying, "He's awake."

"Wait for me here," he called out to the children, some of whom were wandering towards the house. "I'll be back in a sec. I've got to fetch Wenslas."

The girl beat him to the boy and had him in her arms when Jon arrived. In the dim light, Jon could make out the broad grin on the boy's face. That generally spelt trouble. "You are in a school, Wenslas, so you'll have to behave," he told the boy. "And this here is …"

"Becky," she said.

"Becky attends this school." Attend? The word was no doubt inexact. More likely the girl had been forced to be there. Whatever, she didn't seem very happy about it.

"Do you want to ride on my shoulders?" Becky asked Wenslas, all trace of sadness gone. What was that song in his youth? Everybody needs somebody to love.

Wenslas didn't bother with words. He just stretched up his arms. For such a lanky girl, Becky was surprisingly strong and had no problem swinging the boy onto her shoulders. She chattered with Wenslas about landmarks all the way to the house.

Jon brought up the rear, scuffing up dust as he listened to Becky's explanations.

From the top of the main steps of the house, he could make out lights between the trees by the gate. Shadowy figures moved from the gate to the trees and back. Nan must be down there with her wild men. Sam was there too, or rather Sami. He scowled and turned away only to bump his knee on the door which Becky had let swing closed.

In the dormitory the young children collapsed onto mattresses lined up on the floor. By the time Jon had shifted blankets to make sure each child was covered, they were fast asleep. A number of beds remained unoccupied, abandoned no doubt by older boys and girls off exploring new territory. Becky waited outside leaning against the wall, Wenslas asleep in her arms.

"It would be a shame to wake him. He can sleep in my room," she said. "Let me show you where it is so you can find him later."

Jon followed her to the end of the long attic corridor where she pushed open a door with her hip and manoeuvred Wenslas inside. The room was tiny with just enough space for a bed, a small table and a chair.

"Being one of the first, I was able to chose my room. I didn't fancy sharing." She lay the boy on her bed and pulled the covers over him.

"Where will you sleep?" Jon asked.

"There's room enough next to him."

Jon looked at a drawing pinned to the wall above the table. It was a free interpretation of the Centre with a filthy black cloud hanging over it. "I get the impression you are not happy here," he said. Why was he being so inquisitive? What did he care?

She stood up from the bed, avoiding hitting her head on the mansard, and glanced at the drawing. "I'd rather not talk about it," she said, sweeping a pile of dirty clothes into a wicker basket by the bed.

"Sorry. I didn't want to stir up bad memories. I imagine you'd be happy to leave."

She looked up from collecting socks strewn across the floor. "Not at all." She sounded shocked. "This is my home. Where else would I go?"

"But…" he began, perplexed.

"Until yesterday this Centre was not a good place to be. The three horrible girls who ruled over us made a sport of hurting the weak and friendless, me in particular." Seeing how well she handled Wenslas, he found it difficult to imagine she was without friends. "But they have been chased away," she continued. "Life can only be better."

Cilla had told him as much. Apparently Sami the saviour had been at work.

"I'll leave you to sleep," he said. "See you tomorrow."

"Good night," she said, but sounded unwilling to let him go. "Do you mind if I give you a hug?" she asked, looking at her shoes as she spoke. "I haven't hugged an adult in ages."

"Sure," he said and wrapped his arms around her shoulders.

She returned his hug and as she did he could feel the shudder of her body as she began to cry.

"Sorry," she said, pulling away. "Silly, I know, but all this time I have missed being hugged by my parents."

Her heartfelt words had him thinking of all those he missed. Sam, of course. He regretted no longer being able to take his son in his arms. The boy had become a complete stranger. Then there was Jane, his lovely wife, torn from him by a snipper's bullet. And his own parents all those years ago in a different age.

"Good night," he said, his voice catching.

"Good night," she replied looking up into his eyes.

Outside in the corridor he took a long steadying breath and rubbed his face. He needed to get some rest. Looking along the corridor with its closed doors he realised he had nowhere to sleep. He decided to look for Nan. One floor down he spotted Sami sitting on a chair, her head leaning against the wall, her eyes closed.

The sight of his son dressed as a schoolgirl was troubling. It irritated him to see the clothes suited him, her, whatever. He had to admit they did make his son's face look more girlish. It would be easy enough to be mislead. When a stair creaked as it bore his weight, Sami's eyes opened and she turned to see him.

"Hello Jon," she said with a smile, despite her apparent weariness.

"I didn't want to disturb you," he said, wanting to look away, but fascinated by the ambiguity. It was like talking to a stranger with a familiar face. "Do you know where Nan is?"

Sami inclined her head towards a nearby door, her lips pursed as if there was something she didn't want to say. From inside he could hear the sound of running water and the occasional splash. Was Nan washing her hands after dealing with those stinking wild men? The thought almost made him smile. How had she managed to convince them not to attack the Centre?

He lent forward to knock on the door when Sami said, "She's washing Mart." He stopped his knuckles inches from the door. Sami's face was twisted as if the idea pained her. The idea disturbed Jon too. Whatever could Nan be doing washing a boy? He was almost a man. An ugly spark of jealousy kindled in his gut.

"His body was a mess," Sami said, her lips curled in disgust. "He was so dirty we were afraid his wounds would get infected…." Her words trailed off and she closed her eyes.

Jon knocked on the door, saying, "It's me, Jon."

"Come in," Nan called out.

The white-tiled room resembled a bathroom. There was a sink, a shower and a toilet, but in the centre was an examination table on which a young boy lay naked except for a rag that served as loincloth. Jon would never have recognised Mart had not Sami told him who it was. The boy was little more than an ugly collection of bones over which skin had been drawn tight. He had a vicious red wheal about his waist. His legs and arms were peppered with cuts and burn marks and his back and shoulders were a crisscross of crimson lashes.

The smell of disinfectant rivalled with fetid body odours making Jon cough. Nan sponged the boy's chest causing water to run across his stomach, dribble over his hips and drip to a puddle at Nan's feet.

For all his anger at the boy, Jon would never have wished him such a fate. Never. He closed his eyes and bowed his head in shame. The sloshing of the sponge ceased and, apart from the occasional drip splashing on the floor, silence fell in the room. He felt a cold, wet hand in his and Nan pulled him into her arms. "It's alright," she said. "It's not your fault."

74.

Nan shivered. It was the middle of the night and the temperature had dropped. She covered Mart with several dry towels and a blanket hoping they would stave off the cold. Situated as it was in the middle of the Wilds, the Centre was surprisingly devoid of heating.

She looked at Mart's withered face. The filth had masked many of the traces of violence. She closed her eyes and shook her head. What level of hatred and disregard for human life had driven someone as young as that girl to gouge out so many indelible marks in his skin? She pulled up the blanket to cover his neck and shoulders. It would be better if Sami didn't see the full extent of the damage. Nan glanced at Jon. He was leaning against the wall, his eyes closed, his jaw clenched. Opening the door, she peered out and called Sami who was pacing the corridor with her giant dog. "I've finished."

The girl came to the door but hesitated, one hand placed on the dog's head as if for reassurance. "How is he?" she asked, her face pinched with worry.

No point in lying. "I found no substantial internal injury, but he is extremely weak." She took a deep breath, wondering how far to go. "So weak, it is touch and go."

Tears formed in Sami's eyes. For all her determination, she looked exhausted. "You should get some sleep," Nan said. "You will be no good to him if you fall ill."

"I will stay by his side," Sami said, accompanied by the dog's muted growl.

"We can do that," Nan said, glancing at Jon who nodded. "You need the rest far more than us."

"Mart sat by me when I was raving with fever," Sami said, her voice firm and assertive. "I will sit by him."

There was no saying no to her when she spoke like that. "First," Nan said, "you must find pyjamas or a nightdress. A dressing gown would be good too. We need to keep him warm. Could you get him a little broth. He must be dehydrated. Then we should transfer him to a room that is warmer, one where you both can lie down and sleep."

"I will fetch Tia," Sami said, walking away, her dog loping after her. "She will know where to go."

Alone with Jon and the unconscious boy, Nan turned to the former saying, "How are you Jon?"

He frowned. "Pottering along, I suppose. Wenslas will be OK. He's got a girl friend to look after him."

"A girlfriend?" The boy was only six.

"Sort of. One of the older girls called Becky has taken him under her wing. Both seem happy with the arrangement, for the moment. He's sleeping in her bed."

"And the other children?"

"The younger ones are asleep in a dormitory. I have no idea were the older ones are. Scattered around the building with girls from the Centre no doubt."

Nan chuckled. "Didn't take them long."

"What are you going to do now?" she asked.

"No idea. I haven't given it a thought. What about you?"

"I plan to stay a while. Maybe you should too. I fear whoever set up this Centre will wrest back control. For all the maturity and independence of these girls, they are going to need help."

"I'm not sure about staying." He shrugged. "I don't seem to be of much use."

She took a deep breath and kneaded her neck and jaw trying to unclench her muscles. Always the same refrain. She wished she dared shake him. Not that it would work. Most likely he would just get angry.

"It's true," she said. "You are pretty useless."

He looked up shocked and reproachful.

"I mean," she continued, not giving him a chance to reply. "You only raised your son for twelve years single-handed. Anyone could have done that even if your son was severely handicapped and the Food Police were breathing down your neck." She paused. He still looked hurt but confused. "You led a large group of orphans through the jungle and managed to get them to safety. Nothing special in that. I agree. You really are of no use." She paused, trying not to smile as she gave him a chance to respond. His mouth had fallen open but no words came out.

She pulled him into her arms and hugged him. As always his body was tense, but he didn't resist as he often did. "Wake up my friend. Your record has got stuck in a groove. You keep repeating the same dirge. As a concert pianist, I am sure you are capable of more colourful music."

He didn't have time to respond as the chatter of girls came from outside. Jon shifted as if to get free, so Nan let her arms fall and he pulled away looking sheepish. The door opened and Sami and Eileen stepped in followed by the dog, his tail wagging. Eileen was carrying a bowl of soup and a spoon. Sami had a dressing gown over her shoulder and star-spotted night-blue pyjamas in her hands.

Nan took the pyjamas, running the material between her fingers. It was soft, but probably too big. All the better. They would chafe his wounds less. "Give the dressing gown to Jon and place the soup over there," she said. "Now wait outside while we get Mart dressed."

Eileen muttered about being useful, but Sami shooed her out.

Nan pulled the towels from Mart and surveyed his wounds. Some were oozing a clear liquid which she dabbed away. Then she called Jon over to lift the boy's feet so she could pull on the pyjamas. The boy moaned at the movement, but did not regain consciousness. When he was fully dressed she called the girls in.

"What about the soup?" Eileen asked.

Nan took the bowl and the spoon and tested the soup with her little finger to make sure it wasn't too hot. Giving the bowl and spoon to Sami, she said, "Only a very little at a time." Then she propped the unconscious boy up and held his head so it didn't flop to the side.

When the feeding was finished and the boy's lips and face had been wiped clean, Nan was going to suggest she and Jon carry the boy between them. It would hurt him, but she saw no other possibility. Then Tia arrived carrying the stretcher they'd used for Wenslas. Once the boy had been transferred to it, Tia and Eileen led the way along the corridor to a larger room that looked like it was used for informal gatherings. There was even a chimney in which someone had lit a fire. Several armchairs were pushed against the walls. There was also a sofa and a number of upright chairs. Two mattresses had been laid side by side on the floor in the middle at a safe distance from the fire.

They lowered the boy onto the farthest of the two beds and the dog curled up on the floor beyond him. The image of him lying peacefully in his gold-starred pyjamas was misleading. He might well not survive the night.

"I need to sleep somewhere nearby," Nan said. "In case Mart needs me."

"The room next door is free," Tia said. "We put two mattresses in there for you two."

With a grin, she glanced from Nan to Jon. The latter shifted uncomfortably from one foot to another, blushing, but said nothing.

"Come on Jon," Nan said. "We should let these people get a rest. We have a room to explore."

75.

"You need help?" Tia asks, feigning innocence, but there is a glint in her eye.

Yarrow, who has been seated unmoving by my side, nudges Tia towards the door with his head.

"Leave Sami in peace," Eileen says with a chuckle. "Even the dog agrees." Taking Tia by the arm, she tugs her towards the entrance. "She's got a boy to look after." Both burst out laughing and I hear them giggling as the door clicks shut.

:: told you that boy would be a nuisance - now all the girls will pull your leg

You're just jealous.

I begin to unbutton my blouse then remember Mart. I glance in his direction, but he's oblivious to my presence. I resume undressing, carefully folding my uniform on an armchair. I keep my pants on, not wishing to parade the evidence that I am physically more Sam than Sami. Being rarely naked, it's easy enough to ignore the oddity I am. I shiver, despite the fire.

The nightdress Tia left me is warming by the hearth. A thrill of pleasure runs through my body as I pull it over my head and feel it next to my skin. I stare a moment at the play of flames, thankful that in former lives I have no recollection of being tried as a witch. Fire is such a comforting, life-giving force, I'd hate to have it marred by nightmarish memories.

I sit on the bed next to Mart and study his face, not daring to lie down. If you discount Sam - and that really doesn't count - I have never slept with a boy. I shake my head to chase away such thoughts. Hair has flopped over Mart's eyes so I lean forward and brush it aside. His skin is hot and moist. There are so many bruises on his face, he is more blue and green than suntanned brown. The sight is so sickening it pains me. I close my eyes and groan, hoping Nan and Jon will not hear.

Yarrow gets to his feet, pads round the bed and plops down at my side, resting his head in my lap. "Terrible, isn't it boy," I say, running my fingers through the mane about his neck. "To think that girl - what was her name? Priscilla - could do such things to Mart."

Yarrow looks at me, his big eyes probing mine. "I can't understand what would drive anyone to be so inhuman. Vengeance? Jealousy? Hatred? Insanity?" Yarrow lowers his head and makes a sound akin to a sigh.

:: childhood probably - who knows how badly she was treated before she washed up amongst the Baxter refugees

You are probably right. But what can be done for such people? It is as if the humanity has been squeezed from them. Is there no hope? Must they be cast down from the tree like rotten apples?

:: rotten apples might infect other fruit or the tree itself

I just wish something could be done to remove the rottenness without sacrificing the person herself.

:: even a saviour cannot save everyone

I am reminded of the little book in my blazer pocket. I lean over and extract it from its hiding place and open it at random. For a moment I get the impression the words are blurred as if I surprised them before they could take form. But now they are clear enough. I read: No one can be saved against their will. Trying to do so can only cause pain and suffering, if not violence.

So if these people are so far gone they don't want to be saved, there is no hope for them. I close the book and slide it into the pocket.

:: you can't deny the existence of evil - but you can't fight it either - the more you struggle with evil the more evil there is

I look back at Mart. There is a terrible wheal on his neck. How come I hadn't noticed before? I undo the first of the buttons of his pyjama jacket and gasp. The mark on his neck is nothing compared to what I discover on his chest. The skin is torn, lacerated, pock-marked, savagely hacked about, burnt even. My stomach heaves and it is all I can do not to throw up. I clamp a hand over my mouth and look away, seeking comfort in the flickering flames.

Deep inside I feel a surge of power that I take for indignation. It rolls up and out till all is consumed. How dare anyone do such a thing? I am furious, filled with a burning desire to get vengeance, to wreak havoc, to inflict the same marks on that girl's body. I shudder with pleasure at the thought of causing her pain. I am enflamed as rage consumes me. In my mind's eye, I hack about as my fingers become claws digging into the girl's flesh. She pleads for me to stop, but I flay on, ripping, tearing, biting, till all that lies before me is a bloody mass that writhes in my stained hands. I taste blood in my mouth and my body is spattered a vivid red. Her blood, Mart's blood, my blood, everybody's blood, the blood of humanity. And I burst into tears. I sob for myself but also that girl. So had she felt, lost as she was to the world, enraged beyond reach.

With time a calm settles over me. I feel my muscles relax, although inside, deep within, that surge of power is still there, demanding to be used. But how? I am terrified that pandemonium will break loose should I let that power loose. I will become like Priscilla or I will destroy the world with my saintly rage in a crusade against evil. Yet that power is a part of me. I feel it in my chest pulsing with every breath. I feel it vibrate in the muscles in my arms. It tingles right to my finger tips. And I know, as if it is written in each of my cells, what I must do. Why have I not seen it before? I stretch out my hands, my fingers splayed and hold them, trembling, above the wounds on Mart's chest. No thought is needed. I close my eyes and let my body do the age-old work. Warmth flows from me into Mart like a river, a living river, tumbling, bumbling, like a joyful song, from me, no not from me, through me, from a source, here, there, everywhere, a musical, singing river that brings relief and healing.

I have no idea how long I have been sitting like that. Ages

probably. And when the river calms to a trickle and then ceases, I know it is over and I pull back, laying my hands on Yarrow's head. I should probably feel tired, but I don't. I feel satisfied, happy, refreshed, as if I have awoken from a pleasant sleep. And I open my eyes to find Mart looking up at me, a smile on his lips, and my heart skips a beat. All the cuts and bruises on his face and neck and chest have gone. I lean forward and run a hand over his forehead and down his cheeks. His skin is smooth, unblemished. I take him in my arms and pull him in a long hug, savouring the joy of being alive.

76.

"You are glowing," Mart says, sitting up straight, his eyes wide with awe.

"Must be the flickering of the fire," I say, trying to laugh it off, but he pulls away to get a better look.

"No. There's a steady yellow light around your head."

I run a hand through my hair, as if that could rid me of it, but the look of wonder has not gone from his eyes. Why should it? What he sees is there. I can feel the halo, just as solidly as I can feel the fountain of energy pulsing deep inside me or the energy that emanates from him.

"Maybe whatever happened to you has troubled your eye-sight," I say in the hope of distracting him.

"What did happen to me?" He clasps the nape of his neck in one hand, massaging it and his shoulders, as if he could dislodge some memory trapped there.

"I was hoping you would tell me."

:: stalemate - are you two love birds going to dance around each other all night? - I'm tired

When Mart just looks blank, I say, "You were captured by the Wild Men and tortured." His frown indicates he has no memory of the events. My healing must have gone deeper than the wounds. I could keep the healing a secret, but the moment others arrive it will be out. "You were in a sorry state. Nan thought you might not survive. So I healed you."

It's not that he doesn't believe me, I see, but that what I say doesn't fit. "But you told Harriet you knew little of healing."

I nod. I remember. I wanted her to teach me. I was looking forward to it. "True. But seeing you in that dreadful condition worked a kind of miracle and I was able to heal you, just by holding my hands over you. I raise my hands in the air as if to illustrate my words.

Mart stares at my hands hovering inches above my knees. I look at them too as if they belonged to someone else. However had I managed to do that? Then he leans forward, and taking my hands in his, lifts my fingers to his lips and kisses them sending a tingle down my back. "Thank you," he says, his voice husky.

:: call the fire brigade - call out the police, the army, the ambulance men, anyone, but for god sake save us

I ease my fingers free and recover my hands. The memory of the delicate pressure of his lips lingers. It's not just a question of saying thanks. It is more, much more. I can read it in him as if I had access to his deepest thoughts. Maybe I do. Raging desire and wild hopes. A need to prove himself amid a sea of doubts. Can he? Should he? Will he? A sweet tenderness and caring that is almost motherly. Then there's the rampant possessiveness chalking up acquisitions, a jealous owner. And throughout it all, weave dreams of what might one day be...

Only I don't want to go down that road. I cannot. "I'm tired after all that healing," I say. It is not true, but the excuse might work. "You must be tired too. We should sleep."

I lie down on the second mattress and pull the blankets around my neck. Yarrow curls up at my side, his tail tapping out a regular beat on the parquet floor. I lay one hand on his neck, thinking, my old furry friend. The ceiling flickers in the firelight and sparks crackle in the silence. Mart sighs, staring at the fire.

I snake out my free hand in search of his. Finding it, I clasp his fingers in mine. "Lie down," I say.

He does, but keeps a safe distance. I feel his jaw-breaking tension and the constant whirl of turbulent thoughts. They get between me and sleep. Am I condemned to suffer the thoughts and feelings of those around me from now on? I note that Sam has no such problem. He's fast sleep.

"It can't be," I say.

He shifts as if readying to reply, but there is a long silence.

"I can't be what you want," I continue.

He turns to face me, his head not far from mine. "Why?"

I feel his disappointment, his hurt and grumblings of anger.

"There are things I have to do I can only do alone." I think of a phrase I read in the book about saviours: All attachment will be ripped from you. You will be left bare and helpless before you reach the end of the path.

A wave of irritation hits me like a slap in the face. I flinch. He must have felt it, because he asks, "What's the matter?" Irritation gives way to care and concern. I won't survive if I am the brunt of all the emotions around me.

I want to tell him, to shout out, it's your emotions that are killing me, but doing so will only cause more suffering.

"I'm exhausted," I say. "Let's talk tomorrow."

If Sam were awake he would say tomorrow has already come, but his cranky voice of wisdom slumbers. Yarrow too is asleep, snoring quietly. Mart is drifting off and as he does his irritation and perplexity fall away. I reach out mentally and feel Jon and Nan asleep in each other's arms next door. At last. I marvel at my newfound ability. Or is it a curse? I cast away the thought and let myself be enthralled.

How far can I go? I stretch my senses further till I see or feel, I'm not sure which, Tia who has crept into bed with Pri. She is tossing and turning because the young girl talks in her sleep. Becky has wrapped her arms around Wenslas but the boy pushes her away mumbling about needing room and she is pouting with her back turned. Jenna and Eileen are engulfed in a cloud of happiness, cuddled up in bed. As I make my rounds of the Centre, I sift through the sleepers thoughts and dreams, discouraging that which is rough and discordant while nurturing the beautiful and harmonious. I let the tones and colours of those pleasant dreams rock me to sleep. And as I drift off a thought floats into my mind. I have just discovered something very important. But I can't remember what.

77.

"What a wonderful night," a girl said, her singsong voice melodious.

"Me too. First time I've had no nightmares since I got here," another said.

Nan opened her eyes, only to squeeze them shut. The sun was up and a piercing light streamed in the window. They had forgotten to draw the curtains. The voices that had awoken her were coming from the corridor.

"I feel like I could run and jump and sing for joy," a girl exclaimed.

There had to be a crowd of girls outside judging by the pitch of their joy at life. Nan's night hadn't been so bad either. She grinned as she felt Jon's arms laced around her. It had left her feeling refreshed and ready for a new day.

"Delicious," a girl said followed by what sounded like a very demonstrative kiss and a wave of giggles.

If that lot outside didn't calm down, they'd wake Sami and Mart. Nan extracted herself from Jon's arms and tiptoed to the door. Peering out, she discovered a much smaller group than she'd imagined.

"Shhh," she said. "Don't wake them. They need the rest."

Jenna was amongst them, her arm slung around a girl's shoulder. "Let's make breakfast," she whispered, glancing in Nan's direction. It was one of those questioning looks. Approval? Complicity? Absolution?

"Sure," the girl in her arms said and the two set off, giggling as they went with the others traipsing after.

"Join us," Jenna mouthed over her shoulder.

"Later," Nan mouthed back.

She waited till they were gone and all was quiet before listening at Sami's door. When no sound came, she eased the door open and stepped inside. The curtains were drawn, shutting out most of the sun's light and the fire was but a glowing heap of embers. On the mattresses lay Sami and Mart, not entwined as she had imagined, but separated by a wall of covers. Well, maybe it was better that way.

Through an odd trick of the light there was a golden glow hovering near Sami's head. Shifting to get a better look, Nan caught sight of Mart's face. Every trace of cut or burn was gone, wiped away as if nothing had happened. His left arm, which lay outside the covers, was just as pristine. She stood frozen in astonishment for a long moment. Then she sucked in a breath as she realised what must have happened and a bolt of joy shot through her. At last, in her life time, it was happening. She placed a hand over her heart and bowed her head in recognition and gratitude.

When she finally looked up, Sami was awake and studying her, a golden glow framing her head. The girl looked at her for a long, unblinking moment then said, "Nan, I want you to do something you will find very difficult."

Her hand still held over her heart, Nan replied, "That is why I am here."

"Please treat me exactly like you did before."

Nan huffed out a breath. "How can I possibly do that?"

Sami chuckled. "I said it would be difficult."

Nan groaned. How could she pretend Sami was not the Luminary she'd been waiting for all her life? "I will try."

"There are going to be enough people worshipping me that I need at least one person I can talk to and who treats me like a human being and not a god."

Nan looked at the halo glowing around Sami's head. How could anyone possibly treat her as normal when she looked like that?"

Sami's eyes radiated warmth and care, but Nan had the impression those eyes could reach inside her. "I know," the girl said, nodding. "The halo. I will see if I can tone it down."

Nan wanted to laugh, but the laughter stuck in her throat. A part of her wanted to scream with frustration. How was she supposed to treat this mind-reading, miracle-working, twelve-year-old as normal?

"Go and have some breakfast with the children. They are expecting you," Sami said with an authority that couldn't be denied. "I will come later. I have things to deal with here."

Nan wondered if she dared point out the paradox. Had not Sami insisted she treat her like anyone else? Now was one of those key moments. That didn't make it any less daunting. "If you speak with such an authoritative voice and continue to read my mind," she said, "don't be surprised if I react with distance rather than friendship. Not that your are being bossy or issuing orders. But when you suggest something that way it is hard to refuse."

"This is new to me too," Sami said, getting to her feet. She appeared even more impressive when she was standing as if she had grown taller. "There are things I have yet to get the hang of. Like not opening up to people's thoughts and emotions."

A possibility crossed Nan's mind. "Were you responsible for our good night?"

Sami chuckled. "I was trying to get to sleep after the healing. It wasn't easy. I discovered I could skim minds. I wanted to see how far I could reach. I'm not sure exactly what I did. It was like sifting through the emotions, giving preference to all that was harmonious and beautiful." She smiled. "Sam would say I was royally manipulating everyone…"

She paused a moment, her face thoughtful.

"Sam?" Nan asked.

"I haven't heard from him since I…" Her face grew pained and tears welled in her eyes. Nan wanted to encourage her to go on, but she kept quiet. Sami lowered herself into an armchair and put her head in her hands. "It was terrible. I felt the emotions that raged through Priscilla as she tortured Mart. It hurt so much. Not his pain, but my suffering at her actions. I thought I would be ripped apart. That acute awareness brought with it no understanding. I still don't know why she did it. But I felt the evil of it and that will haunt me always."

She broke off as a sob burst from her lips.

Be normal Nan had been told. Now was the time. She went to the girl's side, knelt by the armchair and, cradling her in my arms, she rocked her backwards and forwards. "The only consolation I got from my suffering," she said after her sobs had subsided, "was that it drove me to heal Mart. I just hope I will not be torn apart by pain and suffering each time I need to heal."

"Thank you," she said and, pulling free of Nan's arms, she got to her feet and helped her stand.

Her young face was red and blotchy. Nan rummaged in her pocket, pulled out a clean handkerchief and handed it to Sami.

"Why don't you go down to breakfast. Jenna and the others will be waiting for you," Sami suggested. "I'll come in a while. I have one or two things to do."

78.

The sun has already risen above the treetops. Brightly coloured birds cheep and trill in a discordant chorus as they flit without apparent design or reason over the park. Down by the gate, dull forms shift sluggishly like gray ghosts in the sharp sunlight, encircling a column of smoke that rises unswerving into the air.

I lean my elbows on the window ledge and press my forehead against the glass, letting the coolness calm my feverish thoughts. Must this really be? It might be a tradition engraved in my body, but it feels alien. Could an age-old way of doing things be wrong? Could all my predecessors, including myself in other lives, have been wrong? Now is not the time to doubt.

I turn my thoughts inwards and contemplate Sam. He remains present even when he is asleep. Not just in this body which I use, but as a living separate person that is so different from me. I sigh. The choice is not mine. I move to an armchair, close my eyes and draw in a deep breath.

This is going to hurt. Poor Sam. He's not going to like it. I steel myself for the pain and concentrate on the well of energy inside. Drawing deeply on it, I feel the organs within me readying to shift and change, when all of a sudden my body bucks up and I am flung to the floor.

:: stop that immediately - you are going to kill me

It is for the best Sam. I struggle to get a grip on this body which is writhing on the floor.

:: you are going to rob me of the one thing that makes me me

Come off it, Sam. You are much more than a sex.

:: if so why bother to change? - what difference does it make to you?

I can't go through with my calling if I don't feel this body is mine, wholly mine.

:: of course this body is as much youra as mine - you said so - take it - I gift it to you - but do not denature me

If I stay in a boy's body there will always be a doubt, at least in my mind, and I can't afford to doubt.

:: sure you can - doubt could be your greatest strength

It won't work Sam, luminaries have always changed their bodies the moment they come into their power.

:: well you are going to be the exception

I can't break the tradition.

:: of course you can

In his desperation he has gained complete control of his body. He is much stronger than I thought. I'm not sure I can wrestle it back.

Please, Sam. Be reasonable. This is inevitable.

:: no it's not - you have no right! - does being a newly elected saviour give you the right to trample over me?

At least lie still. I can't think with you jiggling all over the place.

:: only if you promise not to trick me

Blast you, Sam. You make everything so complicated.

:: if one can save the world, surely two can do it even better!

The growing part of me that is uncomfortable about the transformation jumps at the possibility. I wrestle with myself more so than with Sam. *No, Sam. There's only ever one of the chimera that is a luminary.*

:: yeah - look at the success you had going it alone

I've got to hand it to him. He's clever. His arguments feed my own doubts. Was I not saying to myself that doing so felt alien? Maybe I should ask Nan for advice. *Ok. I'll wait till I've asked Nan's advice.*

:: no

His answer has me stumped. *What do you mean?*

:: no means no - you will not put off the decision - you will decide now - either you denature me and have that loss eternally on your conscience and ultimately fail because of it or you link hands with me and we go forward together, with me as I am now, and we will triumph

I huff. He ought to have been a politician or a statesman. My vote would have gone to him. I have regained enough control of my body, our body, to crawl into the armchair. My elbow hurts and I'll have a bruise on my backside.

The commitment is appealing. A new vista. A light opening up, full of promise and the joy at not being alone to bear the burden. I see us breaking new ground and I want it so much the longing hurts.

Yes. YES.

Sam hugs me in a whirling, twirling mental hug. Two become one in that joyful dance amid laughter and a wild beating heart. We spin apart, separate, different, and then reunite in renewed hugs. I am so relieved that I could cry. And I do. Why ever not? Hot tears roll down my cheeks. The depth and breadth of my emotions astonishes me. I was unaware how much I dreaded that transformation. How distasteful I found what it entailed. What's more, I had turned a blind eye on the terrifying loneliness that awaited me. I silence the voice that whispers *you have to face this alone.*

:: Sister, friend, soul mate, I love you

Let's not exaggerate! I give him a mental shove and realise that he can now hear all my thoughts not just those I chose to send his way. *But, yes, I love you too. And I do. I always have. You might be so different from me, but we are intricately bound together for life; two in one.*

"Sami?" Mart's voice is sharp and foreign. It wrenches Sam and I from our euphoria.

:: loverboy is having a hard time grasping you are not for him

I turn to see Mart awake. He is staring at me as if I am a complete stranger, a frown on his face, his lips pursed. How much has he seen? How can I possibly explain my rolling on the floor? Or the wild joy on my face?

"How do you feel?" I ask, trying, but failing, to sound casual. His frown deepens. "Who are you?"

"I am Sami."

"You are not the Sami I know. I see it in your eyes, I feel it in my bones. If you are Sami, you have changed so much I don't recognise you."

Should I overawe him with my halo and a show of power?

:: unwise - keep that as a last resort - better to tell him the truth, or at least part of it

"You are partly right, Mart. This is still the same body you escaped from Baxter with, but I am no longer the person you knew. I was destined to change, to become something else and that transformation has just happened, thanks to you."

"Me?" His disbelief says, 'What have I got to do with it?'

"Like I told you last night, you were terribly wounded. We weren't sure you would live. The sight of your ravaged body was so terrible it sparked the transformation that awaited me and, thanks to that, I was able to heal you."

He shakes his head, rubbing his arm as if it itched. "So I am to blame for the change?"

"Blame is not the right word." After the joys of what just happened with Sam I really don't want to have this conversation. "For me the transformation was a blessing - did it not lead to me saving your life? - I would prefer to thank you than blame you."

Mart scowls.

:: why don't you take him down to breakfast - he must be starving - hunger can make boys grumpy

"I'm hungry," I say, getting to my feet. I make an effort not to groan at the pain in my knee.

:: why don't you heal yourself?

Why didn't I think of that?

"Let's go and eat. Friends of mine have prepared breakfast. Are you coming?"

He reluctantly gets to his feet only to realise he is wearing cosmic blue pyjamas spattered with gold-stars. His face is a picture of disgust and loathing. "I can't go down like this."

:: if anyone has changed, it is him - the damage that girl did goes much deeper than you thought

I'm not sure I can cure that.

"Here," I say, unhooking the dressing gown from behind the door. It the one Tia brought. It is the same blue as his pyjamas, but without the stars. "This will hide your milky way." I want to grin, but I dare not for fear he thinks I'm poking fun.

He shrugs it onto his shoulders, struggles with the sleeves into which he finally manages to stuff his arms and ties the belt as tight as he can. "OK," he says sounding like a grumpy old man.

79.

Linked arm in arm with Jon, Nan stepped into the dining hall to find a noisy group of girls sharing a copious breakfast with some of the boys from Baxter. So much for the mature attitude of these youngsters. Shame. She'd admired them for it.

Nan stepped round a cup that lay smashed where it had fallen. Used plates and cutlery were heaped in a corner of a table and food had dribbled onto the surface nearby. Wenslas, who thrived on disorder, was crouched under a table eating his toast and jam despite the entreaties of a lanky, bespectacled girl begging him to come out. Chaos was lurking in the wings, waiting for a pretext to prance onto the stage.

The moment they saw two adults arrive they calmed, especially the boys from Baxter. Wenslas finally obeyed and crawled from under the table, but left behind a plate of half-eaten toast.

"Wenslas, the plate!" Jon said, his voice sharp and authoritative. The night had done him good. Taken aback, the boy looked at Jon alarmed and hastened to crawl under the table in search of the plate. They passed close to a catastrophe when Wenslas pinched a girl's ankles as he picked up the plate. She kicked out, narrowly missing his head but sending the plate skittering across the floor. Luckily it didn't smash. He retaliated by punching her leg and the girl was about to lay in with feet and fists when the lanky girl dragged him out by the scruff of his neck and held him up one handed, his feet dangling in mid air, as she wagged a finger at him.

It was Jenna emerging from the kitchen with a chef's toque

on her head who rescued Wenslas and scolded him before handing him back to the tall girl who was apparently called Becky. She cuddled him then sent him to fetch the plate. Happy to be the centre of attention, Wenslas did as he was told for once.

Following Jenna from the kitchen came Eileen the cook. Nan had met her the day before when she had so efficiently coped with feeding the wild men. Seeing the chaos in the dinning hall she collared one of the younger girls and told her to clear the plates away. Another was set to cleaning tables and several girls were commandeered to right chairs.

"Girls, you should be ashamed of yourselves," she said, raising her voice to address everyone in the room. "All it takes is a couple of boys." She shook her head in disgust. "What happened to all the hard work we've done these past months? What will Nan here be thinking of us?"

Nan had no wish to be held up as the figure of authority to scare the girls into obedience, especially as Eileen managed quite well on her own.

Sami's friend Tia entered only to halt, no doubt struck by the tense atmosphere in the room. "What's going on here?"

"Just ensuring a little order," Eileen said.

"Where's Sami? I thought she'd be here already," Tia said.

"She had things to do," Nan told her. "She'll be down soon."

Seeing everyone look past her their mouths fallen open, Nan turned to find Sami entering followed by Mart. The boy looked unhappy but Sami smiled. The glow around her head was less pronounced than earlier, but it was still clearly visible.

"I like your shampoo," Tia joked. Nan liked her all the more for making light of what must appear miraculous. "Can I try?" Then Tia saw Mart and gasped. Her eyes flicked to Sami then back to the boy. "Did you do this?

"Yes," Sami said, joining Tia at a table. "I was so shocked when I saw what they had done to him I healed him."

Nan glanced around. Those who understood were awed. A few whispered, but most sat or stood in silent reverence.

"Eileen," Sami called out. "I'm starving after all that healing.

Have this lot left me anything to eat."

Sami's casualness went some way to unknotting the tension. Girls sat back at their tables, finishing their breakfast or talking quietly. But as she joined Sami at the table, Nan couldn't help noticing the girls frequently glanced at Sami as if to verify they hadn't been dreaming.

"How are the wild men settling in?" Sami asked as Eileen put a plate of buttered toast in front of her.

"Fine," Saskia said. "All the wives and children are here and I have switched the electricity back on."

"Do we have a map of the centre and the surrounding area?" Sami asked accepting a mug of tea from Jenna.

It was Pri that answered. "There are several in the main library. I can get them for you. Why do you want a map?"

Sami chewed on a piece of bread and swallowed it before answering. Nobody spoke. "Several reasons. I want to see where best to house the wild men and their families. And if news gets out about us granting refuge there are likely to be others."

This caused a stir. Nan glanced at the girl's faces. The possibility clearly hadn't occurred to them. The more that came, she thought, the more the authorities, whether the Food Police or those who had set up the centre, would want to regain control and the more they'd be tempted to use force. In a way, taking in refugees was a declaration of war.

"We can't possibly feed them all," Eileen said, sounding distraught. "I have been very careful, but our supplies are running low and I doubt we'll receive any more."

"And if any are ill, we'll be needing more medical supplies," Cilla commented.

"There may be other solutions," Saskia said. "The wild men went out foraging early this morning and came back with game and fruit and even wood for their fire."

"But if lots more come, there will soon be nothing left to forage," Jenna said.

She was right. And the further afield they went, the more they risked being intercepted.

300   Alan McCluskey

"That's why I want to see if we can plant food within the grounds," Sami said, "and even raise livestock."

"Wow!" several girls exclaimed, their faces lit up with excitement.

"Won't that take time?" Pri asked.

"Yes. But we need to plan for the longer term," Sami replied, pushing away her empty plate

"Couldn't we extend the grounds?" Mart asked. "To have more room for people and crops."

Nan was glad to hear him intervene. Sami smiled too. He had been sulking over his breakfast as if someone had stolen his favourite toy. He used to be such a resourceful child.

"How would you do that?" Pri asked.

"I'm not sure," Mart said, straightening his back as all eyes turned on him. "We need to be able to protect our land. The electric fence I heard you talking about does that now. But maybe natural landmarks could help us defend more territory."

"That's all very well," Jon said. The smile that had lingered after their night together was gone, replaced by a grim, almost sour face. "But I have seen what the Food Police can do with their spray. It kills crops, people, everything."

Nan was annoyed at him for heaping poisonous reality on the children's dreams. She suspected he continued harbouring a grudge against Mart. What was more, as adults, weren't they always setting limits in the name of the possible and reasonable. Something exceptional was needed. A miracle.

"Can you not do something against that?" Pri asked Sami.

A momentary grimace crossed Sami's face, as if she was upset at being taken for a goddess, but then she grinned. "I might have healed one person, but I am no superwoman."

"Sure you are," Tia contradicted. "We are all superwomen."

Several girls laughed. A number puffed out their chests.

"What about us?" one of the Baxter boys asked.

"You can be a superwoman too," Tia said and cupping her hands over her breasts, added, "With a little effort." Her quip brought widespread laughter.

80.

Jon sat by the window staring at the park with its expanse of grass, its tall pines from another age and the jumble of rags strung up from crooked poles masquerading as an encampment. Beyond the fence, the jungle crowded in as if in search of a breach through which to reclaim what was rightfully its.

Behind him, in the library, the scene was just as unlikely. Row upon row of books ranged from floor to ceiling, a display of cultural riches unequalled in the remains of the so-called civilised world. Jon wondered if the group of girls gathered had any idea how fortunate they were. In more ways than one.

Several maps depicting the Centre and the surrounding area were spread across a large table, weighted with books at each corner. The group of girls, along with that irritating boy Mart, were huddled around Sami discussing where to build lodgings and where to plant crops.

"Didn't you say you found a hot spring, Tia?" Sami asked. "Where is it?"

"Here," Tia said, pointing to the map. It was off to the north at the foot of the mountains.

For all his pessimism, Jon was intrigued. To his knowledge there were no geological faults near the city, so that one existed surprised him. He abandoned his window seat and looked at the map over the shoulders of the smallest girl.

"That could be a useful source of energy," Mart said, examining the surroundings. "What's this?" He pointed to rough markings filling a large area.

"Scrublands," Tia said, "and rocks, maybe caves."

"We should have a look," Pri said. "Might help us decide where to put what."

"Good idea," Sami said. "We'll tour the grounds this afternoon."

She moved from the table and, as if by instinct, the group shifted, leaving a conspicuous space around her. Sami contemplated each person, pronouncing their name as she did. Jon had the impression he was an uninvited witness to a sacred ceremony. Tia, amongst the youngest of the girls present was the only one who had not shifted away. Sami linked arms with her and stayed that way as she continued to look from girl to girl.

Pri, another small girl that had already impressed Jon by her penetrating questions and the intelligence of her ideas, was next. The girl grinned at the sound of her name and linked arms with Sami on the other side. Then came Eileen, the chubby cook, and Jenna that Jon had got to know during their flight from Baxter. The two girls stood arm in arm like old friends. Saskia, the girl who carried a bunch of keys at her waist, nodded to Sami as Sami mentioned her name. He recognised her as the girl who had unlocked the gate to let them in. Then came Cilla who had tended Wenslas so well and a girl called Rachel that Jon didn't know. She had a quiver of arrows slung over her shoulder and was clutching a bow in her hand, a non-nonsense look on her face.

"I want to name Becky, too," Sami said. "She is tending the little ones."

Sami halted a long moment in front of Mart as if taking the measure of him. The girl frowned. Was she unsure of him? At least, that was how Jon interpreted it. The boy's sour face was back, no doubt feeling neglected amid this bevy of girls. "Mart," Sami said as she had for each of the others. "Will you join us?"

He screwed up his face, saying, "Of course."

Sami appeared unsatisfied and, freeing a hand from Tia, placed it on the boy's forearm. He sighed and the tension in his face melted. "Yes," he replied to an unspoken question.

"Tia, Pri, Eileen, Jenna, Saskia, Cilla, Rachel, Becky and Mart.

Nine children. The Council of Nine," Sami said. "It falls to you to manage this place and to care for all that live here. We will talk later about what each of you must do. I look to each of you for your support in the difficult times to come. And if ever anything happens to me..." There was a mutter and a shaking of heads. "...you will make sure to get as many of the people here, both children and adults, to safety."

"What ever could happen to you?" Jenna asked.

"All sorts of things," Sami said, sounding old and tired. "If we are beset by enemies, as I fear we will, I will be their target."

"The fence will not be enough," Mart said. "We need more."

"I agree," Sami said, her face grim. Turning to look for Jon, she said, "You talked about gas."

It was so strange to have this person that had once been his son, talk to him as if he were a stranger. She might be only twelve, but she was without doubt in charge.

"Do you know anything that might help us deal with it."

Jon flinched at the memories of the gas. "It's not very pleasant," he said, curling his lips in disgust.

"Tell us what you can," Sami said, her face serious. She caught his eye and he had the uncomfortable feeling she was reading his thoughts. The moment he thought it, she looked away, as if in confirmation.

"It is toxic for plant life, for human beings and for animals alike," Jon began. "I saw it used close up…" he shuddered and saw Sami shudder too. "It kills almost immediately."

"Is it a gas?" Pri asked.

"It's a powder, I think," Jon replied. "The Food Police wear masks and full body suits when they handle it. I guess it must be fatal in contact with the skin."

"Is there an antidote?" Pri asked.

"Not that I know of," Jon said.

"There is, actually," Nan said. She been standing next to Jon listening but had said nothing. A noise at the door interrupted her. Then Becky burst in, with Wenslas straddling her back and a couple of little children at her feet.

"There's a delegation of wild men outside," she said. "They heard about you healing the boy and want you to heal a girl they think has the plague."

A stir of panic rippled round the room as girls got to their feet and everyone began to talk.

"Quiet," Sami called out. "Panic will not help." The chatter ceased.

"If it is the plague," Nan said, "we'd better act quickly before it spreads." She looked to Sami for approval. The girl nodded. "Only Sami, Jon, Mart and myself will go."

Several people objected including Cilla. "If I am to deal with health I need to come," she insisted.

Nan silenced them. "All four of us are immune."

"Cilla can come," Sami said. "She will not catch the disease."

The girl looked delighted. The others stared at Sami, expectant.

"This is going to take some time so we need to get things rolling," Sami said, then turning to Eileen she went on, "You and Jenna check our supplies. Make a list of what we will need over the next six to twelve months. Include the wild people in your calculations and add about fifty percent more. Think about where and what we can forage for food. Talk to the wild men. Oh! And think about getting water too." Addressing Saskia, she said, "You and Mart track the fence and check for weak points. Maybe you can find ways to increase or extend our defences. Take Rachel with you, if ever you get into trouble she can shoot you out." Turning to Pri and Tia, Sami said, "You two go and investigate those hot springs. I'm sure you'll have some brilliant idea how to harness them."

"What about me?" Becky asked, setting an irritated Wenslas down on his feet.

"Gather up all the children and get them to help you with the little ones. Get the older ones to carry the gardening tools to the garage and begin weeding and turning over a patch behind the garage."

81.

Nan is deep in conversation with Cilla about remedies for the plague as we walk down the drive. Jon and Mart walk a little apart, engrossed in their thoughts. I am glad to be left to think.

:: good that they don't depend entirely on you

Indeed. For when I'm not here, I remind myself. A wave of sadness washes over me but I shoo it away.

:: you are far too fatalistic - it doesn't have to end like that - in the same way you didn't need to shrivel up my willy

I smile at his baby language. Sex and gender are subjects we avoid. Maybe we should talk about it, while we have the chance.

:: cut that out!

Those who brought the call for help have run ahead to warn the others. A wave of excitement and expectation stirs near the gate. There's also a great deal of anxiety. They remember how poor people were driven out, or worse burnt alive.

A crowd greets us. Some fling themselves to the ground in awe, others bow their heads, most just stare.

"Get up," I say, helping those on the ground to their feet.

"Where is the person who is ill?" I already know but they need to tell me. Borg steps forward and bows. He points beyond the crowd to a makeshift tent strung from rags and blankets.

"What's his name?" I ask.

"Anais." A girl then.

"We find out who had contact with the girl," Nan whispers.

"Too complicated," I reply. "Bring Anais to me," I call out. No one moves.

:: they are petrified they'll catch it.

Half of them already have, Sam.

:: thank heavens they don't know - we'd really learn what wild means

"I am going to heal Anais," I say to the crowd. "But I will need your help. Here's what I am going to do. I will fetch her and bring her here." Several people groan and a number shift further away. "While I am with you, you have nothing to fear. I will ask you to pray for her and your prayers will help heal her. OK?"

Grunts and nods are their only response. Many doubt I can protect them. They are on the verge of fleeing. I reach out and let a drowsiness settle over them. Once their desire to run has calmed, I advance on the crowd and they part to let me through. Nan, Jon, Mart and Cilla follow. At the top of the small rise we reach the tent and I push aside the rag that serves as a flap to be greeted by a sickly stench.

"It's the plague alright," Nan says.

I don't need her confirmation. I can feel it. We are almost too late. The girl is coughing violently and blood dribbles from the corner of her mouth. Her lungs are in a pitiful state and lack of oxygen is affecting key organs. She must have been ill for a while. No wonder so many others are infected. I hope none of the children in the centre have been infected. I'll have to check.

"I will have to heal her before we can move her," I say. "She won't last the short journey otherwise."

"Then why bother to move her?" Mart asks.

"Because I need the pretext of healing her to heal those who are already infected."

"Others?" he asks amazed.

"Over half of them," I reply. He gasps.

The girl coughs, her whole body arching up. Enough talk. This can't wait. I kneel by the girl's side and let my hands hover over her body. Drawing on the power in all things, I let it flow through my body into the girl. I drive the illness from her. I repair most of the damage to her lungs and strengthen her heart. If any more is needed I can do it later. We need to return to the wild people before they become impatient or suspicious.

I slide my hands under the girl and lift her up. She might be featherlight, but she is still an armful. Jon and Mart help me to my feet and steady me as I retrace my steps towards the crowd. They shy away like animals fleeing a fire.

I place Anais on a patch of grass and kneel beside her.

"Now is your turn to help," I say, raising my voice. "Kneel with me. Close your eyes. And pray for good health to come to her and to you. If you don't know how to pray, just imagine you and all those gathered here are in good health."

They fall to their knees, bow their heads and close their eyes. Seeing that not one remains standing, I lift my arms from my sides till they are slanting upwards and I let the energy of the world flow through me and into those kneeling before me. Alone I could never have healed them, but an immense force lends its aid and the sickness is nothing against it.

"Jon," I whisper. I turn to see that he and the others are also kneeling. He looks at me questioningly. "Do you know a simple song?" He nods. "Then sing it now. Sing it with all your heart."

He clears his throat and begins to sing, his tenor voice strong and clear. I swear his voice is so moving it would raise the dead. The melody is familiar and catching. Nan, Mart and Cilla join in. Finally the wild people begin to sing too, till the crowd swells with the music and I seize the opportunity to finish curing Anais. I wipe the blood from around her mouth and stroke the hair from her eyes. They open and she looks at me, all wonder and joy. "Do not be afraid," I whisper close to her ear. "You are healed. All is well." I help her to her feet and when the song is over I say, "Your miracle has worked. You can open your eyes."

There are gasps as they see Anais, her hand in mine. Her parents rush forward, dashing her off her feet to embrace her. Borg shakes my hand. Others jostle, wanting to touch me as if I were a saint. Many whisper their gratitude. Others pass, eyes down. Nan has tears in her eyes. Mart and Cilla look at me as if I come from another planet. Jon is the most affected. Singing has brought welcome release that has done him immense good.

82.

"Did you really heal those people?" Cilla asks, her eyes wide as we saunter up the drive. Nan and Jon have remained behind to make arrangements so no new arrivals bring in the plague. Mart has hurried off to find Saskia to tour the electric fence.

I nod. "Nearly half had the beginnings of the plague. It spreads so quickly once it has taken a hold. That girl must have been ill long enough to contaminate so many."

"You must be tired," Cilla says.

As we walk I take stock. "No. Not all," I reply, spinning round a couple of times on my heels to prove my point.

Cilla laughs. "Wow! Could you teach me to heal like that?"

"With a pirouette, you mean?"

Her eyes are bright with laughter. "Just as simply and apparently effortlessly as you."

:: it would be good if others knew

I catch some of the thoughts behind his comment. *Now who is being pessimistic? But you are right. Better if I am not the only one.*

"I'm not sure it can be taught. To be honest, I'm not even sure how I do it. But we can try. Ask me again this evening."

As Cilla climbs the steps, I say, "Could you organise an assembly before evening meal? I want to check no one has been infected, so make sure everyone attends. But don't tell them why. Say it is to discuss the tasks to be done. Let's not spark a panic."

With an "OK," over her shoulder, she pushes open the door. I continue round the house in search of Becky and the children. Yarrow, who has been off on errands, runs circles around me, delighted we are together. I glide my fingers through his shaggy mane and pat his back. "Where have you been?" I get no answer.

At the corner of the house I pause, cupping a hand over my eyes to peer at the mountains. Inhospitable peaks capped with snow surge amongst giant clumps of rocks. From what Nan told me, it was at the limit of that godforsaken terrain that the adults from Baxter perished. If it is any consolation, at least we are unlikely to be attacked from that side, lest it be by polar bears or wolves. The thought has me shivering.

:: let's hope you are not gifted with precognition

Very funny, Sam. I shiver. *I believe some of my predecessors did have such a gift but it didn't help much. Most people wouldn't believe a word they said.* I shake my head to bring me back to the present.

Rounding the garage, I discover a crowd of busy girls and a few no-less-busy boys. Becky has gathered the little ones, including those from Baxter, and has them collecting small stones which they use to lace a line around a large plot of land. Older children are at work digging a patch of dark earth within that plot, while others weed out grasses and pile them in a wheelbarrow. One of the Baxter boys called Kred is at Becky's side, much to Wenslas's disgust.

Seeing me, Becky waves and a lot of children look up, more intrigued by Yarrow than by me. "We are lucky. Kred's done some gardening," Becky says.

I nod to Kred who smiles shyly. He's as tall as Becky. They could be twins, what with their mop of brown hair and pasty complexion, although he is a few years younger and doesn't wear glasses. He continues telling Becky what to plant so I move away.

:: competence

Sorry?

:: you should find out who knows what - there's a mass of unused talent here and tons of useful knowledge - you are going to need every last drop of it

Sam's thoughts spin off in wild scenarios of neglected knowledge muddled with plans to identify and harness available knowledge. *You sound like you are laying the foundations for a future city.*

:: is that not what you are doing?

I turn back to Kred. "Where did you learn about gardening?"

"My father was a botanist. He organised growing fruit and vegetables as well as medicinal herbs in Baxter. There were no schools, we learnt from adults. He taught me a lot before the Food Police got him."

He brushes tears away with a muddy fist. I place a hand on his arm, taking some of his sadness as tears well in my eyes.

"We will meet later about the work to be done. Come with Becky. I am sure we can put your knowledge to good use."

I spot Cilla hurrying from the house. "See you later," I say and head to intercept her with Yarrow running circles around me. She waves, her face pinched with worry. Yarrow greets her, licking her hand. She tries to smile but her lips barely curve.

"I found Magalie in the attic room coughing violently. I think she's got ... You know."

"Is anyone with her?"

"No. She's alone. I would never have spotted her, hidden as she was in a heap of bed clothes, but I heard her cough."

Yarrow choses that moment to bound off, as if he doesn't want anything to do with the plague. I don't blame him.

The moment Cilla pushes open the bedroom door a telltale odour greets us.

The sick girl's eyes are wide with fear. "Hallo Magalie," I say. "We've come to make you well."

A violent fit of coughing has her close her eyes in pain. I kneel beside her mattress and, placing my hands above her chest, I take stock. She is not as far gone as Anais, but her lungs are badly infected. I turn to Cilla. "Do you still want to learn?" She nods enthusiastically.

"Place your hand here," I say indicating a space just above Magalie's chest. I place a hand over hers and close my eyes.

:: I hope you know what you are doing

I'm improvising. Now keep quiet if you don't want her to know there are two of us in here. I am going to talk in her mind.

Cilla, I say in her head, like I might talk to Sam. She must have heard because she gasps and jerks her hand away.

:: are you sure about this? - maybe this knowledge is not meant to be shared

Shhhh.

"Don't be alarmed. That was just me talking into your mind," I explain. "We will be able to work better if I do." She puts her hand back under mine, muttering, "Sorry." Her fingers tremble. I steady them.

Good. Now try talking to me in your head. I will be able to hear.

"Like this," she says.

No, without speaking out loud.

This is so strange, she says and giggles when it works.

Good. Now concentrate on your hand. I sense her doing so. *Turn your attention to Magalie's chest. Exactly. Can you see the way the illness is attacking her lungs?* I feel her perplexity. She can't see anything. *Let me show you.* She is so startled, I almost lose contact. When her pulse calms, I continue. *I am going to draw on my energy to chase away the illness and repair the damage done.*

When the healing is finished I remove my hand, releasing Cilla's as I do. Magalie is smiling. "You'll need to rest, miss. But in a few days you won't even know you were ill."

I clamber to my feet and am surprised to find Cilla still kneeling. I take it for shock and help her to her feet. My arm linked in hers, I head for the door saying, "Sleep now, Magalie."

Once outside I halt and take a closer look at Cilla. She seems dazed. "Cilla?" I say, but she doesn't respond.

:: I think you've blown her mind

I try to ignore Sam's alarming words and lead Cilla down the corridor to her room. She lets herself be led and lays down on her bed as if she had no will of her own. What have I done? She acts like some essential part of her has vacated her head, but I don't want to probe her mind for fear I'll make things worse.

:: check her energy level - I think she drained

How could she have done that? I didn't touch her energy.

:: I suspect she used hers to help you

I am flabbergasted. I hadn't even noticed. *Let me check.* I place a hand on her forehead. Sure enough she has next to no energy left. *You are right, Sam, she's drained. No wonder she's barely here.*

:: careful about replenishing her energy - maybe it is like hypothermia - if you heat someone up too fast it has disastrous results

You do well to warn me. I hadn't thought of that. I let a trickle of energy flow into her and immediately sense her presence grow. I check the rest of her body. Everything is fine. So I dribble more energy into her and her eyes flutter open. She goes to sit up, but I put a restraining hand on her shoulder. "Lie still for a while."

"What happened?" Her voice is weak and she hesitates over her words.

"You tried to run before you could crawl and exhausted yourself."

"But I don't feel tired."

"Not your body. Let's say your soul."

83.

Nan stood at the gate surrounded by wild men, brandishing crude clubs and other makeshift weapons, threatening her because she wouldn't let them out.

"We have to hunt," Borg said, the ring in his nose bobbing up and down. "How else are we to feed everyone?"

The keys that Saskia had entrusted to her weighed heavy in Nan's pocket.

"Just a minute," Jon yelled to the wild men in an attempt to be heard over the uproar. He took hold of Nan's elbow and pulled her away from Borg. "If they keep going in and out," he whispered, "how are we to stop them bringing back the plague?"

"They don't realise there is a threat," Nan said. "Sami should have told them what she did."

Nan went to Borg and raised her hands for silence. The men ceased their brouhaha just long enough for her to say to Borg, "Let's take a walk."

As always he looked confused, unable to grasp what was required of him. She grabbed him by the arm and marched him along the path. He didn't flinch. Nor did he try to stop her. He trotted at her side uncomprehending. She wondered how he managed to lead his people. Brute force probably.

"We need to talk," she began, when the commotion of the wild men was far enough away.

"Anais was ill. She had the plague. You know what the plague is like?"

He grunted by way of response, glancing over his shoulder

to see if perchance his men were following. They weren't.

"Sami cured her although the girl was close to death. Do you understand?"

"Yes," he said, sounding annoyed. "I'm no idiot."

She was hoping as much. "She must have been ill for a while. Where was she all that time?"

"She cooked."

"She was in contact with many of you. You know what happens when someone with the plague is in contact with other's."

Borg halted in his tracks. She could almost see his mind at work. That he understood was clear from his shocked look. Once again he glanced over his shoulder at the encampment.

"Nearly half of you were infected," she said.

She had to hang on to his arm to stop him running back to the camp.

"Let me finish. When Sami made you all kneel and close you eyes, when Jon sang that song and you all joined in, Sami healed those of you who had the plague."

He stopped and stared at her, shaking his head in disbelief. "How could such a little girl do that?"

"She is very special," Nan said, a shiver running down her spine. "Have any of you got the symptoms?"

He stood unmoving as if sorting through the wild people in his head. "No," he said. "No one." He scratched his head, making Nan wish they washed from time to time. Then he nodded. "Thank her for me."

So far so good, Nan thought. "The plague is waiting out there in the jungle." She let the thought sink in. When his forehead frowned, she guessed he'd grasped the implications. "That is why we can't let your men out. Not yet. We have to find a way to ensure no one entering the grounds is infected. Once we have that figured out, you can go hunting. In the meantime, we'll provide food from our supplies."

He halted again, as if he couldn't walk and think at the same time. "I see. How long?"

Nan shrugged. "Not long." The food would dwindle rapidly.

"Many new people will be arriving. Refugees. They will come for the same reasons as you. But we won't be able to feed everybody." We can hardly feed ourselves, she thought. "We will need your help to find food."

"Why not shut 'em out?" he grunted.

"For the same reason we let you in, because we have to help those in need."

She halted and released his arm. "Do you agree not to go hunting?" He held out a tentative hand and she shook it. "It would be better if you didn't tell anyone how ill people were," she suggested. "They might panic."

He frowned. "How do I explain?"

"Talk of the threat of catching the plague like Anais."

"OK."

"Someone will visit you about food," she said, "probably Eileen or Jenna."

They returned in silence till they reached the men seated on the ground, clubs at their sides. Jon stood some distance away looking worried. She smiled at him. "Let's go see about food for these good people," she said, and linking arms with him, led him up the drive.

She had finished telling him what happened when they reached the house. Seated on the steps was Cilla. Sami sat next to her, one arm slung around the girl's shoulder. Sami smiled at their arrival but Cilla looked weary.

"Cilla has had an adventure," Sami said. She slid her fingers across Cilla's forehead, brushing the hair from her eyes, the sort of gesture a mother might make. Nan had to smile. Physically at least, Cilla was several years older than Sami.

"Can I talk about it?" Sami asked.

Cilla nodded.

"Cilla discovered one of the girls had the plague." Nan and Jon gasped. "Don't worry. It's alright. As Cilla asked to learn to heal, I gave her a first lesson. I must admit I hadn't thought it through. People like me have never taught others how to heal. So I had no point of reference. I showed her healing from the inside, as it were. Then when we had finished imagine my surprise to discover Cilla had become a zombie." She chuckled, but Cilla didn't smile.

"It took me a while to realise what had happened." She pulled Cilla closer and planted a kiss on top of her head. "This wonderful girl wanted to help me so much she completely drained herself. But now everything is alright."

Cilla looked up at Jon and Nan and grimaced. "It was horrible. I felt so empty." She became pale. "We talked about the soul in a study group. I remember arguing with Pri about what it was. I never thought I would experience it first hand. That's what zombies are: people without souls." She shivered, at which Sami hugged her. "Let's go find a place for the Council of Nine to meet," Sami said, getting to her feet and pulling Cilla up with her.

"Why do you say nine?" Cilla asked, brushing the dust from her skirt. "There are ten of us with you."

"I'm here only for a short while," Sami said. Cilla began to object but Sami placed a finger on her lips. "Once I am gone, you Nine will manage well enough." Cilla flung her arms around Sami's neck and burst into tears.

84.

Jon turned to leave at the Common Room door. "I'll check on the children," he said, feeling second-class and unwanted.

"They are fine," Sami said. "Stay with us. Your advice will be welcome. You too, Nan."

He shrugged and followed her into the room. It must have been designed to entertain special guests because it was enormous. A large number of armchairs were scattered in front of a giant hearth, a thickly woven carpet covered most of the floor and outlines on the walls hinted at paintings or portraits that must have hung there. The room was warm enough without a fire burning in the grate. Sunlight steamed in several floor-to-ceiling windows looking over the park.

Jon took a seat farthest from the fire, but the sun's rays beat down on his head and shoulders and he quickly felt too hot. Shifting to an armchair in the shadows close to the door, he was the last to be seated. Pri and Tia were on the floor at Sami's feet. Cilla, the girl they had met outside on the steps, had pulled up an armchair next to Sami. The others were seated in a tight circle around Sami talking quietly amongst themselves.

"Let me introduce Kred," Sami began, indicating the boy seated next to Becky on the settee. "His late father was responsible for agriculture at Baxter and Kred learnt from him. I suggest we welcome him into our group. If he is responsible for gardening that will leave Becky time to look after the children."

"Unless she prefers gardening with Kred," Jenna said. Both boy and girl blushed.

"That time will tell," Sami said with a hint of a smile.

"Welcome, Kred," Pri said. "That makes us the Council of Ten."

Sami nodded. "Let's turn to the situation here," she said. "It is getting more and more complicated."

"You bet," put in Tia, her head leaning against Sami's knees.

Sami tousled Tia's hair, bringing several envious looks from around the group. "That's why we will have to meet several times a day to tell each other what is going in." She looked around the room, lingering at the sight of the large windows. "This is a really inspiring place to meet. Thanks Cilla for suggesting it."

Cilla leaned closer to Sami and grinned. She still looked fragile but judging from the way she followed the conversation, she had got over the worst of her fright.

"So who is going to begin?" Sami asked, her eyes settling on Cilla.

"We have had to deal with a serious outbreak of the plague," Cilla began, causing gasps of dismay. "As you know…" and she went on to explain what happened with the wild people.

"So many!" Tia said, her eyes bright with admiration.

"Then I stumbled on Magalie. She was coughing violently. It was clear she had the illness. Sami cured that too. She has suggested we organise a gathering after this evening's meal, ostensibly to talk about who does what, but in reality so she can detect if anyone has the plague and cure them."

A buzz of talk rippled around the room.

Sami raised a hand for silence. "Cilla asked me to teach her to heal." Her words set off a new round of talk which Sami had to quieten. "I wasn't sure it was possible and we had some problems." Cilla nodded vigorously. "But now we've figured it out. I suggest I teach all the council." This time Sami made no effort to silence the discussions that broke out as people speculated about being able to heal.

Clever move, Jon thought. It will give the Council authority and help them be accepted, especially if more adults join.

"The meeting Cilla mentioned will be about work. Each of

you should be looking for someone to second you and others that can help, especially those who know something about what you have to do."

"This is all going so fast," Becky said. "So many new prospects, it makes me giddy."

"You been filching wine from my kitchen?" Eileen asked, imitating the voice of a severe matron.

"Well, just a little," Becky replied, her voice contrite. Everyone roared with laughter.

"Talking about kitchens," Eileen continued. "Jenna and I made a list of supplies. The situation is worse than I thought." Several people groaned.

"How come?" Pri asked frowning.

"We were so used to receiving regular supplies that when they stopped it took a while to realise we needed to be more careful."

"It'll take a while to grow thing in the gardens," Kred said.

"We went down to see the wild people about foraging," Jenna said, "but they told us they are not allowed out."

"Yes," Nan said. "If they go out they are likely to bring the plague back."

"However did you manage to convince them not to hunt?" Pri asked.

"By telling their leader how many had been infected before Sami healed them," Nan said

"Was that wise?" Cilla asked.

"I couldn't see how to do it otherwise. I insisted he didn't tell anyone."

"So we need to check everyone who enters," Saskia said. "A small group of the wild people wouldn't be too difficult. Sami could scan them… But if more arrive we could have a problem."

"That's another reason why I want to teach you all to heal," Sami said. "I cannot possibly spend all day down by the gate, but if all of you can check, we can take it in turns."

"If new people want to force their way in when the gate is open we might find it hard to stop them," Mart said. Faces around the group became thoughtful.

"I would like to teach more people archery," Rachel said. "There was a group in the Centre, so a good number of us can shoot and we have quite a supply of bows and arrows."

"That's a really good idea," Mart said, grinning. "I'd love to learn. In return I could teach unarmed combat and self defence."

"Wow! Our own army," Tia said, clapping her hands.

"Not exactly," Sami said, laying a friendly hand on Tia's shoulder. "Defence not attack."

Pri boxed Tia on the shoulder and Tia mimed pulling an arrow from her quiver.

"We don't have much time before evening meal," Eileen said. "What did you discover at the hot springs?"

"We couldn't find them," Pri said, trying but failing to keep a straight face. It was Tia's turn to pummel Pri's shoulder.

"They are wonderful," Pri admitted.

"Did you have a bath in the hot water?" Cilla asked. "Such sulphur-filled water is supposed to be very good for you."

"No thank you!" Tia exclaimed. "The water was boiling. The whole place was shroud in steam and smelt of bad eggs."

"If we can channel the water and keep it hot, we might have a way of heating the house…" Pri said.

"Or hot houses to make plants grow in winter," Kred added.

"Great idea," Pri said.

"How far away is it?" Becky asked.

"A good couple of miles," Pri replied. "All up hill, so we could channel water here if we wanted."

Eileen got to her feet and Jenna joined her. "We have to oversee preparations for the meal," Eileen said, "but before we go I'd love to hear news from the fence. It could be our best friend."

Saskia and Mart exchanged looks and the boy nodded. "We didn't have time to complete the circuit," Saskia said. "It goes on for miles. But what we did see was intact."

"Our main concern," Mart added, "is the electricity. We have no idea where it comes from. If someone decides to cut it we could be completely exposed."

There was a hushed silence as worried faces looked at worried faces.

"I have no idea who set up this place," Mart said, "but for the moment they continue to protect us. We can't count on that for ever."

"We must do two things," Saskia said. "Trace the source of electricity. Who knows, it may be coming from within the grounds. In which case it will be less of a worry."

"And the second thing?" Pri asked.

"Give them a chance," Tia said nudging her.

"I'm hungry," Pri replied, at which everyone laughed.

"The second thing, " Mart said, "is to dream up an alternative way to electrify the fence. It is so long we can't imagine replacing it."

"Ok," Eileen said, heading for the door with Jenna in tow. "Dinner in fifteen minutes. Don't be late. It's special."

85.

"Why here?" I ask pointing to a spot on the map three miles from the main gate.

"Because there is another gate there. It is unused, but once it must have been the main entrance. Opposite is a wide road leading straight to the city," Mart says.

"It is where most refugees or attackers will arrive and, as it is unwatched, it is a weak spot," Saskia adds. "But it could also be a godsend."

It is so far from the Centre I wonder how it could be of use.

:: hard to keep an eye on

"If we channel refugees through that gate," Saskia explains, "we keep them at a safe distance. We would have to make it more difficult to take the track leading to our gate."

"There is another reason why this is a good choice," Mart adds tapping the place on the map. He grins, challenging me to ask him why, but I make no move to do so.

:: boys and their power games, will they ever learn

Not interested in such trials of force, I turn to Saskia, who is more forthcoming.

"All around the gate are abandoned warehouses and work-shops. There are also at least ten small houses and even a hotel or hostel," she says. "They are dusty and have suffered from the weather, but whoever lived there took good care of the place."

"There must have been some sort of industry," Mart puts in. "We should explore and see what else it has to offer."

"We could accommodate a large number of people comfortably in those buildings," Saskia says, "with a few minor adjust-ments." She grins, delighted at their discovery. "There is even a considerable stock of timber in what must once have been a saw mill. All the equipment is still there, abandoned, as if the people upped and fled from one day to the next."

"It is a shame we don't have more time. This place," he waves his hand over the map, "may develop into a future city and we have a unique opportunity to rethink how such a city might be built and organised-"

:: a man with big ideas your lover boy but they are a bit dis-connected from the real problems we face

I snort mentally at Sam's irritating habit of casting Mart as my suitor. I am about to scold him when Pri appears in the entrance saying, "Sami, everyone is waiting for you. They are hungry."

As I enter the dining room everyone gets to their feet.

:: respect or adoration

I halt at the first tables. "Please sit down," I say and wait till all are seated. "I am no different from you. If you must show me respect, do so by treating me the same as the person seated next to you."

"Lord no!" Tia exclaims, boxing Pri's ears. "I would never treat you like Pri."

A number of people laugh, but I see several wince.

:: I doubt they will ever be able to treat you normally

That's why I need to catch them unawares. I turn to the people seated at the table next to me where there is a spare place. Their faces are petrified, afraid I will join them.

"Whose place is this?" I ask, struggling not to sound accus-ing as my worry about a possible missing girl grows.

They look for one to another as if vying to avoid having to reply. "I'm not going to bite you," I say with a chuckle that sounds forced even to my ears. "It's just that if someone is ab-sent that might be important."

A tiny little girl, even smaller than Pri answers in a voice so weak I can hardly hear. "Arkady."

"What's your name?"

"Ronia," she replies like a phantom. I want to tell her to speak up, but that would never do. She'd shrivel up.

"Ronia, do you know where Arkady is?"

"She said she was too tired to come down," she answers then coughs. Her eyes are wide with fear, as if I am going to flay her.

:: sounds ominous - the plague?

Indeed. I spot Cilla across the dining hall and beckon to her. I hold out my hand to Ronia. "Let's go and see if Arkady is OK. You can show me the way."

She gets to her feet, steps over the bench and places a trembling hand in mine. She is so tense and brittle I am afraid I will break her fingers. I let a dribble of energy flow into her, bringing with it a boost of confidence. Not too much. Better if she builds her own.

I turn to address everyone. "Is anyone else missing?"

A sea of shaking heads and blank faces reply.

Cilla has joined us and we head out of the refectory. From the corner of my eye I spot Eileen flinging her arms up in despair. Poor thing. So much for her surprise. I let Ronia go up the familiar spiral stairs first. Progress is painfully slow and she has a hard time breathing.

:: she's ill too, isn't she?

Yes. In the very early stages.

I would like to ply her with questions as we climb, but talking is impossible in her condition. "Arkady is your friend?" I ask when we halt for a rest on the landing to the attic.

"Yes, she befriended me when I arrived."

She halts in front of a door and pushes it open.

"Maybe you should wait outside," Cilla suggests.

"No. It's alright," I say, planning to heal both girls. "I will protect her."

The curtains are drawn and I don't at first see Arkady in the deepening shadows.

"Arkady," Ronia says. "I've brought help."

A groan comes from a corner where I spot a girl rolled up in a blanket crouching on the floor. "Can't get into bed," she croaks. "No strength."

With Cilla's help I lift her onto a bed. "Lie down next to her Arkady and hold her hand," I say. Cilla shoots me an alarmed look. "You are also a little ill, Ronia, so I will heal you both."

I kneel next to the bed and Cilla joins me. When I stretch out a hand over Arkady, she does the same after a brief hesitation.

Is it safe for me to do this? she asks mind to mind.

Yes. They say when you fall from a horse the first thing to do is get back on. Can you see the illness?

"Oh!" she says shocked into talking out loud. *Yes. It's so ugly.*

This time we will take energy from the world around us. That way your supply will not be depleted.

Once Arkady has been cured we turn to Ronia.

There is hardly anything there, Cilla says.

I'll let you call on energy to get rid of it, I say. She draws a considerable pool of energy which rushes eagerly to her. I realise how intoxicating that must be for those not used to it. Gently, I say. *Just a small drop will do.*

What do I do with the rest?

Keep a little for another time and let the rest flow back where it belongs.

When we open our eyes, two young faces are looking up at us full of wonder. "You were both ill," I say. "Cilla and I have healed you. Now, if you have the strength we can go down and eat. Apparently there's a surprise."

"Should we not disinfect the blankets?" Ronia asks.

I laugh. "Good thinking! I think you just found yourself an assistant, Cilla."

"Me too," Arkady insists.

When the four of us enter the dinning hall everyone begins applauding. Some even cheer or whistle. Arkady and Ronia are intimidated. I show them to their table where they are beset by questions.

I raise a hand for silence. "Arkady and Ronia were ill," I say. "Cilla cured them, with my help."

:: good - the more you keep them informed the less they will surround you with myth and speculation

And worship. It always gets in the way.

:: well, sharing your abilities is a good strategy

There is renewed cheering as Cilla and I join the other members of the council along with Jon and Nan.

"Sorry about the food," Eileen says. "It wouldn't wait."

"And neither could we," Pri added, making a show of licking her lips.

"You should have been an actress Pri," Tia says.

Pri gets to her feet and makes a bow worthy of a prince. "If Sir Tiatray would grant me the next dance?" she says, forcing her voice down an octave. Her performance sparks more laughter.

I glance around the room. So many smiling, happy faces. I only wish it could continue like that.

Eileen places a plate of roasted chestnuts in front of Cilla and I. "Pri and Tia collected them en route for the hot springs," Eileen says, "and the cream is the last we have. I whipped it myself."

"Where are we to hold the meeting?" I ask Cilla between chewing chestnuts.

"I haven't had time to organise anything yet," she says.

"Why not here?" Pri asks. "A meeting in the hall might bring back bad memories."

I shudder at my own fearful memories of the place.

"Here it is then," I say. Turning to Nan who is seated at the far end of the table I beckon her over. She manages to squeeze on the bench between Cilla and I.

"Should we disinfectant rooms where the plague has been?"

"It is propagated by touch and breath," Nan says. "It doesn't survive long outside a human body."

"So we don't need to disinfect," Cilla says. "That's a relief."

86.

The dishes have been cleared away and most of the tables shifted against the wall so the chairs form concentric semicircles around a long table at which sit the council. Eileen's helpers have finished serving herbal tea and take a seat.

"Oh that we could live forever like this," I begin, giving voice to the wistfulness the moment evokes. My words bring smiles all round. "Delicious food, a comfortable house, excellent company and lots of stimulating conversation. But things around us are changing fast." The smiles fade as they sense that less pleasant news is on its way.

:: you scare them

"The wild people are just a beginning. There will be others. Many others. Conditions are getting worse outside, mainly because the plague is on the rise. We urgently need to prepare."

There's a tense silence in the room.

"We can do nothing against the plague," an older girl says.

"That is not true," Cilla says, getting to her feet.

It is good to see her taking a stand after her setback earlier. I sit on a chair off to the side and close my eyes. Letting my senses reach out, I scan the gathering in search of those that might have the plague. Several are in the early stages. I set about healing them. It is more difficult at a distance but not impossible.

"There are three people in this room who had the plague," Cilla continues, "but Sami and I have healed them."

Her words spark a buzz of conversation as heads swivel in search of who it could be.

"That's not all," Mart says. "You may know that one of the wild people caught the plague. It turned out a large number of them had it. Sami cured them all. She cured them all."

Rather than reassure them, Mart's words make them more agitated. I will have to intervene if he and Cilla can't calm them.

"You are missing the point," Cilla says, raising her voice. "The important thing is not who was ill but that they have been cured and we know how to do it."

I have my eyes closed but I sense her glance in my direction.

:: she wants to show those who have been cured - they might get lynched or shunned

I know, I tell him. *Go ahead, Cilla,* I speak into her mind. *I need time to heal the few people who are still ill.*

Cilla goes to Magalie's table. "Tell them, Magalie," Cilla says.

"I felt exhausted," Magalie begins, her voice trembling, daunted at having to speak before so many. "I couldn't stop coughing and each time I coughed it was like an explosion in my lungs. Then Cilla and Sami healed me. It was very strange, like a force moving inside my body. The coughing stopped and my lungs ceased aching. I felt like I could run and jump for joy, but Sami told me I needed to rest."

"It was the same for me," Arkady said, getting to her feet. "It wasn't as bad as Magalie, but I felt lousy and started coughing. Cilla healed me and now I am right as rain."

"You can too?" someone called out.

"Yes. Sami taught me," Cilla says.

I open my eyes to see she has returned to the table.

"Sami said earlier that things are changing and we urgently need to prepare," Cilla said. "Well our first step was to set up a Council to look after the preparations."

She waved a hand over the Council members. "It was Sami who chose us and we accepted."

"Do you get more cake at dinner?" someone called out and several people laughed.

Cilla's face was grim. "No extra cake, no special privileges, just a lot of hard work and a great deal of worries."

Tia gets to her feet and joins Cilla. "In our Council, Cilla is responsible for health. You have just heard she was the first to learn to heal from Sami."

"The first?" a girl asks.

"Sami has agreed to teach the Council to heal so we don't have to rely on her," Tia replies.

"I already have two helpers, Arkady and Ronia," Cilla says. "If others are interested, we will need all the help we can get. And Nan has agreed to teach us what she knows of healing."

Several girls get to their feet, a boy too, their hands raised. "Me!" they say.

"Not now," Cilla says. "We have a lot to talk about. Come to me afterwards."

"You can imagine what responsibility Eileen has," Tia says.

"Loved the cream," someone calls out. There's laughter then the girls begin clapping, a few at first then more and more, several even cheer. Eileen gets to her feet and, pulling Jenna up beside her, the two girls take a bow.

"We have a difficult task," Eileen says. "Our usual supplies have dried up so we need other sources."

"We've talkied to the wild people about foraging," Jenna says.

"And we have started a garden to grow vegetables and herbs," Becky adds, standing too. "With the help of Kred our resident agricultural expert."

Kred shakes his head, but Becky hauls him to his feet and has him bow amid cheers.

"We are thinking of building hot houses," Kred says. "So we can grow vegetables even in winter."

"That's where Pri and I come in," Tia says, beckoning to Pri. "We've found a source of unlimited hot water and Pri has been burrowing through the library for ways to use that energy."

"Burrowing!" exclaims Pri. "Anyone would think I am a mole. And before anyone says I look like one, let me tell you how important those hot springs are. They could mean heated accommodation and running hot water for baths and showers."

The image of hot baths sends a shiver of excitement around

the room that in turn sparks a buzz of talk.

"There is at least one more thing we desperately need to do; reinforce our defences," Saskia says. "We cannot be sure the electricity for the fence will continue. With Mart, we are looking into generating our own and adding additional protection."

"And we are thinking of shifting the main entrance to anther gate at a safer distance from us," Mart says, "in a place where there are already many buildings we can adapt to house the wild people and anyone else who seeks refuge. So we will need help from anyone with skills in carpentry or building."

"As part of our defence efforts," Saskia says, "Rachel will be training us in archery."

"I will organise practice every day," Rachel says. "I suggest you either do archery with me or unarmed combat with Mart."

"Can we do both?" a boy from Baxter asks.

"Sure," Mart and Rachel reply together.

"Cool," the boy says, "our own militia."

"As Sami said, we are not forming an army," Saskia say, "but preparing a force in case we have to defend ourselves."

:: how about that - they held the meeting on their own - soon you'll be out of a job

Good. I'll be able to retire to a cottage in a clearing and play chess with you. I get to my feet feeling very proud of them.

"Some good news to end on," I say returning to the Council. "While these ten council members have been so admirably holding this meeting and planning our future, I have checked every one present. A few of you had the beginnings of the plague but I have cured you. So we can safely say there is no plague within the grounds."

"What about those coming from outside?" Ronia asks.

"We still need to work on that," Saskia says.

Her reply provokes a thoughtful science.

:: they hadn't realised how difficult their task will be

"If you want to ask questions about the work or sign up to help," Tia says, "and we hope you will, now is your chance."

87.

The track crested a hill and burst from amongst the trees. The group halted, awe struck. "It's enormous," Pri exclaimed. She was right. Jon had not expected anything like it.

Below, in a wide valley, a road serpentined from a gate in the electric fence, slithering between rows of houses, passing what looked like a hotel in the shape of giant U and on amid factories and warehouses ending in front of a brick building that stood apart. The sawmill was easy to identify with its stock of planks piled high. Beyond lay a series of greenhouses overgrown with plants. On the far side of the valley, a dense forest stretched to the foot of the mountains. To the left, on the far side of the greenhouses, a dense cloud of smoke rose.

"The hot springs," Pri said.

"Looks like someone already had the idea of heating the greenhouses using the hot springs," Kred said. "See those pipes." He traced the line with his out-stretched hand.

He was right. Jon could make out two large black pipes running parallel that surged like ghosts from the mist and rose and fell with the lie of the land till they plunged into the waiting greenhouses. Vegetation flourished all along the pipes partly concealing them within a hedge of plants and flowers.

"I sense no human presence," Sami said. "Let's go and explore this Eldorado."

"Eldorado?" Rachel turned to ask as they headed down the hill.

"It was a realm in which the king was said to cover himself

in gold," Sami explained. "It became a legend and many people came in search of the promised gold, but never found it. In reality, it had existed. The king was a despicable tyrant whose only interest was riches. For years, his greed fed off his people till rage and suffering became too much and the people slaughtered him and his family. The killing didn't stop there. Fighting broke out as individuals vied for a share of the gold. Some say the gold was cursed. Not even the intervention of the most gifted of souls could save the situation. Very few survived."

Sami's story was like a freezing downpour on an otherwise sunny day. Everyone shivered. Jon wondered how she could know such things. She spoke as if she had been there.

"So why call this an Eldorado?" Rachel asked. "There is neither gold nor king, thank heavens."

"True," Sami replied, chuckling. "The word has come to mean a promise of riches that is much needed but quite unexpected. If I am not mistaken, this village brings solutions to many of our insurmountable problems." Her words lifted some of the dark shadows her tale had cast.

Reaching the first buildings, they were enveloped in a cloud of flies that buzzed wildly about their heads. To make things worse, the air was thick with a sickly smell. Tia wiped her hand across a window as they walked between two low storage buildings. "Fruit," she said, peering inside. "Rotten fruit. Unending piles of it."

"And shelf upon shelf of jars and cans," said Pri, who had clambered onto a stone to see inside the opposite warehouse. "I have never seen so many."

"This must be the canning and bottling factory," Mart said. "All the machines seem intact. Ugh. Disgusting. It will take some time to clear up. Whoever worked here left in a hurry. There is a line of half-filled bottles in the machine, brimming over with fungus and a world of crawling beasties."

"Look over there," Kred said hurrying between the warehouse and factory. "It's an orchard."

"Trust Kred to find an orchard," Tia said.

When everyone caught up they saw he was right, though there was little left of the orchard. Most of the trees had gone wild and needed a severe pruning. The ground lay strewn with several years of apples and plums and pears amid a buzz of wasps and bees.

"Can you do anything with all this?" Sami asked.

"Sure," Kred replied, grinning. "If I can find pruning shears and a stone to sharpen them."

A road ran between the orchard and the factory, they followed it a short distance till they reached a crossroads. Opposite were the greenhouses they had seen from above. Close up, Jon could see they were bursting with outsized plants that had pushed their way out every open window and seemed set on conquering the outside world. Judging from the noise, the buildings were teeming with life, not all of it friendly. Turning right, Rachel said, "I want to look at the gate." She unslung her bow and cocked an arrow. Tia and Pri did likewise.

Despite the years it must have been unused, there was a strong smell of wood in the air as they passed the piles of timber and then the sawmill that crouched in a hollow. Several lumber trucks lay collecting dust in front of the main entrance. Maybe there was a supply of petrol or diesel somewhere.

They reached a second crossroads. To the right, the road curved back the way they had come. To the left it went past the sawmill on one side and a low squat building on the other from where it continued to the forest. Rachel went straight ahead. They passed several rows of squat houses to their right that had probably lodged workers. The windows were tiny and the front doors narrow, each house having a minuscule garden out front.

On the left was the hotel or hostel they had spotted from the hill. Judging by the balconies and windows, it promised more space than the houses. Tia tried the front door. It was locked. Beyond, the road widened into a large square devoid of buildings that abutted the fence and the gate.

Peering through the gate from a safe distance, Jon could see a wide avenue sloping down, flanked by a riot of trees. In the distance, above the dense foliage of the jungle, through the haze, he could make out the ruins that marked the beginning of the city. The Food Police could easily drive up that avenue with several of their armoured vehicles abreast. The image left him feeling sick. He turned away.

"However are we going to open the gate if it is electrified?" Pri asked.

"We'll have to ask Saskia. She will know," Rachel said.

Turning towards the village, the low building wedged behind the hostel and its carpark on one side and the massive forest beyond was clearly visible. It was much bigger than it had at first appeared.

"It's enormous," Rachel said, pointing to the building. "Let's explore." Seizing Tia's hand, she tugged her across the carpark. With Rachel's tall body reaching ever more skyward and Tia, short and round-faced and very much down to earth, they made a comical pair. Odd really because Rachel, for all her adventurousness, was by far the more down to earth of the pair.

There were no windows and no doors on that side of the wooden building so they had to walk its full length and only when they reached the entrance opposite the sawmill did they find a door flanked by windows. Tia tried the door, but it was locked.

Jon rubbed the grime from a window and peered in. A wooden counter ran the breadth of the building, behind which were numerous shelves and doors that opened on the rest of the building.

Several cardboard boxes lay open on the counter. Piled next to them were dusty stacks of brightly coloured shirts and trousers. Suspended from hangers amid abundant cobwebs was a large assortment of jackets. He recognised the styles. They dated from prior to the Disaster. Out of necessity, such colours had since been replaced by grey. The girls' uniform was an exception.

"Wow!" Tia exclaimed. "Beautiful clothes."

"It'll be too big for you," Rachel said.

Tia took a swipe at her, but Rachel was far too quick to get caught.

"I'd like to explore the building beyond the greenhouses," Mart said, grabbing Tia's arm to stop her from running after Rachel. "Anyone want to join me."

"I'll come," Tia said, shaking herself free, "but only to make sure you don't get up to mischief."

"Mischief? Me?" Mart exclaimed, grinning. "You can talk."

"I'd better come too," Pri said. "To make sure the two of you don't get up to mischief together."

Sami laughed. "Let's all go. Then we can get up to mischief together." All the children laughed.

Jon hung back, wondering what he was doing with all those young people. He felt stodgy and slow with age. How could they possibly joke when a catastrophe was lurking around every corner? He glanced at Sami. No. She was different. She might smile, but the weight of concern was there if you cared to look.

The road, which curved to the right after the greenhouses, was lined with trees concealing much of the building they wanted to explore. Up a slight incline then a sharp left, they stood in front of a majestic one-storey building sporting large bay windows and a massive oak door.

The group climbed the steps to the door. Jon turned hoping to see the village but the trees and greenhouses got in the way.

"Look," Pri exclaimed. "A plaque."

Sure enough, when she pushed aside the ivy clinging to the walls, there was a weather-worn plaque.

"What does it say? Tia asked.

Pri pulled a handkerchief from her pocket and rubbed the plaque till the handkerchief became the same dark grey as the plaque. "Trey," she read out. "That's spelt T-R-E-Y. Oh! And it says these are the municipal hot springs and baths."

Tia clapped her hands. "Hot water! My dream come true." She stepped forward and tried the door. It wouldn't budge. "Blast. So much for dreams. It's locked."

"Let me try," Mart said. "Maybe it's just very heavy or stuck with time." But, much to Jon's satisfaction, the boy's youthful strength couldn't shift the door.

"There must be other doors," Pri said, shaking out the filthy ruins of her handkerchief before stuffing it in her blazer pocket.

Both Kred and Mart were tugging at the door with Rachel's help when suddenly it cracked open and the two boys tumbled down the steps. It was only thanks to Rachel's efforts that it did not snap shut.

A strong smell of rotten eggs greeted them as they entered the white-tiled hallway. On either side were offices, but the young ones were set on visiting the baths. Through a revolving door they entered a hallway with a low bench running the length of the wall on both sides.

"It's to leave your shoes," Jon told them.

"Have you visited baths like these?" Pri asked.

He found the straight-forward way she addressed him endearing. She might joke with Tia but he appreciated that when she questioned him, she was motivated by a desire to learn.

"Only once. A long time ago. It wasn't as sumptuous."

"Sumptuous," Pri said as if tasting an unfamiliar word.

They took off their shoes and stood barefoot before the sign which said men to the left, women to the right.

Sami hesitated but Tia and Pri took her by the arm and bustled her into the women's changing rooms. Jon wondered what Sami, alias Sam, would do when it came to getting undressed.

88.

:: that's torn it - what will you do?

I sit on the bench, my arms folded over my chest, my skirt pulled tight around my legs. *I have no idea.*

"Hey, Sami. Come on," Tia says. "You are not going to tell us you are afraid of warm water."

All the girls have stripped to their pants, not in the slightest embarrassed at being half-naked. None have much in the way of breasts, but I sense Sam's interest and look away. I wonder what they'll think when they know that I am physically a boy.

:: don't blame me - I can't help it if I want to look - it's only natural

"I have a problem. Well. Not a problem. A difficulty," I say, staring at my bare feet. "Why don't you put your blouses on while I tell you. You'll get cold."

"Cold? But it's warm in here," Pri objects.

"Humour me," I say, squirming. "Believe me, when you hear my story you'll be grateful I insisted."

I glance up to gauge their reaction. They look at me as if I am mad, except Pri. I can see her brain working overtime. But they pull on their blouses, to my relief. I'd better begin before Pri starts in her questions.

"You will have gathered I am not quite like everyone else," I say, taking the most roundabout route possible.

Tia pats my knee. I almost cringe. "How could we not notice?" She grins, meaning well. She has been the one to react the most normally to me.

"I am even more different than you think."

:: get on with it, if you must

"I am what they call a chimera."

"Isn't that a mystical beast made up of parts of different animals?" Pri asks.

"Yes. But I am not made up of different animals." Tia chuckles while I take a deep shuddery breath. "I am both a boy and a girl." There it is out. Why don't I feel relieved?

"Wow!" Tia says.

I look at them in their pants and blouses, their legs bare, vulnerable.

"Is that why you won't get undressed?" Pri asks.

I nod.

"So… do you …" Tia falters. "I mean … are you more boy than girl?"

"I am one hundred percent girl," I say. "But…"

I can see from their tense look they expected my 'but'.

"But this body is a boy's."

"So you have a …" Rachel can't go on.

"Yes," I reply. "I have all that a boy's body would have."

Rachel makes a silent 'O' with her mouth.

Pri is frowning, thoughtful as ever. "Are you just a girl born in a boy's body or is there a boy in there with you," she asks.

Rachel giggles nervously.

"A fully-fledged chimera has the genetic material of two people. That is what I am. Or rather I should say we are. We are both boy and girl but this body is physically a boy."

"That must be awkward. Do you close your eyes when you undress?" Tia asks.

In other circumstances, I would laugh. "I try to avoid it."

"But…" Tia is struggling. They are all struggling. "Does this boy have a name?"

"Surely you are not going to chat up the boy in Sami?" Pri exclaims, a mischievous glint in her eyes.

"Sam," I say, trying not to think of Pri's suggestion.

"Can we talk to him?" Tia says.

"What did I tell you!" Pri exclaims, feigning indignation.

"Pri," I say. "This is very difficult. I love your jokes. But at the moment they are…" I hesitate. "…embarrassing. Please…."

"Sorry," she says, not daring to look at me.

"It is not your fault. I just feel uncomfortable."

"How do you decide who controls your body and who speaks?" Pri asks, her inquisitiveness triumphing over her guilt.

"Sam has great difficulties talking and moving. He's autistic. So I do the talking and moving for him."

"That must be terrible being shut up in a boy's body when you can't even talk to him," Tia says.

"Oh, Sam talks. To me. He is eloquent and perspicacious."

:: thanks for the compliments - tell them once I got over the monster in my head I enjoy having someone who understands

"He says…" and I repeat his words.

Once they absorb being talked to this way, Tia asks, "A monster?"

"Waking up to find me in his mind was a nasty surprise."

"I don't understand," Pri says. "Are you saying you weren't always there?"

"No. The second half of the chimera can lie dormant for years. I woke up, as it were, only a short while ago."

"So does he tell you about the girls he fancies?" Tia asks.

Pri huffs, muttering, "A one track mind."

"He did once fancy a girl. At least I think he did. But you shot her."

:: thanks for blurting my private business to a bunch of girls

Their mouths fall open, the eyes wide in horror. "No!" Pri says. "Not her."

"She was not the same back then," I say.

"You lot coming?" a male voice calls outside.

"So," Pri asks, "are you going to get undressed?"

I screw up my face. *Sorry Sam. But to be honest I am ashamed of this body.*

:: what do you want, an athlete? - I don't get to use it much

"I have a suggestion," Pri says. "It may sound crazy, but here goes. I suggest we all take off our clothes."

Tia snorts. Rachel gasps.

"So we know we have nothing to be ashamed of," Pri finishes.

"You are weird Pri," Rachel says.

"No," I say. "I think she is right." I try to ignore Sam's lurch of enthusiasm. "As I said to Sam, I am ashamed of this body. Maybe if we do as Pri suggests, I can feel accepted as I am."

"So?" Pri asks.

I unbutton my blouse and fold it on the bench next to me, taking far too long. I feel my face heating and I want to clasp my hands over my chest but I resist. The other girls take off their blouses but with none of the nonchalance they had before. I get to my feet and unzipping my skirt I let it fall to the ground.

"On the count of three," Pri says. I glance at her beseeching her to spare us. "One … Two …. Three."

All four of us stand naked, our pants in our hands.

"I have never seen a boy naked," Rachel says. "Turn round so we can get a better look."

"It's not a cattle show," Pri protests.

"No. But I want to admire Sami's body or rather Sam's body. So Sami knows it is not bad."

I sense no lust or desire, just inquisitiveness so I turn several times.

"You have a very nice body," Rachel says.

"I agree," Pri says.

"Me too," Tia adds. "And do you like mine?"

Pri swats her over the head with her pants and everyone laughs as we hastily pull on our underclothes

"Come on you lot. Surely you don't need so long to get ready for the baths," Mart says outside.

89.

Nan sat on a stool in the tiny infirmary with Cilla. On the examination table in front of them were laid out pots of unguents, glass jars of potions, material for poultices, a makeshift splint and packets of dried medicinal herbs. Each carefully labelled in neat script with not only the name but also when Cilla made it or received it.

"We should make a list of all that is missing," the girl said.

It would never suffice in an emergency. Needs had changed and would do so even more. Nan shuddered. How would they handle the aftermath of an attack? "Let's limit ourselves to basics."

Cilla gasped, a distant look in her eyes.

"What's the matter," Nan asked.

"Something is wrong," Cilla said, her head turning in every direction as if searching for the cause. "Since Sami taught me to heal I can feel things at a distance. But they are never quite in focus. I hope nothing is wrong with Sami."

Nan did too. She had been worried about Sami going off, even if she was surrounded by some of their best archers.

The door burst open and in hurried Rona, closely followed by Arkady.

"Down by the gate…" Arkady gasped.

"Get your breath back," Cilla said.

"People," Ronia said, ignoring Cilla's instructions. "Lots."

"They want in," Ronia added.

"I'll come," Cilla said, "but I need a moment alone."

Nan glanced at Cilla to know if she should leave. "Please," Cilla said in a whisper. "I'm going to call Sami."

Nan waited on the steps of the Centre with Ronia and Arkady. A growing crowd was milling on the far side of the fence. Even from that distance she could hear their demands mixed with the cries of infants.

"We are not to let them in," Cilla said the moment she pushed open the front door. "I will check them from a distance and, if I can, I will heal them, but Sami says that they are to stay outside. She will be here in a short while. They are bringing food and supplies."

The news astonished Nan. Where could they possibly have found food? And how would they transport it?

Down by the gate, the plague was in the air. Even Nan could sense it, like a malignant cloud clinging to the people packed into the narrow track between the jungle and the fence. Several refugees had been pushed against the gate in the crush and were lying electrocuted.

Cilla raised her voice and shouted, "You will come in later." She had to repeat herself several times before they quietened enough to hear.

"Who are you?" One burly man brandishing a large stick asked. "We don't want to talk to no kids. Where are the people in charge?"

"I am in charge," Cilla said.

"If this blinking fence weren't here, we'd soon show you who was in charge," a woman at the man's side said.

"What about healing?" a young woman called out. She had what looked like a bundle of rags in her arms. "My baby is ill. Can't you help?"

"We will help," Cilla said, taking a step forward. "But you must wait."

"The bloody plague waits for no man, or child," a tall man at the back called out and began pushing forward. A resounding crack rang out and a scream went up as the woman with the burly man was pushed against the fence and collapsed.

"Stop pushing!" Cilla shouted. "You'll kill each other."

Nan could hear the rumble of a distant motor and turned to see an old, open-backed truck emerging from the forest above the Centre. The crowd had heard it too and pulled back in panic, some hurrying away from the gate.

In a world in which only the Food Police had petrol for vehicles, they must have thought the police were on their way. The vehicle was close enough for it not to be mistaken for the police. A rusty red truck, with a large exhaust pipe sticking up behind the driver's cabin, chugged its way down the drive. Jon was at the wheel. Mart was next to him with Sami. Rachel, Pri and Tia were seated an piles of boxes in the back. Rachel and Tia had their bows cocked and ready.

Jon swung the truck to a halt close to Cilla and Nan and the three girls jumped from the truck joking and laughing. Sami clambered out and joined Cilla.

Sami immediately addressed the crowd. "Before we let you in we need to check for the plague."

"And what if we have it?" the tall man at the back asked. He had ceased his efforts to get to the front.

"Then we will heal you," Sami replied.

"No one can cure the plague," the man said. He struck Nan as different from the others, more sophisticated and less harassed. Unlike the others, he looked fed and rested.

"Yes they can," Borg said, coming to stand with Sami. "Many of my people were ill. She cured them."

No sooner had he pointed at Sami than a shot rang out. Pri dived in Sami's direction, knocking her to the ground. Several people screamed. Nan turned to see Sami lying on the floor covered in blood. Pri lay at her side unmoving. "Oh no!" Nan screamed as she rushed to Sami. Tia, Rachel and Saskia were standing around her, the bows pointed at the crowd.

"He's going to fire again," Saskia said. Her words were followed by a chorus of twangs and a piercing scream. Nan could just make out the tall man stagger forward as the crowd scrambled to get out of his way. A limp gun hung from his fingers.

An arrow stuck in his chest amid a growing red stain. A second pierced his throat. A third was lodged in his skull between his eyes.

"There may be more," she heard Saskia.

Nan placed a hand on Sami's chest searching for a heart beat. She was shocked and delighted to feel the girl stir. "Where are you wounded?" Nan asked.

"Nowhere," Sami replied. "What happened?"

"You are covered in blood,"

Sami glanced at her hands and her clothes amazed, then looked around. The moment she spotted Pri, she crawled to the girl's side and rolled her over revealing a bloody gash in her chest. Sami let out a heartrending cry that had tears springing to Nan's eyes. Sami scurried to her knees and lay her hands next to the wound. There was a long moment of silence. Nan had none of Sami's ability, but she could feel the rush of energy as it responded to Sami's call. The halo around her head blazed. But despite her efforts, Pri remained unmoving.

Sami lowered her head and wailed. "I can't cure the dead!" Her body shook with grief and the girls who stood in a close knot shielding her cried too.

"See what happens when you let kids try to run the world," the burly man in the crowd said. "A real mess."

Sami took her hands off Pri and got to her feet, refusing Nan's help. She pushed her way through the ring of girls and fixed the man across the gate, her face torn between grief and hatred.

"How dare you say such a thing," she hurled. Her whole body was trembling with rage but her voice was firm and incisive. The crowd fell back as if battered by her words. "You bring nothing but death." People were looking around at each other in disbelief. Nan could imagine them thinking, "Not me!"

"Yes. You. All of you," Sami continued. "More than half of you have the plague and all of you will die in the next few days if we don't heal you. You conceal a killer sent by the food police. That man has killed my dear friend. A gentle person who would harm no one. A real fountain of knowledge. A joy to life. And thanks to you she is gone for ever." Unable to contain her grief, Sami lowered her head and broke down in sobs.

Nan went to take her in her arms, but Sami pushed her away. Wiping the tears from her eyes, she continued to harangue the burly man. "You." She pointed at him, causing the man to cringe. "You are incapable of having children and now your wife lies dead at your feet. How dare you say children cannot make a better world. Look at the one you left. Poisoned by deadly gases and foul industrial fodder. On fire and in ruin. No food, no houses, no security. No future. Nothing. Just misery and suffering. Who is responsible for that? Certainly not these children." Sami gestured to all the girls from the Centre who formed a tight group around her along with the children from Baxter.

"I declare a day of mourning. Tomorrow at sunrise we will bury our beloved Pri," her voice caught on the name, "with all the honour she merits. If any of you are still here and alive tomorrow we will set about curing you and will organise a place for you to live. Until then I suggest you meditate on what has happened and whether you merit a future."

90.

Alone. I am abandoned to my miserable thoughts. Even Sam is voiceless. I haven't felt so desolate and forsaken since the wave hit Atlantis. A cloud passes in front of the sun. I shiver and clasp my arms about me.

OK. Not entirely alone. Somewhere in the shadows, unseen, Tia and Rachel keep pace, bows at the ready, arrows cocked. I feel their love and concern as if they were shouting it to my face. They mean well. After what happened they feel responsible and want to protect me. With that one shot they have become much more vulnerable. They can't know that precariousness was always my lot, but it was never meant to be Pri's. Poor Pri. Such love and devotion. Not that I am ungrateful for Tia and Rachel's care and attention, I am not, but I shut out their emotions as that only heightens my own.

The trees in the forest beside the path to Trey sag under the weight of years of creepers and vines. Age-old kindred spirits. I feel like I too sag as I plod the grassy slope. Birds hop from branch to branch, splashes of colour in the grey-green, cheeping excitedly, oblivious to my grief. Can birds feel sadness? Do they pine and waste away at the loss of a loved one?

:: come off it - have you ever seen a bird with its legs in the air crying its heart out at the loss of a young one fallen from the nest? - if you get any more melancholic you will be wading through your own puddle of misery

You can't understand. Pri didn't mean so much to you. There is vehemence in my words and my teeth hurt as if I am grinding them. Maybe I am. *Pri gave her life for me. Sami not Sam. She hardly knew you.*

:: she saw a good deal more of me than I would have liked

That's not funny, Sam. Yes. It was Pri that had us undress. There was an artless earnestness to her approach to life. Yet she knew how to be playful, like these tiny birds. She had such a delightful laugh. Tears roll down my cheeks. *I loved her, Sam. Life shone from her like a warm light.*

:: I loved her too - for someone so little her presence had a punch to it

I never know if you are joking or not.

:: I often kid you, but I am deadly serious - I really did like her - more than you can imagine - if I didn't have to depend on you as my bridge to the world, I would have showed much more interest

I am astounded and saddened by his admission. *Oh Sam! I am so sorry. I had no idea.* I walk on. Sam and Pri. I like the idea only to be reminded that Pri is no more. I kick a stone. It ricochets off a low branch sending a rabbit scuttling away.

I wonder where Yarrow is. Has he abandoned me?

:: he is wild and knows when to avoid the plague

Sometimes I feel him moving around. Although I have no idea what he does. I wish he were here.

:: call him

I will. But how? I can't just shout his name.

:: try mind to mind

Do you think he'll understand? Sam nods mentally. *OK. Yarrow.* I feel silly. *Yarrow.* I call again. Nothing. Maybe he is too far away. Then I sense him and I feel an echoing tension in Tia and Rachel. Oh no! I couldn't lose him too. "Don't shoot," I call out. "It's Yarrow."

"OK," Tia calls out and Yarrow pads along the path and greets me, licking my hand. I kneel next to him, sling my arms around his neck and bury my face in his fur. He whines softly at my muffled sobs. When he tries to lick my tear-covered face, I push him away saying, "Who knows what you've had between those teeth."

Yarrow sits back on his haunches, his tongue hanging out, and looks at me reproachfully. I laugh. Guilt grabs me, but it feels good to laugh. No doubt hearing my laugh, Tia calls out, "Are you alright?"

"Yes. It's Yarrow. Come and join us."

When I see their determined, tear-streaked faces I remember why we are here. They too have lost a dear friend. One after another I take them in my arms while Yarrow tries to nuzzle his way between us. Then hand in hand the three of us begin our descent to Trey.

"I am glad Nan and Jon took charge of the funeral," Tia says. "I don't think any of us could have faced organising it."

I too am relieved. "They will do her proud."

We pass between the fruit warehouse with its insane buzz of insects and the bottling factory part of which we cleared during our last visit and arrive at the crossroads not far from the hostel. To the left the road leads to the baths, but none of us want to go there. Memories of Pri are still too fresh that way.

"We should be getting back," Tia says, winding her fingers through her long hair as she peers around the abandoned village. "We don't want night to fall before we reach home."

"There's still time," Rachel replies, looking at the cloudless sky. "Let's have a quick look at the hostel." Not waiting for an answer, she strides in that direction.

Tia glances at me, shaking her head. I shrug and we follow.

We know the front entrance is locked, so we walk to the back. The hostel forms an U with the car park snuggling between its two arms. One of the remaining sides is flanked by the windowless façade of the clothes store and the other, at some distance, opens onto the electric fence and the jungle beyond.

There are several doors, but all are locked. The residents might have left in a hurry, but they didn't forget to lock up.

"There," Rachel says, pointing to a ground floor balcony. She's right. The door is ajar. She scales the railing with ease and vaults onto the balcony then turning she offers a hand up.

"My Romeo," Tia says grinning at her.

Rachel purses her lips and stuffs her hands in her pockets. "I'm nobody's Romeo?"

Tia's grin widens. "Shame. You'd make an excellent boy."

Rachel turns her back on Tia and makes a point of helping me. Tia is too short to reach the railing as Rachel had. When she finally manages, Rachel mutters, "Girls!"

Inside the place is in chaos. An army of animals has preceded us. The mattress has been ripped apart scattering feathers over the narrow bed frame, the rickety table, the upturned chair with one leg broken and the carpet which is more stains than carpet. The remains of a large rodent lie curled in a corner abuzz with flies. It stinks.

Rachel opens the door onto the corridor and peers out then turns back to give the thumbs up. We hurry out and shut the door, trading the stench of death for the musky smell of stale, forgotten air. None of us speaks. I imagine armed thugs lurking in the shadows waiting to jump out. The corridor, which stretches the length of this arm of the building, is lit by light filtering from the reception. We head for the light.

The reception is large and doubles as bar and lounge. Limp curtains hang drab and dusty at the windows obscuring most of the road. In the shadows I make out low tables each with its assortment of armchairs.

"Let's see what the bar holds," I suggest.

"I could do with a drink," Tia says, grinning.

"Now I understand," Rachel quips. Tia makes a sound that is meant to be a hiccup. "You need more practice," Rachel says.

"Girls!" I say. "This is neither the time nor the place…"

We are about to step out of the corridor when Yarrow growls deep in his throat. Halting, I listen but hear nothing. The hackles are up on his back.

:: maybe we should scoot out of here while we can

"Let's…" I begin when there's a distant roar. We glance at each other, alarmed. The roar halts a moment then takes up again coming closer and closer only to take the form of a jeep that swerves to a halt in front of the hostel. Four food police climb out and stretch their legs. Three are brawny specimens. Exactly what you'd expect. The fourth is a frail youth whose uniform hangs loose on his frame.

The four climb the steps and I hear them rifle through what must be a box by the door. Then they stroll in as if the hostel was their second home.

"Jake, fix us a drink," one of the bodybuilders says.

"Shouldn't we go to the generator," the young one says in a high-pitched voice. "We are supposed to blow it up."

"Shut your cake hole, squirt," the first man says. "We've got loads of time. They've got enough problems at headquarters without bothering about us."

"The usual, Brandon?" Jake asks. Brandon grunts. "And you, Damast?" Damast looks out the window with his hand over his mouth to conceal a cough.

:: he's got it

Yup! I hold on to Yarrow by the scruff of his neck to stop him slinking away.

"A whiskey," Damast replies.

"And you squirt?"

"I don't drink."

The men burst out laughing. "Fix him a double scotch," Brandon says. "It'll toughen the baby up."

The bar is only feet from where we are hidden and Jake stands so close I can smell his sweat. Thank heavens he is too busy mixing drinks

91.

Jake pulls a folded cloth from a drawer, shakes it out and polishes four glasses, holding each up to the light. He shifts several books on the shelf, revealing a bottle of whiskey. These men have been here before. He sniffs the contents, making a satisfied "Mmmmm". I mentally nudge his enthusiasm making him pour more than he intended. He is no longer used to alcohol and just the whiff makes his head spin. He giggles as he fumbles to screw the cap on the bottle.

:: can't you make the drink stronger?

I can't influence inanimate objects and I doubt it will be necessary.

Jake stumbles and the glasses slither across the tray, but he manages to right it in time.

"Careful," shouts Brandon, jumping to rescue his glass. Off balance, the three remaining glasses slide in the opposite direction as Jake struggles to stop them. Brandon peers into his glass and sniffs the liquid. "Continue to be so generous and we'll have to find a new supply."

If Brandon turns he will see us huddled in the corridor, but to my relief he plops in an armchair, sticking his feet on a table.

Tia is holding my hand so tight her grip hurts. I wish I had taught them to speak mind-to-mind. If I talk in her head she'll probably scream. All I can do is send her and Rachel calming energy. Yarrow has his hackles up but sits still at my side.

"Cheers," Damask says, raising his glass. Jake and the boy raise theirs. Brandon ignores them. The boy pretends to drink, but I make his hand tremble causing him to swallow a mouthful.

He coughs violently as the liquid burns his throat.

"You ain't got the plague, squirt, have you?" Damask asks.

:: you can talk - nothing like shifting the blame on others

"Take another swig. It'll kill the germs … if it doesn't kill you," Jake jokes. No one laughs but the boy down a mouthful causing him to splutter again.

"What a mess," Jake says.

"He'll get over it," Brandon replies.

"No. I meant at headquarters. They can't beat the plague."

"We should never have gone to Baxter," Damask says. "Everyone knows the place is rife with it."

"Sure sent them witches scurrying," Brandon says. "Those we didn't kill."

:: they are in no hurry - I doubt my nerves will hold out - can't you nudge them out the door?

Your nerves! What about ours? I whisper in Jake's mind that he is thirsty. He zigzags to the bar. Grabbing the bottle, he turns and waves the whiskey at the men. "Anyone for more," he slurs.

Brandon frowns. He is more difficult to influence. Damask grins and holds out his glass, but Brandon refuses. "We got work to do," he says standing. His feet firmly planted on the floor, he is as steady as a rock. Damask and Jake knock back the remains of their whiskey and struggle up. "Let's put that generator out of action. Headquarters are waiting for that to launch their attack."

Generator? Where could that be? We saw no signs of it.

The boy extracts himself from his seat and stands on wobbly legs before leaning against the wall. Brandon shoves him into the chair. "Not you brat! You stay here." He pulls the boy's gun from its holster and for a moment I'm terrified he's going to shoot him. But he shoves it into the boy's hands, then jerks a thumb at the vehicle. "Keep an eye out till we get back."

"'nd don't drinkallthewhiskey," Jake mumbles, burping.

The three exit amid curses and cries as two lose their footing and tumble down the stairs. Brandon swears before striding off towards the baths. The others hop after.

:: whatever they are up to, you'd better stop them - fast

I concentrate on the boy. His eyes droop and his mouth falls open. He is so easy to influence. I send sleep rolling over him. His eyes close, his head sags and he begins to snore.

:: take the gun

Sure. How easy. I signal to Yarrow to stay put and tiptoe to the boy. Hovering over him I check his mind. He's long gone. Extending a hesitant hand, I ease the gun from his fingers. His snoring continues.

"Tie him up," Tia says, looking for rope.

While she searches, Rachel and I rifle his pockets. We find a key which I pocket, a badge bearing his name, Knut Langenbrooke, and a pair of handcuffs hanging from his belt. The three of us trundle him to the nearest bedroom and handcuff him to the bed posts. Rachel tears a strip from the sheet and wedging it in his mouth she tears off a second strip to hold it in place.

"We need to follow those men and stop them," Tia says. "If they destroy the generator, we are dead."

I agree although I don't like it. "I must do something first. It shouldn't take long." I take hold of Tia and Rachel's hand. The two look perplexed. "I am going to teach you to speak mind to mind. We may need it."

Both are so excited, their minds bubbling with ideas about what they could do with such a gift, not all of it very healthy. I have to calm their thoughts before I can begin. I am conscious that all this time the men are getting closer to the generator, but this can't be rushed. *Can you hear me,* I ask. Both nod. *Try talking back.* As always they talk out loud but quickly catch on. *Good,* I say. *We can practice on the way.*

Front door or back? I ask.

Front, says Rachel. *We can't be sure which way they went.*

She eases open the door and peers out. No one is in sight. We creep in the direction of the bath house keeping close to the wall of the hostel. At the crossroads we have no choice but to continue in the open. I extend my senses. The three men have reached the baths.

Beyond the saw mill and bottling factory we keep to the

shadows as we round the corner by the greenhouses and climb the curving incline to the bathhouse. Yarrow pads at my side his nostrils flaring. Ahead someone swears.

"Blast you Jake." It is Brandon. "You can't hold you liquor." There's a dull thud followed by a groan.

Peering round the last tree at the edge of the clearing that serves as a car park, I see Jake balled up on the ground, his head in his hands.

"Blinking' hell, man, get up." Brandon shoves Jake's foot with his boot.

Jake screams. "My ankle! It's broken."

Damask goes to help him up. "Leave him," Brandon snaps. "We'll pick him up on the way back. If he's still alive."

Jake whimpers, but Brandon leaves with Damask trotting after him.

Can you send him to sleep like the other one? Rachel asks.

Risky. Out in the open anything could eat him, including ants.

We could tie him up in the bathhouse, Tia suggests.

Take too long, Rachel says nodding to the two men disappearing into the trees behind the baths. She marches over to the man, rips his gun from his holster and points it at his head. He cringes wide-eyed at this sudden apparition.

"I'm going to shoot you," she says. "Is there any reason I shouldn't?"

Don't Rachel, I say, preparing to stay her hand mentally.

Trust me, is all she says.

"Please don't," the man snivels.

She presses his ankle. He screams.

"I'll do anything," he whimpers.

"Ok. Where are you friends going?"

"To destroy the generator."

"Where is it?"

"A mile beyond the baths. There's a path between the rocks."

"How will they destroy it?"

"Explosives. Brandon has them in his bag."

"Detonation?"

"A small silver keypad in his pocket."

"Good. Now we will help you into the bathhouse where you are to wait for us. If you obey we will cure your ankle and also get rid of the plague you have caught." He whimpers at the news. "It's in the early stages, so you ought to survive till we get back."

But he hasn't got the plague, I say.

It doesn't matter, is her reply. *You can send him to sleep now.* The three of us cart him up the steps, almost dropping him several times. His body is all the heavier that he is profoundly asleep and the armour under his uniform makes him slip through our fingers. In the entrance we dump him on the floor and Rachel padlocks his hands behind his back with his handcuffs.

Now let's do something about the two remaining men, she says.

92.

Beyond the bathhouse, the path winds beside a noisy brook from which clouds of steam billow up. Spruces and pines with their telltale odours give way to coarse shrubs full of needles that jab my bare calves. These in turn are replaced by stones and rocks some bigger than me. Underfoot, gone is the soft turf. Stones roll beneath my soles threatening to twist my ankle.

How far ahead are they? Tia asks, pausing in the shadow of a rock to check her bow.

I close my eyes and reach out. The rough terrain troubles my mental vision, as my thoughts weave between the rocks. Half a mile, I say. The men are smug. They have almost reached the generator. We are not going to arrive in time.

At my words, Yarrow bounds off down the track. "No!" I shout. "Come back." But he is gone.

:: he's gone to play his part

Whose voice was that? Tia asks, sounding alarmed.

Blast you Sam, I say only to him. *Did you have to complicate things?*

:: they knew anyway

It's Sam. Sam, meet Tia and Rachel.

Ooooh! The boy. Tia says. *Must be strange having a boy in your head.*

At least you would not need to explain why you enjoy climbing trees and playing with bows and arrows, Rachel says, her words heavy with emotion.

I want to say we are grateful she is so good at archery, but Tia says, *I wonder if I could kiss him without kissing Sami.*

Tia! Rachel exclaims. *Have you got no restraint?*

Oups. You weren't supposed to hear that.

Liar, I feel like saying. Who are you kidding? Worse, I can feel Sam grinning, the blind fool. Thank heavens my thoughts are my own and I can stop his grin spreading to my face.

Maybe I'll let Sam take over when we haven't got killers to stop.

:: that's not fair - do you have to rub in how dependent I am on you?

I make sure I block his thought so that only I can hear.

Don't get your hopes up, I tell him and only him, *Tia is making mischief at your expense.*

Maybe some other time, Tia says. I doubt her look of alarm is due to the killers.

Now you've upset Sam, I say.

A shot rings out followed by a yelp bringing a brutal halt to our bantering. A sharp pain stabs me in the side causing me to gasp and bend over double.

"What's the matter?" Rachel asks. "Are you hit?"

"It is Yarrow," I say, closing my eyes. I reach out to him. He's hurt but alive. As for the men, one is wounded, the other, Brandon, is fighting off Yarrow. I hammer Brandon with a wave of tiredness and sleep, but he proves impervious. I get to my feet and break into a run but my foot buckles on a stone and I plunge forward only to be caught by the two girls. My ankle swells. When I put weight on my leg it gives way. Tia and Rachel lower me to the ground and I place my hands around my ankle letting healing energy do its work.

We find the two men at a widening of the path. Damask is rolling on the ground clutching his arm. Brandon, whose right arm hangs limp at his side, tries to aim the gun in his left hand at Yarrow who swerves seeking an opening to attack. I hear a twang as Rachel and Tia let fly their arrows. Brandon, who is caught off guard, not having seen us arrive, is lucky. He staggers and the arrow soars over him. The other, which would have pierced his heart, digs deep into his left shoulder. He turns to face us with a snarl, brandishing his gun in our direction. Yarrow leaps for the man's arm as the gun goes off. All three of us dive to the ground.

There's a yelp and I look up to see Yarrow lying motionless at the Brandon's feet. No! Not Yarrow. I want to rush to his side, but Brandon stands over the dog. Blood is streaming from the man's shoulder. His right arm is also bleeding. In his left hand he brandishes an object that glints in the sunlight. It is too small to be a gun. Then I see the gun on the ground yards away.

"Don't move, or I'll blow us all to smithereens." He gesticulates to a low building amongst the rocks, half concealed by whirls of steam. "And the generator with us."

Keep still, I say to the girls. *But be ready to shoot.*

I get to my feet, holding out my hands to show I am not armed. All the time I work on Brandon's mind trying to convince him to put down the detonator. He is a stubborn beast.

"Brandon. That is your name, isn't it?" I have no idea how to do this. I rummage through his memories. What a mess. Pain has shredded his thoughts and the past is a jumble of moments that makes no sense.

His face is twisted in pain and he sucks in a deep breath before he can reply. "Back up and put away those weapons."

"Edith sent me," I say, plucking his mother' name from afar. the memory seems happy. Let's just hope he doesn't detest her.

"How the hell?" He winces, one good hand clutching the detonator, the other clamped over his shoulder. "You're one of those witches." Horror and fear are added to the pain. "Keep away from me."

Witches? So much for my clever idea. Now what? I could paralyse him, but I am loathed to hurt him. That is not why I am here. Whatever happened to my mission to do good?

:: come off it - if you don't stop him, everyone here will die - hundreds of people, most of them children - is that why you came into the world?

Brandon takes a step forward, his eyes wild, his mouth hanging open. "To hell with this," he mutters. "I'm going to die anyway." He peers up at me, a haunting, beseeching look, almost as if looking at someone else, and says, "The end of the road, mother."

It's now or never. I slam into his mind, severing all communication between his brain and arm. He hurls in frustration, straining every muscle to move an arm that refuses to budge. He looks at me, pure hatred in his eyes. Then he twists and turns, like a contortionist gone mad, trying to use his teeth to set off the detonator, but to no avail. "You bastard," he splutters, "I curse..."

Rachel's arrow sinks into his chest, cutting off his curse, and he falls forward with an inarticulate thud. I have a horrified image of the fall setting off the explosion and fling myself to the ground, but there is no deafening bang, just the twittering of birds and the muffled babbling of the brook.

"Everyone ok?" I ask as I crawl to Yarrow's side. I hear their yeses like distant hisses as I kneel by my friend. His flank is a shocking red, his fur matted where the blood has started to dry. I place a hesitant hand on his neck and reach out in search of life. Yes. A faint echo, born maybe of my desperate hopes and prayers. I channel healing energy from the brook, from the trees, from the rocks, from all the birds and beasts. I call on the cloudless sky, on the distant mountains, on the sun and moon. Save my friend. Please.

A bullet is lodged in one of his ribs. I feel his heart beat in fits and starts as if tottering on the edge, hanging suspended the time to say goodbye. *Hold on,* I plead. His lungs hardly rise and fall, the weight of impending death crushing them. Frustration and despair have me in a vice-like grip. I cannot do this alone.

"Tia. Rachel. Please. Help." They kneel beside me and as if guided by some deeper knowing, they lay a hand next to mine, each of us a conduit struggling to shore up life against the inevitable. Unmoving. Silent. Free of thought. An immense force to move mountains, to roll back time, to bring back life.

Night has fallen when the animal beneath our joined hands stirs and turns its wide eyes to contemplate us, yawning as if awaking from sleep. We too awake to a boundless joy that runs wild in our veins although our limbs, which have long given up hope, will require more time to return to life.

93.

Nan sighed, shifting to a more comfortable seat on the steps. Not the slightest sign of movement on the track behind the Centre that wound to Trey. Interrupting her vigil, she faced the setting sun and basked in its warmth as the fiery disc hung over the tree tops. Maybe its rays would help unwind the tension in her shoulders and neck. Sami had not returned and night would soon fall. She wished she'd opposed the girl's pilgrimage to Trey.

Jon was engrossed in organising the funeral. Music was to play an important part and the contact with the young ones would do him good. If only he could get over the feeling of uselessness. She like him a lot, but that moroseness wore her down.

She glanced at the road. Just lengthening shadows.

Snatches of singing wafted from within as an improvised choir rehearsed to accompany Pri on her last journey. Nas was reminded her of her own losses.

The front door opened and Cilla and Saskia stepped out, deep in conversation.

"If we don't, they'll die of starvation even before the plague gets them," Cilla was saying.

"But Sami categorically refused to help them before the funeral," Saskia replied.

"Yes, but Sami is not here."

"Have you had any news?" Nan asked.

The two turned, surprised to find her sitting in the gloom.

"No," Cilla said. "I have tried to reach her several times, but I get no reply."

Nan kept a brave face. "You think we should feed the refugees?"

"Yes. I can't bear to see them starving." Cilla said.

"But Sami…" began Saskia.

"There are more," Cilla said. "Their needs have changed."

"Have you checked for the plague?" Nan asked.

"I started," Cilla said. "But I was called away. One of our girls got hurt."

"Nan is right," Saskia said. "You can begin screening them and healing those who are infected."

"But those that are healthy need to be brought inside. I can't see how to without others trying to storm the gate," Cilla said.

"That's easy enough," Saskia said. "In batches."

Cilla looked perplexed. "Take a small number. Separate them, check them, cure those who need it and let them in."

"But what if some are like that man who shot Pri…" Cilla shuddered, as did Saskia and Nan. "Armed and out to do ill?"

"You make them walk a narrow corridor. Could you check and cure them as they walk by?"

Cilla nodded.

"We could search them, but that might be difficult. What if we made them undress, pretending their clothes are infected? We could rig up a shower. Let them believe the water has special properties. That way we would be sure they have no arms."

Nan had to admire Saskia's inventiveness.

"But what about clothes afterwards?" Cilla asked. "They'll freeze. Night is falling."

"There are loads of clothes in Trey," Saskia replied. "…and wood for the fence."

"You can check on Sami while you are there," Nan said.

"Good idea. Can you drive a truck?" Saskia asked.

"Sure."

"Great. In the mean time, can you ask Eileen to make a giant soup? And have Jenna bring us as many spare blankets as she can, just in case," Saskia said. "And tell Jon and the children what we are planning."

With that the two hurried down the steps talking earnestly and strode off in the direction of the camp, leaving Nan staring after them. A young girl who had barely reached puberty had just given her, a woman who had survived the plague, who had trained as a healer and who worked undercover against the food police for over ten years, a set of orders as if that was as natural as breathing. A part of Nan objected. Damn it! They couldn't even drive a truck. She felt slighted, her talents wasted. At the same time, she was full of admiration. These girls rose to the challenge of an impossible situation without apparent hesitation when most adults would whine and complain.

Nan clambered into the driver's seat, turned the key and waited for the truck to respond. Nothing happened. At the fourth attempt the motor sputtered into action, died, restarted, then roared. Mart and Jenna joined her in the cabin while a group of girls she didn't know climbed into the back. They were to load wood and clothes. Several sported bows cocked and ready to fire.

The truck lurched from side to side on the rough track as they entered the forest, the headlights sending dislocated shadows jumping from tree to tree. Nan glanced over her shoulder through the tiny window making sure the girls were OK. One gave her the thumbs up.

Nan would have liked to get news from Mart and Jenna but the racket of the engine made conversation impossible. When they cleared the forest above Trey, lights were blazing in the hostel below and a vehicle was parked outside. Nan cut the headlights and halted the truck.

Mart wound down his window and whispered "Food police." The girls behind jumped down and worried faces appeared at the window.

"What do we do now?" Jenna asked.

"They must have caught Sami and the others," Nan said.

"Then we'll rescue them," Mart said. "How many archers have we got?"

"Three," a voice in the dark said.

Nan wanted to refuse. The thought of a group of children against the food police sent cold sweat running down her back. But Mart and Jenna were clambering out and several of the girls had already set off down the track. She hoped these archers were all markswomen like Tia and not Rachel 's recent recruits.

When Nan caught up they were huddled around Mart and Jenna. "At most there could be four in that jeep," Mart said. "We need to be careful none are wandering about." Mart was the only one who had already visited Trey. "If we follow this track it will come out between the fruit storage and the bottling factory. The buildings will give us cover to the crossroads from where we should be able to see into the hostel."

The night was peopled with noises. If anyone were to creep up on them, they would never know. No doubt aware of their vulnerability, Mart increased the pace till they were jogging.

Light streamed from the hostel, leaving the crossroads dangerously exposed. Mart led them across rough ground till they reached the cover of houses. Peering over a low wall, Nan saw the jeep parked at the main entrance. The curtains were drawn, but she could make out two forms pacing inside. Long minutes passed as they surveyed the road, expecting one of the police to surge from the shadows at any moment.

"We need to get closer," Mart whispered.

A scream pierced the night. It was clearly that of a girl. Then a dog barked. The whole group vaulted the wall, sprinted across the road, up the steps and burst into the hostel. Nan was more cautious. She stole up the stairs carrying a heavy wrench she'd taken from the truck. To her amazement laughter rang out. When she entered she found Mart bent over double laughing and the girls were giggling. Across the room two policemen sat handcuffed to a chair looking bewildered. Opposite stood Tia and Rachel their backs turned to the men. They were laughing at Sami who had her hands clasped over her eyes, while a giant dog tugged at her sleeve. "It was a snake," she said. "I hate snakes."

94.

Nan put down the wrench, but not too far away that she couldn't grab it in an emergency, and accepted a glass of an orange liquid Rachel offered. She sniffed it, not believing her eyes. "Orange juice?"

"Great isn't it," Tia exclaimed. "We found some in that fridge." She pointed to a white door concealed under the bar.

Nan sniffed the liquid. It smelt like all those years ago.

"It's OK," Rachel said. "We've tried it."

Nan took a sip. The taste conjured up a host of memories. She was tempted to indulge, but now was not the time. She turned to Sami who had got over her fright and was staring at the boy in police uniform as she caressed Yarrow's head. Nan wasn't sure if the boy cringed at Sami's scrutiny or because of the dog.

"Before that snake gave me such a fright, Kurt was telling us about police headquarters," Sami said. "Apparently a unit brought back a present from Baxter and now they are struggling to avoid being wiped out by it."

"I know about that visit," Nan said. "I was there. I overheard their commander saying one of them had the plague."

"But!" Kurt eyed her in disbelief. "The officers told us everyone had been killed."

"Either they lied or they didn't know. Many were butchered, but many escaped."

She wasn't going to tell him that most of those who got away had perished in a landslide.

"So how are they handling their home-grown disaster?" Nan

asked not bothering to hide her anger.

"Home-grown?" Rachel asked. "Weren't they against growing."

"It was a disaster of their own making. They slaughtered those who could have helped," Nan said, remembering how her friends had been savagely eliminated. "Now that they are most in need, they have no one to turn to."

"Apparently there is some magical saviour on the loose," Kurt said. "They are hunting him down everywhere."

Him? Typical! Nan glanced at Sami, but she was intent on the men.

"Some say the saviour's 'oled up 'ere," the older man said.

"Meet Jake," Sami said.

"Where there only two of them?" Mart asked, taking in the two men with a wave of his hand.

"No," Rachel said. Nan could have sworn the girl shuddered. "The other two are dead."

"We'll be dead soon too," Jake said. "For all I know we might already 'ave the plague."

"You don't," Sami said in a way that left no doubt. "But your friend... What was his name? Damask, he had it."

Kurt lowered his head in an attempt to conceal his tears. "We're condemned," he muttered.

"Come off it, Kurt. You should be laughing," Tia said, patting him on the shoulder. He shrugged her away. "You never liked the police and now you are rid of them."

This was no time for commiserating. Material and supplies were urgently needed back at the centre. "If we can talk," Nan said to Sami.

Rachel had the three armed newcomers keep watch, while she followed Nan and Sami outside with Tia, Mart and Jenna.

Nan outlined Saskia's plan which had Sami chuckling. "Such a fertile imagination," she said. Sami was quick to size up the situation. Nan was to drive Mart and half of the girls to fetch timber, then leave them there and return on foot to be with Sami who wanted to question the men. Tia was to go with Jenna and the remaining girls to pick clothes for the refugees, while Rachel stayed with the three archers to guard the prisoners.

Rachel's parting words to Jenna were, "Don't let Tia try on any clothes. We'll never get home tonight."

"I love you too," Tia called out, blowing Rachel a kiss.

On her walk back from the sawmill the night noises had calmed somewhat and Nan could hear the girls in the clothes store laughing. She wondered if they'd be ready in time, but it was not for her to intervene. Jenna would sort it out.

"So what are people doing for food?" Sami was asking when Nan entered. She nodded to Sami and lent against the reception desk, unseen by the man. Rachel and her archers had retreated to behind the desk where they stood, bows at the ready.

The two policemen were untied and sat in armchairs each with an orange juice perched on its arm. They were like a two-man act. One, a snivelling youth with a posh accent, was chewing his nails. The other, a hardened, uneducated man in his forties, was perched on the edge of his seat alert, as if ready to jump into action at the slightest threat. They were both talking in earnest tones to Sami who listened with a hint of a smile on her lips.

"The police 'ave got piles in the basement," Jake replied.

"Stock enough for a week," Kurt said sipping his drink.

"But it's 'ell out on the streets. Folks're starving."

"Anyone with the slightest ounce of energy attacked headquarters hoping to steal food."

"They shouldn't 'ave 'ad a chance, what with us 'aving guns and all."

"But shots rang out. No idea where they got the guns."

"Big uns too. Some say they 'ad 'em from a rival town."

"When they heard the plague raged inside headquarters they scattered like squealing mice."

"What happened to that synthetic food they were so fond of?" Nan asked, moving into view.

Jake who had been engrossed in talking to Sami jumped at the sound of another voice. "The blinkin' lot went up in smoke."

"The officers said it was saboteurs from a neighbouring city."

"Hogs wash. More like a cock-up at the factory."

"Your are right. There's been tension amongst workers."

"Apparently the food 'as been bringin' them out in spots."

"But it was definitely saboteurs that set fire to the pesticides."

"What?" Sami and Nan exclaimed together.

"Yup. Smoke killed 'undreds."

"I couldn't sleep for the wailing and groans."

From their description, the town must be littered with bodies and toxic waste. It was worse than the disaster. "If there are survivors, they will be desperate to find refuge," Nan said. "They'll be terrified and probably aggressive. That's why we need to get back to the Centre, now."

"You are right," Sami said. "The threat is probably no longer the food police but the refugees."

"I wouldn't discount the food police," Kurt said. "They are as desperate as the refugees."

"And don't forget them saboteurs'" Jake added. "We 'ave no idea what they'll do."

Mart, who entered at that moment, pointed at the two men and asked, "What are we going to do with them?"

Sami ignored the question, asking Mart, "Is the timber stowed?"

He nodded.

"The clothes too," Tia said, pushing past Mart.

"We tied Tia up," Jenna said. "To stop her trying the clothes."

Tia pouted. "What have you lot got against me? I like clothes. Is that a crime?"

"We should appoint you head of clothes," Sami said feigning innocence.

Tia huffed and stamped out the door.

"Go give her a hug, Mart," Rachel said, grinning. "Otherwise she'll be unbearable."

"Girls!" Mart muttered as he went in search of Tia.

95.

Reaching the top of a slight rise, Jon halted and stared round the broad circle of stone pines which could easily hold a hundred people. The red trunks stood like the pillars of a natural temple. He peered upwards seeing them stretch up and up to the flattened crowns above.

"Will this do?" Becky asked, peering up at the trees through bespectacled eyes. With her shoulder length auburn hair and her finely chiselled features she resembled a Celtic goddess.

"It's wonderful," Jon replied.

None of the places in the Centre were large enough. They might have used the lawn, but it was too exposed, what with the wild people near by and an ever-growing crowd of refugees at the gate. Such a celebration required peace and majesty.

"I thought we'd set up a table in the middle…" Becky hesitated. "… for Pri."

"What do you think of a procession?" he asked.

"Beautiful," she said, only to add in a shaky voice, "I think she would like that." There was a thoughtful pause during which the girl wiped her eyes. "I will have girls clear the path."

"Good. I have to get back for choir practice," Jon said as they wound their way down the path.. "Do you sing?"

"I love to, but singing in front of anybody has my throat clam up."

He appreciated her forthrightness. What if she could sing? Wouldn't that be wonderful. On an off chance, he decided to take the risk. "Do you know this?" He began singing a lullaby.

Midway through the first verse, he heard a timid voice join his. He sang on, intuition advising him not to break the magic. When the lullaby came to an end they walked in silence. He heard her sigh. "Would you like to sing more?"

To his surprise she halted mid-step. "I've never sung like that," she said, a son in her voice. "Never. Ever."

"It was beautiful," he said, moved. "Shall we try again?"

She pulled a large handkerchief from her sleeve and blew her nose then wiped her glasses on her blouse. "Yes. Please."

He began the same lullaby and this time she sang with more force, her voice a real pleasure. The third time he let her sing alone. She hesitated at first, but, with growing confidence, she sang the whole lullaby unaccompanied.

As they arrived at the steps, Jon turned to her. In the light over the door he could see her face aglow. "I plan to use this lullaby once we have laid Pri up there. I would very much like you to sing it for her."

"On my own?" she asked aghast.

"The choir will hum the tune and you will sing the words."

She shook her head. "I couldn't possibly do that."

"Not only can you, but you will," he said. "You have such a lovely voice. We are not going to let that slumber any longer."

She was still shaking her head when Jon took her by the arm. "Come and meet the choir. It will work. I assure you."

"But I have to see to clearing the path and so many other things," she said. "And the little ones."

"This will take half an hour. Those things can wait."

Two hours later when he had finished with the choir, he discovered Becky, her brow furrowed with worry, deep in conversation with Cilla and Saskia. "What's wrong?" he asked.

"We are concerned about Sami and the others," Cilla said. "We sent two parties to Trey and neither have returned."

"We can't afford to send anyone else," Saskia said. "The gate could give at any moment." With her heavily lidded eyes and her fleshy mouth she looked a little drowsy, but even in his short stay, Jon knew her appearance was deceptive. She was sharp-witted and extremely attentive.

"Have you tried contacting Sami?" Becky asked Cilla.

"I've been so busy," Cilla replied. "Give me a moment." She withdrew to a bench along the wall and sat down.

None of them spoke, not wanting to disturb her. Instead they stared at Cilla, her hair had fallen over her eyes forming a screen that made it impossible to read her expression. When she did look up and swept her hair back behind her ears she was grinning.

"They will be here in a few minutes," she told them. "With two policemen they captured. No. Wait. Sami said 'converted'."

The girls looked delighted and confused by this news.

"What are we waiting for? Let's go and see," Becky said, preceding them down the corridor to the entrance.

Outside a crowd was gathering on the steps. How could they possibly have known? The excitement was palpable and conversation buzzed and crackled like electricity. When the first lights broke from the forest and began winding down the track, a cheer went up.

It might not be wise to openly announce the arrival, but even Saskia appeared unwilling to dampen their relief.

When the heavily-loaded truck ground to a halt in front of the steps and Nan, Mart and Tia climbed out people began to applaud. Those perched amongst the clothes and boards climbed down and were greeted like heroes.

The arrival of a second vehicle bearing the markings of the food police brought an abrupt end to the jollity and a tense silence hung in the air. A stocky man in police uniform was driving causing Saskia to cock her bow and point it at him.

"There will be no need for bows and arrows," Sami said, stepping out of the jeep. "This is Jake and his colleague…" A young man got out of the back of the jeep accompanied by Rachel. "… Kurt. They have come to join us. I want you to make them welcome. They have brought us much news which we will share with you as soon as possible."

96.

Candles flickered in the predawn breeze. In the east, faint streaks of pink brought the promise of a new day. Birds were stirring and their calls rang out in the dark. All along the torch-lit path, children stood silent, heads bowed, hands clasping a blazing torch. They must be exhausted. Many had not slept all night.

Jon watched from the steps, tense, his hands folded across his chest. He hadn't experienced such stage fright in a long time. He wanted the ceremony to be a resounding success, for Pri, for Sami but also for Sam. All was ready. He'd managed to write some music; a lament to accompany the procession. Around him the choir waited, nervous and excited. He was delighted that children from Baxter had joined girls from the Centre to sing.

Inside the four wild men who were to carry Pri would be shouldering the improvised coffin festooned with flowers. Like many others he had spent a moment at Pri's side. Her eyes were closed, but she looked so full of life he expected her to sit up and ask him one of those penetrating questions she had the art of. If only she would.

A soft knock came at the door. The sign. He turned to the choir and raised a hand. Their attention snapped to him. As the door opened and the pall bearers stepped out, he marked the beat with a downward movement of his hand. The choir began pianissimo. As the pall bearers descended the steps and set out for the hill, the choir fell in behind, their voices swelling in volume. One by one the children lining the path joined the procession, forming a slow serpent of light snaking up the hill. A delegation of wild people brought up the rear, some accompanying the music with their drums.

Once inside the ring of trees the four wild men laid Pri on the table, then stepped aside. Jon ushered the choir behind the table. The members of the council stood in front and the others stood in rings that encompassed the table several times. He caught sight of Nan and Mart accompanying the two policemen who had changed to more casual attire.

Sami stepped forward. Silence fell. Even the birds ceased their noisy welcome for the coming day. Turning to the east, Sami raised her arms in salute as the sun rose majestically above the jungle. "Please accept our dear friend, Pri," Sami called out, lowering her arms as she did. Her voice was transformed, older, wiser, neither male nor female, but deeply human and touching, as if she spoke for each person. "With her going we have lost an important part of ourselves. Each of us feels the pain and suffering of that separation, when all we want is to belong and be one. Oh that we could hold Pri in our arms and delight in her smile, in her joyous youthfulness. So small, yet so full of life. She gave us a gift of immense worth: an unending joy in life. She has been torn from us by senseless violence, by forces that have no respect or love for life. Yet in that loss we have gained far more. An awareness of ourselves as frail and fragile, of an urgency knowing that our lives are short indeed. But now is not a time to be bitter. No good will come of taking up arms, lest it be in self defence. As I speak, those who brought about this disaster are already being consumed by a fire of their own making. As we go forward and welcome all those who sorely need our help, as we lay the foundations for a better world, let us each, you and me, carry within us and cherish that joy of life that Pri so generously shared." Sami turned back to the coffin and knelt in prayer.

It was time for the lullaby. Jon glanced at Becky who looked petrified. Crossing the space between them, he took her hand and led her to the front of the choir. He hummed the first note and waited for her to begin. But no sound left her mouth. Raising one hand in the air and holding the index of the other to his lips he launched the choir as they hummed the first verse. Still Becky did not sing. Instead tears were streaming down her cheeks. "I can't," she mouthed.

A breeze stirred about the table lifting stray leaves as it did and a girl's voice whispered, "Do this for me, Becky."

Jon wondered if it was an illusion, but everyone gasped, torches trembling in their hands. Pri had spoken. Jon recognised her voice. Yet her body remained motionless, bedecked as it was with all the flowers the children could find.

Becky looked at him, her eyes wide with awe. He nodded. Taking her handkerchief from her sleeve she blew her nose and took a deep breath. No one moved. No one spoke. Jon raised his hand to give the beat and the girl closed her eyes and sang. There was not a shadow of a doubt in that voice, no hesitation, just raw emotion that had tears in everyone's eyes, including his own. The choir hummed the melody laying the foundations on which her voice could rise and soar like a musical cathedral full of light and sound, solemn and majestic. Yet there was also something home-ly in that lullaby that wrapped its arms around each and everyone of them bringing comfort and love.

Onlookers and choir alike stood a long time entranced, un-aware that the music had ceased and that bird song had taken its place. It was the sound of the four pall bearers coming forward to take the coffin that brought people back to their senses. The four men stood, each at one corner of the coffin, waiting. Jon glanced at Becky. The girl was glowing. He wouldn't have been surprised to see a halo surrounded her whole body.

She came forward and rounded the table to where Sami was still kneeling. She leaned over Pri, kissed the girl's forehead and turned away. As if that was a signal, a line formed in front of the coffin as each person came to bid Pri farewell. When all had filed away and the choir had done their part, Jon went to stand by the coffin and stared a long moment at the girl's peaceful face. Then he laid a hand on Sami's shoulder. The girl turned and looked up at him, her eyes filled with tears. He helped her to her feet and took her in his arms.

97.

"I'm tired of all this, Jon," I say snuggling up in his arms. The early morning air is cold and I feel exhaustion wash over me.

Out of the corner of my eye I notice faithful Rachel and Tia hanging back at the edge of the ring of trees, their bows ever ready. Struggling to stay alert, they too are exhausted. Such devotion. Everyone else is making their way back to the Centre where Eileen has prepared breakfast and then on to a welcome bed.

"Of what?" Jon asks, running his fingers through my hair. The feeling is so comforting I pray he won't stop.

"All the pain and suffering," I say. "Being there to save the situation. Nudging people into doing what they should have done all along. Incapable of preventing lovely people like Pri being sacrificed. But above all I loath the unending return. What's the point? It will only happen again and again and again. Are humans incapable of learning? Tell me Jon, are they really worth saving?"

"How should I know? I'm no saviour."

"But you are my father."

His fingers cease their movement in my hair. He makes a sort of choking sound and I realise he is crying.

"Why do you cry?"

"I'm not sure. Deep down I longed to hear you say I was your father. I fathered Sam, and mothered him too." He chuckles through his tears. "But I didn't feel I fathered you."

"Who else could be my father, our father?"

A sob catches in his throat and he hugs me tighter.

I am glad Sam sleeps. For once to be alone with my father,

even if all humanity fathered me.

"Sami!" A voice calls out. "Come quick."

Here we go again. I free myself from Jon's arms and turn to see Saskia running up the path. "There's trouble at the gate."

Jon, Tia, Rachel and myself hurry after Saskia down the path. "There's a group of food police amongst the refugees," Saskia says. "Not many. Five at most, I'd say. They are stirring up trouble. Telling everyone we have a saviour but we won't share you. That is why they are being held outside the fence. Some of the refugees are so furious they fling themselves at the fence. Others keep calling out your name. I don't know how they found out."

As I reach the steps I find almost all the members of the council waiting. Their faces are grim, but determined. Those that can use bows and arrows are armed. I am about to set off for the gate when Eileen pushes open the door. "You are not going down there without eating something first," she says. I start to refuse, but she takes me by the arm and marches me inside.

She heads for the canteen when I say, "Is there not a smaller place where the council can eat?"

Without a word she changes direction and leads me to the common room. It is hardly a suitable place for breakfast, but why not? When I go to sit down she says, "Not here." Opening a door on the far side, we enter a spacious dining room with a long table topped by flickering candles and surrounded by twelve chairs. The council members follow us in.

"Ask Jon and Nan to join us," I say to Saskia and sit at the head of the table. As the others jostle to get a seat, Eileen and her helpers carry in food. I see she has not heeded her own advice and prepared a feast. One of her helpers looks longingly at the pile of bananas. Goodness knows where Eileen dug them up.

"Have the other girls eaten like this?" I ask.

Eileen shakes her head, "I wanted the best for you."

"Do not feel guilty," I say. "I appreciate your efforts and recognise your love for me. But we will eat like the others."

Eileen looks about to argue, but I get to my feet. Jon and Nan arrive at that moment and I invite them to join us. Eileen makes the most of the interruption to order her helpers to remove much of the food but continues to hover near my chair.

"Close the door after you," I say to the last helper and then turn to Eileen. 'You did nothing wrong. You acted from the depth of your heart." I lead her to her place. The twelve chairs are filled except mine.

"Things have to change," I say, walking round the table, placing a hand on each of my friends. "I am not here to be treated as special. I am no saviour. Only you can save yourselves." The truth of my words hits me. I can only do this with them.

"But you are special," Tia and Rachel say in chorus.

"I intend to change that," I say, reaching my chair, but I remain standing.

"You probably don't know, but this is not the first time I have come into the world when things are going wrong. I am a luminary. My task is to bring light when darkness threatens. Time and time again I and my fellow luminaries return to set things right. We do not always succeed. Far from it. But one thing is certain, sooner or later we will have to return because the world is in crisis again. Each time we struggle with the help of people like yourself, but even if we win through you can be sure that in a hundred or a thousand years it will start again."

There are many astonished faces around the table. Why should I burden them with my problems? They have enough of their own. Not the least a seething mass by the gate, some armed and ready to kill. Tomorrow many may be dead. Life is so fragile.

"Something has to change. I do not want to leave another Atlantis behind me." I halt and look at each in turn. Tia, Rachel, Cilla, Saskia, Eileen, Jenna, Kred, Becky, Mart, Nan and Jon. Serious, thoughtful faces. Some hopeful, others not. Must I do this to them? "I have decided to share my gifts with you." My words cause a stir.

"Do not rejoice too quickly. In some languages the word 'gift' means poison. What I am offering will be more of a burden than a present. Above all, you will share my concern for the world and those who live in it, today and for ever more. Most of you are still children. Childhood can be a time of joy and discovery, of heart-rending loves and unbridled passion. But if you accept what I am offering, you will leave childhood behind. Although I hope you will continue to cherish that inquisitiveness and joy that was so characteristic of Pri. Never forget that someone apparently small and insignificant may be the very treasure you are looking for."

Evoking her name makes Pri all the more present. I picture her smiling at her friends. Tears well in my eyes.

"Pri's first act, for me at least, was to ask to belong. She dared. Will you? I am not going to force you. It is up to you to chose." I return to my seat and wait. I might well be going against all the luminaries have worked for. I have a terrible vision of a wave far more vengeful than that of Atlantis rolling over us. Or maybe I am opening a door to another world, possibly a better one.

They are brimming over with questions. Above all, they talk about the gifts. Some dream of power, others imagine being able to heal or help. Although I spoke of gifts, they are not as important as personal engagement. But I say little and let them talk.

After half an hour of intense discussion, Becky gets to her feet and holds up a hand for silence. I see a look of pride on Jon's face. Singing for Pri has transformed her and Jon has found a musical soulmate in this talented girl. "This morning I have already received the most wonderful gift imaginable," she says. "I need no other, but I accept Sami's offer."

When she sits down, people look around wondering who will be next. "I too have already received the very gift I always dreamed of," Cilla says, "to be able to heal. I accept Sami's offer with my whole heart."

Rachel gets to her feet. "I always wanted to be a boy," she says and blushes bright red. "But getting to be an angel is almost as good." Everyone laughs. "I accept."

"Since Sami joined us," Saskia begins, "I have discovered a whole new side to myself and I look forward to discovering much more. I accept."

"You know me," Eileen says, "my home is in the kitchen. Without it I might be a little lost, so bear with me. You will have guessed, I willingly give up my beloved kitchen to join Sami. I accept,"

Jenna springs to her feet saying, "And my home is with Eileen, with or without the kitchen." Several people chuckle. "So I accept too. Someone has to do the cooking when she is busy."

Kred gets to his feet, looking intimidated. "I have nothing to offer, no wonderful gifts to bring to the table, just a little knowledge of gardening," he begins. "But if you will have me, I will willingly be one of you. I accept."

"I confess," Mart says, getting to his feet, "that from the moment I saw Sami I was in love." He stares down at his hands. "I would have preferred to have her all to myself." He glances up at me as if seeking approval. I return his look, unflinching. "But that is not going to happen. So I will share that love with you all." He blushes. "If you will have me that is."

"My whole life has been devoted to the coming of Sami, or a luminary like her," Nan says. "And although my intervention saved her life, I wonder now if we weren't misguided spending all that time waiting and preparing when we could have played a more active part in the world. If you will have me, though I am old enough to be your mother, I whole heartedly accept Sami's offer."

All eyes turn to Jon who is the last but one to stand. "If Nan is old enough to be your mother then I could be your grandfather." A couple of people laugh. "I am in fact Sami's father." Many of the children look surprised. "How could I not accept my ..." He hesitates over the word. "... my daughter's offer?"

As he sits everyone turns to Tia who is curled up in a ball on her chair, her hands over her face. Rachel places a hand on her shoulder but Tia shakes it off. "I can't," she mutters. "I won't." She stamps a foot on the floor.

"Tia!" Becky exclaims. "You are not going to abandon us now. We've all accepted."

98.

Tia looks at Becky, then at me, then at all the anxious faces. "It's easy enough for you lot, but I know you don't want me." She bursts into tears.

Becky, Cilla and Rachel move to get up, but I shake my head. She has to do this alone.

"You poke fun at me 'cause I go wild over clothes. You mock me because I mess around. You dislike me because I fancy boys." She dares a furtive glance in Mart's direction. "You..."

A deep growl stops her. No one has seen Yarrow enter except me. He advances on Tia growling. She backs away only to trip over a cushion and fall on her backside. Yarrow pounces and pushes her over, planting both paws on her chest, nailing her to the floor. His muzzle inches closer to her face. I hear Becky squeal in fright, but I hold up a hand to silence her.

Yarrow sniffs the girl's trembling face. She tries to turn her head away but he butts her with his muzzle. Then he licks every inch of her face, even her nose and ears.

"Ugh," Rachel whispers.

As if satisfied, Yarrow removes his front paws and curls up next to her planting his head squarely on her chest, pinning her to the floor. With extreme caution, Tia brings her hand to her face and wipes away some of the slime. "What do I do now?" she asks, hardly daring to move.

"Don't know," I say. "It's still your call."

"I'm sorry," she mumbles. "I've been so silly." She pauses. "When Mart said... you know ... that he loved you .... it was too much. I can't help it if I am a jealous moo." Yarrow snorts. "Well maybe I can." She groans. "Of course I accept." She takes a deep breath. "If you'll have a silly little girl for friend."

Several girls sigh with relief.

"Good," I say. "That's enough Yarrow." He lets out a disgruntled humph, stretches and finally frees Tia. The girl scrambles to her feet and, with the sleeve of her blouse, wipes her face.

"OK. Now let's get down to serious business." I grin in case they believe I am belittling what has just happened. "I'm going to reveal millennia of secrets in a single flash." I laugh at their alarmed faces.

"Will we keep coming back like you?" Becky asks, raking fingers through her hair.

"I don't know. This has never been done before."

She doesn't look reassured.

"The secret of life is in the breathing. It is the door to the unknowable," I begin. "Most religions and esoteric thinkings are built on this, although they generally wrap it in their mumbo jumbo." Tia and Kred look alarmed. "Don't worry. I'm not going to lecture you, although that would be fun." Tia groans. "I'm going to use breathing as a short cut to teach you what you need to know. And what better way than to use the voice and singing. Jon can you sing a note?"

He raises his eyebrows. "Any note?" I nod. He clears his throat and sings a resounding low note that sets the air vibrating. "Close your eyes and keep going, Jon. All of you close your eyes. Now you Becky. Sing your note." Hers blends with Jon's, the two pulsing together. One by one, I have each voice join the dance till all are singing in a strange but moving chorus.

I too close my eyes, and reaching back across the centuries, I call upon all the luminaries that have ever been, inviting then to join us. This too has never been done. Will they answer my call? Yes. I sense them coming. Some are known to me, most are not. Why have I never done so? I could have called on their help.

There is a deep whoosh like rushing air and the room is dense with a thousand voices talking softly, some not so softly, disgruntled, disturbed, shocked but also intrigued, excited, enthusiastic. Several children gasp, their song broken off. "It's OK. You can stop singing." Energy is building and crackles in the air. It is as if we are being lifted up and away.

Some luminaries rear up against me, furious at my initiative, but we have no time for futile debates. As the current luminary, I am surprised to realise I have sway over them. I had no idea. How could I? Never have we come together in such a gathering.

"Down the centuries we have worked as one to keep this planet on course. We bring light to the dark. But time and time again the dark creeps back. As long as there is light, there will always be dark. I know. We are not here to eradicate darkness, but to make sure it does not eradicate life. Yet I refuse to believe we are condemned to this futile round till the end of time. We need to break the cycle. That is why I called this gathering. To join forces with mortals and share our knowledge with some amongst them. I have chosen those gathered here to take on this task. They all do so willingly. I will not order you to hand over your powers to them."

There are huffs and cries of indignation, but they are drowned out by the clamours of luminaries who want to hear. "I ask those who heed my call to flow amongst them and bless those you see fit with your knowledge and gifts. That together they form the foundations of a new world."

I expect no answer and none comes. Those who disagree go with my blessing. The host that remains moves amongst the group like a knowing wind whispering in the tall grasses, swirling round the heads of awestruck, joyous children, young and old. Each one, Tia, Rachel, Cilla, Saskia, Eileen, Jenna, Kred, Becky, Mart, Nan and Jon, has their own whirl of luminaries, some more than others, sharing secrets in the minds, in their hearts. Even I, much to my surprise and delight, have my own group of whisperers that my soul expands to embrace. I would dearly love to explore the riches gifted me, but time is running short and another appointment awaits us down by the gate.

As the last of the luminaries speeds away, I open my eyes

and look round the table. Eleven people turn to face me, eleven people to set the world right. Their faces are familiar, I can put names to them, but they are no longer the same. They are so much more. Layers upon layers of richness, of history, of experience. Like me, each of them is humanity incarnate or at least a facet of it. I get to my feet and kneel before them.

99.

Nan's mind was in turmoil. The luminaries had whispered so much in her head, in her soul, she felt she might burst. She needed time. She looked at the others. They needed time too, time to think, to explore. But no time was forthcoming. Girls came running from the gate reporting that the situation had turned ugly. Several people had been trampled to death, the horror lingering in their haunted eyes.

Nan pushed open the front door, closely followed by Sami, only to find Jake sitting on the steps, his head heavy in his hands.

"Are you alright?" Sami asked.

"I just 'eard the story. That poor girl," he said to Sami.

At first Nan thought he meant someone in the stampede, but then she realised he was talking about Pri.

"I'm so sorry," he said. "I wish I could make amends." He glanced around as if afraid of being overheard, then said, "I 'ave a present for yer. Something right special that I 'ave to give yer in private." With which he got up, signalling for her to follow.

"Should I come?" Nan asked. The hint of conspiracy worried her. She was not entirely confident he was safe, especially now part of his personality lay open to her. He was like a book, the darkened pages of which she could dimly read. Despite her alarm, she couldn't help being distracted by her new-found clairvoyance.

"No," Sami said. "I'll be fine. Go. I will join you at the gate."

Nan was inclined to stay, but Sami insisted. Shrugging, she joined the others. Their usual banter had been banished. Tia was silent, as was Rachel. It was not that they had lost the joy of life so characteristic of them, Nan realised, but rather the situation was so grave a numbing foreboding hung over them, her included.

She had heard enough of luminaries, and her newly gained knowledge confirmed it, to know that their lives rarely ended without violence. It was that she dreaded. And violence was just what she could sense seething down by the gate. Like a disgusting black monster that writhed and hissed and mocked her, it filled her with apprehension.

With an effort, she turned her attention to the young people. Although they were subdued and anxious, she delighted in the light that danced in and around them. It gave her hope. In all her time preparing for the next luminary she had never once wondered how those beings of light might see the world. Of course, people spoke of good and evil and the battle that raged between the two, but now that she had seen both sides she felt her soul yearning for the light.

The closer they got, the louder the jeering. Angry adults, men mostly, but women too, snarled like animals, their teeth bared. Was this the humanity they were to save? Were these the people luminaries repeatedly gave their lives for?

"Sami! Sami! Sami!" the crowd brayed. "Hand him over," they shrieked. It was more like the ritual slaughtering of a wild pig or a public execution gone berserk than a crowd in search of healing and redemption. The foreboding that clung to Nan tightened its grip.

Sickly infants wailed in the arms of fraught mothers. Men with their hair bleached white and skin crumbling from pesticide burns flung themselves in desperation at the electric fence adding the stench of roasted flesh to the horror. "Sami! Sami!" the crowd hurled, the words devoid of sense.

All the time, the girls of the Centre and the children of Baxter, a sea of bright blue, stood horrified, enduring a nightmare that refused to end. As Nan watched, the girls parted and three people walked between them. Sami strode undeterred, her steps firm and decisive, her head held high, flanked by the two police-men, nervously looking this way and that. Even though they no longer sported their uniforms, Nan had a vision of them leading Sami to her execution.

The crowd roared at the sight of her as if they had spotted the sacrificial lamb. Nan imagined saliva dripping from their jaws as they chanted Sami's name. She could feel the darkness gaining her and she had to fight not to be dragged under. A glance left and right showed the signs of strain on the faces of her fellow councillors.

Sami and her guardians halted a few steps in front of the Council. She raised a hand for silence causing many to cower, terrified she would strike them down. "You called," she said. "I have come. What do you want?"

"We don't want no blinkin' girl," a man shouted. "We want the saviour."

"The only person who can save you is yourself," Sami replied.

"Sami! Sami!" the crowd chanted.

Sami raised her hand a second time. "I am Sami. I have come to help you but only if you will accept me as I am."

A man pushed his way through the crowd, brandishing a gun. He was wearing the tattered remains of a food police uniform. Two others shoved their way after him. Kurt and Jake drew the guns, aiming at the three men.

Sami turned to them, saying "Do not reply to their violence with your own. That is what violence wants. Violence feeds on violence."

Kurt and Jake glanced at each other, unsure, then lowered their guns, their faces betraying their doubt and confusion.

The crowd jeered and the first gunman, a grin plastered on his face, turned to salute them waving his gun in wide circles above his head, firing several shots in the air. Turning back, he shouted, "Don't waste our time little girl. Hand over this saviour you are harbouring."

"How dare you doubt my word, you who have only lies to

spread," Sami replied. "Who drove these people to starvation? Those you didn't poison. Who slaughtered the only people who could help them? Who..."

A resounding bang rang out, cutting off Sami's accusations, followed rapidly by two others and Sami, Kurt and Jake were hurtled backwards.

Many of the girls around Sami screamed, others burst into sobs, while opposite the crowd cheered in delight and writhed in a crazed dance of victory. The three men strutted up and down, crowing like cocks before their hens.

"Now we will have our saviour," the leader said.

Nan felt numb. The unthinkable but inevitable had happened. Again. Despite all their hopes. She stared at the three bodies crumpled at her feet. All three had been shot in the chest. Shock and grief were not words enough to name the feelings that overwhelmed her.

Jon took her hand and when she looked at him, she saw that all eleven surviving council members were holding hands in a line. Together they took several steps forward forming a protective cordon in front of Sami's body. As they did she felt the whoosh of the host of luminaries flood into them, banishing the doubt and darkness that had crushed them only seconds before.

It was Saskia that spoke. "These three fools have killed the one person who could have saved you all," she said, her voice ringing out like thunder rolling over the crowd as the host of luminaries spoke through her. "Blind they were and blind they will ever be." Saskia raised a hand in their direction. "They will be condemned to darkness and despair for the rest of their days." The three men screamed and fell to the ground, groping blindly about the space that opened around them. People elbowed each other in their panic to get away, terrified they too might be cursed.

"It is tempting to condemn you all," Saskia said, her voice calmer now but still like a distant rumble of thunder.

A groan went up from the crowd. "Please," some of them said and got down on their knees.

"To call you animals would be an insult to animals. You have forfeit the right to be human and if I listened to the anger that burns in me I would condemn you all to a time as inanimate objects. But a light still shines in a lot of you, albeit tiny, that we would not willingly snuff out."

It was Cilla that then spoke. "Those of you who wish to join us will form an orderly line in front of the gate. We will let you in one at a time. You will receive clothes and food and those who are ill will be healed. We will provide a home for you and you will join us in our efforts to make this a good place to live. Those of you who refuse will leave and return to the city. There will be no second chance."

As Cilla, Saskia and Rachel headed for the gate accompanied by a number of archers, Nan turned to find what had become of Sami. Someone must have gone in search of a several small trollies because Sami and the two men were being transported up the path beyond the house towards the circle of trees where Pri had been buried.

Her hand still in Jon's, the two fell in with the girls trudging up the hill to another funeral.

100.

Jon trudged to the breast of the hill with its giant circle of trees, his body numb, his thoughts dull. The colour had bled from the world.

"What now?" he asked Nan.

"Life goes on," she replied, her tone one of defeat.

"Are They going to arrive too late each time?" he asked, feeling a burst of anger that faded almost immediately. He and his fellow council members were akin to survivors of a silent shipwreck in a sea driven wild by unanswered questions.

"I don't know," she said, halting at the foot of the stone trees unable to advance. "I don't know." She shook her head, her eyes downcast.

He stared at her, startled at what he saw. Her face was grimy and streaked with tears. Lines had formed on her forehead and radiated from the corners of her eyes and mouth. Her hair was flecked grey. She looked old, ages old. Yet for all her weariness, a light shone in her that called to him. When their eyes met, he knew she was seeing that same light in him. The clamour of questions in his head abated. One thing was clear; he wanted to be with her and she wanted to be with him. Their hands joined and they took a step closer.

They must have been standing for ages, their eyes locked in mutual appreciation, when he became aware of others. A couple of girls nearby spoke in whispers. "It looked like her. I could have sworn it was Marge."

He knew that name, but who was it? And why was it so

important?

"Where?"

"Amongst the refugees."

"You didn't see the other two, I hope."

He strained to hear more, but they shifted away. Then the singing began, soft and caressing, and all talk ceased. He recognised Becky's voice. She and the choir were singing Pri's lullaby. He and Nan stepped apart, but their fingers remained intertwined. Looking around he was amazed to find the children of the Centre and Baxter standing in silent vigil around the bodies of Sami, Jake and Kurt; three smiling sleepers on their trolleys, bedecked with flowers. Yarrow sat on his haunches by Sami, unmoving, his muzzle resting against her side, surprisingly unconcerned by the girl's death. Becky and the choir were gathered in a semicircle behind the three, swaying in song.

Then, as if awaking from forgetful sleep, the suffering hit him. Sam and Sami were dead. Tears flooded his eyes and rolled down his cheeks. Not tears of sadness though, but of joy. His wayward feelings had him troubled. What was wrong with him? Was he so callous that he rejoiced in their parting? He didn't feel callous. He didn't feel sad either. He looked at those who stood in silent vigil. They too looked joyously perplexed.

A gasp went up and the singing stopped. Like everybody, Jon's head swivelled to Sami. Her eyes were open and she was staring up at the sky. Only the faint rustle of the wind in the tree could be heard and the occasional cheeky chirp of a bird. It was as if the whole world stood suspended in one in-drawn breath.

Slowly, ever so slowly, Sami raised her head and peered around, taking in the astonished faces staring at her and she smiled, a smile like the sun cresting the horizon on a joyous dawn, full of promise and hope. Her smile was so infectious, Jon felt an echoing smile form on his own lips.

"Anyone got anything to eat? I'm starving," she said.

"Sami?" Becky exclaimed, voicing the surprise and joy of everyone present.

"No. Sam actually," came the answer. "Sami is asleep. It's

been an exhausting day."

"But…?" Becky began, only to falter.

"Jake gave us a bullet-proof jacket. All three of us had one," Sam said and, lowering his legs over the edge of the trolley, he sat swinging his feet backwards and forwards in evident delight. "That's the first time I have ever been able to control my legs." He chuckled, taping his thighs. "It's also the first time I have been able to talk." He turned to Becky, but then spotted Jon and said, "Hallo, Dad. You must teach me to sing. I'd love to do that." Jon clutched his chest afraid his heart would burst. Then Sam saw Nan with her hand in Jon's and, getting to his feet, he took a hesitant step forward, saying, "At last."

Annexes

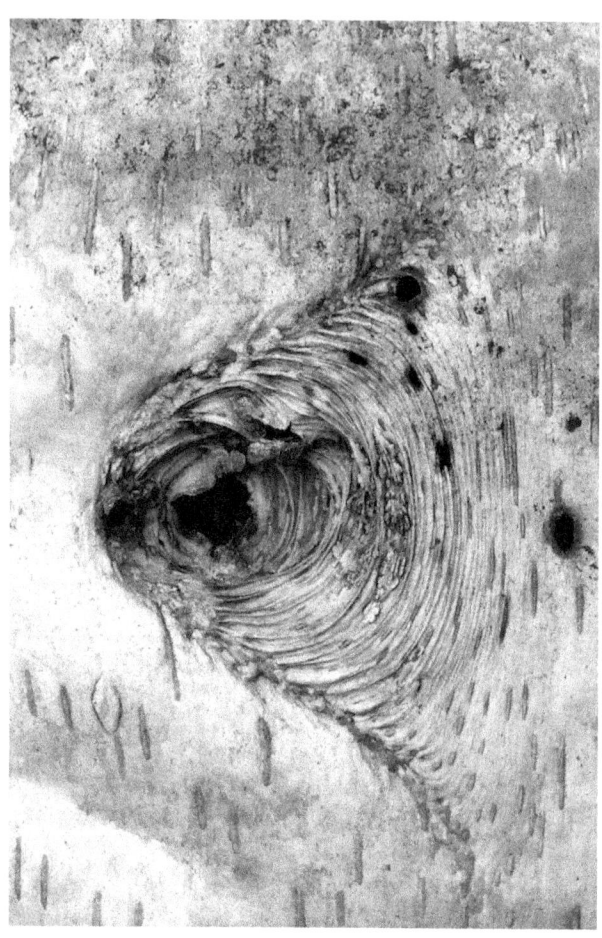

Thanks and more

Girls can and will save the world. Such was the conviction that
inspired Chimera, a tale unfolding against the real-life backdrop
of anxiety about the disastrous impact of increasingly unhealthy
industrial food and the rampant abuse of pharmaceuticals including antibiotics, antidepressants and painkillers.

The scene set, giving form to Chimera took unexpectedly long. I embarked on the book in February 2014 only to decide, a third of the way through, to retrace my steps and begin again. A tough decision when you have already written over forty-thousand words. In my approach to novel writing, being convinced of the story is key. It is the force that drives me to continue telling it.

I enlisted the clear-sighted advice of Emjay Holmes about the initial chapters and I am very grateful for her input. A few chapters were read and discussed in critiquing sessions in the Geneva Writers Group. Thanks go to those members who attended and particularly to Susan Tiberghien for chairing the sessions. Thanks also to Anita who read an early manuscript in instalments. I finally finished the first version a year and a half later, in September 2015.

Editing the draft was halted by health problems. Heartfelt thanks for their care and attention go to the staff at the Inselspital, Bern and Pourtales Hospital, Neuchâtel, as well as Dr Nathalie Calame, our family doctor. Ill-health, however short-lived, brings with it a feeling of vulnerability. It heightened the urgency to write my stories and make them available to readers.

Back on my feet, I set aside the draft of Chimera and prepared In Search of Lost Girls for publication. The writing of five other novels (World o'Tales, Forget Me Not, Stories People Tell, People of the Forest and Local Voices) filled the interim before I finally picked up Chimera again, in March 2019, delighted at what I (re)discovered.

Alan McCluskey, Saint.-Blaise, May 2019.

396   Alan McCluskey

The author
Alan McCluskey

One of his former pupils once confessed, with typical candour and ambiguity, that Alan McCluskey had taught her the creative value of madness. His work, whether as a teacher or a video artist or a company director or a scientist or a novel writer, has always been marked by a need to question the obvious, adopting what he calls the Martian perspective in which the self-evident is not taken for granted. He has brought that questioning perspective, along with a passion for images and what they can reveal, to novel writing, together with a long-standing fascination for the dream world and the magic of fantasy.

For information about Alan McCluskey, his books, short stories and artwork, see:
Secret Paths: https://secret-paths.com
Facebook: https://www.facebook.com/Secret.Paths

Secret Paths Editions presents
Stories People Tell
A novel by **Alan McCluskey**

"We raise our fists in salute, not in threat but as a sign of solidarity. In those fingers held tight we embrace everyone however different they may be. Gay. Trans. Straight. Black. Brown. Yellow. White. All colours of the rainbow. All are welcome in our London."
Annie Wight, London Whatever

Stories People Tell
by Alan McCluskey

Stories People Tell is a tale about Annie Wight, a shy schoolgirl who, despite sustained, cruel treatment and personal doubts, blossoms into a major voice in the grassroots movement 'London Whatever' celebrating gender diversity while struggling to end violence against women and care for the weak and marginalised.

Annie wasn't expecting to stumble on love or notoriety when she got swept up in 'London Whatever'. Nor could she have known that, right from the outset, she would become the number one target of Nolan Kard, the homophobic Lord Mayor of London. who was campaigning to 'Keep London Straight'. She bore the brunt of attacks from his rogue police, not to mention from a sinister gang of ghost-writers, the nightmare of all Kard's enemies.

The Storyteller's Quest ~ Book One
The Reaches
Alan McCluskey

The Reaches
The Storyteller's Quest Book One

by Alan McCluskey

The quiet town of Avan with its port, its provincial university
and its conservative seafaring folk would hardly be the place
you'd expect to run into an adventure and frankly neither Brent
nor Sally nor Keira were going out of their way to have one.
At least nothing more than the occasional torrid love affair and
the awkward self-questioning typical of many young adults like
themselves. Sally was finishing her studies in the Theosophy
Department of the University hoping to become Professor
Rafter's assistant, Keira, Sally's best friend and lover, was a young
librarian who occasionally sang in a popular folk group and Brent
was a would-be writer who couldn't quite get his act together and
who spent hours wandering the streets and lanes of the town
in search of inspiration. Yet unbeknown to them forces had
long been at work that would throw them together in a series of
adventures that were going to tax them to the extreme forcing
them to develop abilities that went way beyond what would seem
possible. Their journey would take them from the real world to
the realm of dreams and on to another world called the Reaches
that at first sight looked deceptively like their own.

The Storyteller's Quest ~ Book Two
The Keeper's Daughter

Alan McCluskey

The Keeper's Daughter
The Storyteller's Quest Book Two

by Alan McCluskey

It wasn't Brent's fault if he was stuck in the form of an owl, at least he didn't think it was as he sat on a branch preening. The threads of his stories had become inextricably muddled in his owlish head. To think that he'd once prided himself on being a storyteller. His stories had become adventures and some of those had become nightmares, and now he was stuck with them. He'd flown in search of his friend and lover, Mia. She'd been dragged off by a band of thugs just when it was time to return to their world. Only Sally, their mutual friend and lover, had made it back to their hometown of Avan. Hearing her story, despite the dangers she'd had to face, her friends suggested Sally teach them to travel to the Dream Realm and beyond to the Reaches. The idea appealed to everybody. Not that Sally knew how to get back to the Reaches, but the idea of a 'dream class' as they called it pleased her and, above all, she wanted to return to the world where her newly-found half-sister lived and where her two friends had so abruptly disappeared.

The Storyteller's Quest ~ Book Three

The Starless Square

Alan McCluskey

The Starless Square
The Storyteller's Quest Book Three
by Alan McCluskey

A weekend of joyous festivities! Such was the Theosophy department's response to a group of fanatics bent on destroying their reputation and having them shut down. Theosophy? Professor Rafter, head of the department, called it "the study of our direct relationship with that which is beyond and above the normal range of human experience". He could just as well have been describing the adventures of the group of young friends who had been called back from their travels in another world to defend their department with their new-found abilities. But how could entrancing singing or breath-taking storytelling or exquisite cooking possibly stand a chance when pitted against the evil black cloud that threatened to obscure the Starless Square?

Boy & Girl
Revised edition
Alan McCluskey

Boy & Girl

by Alan McCluskey

When Peter awakes in the head of a girl, he is both delighted and alarmed that his secret yearnings have become reality. Very quickly, however, his error is apparent; this girl is not him. Kaitling –that's her name – is twelve years old, like Peter. She's the daughter of a magician, a prominent figure in another world. Boy and girl travel back and forth from each other's minds, but have little time to get acquainted before Kaitling's island is overrun by warrior priests and she has to flee. At home, a conflict erupts in Peter's family forcing him to take refuge at a friend's place. Meanwhile at school, a haughty new girl goads him about his girlishness and, spitting in his face, vows to rid the earth of people like him. The stage seems set for a desperate struggle to survive, but will ingenuity and youthful fervour be enough against folly and fanaticism?

A sequel to Boy & Girl

In Search of Lost Girls

Alan McCluskey

In Search of Lost Girls
by Alan McCluskey

If you listen carefully you can just hear the mournful tolling of a convent bell over the shuffle of girls' feet as they traipse to Mass, nursing bruises and numbing despair. No one cares. No one is there to stem the torrent of injustice and abuse. They are lost and forgotten. In another world, the walls of the cathedral still reverberate to the sound of angelic singing as the mourners make their way to the exit, heads bowed, voices hushed. If only they knew that those girls who delighted them with their music were really boys in disguise, sanctity would flee in the face of raging indignation. The scene is set. The author picks up his pen with trembling fingers and begins to write. Time to tear Kate and Peter apart. The thought of making her life hell has him dribbling in anticipation. He ought to know better. Things rarely turn out as an author expects.

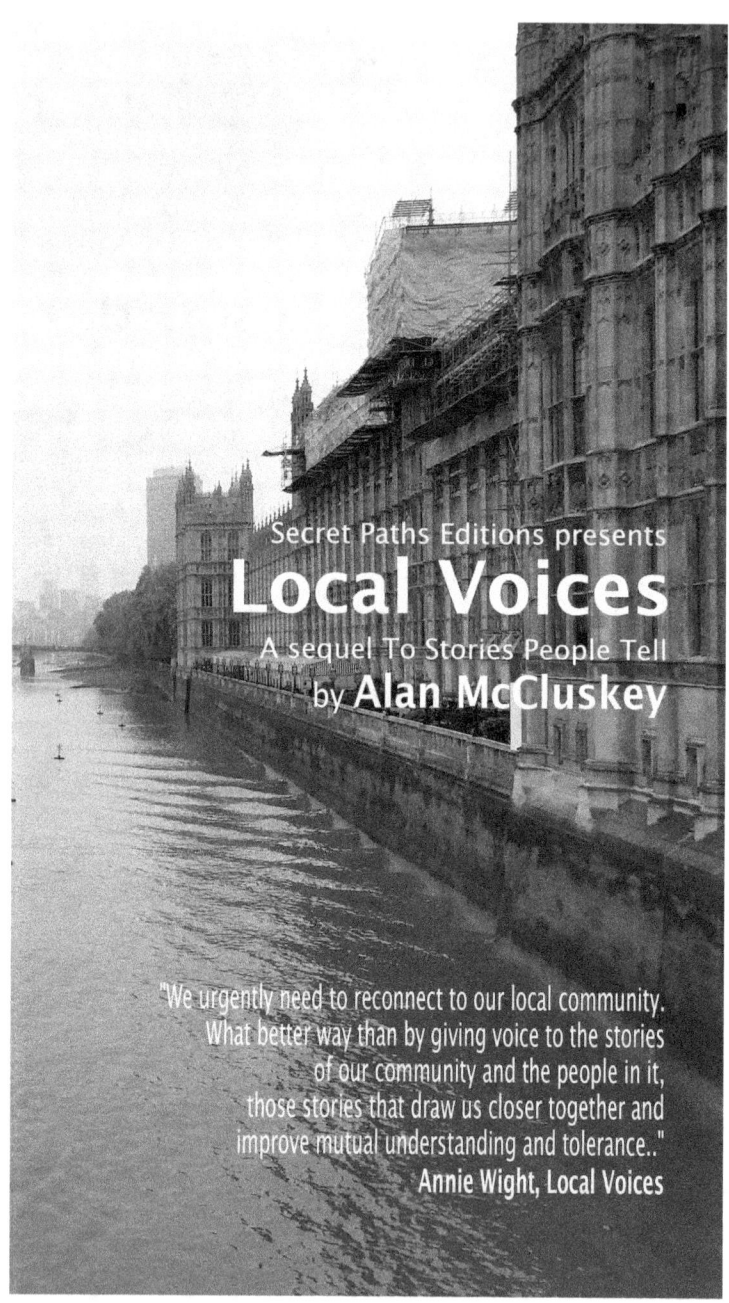

Secret Paths Editions presents

Local Voices

A sequel To Stories People Tell

by **Alan McCluskey**

"We urgently need to reconnect to our local community.
What better way than by giving voice to the stories
of our community and the people in it,
those stories that draw us closer together and
improve mutual understanding and tolerance.."
Annie Wight, Local Voices

Local Voices

by Alan McCluskey

Coming soon: a sequel to Stories People Tell

In her campaign to re-assert and strengthen the role of women at the heart of hearthside healthcare, seventeen-year-old Annie Wight finds herself pitted against Health England, a conservative think-tank backed by pharmaceutical giants and private healthcare providers. Pretexting the defence of the National Health Service, they stop at nothing to stamp out Annie's efforts. They target not just her but those close to her, wreaking havoc in friendships and affairs of the heart. As part of her response, Annie launches a project to share the stories of those that never figure in the spotlight. By celebrating local voices, the project fights against isolation and disempowerment.

412   Alan McCluskey

www.ingramcontent.com/pod-product-compliance
Lightning Source LLC
Chambersburg PA
CBHW070353260626
47161CB00001B/118